Amanda
Wakes Up

Alisyn Camerota

Amanda Wakes Up

VIKING

VIKING

An imprint of Penguin Random House LLC
375 Hudson Street
New York, New York 10014
penguin.com

9780399563997 (hardcover)
9780399564017 (e-book)

Printed in the United States of America
1   3   5   7   9   10   8   6   4   2

Set in Jamille ITC Std Book

For Ale, Cessa, and Nate—the lights of my life.

May you each find your calling.

PART I

Setup Piece

Chapter 1

Breaking News

My eyes snapped open. I'd been dreaming that an alarm was going off somewhere just out of reach. Only now as the fuzzy room came into focus did I realize the sound was my cell phone chirping next to my head. I fumbled around on the nightstand, almost knocking over my water glass, then croaked, "Hello?"

"Hey," Laurie said, wide awake, as though it weren't a Saturday morning in August. "You're not asleep, are you?"

"Sort of," I said softly, trying not to wake Charlie.

"Are you still at Patricia's house?"

I was grateful for the memory jog because my brain hadn't yet squared why the pale curtains with the sun streaming through them looked so different from the blinds in my apartment, which faced a brick wall.

"Yeah, we're still here," I said, rubbing my left temple. "We stayed out late last night. There was this great beach bar that had this fantastic ska band. And we were dancing, and it's possible we were overserved, so we decided to stay over."

"There's something going on at the post office in Smithtown."

"There's something . . . going on . . . at the post office . . . in Smithtown," I repeated slowly, as if learning a foreign language.

"Dataminr has something about a gunman inside the Smithtown Post Office. It's just a couple of weird tweets. I can't find anything else online and the PIO at the police department is useless. She's not returning my calls. Don't you have a contact at the PD there?"

"Uh, yes, I do," I said, waiting for my brain to connect and retrieve his name from six months ago. A cop contact was always better for real info than the public information officer. "He's a good one, too. I helped him find that fugitive, whatever his name was. I can call him."

"Why don't you just drive over there and see what's going on?" she said.

"What am I, your intern?"

"Hey, I'm giving you a hot tip. An active-gunman story could catapult you to the top of Newschannel 13. You could leapfrog that guy who loves the walk-and-talk stand-up. 'Look at me! Reporting live from the scene, I'm Dave Jeffries,'" she said in a fake TV voice.

"It's Jeff Davis!" It cracked me up that Laurie couldn't be bothered to learn the name of the guy who considered himself king of the hill at my lame local station. "I'll call my detective and call you back."

"Good. I'm in the truck. We're heading there."

"Are you kidding?" I said. "BNN is already rolling a truck? What if it's nothing?"

"We got nothing else going on. Maybe we get lucky and it's a hostage crisis."

"Doesn't get luckier than that."

"You know what I mean," she said. "I'll take a hostage situation any day over some dumbass election story. This'll be refreshing."

"Fly in, get the gore, fly out," I said, quoting Laurie's own favorite expression back to her.

"Exactly," she said. "See what you get from your source and call me back."

"What was that about?" Charlie asked, his eyes shut and voice thick with sleep.

"Sorry," I whispered, as though that would make up for just having had a phone conversation next to his ear. "That was Laurie. She read some tweet about a gunman or something at the post office in Smithtown and she wants me to call my source."

"That sounds like it can wait," Charlie said, putting his arm around me and pulling me toward his warm body.

"Hold on, hold on," I said, laughing. I always found it funny, and a little annoying, when people not in the news business thought breaking news could wait.

"Let me call my detective and confirm it's nothing," I said, pulling my arm back from Charlie so I could scroll through my contacts until I saw one that rang the right bell. I dialed.

"Pultro," he answered.

"Hey, Detective Pultro. It's Amanda Gallo, Newschannel 13. Sorry to bother you on a Saturday. I just got a tip about something possibly happening at a post office in your area."

"I can't confirm anything, Amanda. You know that. You gotta go through my PIO."

"Yeah, I'm having a hard time getting in touch with her right now," I said, neglecting to mention I hadn't tried. "I just need to know if there's a situation that would warrant my driving over to Smithtown right now."

He paused. "Yeah, that'd probably be wise."

"Oh. Okay. Really? So is there a gunman at the post office?"

"I'm on my way there. That's all I can tell you."

I hung up and turned to Charlie. "I think I have to go. It sounds like something's happening."

"Really?" He rubbed his eyes and sat up.

My heart was starting to race as I looked around and tried to figure out the steps necessary to get from bed to a live shot location. In situations like this, I always wondered what it must be like for regular people: people who could wake up and get the news about a crazed gunman or a plane crash or a hurricane, taking it in at their leisure, maybe even from bed; people who could let someone else handle it. How easy and effortless it must feel to "watch" the news rather than deliver it. And sometimes, like this morning, I envied the numb listlessness of letting news wash over you, rather than taking a heart-pumping dive into the middle of it. My hands were shaky as I dialed the number to the newsroom.

"Newschannel 13!" Zeke answered like his hair was on fire.

"Zeke, it's Amanda."

"Amanda, I'm in the weeds! We're getting reports of a gunman at a post office on the Island, but I haven't been able to confirm it."

"I know!" I told him. "I just talked to my detective source there. It sounds like it's for real."

"Shit, really? Okay, I'm going to roll the truck. I wish I could send you, but I already gave it to Jeff. He's ready, but none of my fucking fotogs are answering their fucking phones. Call me in an hour. Maybe

I could have you do a setup piece from the studio tonight or something. We have to see what happens. I just don't know yet."

"But Zeke, I'm here! I'm already on Long Island. I'm like ten miles away from Smithtown."

"You are?"

"Yes! I'm here. Don't send Jeff!"

"Gallo is there! She's ten minutes away!" Zeke yelled to the newsroom. "Jesus, that's fantastic! How quick can you be live?"

"I'm leaving right now. Maybe fifteen minutes?"

"Make it ten. Call me as soon as you get there. You won't have a crew, but you can do a phoner. No other station is at the scene yet, so GET GOING!"

I jumped up, beginning to scour the floor for my clothes, suddenly feeling self-conscious and silly to be undressed in the face of such a serious news story, as if the camera crew were in the room and the viewers were watching me look for my clothing. What the hell? Had someone hidden my clothes?

"Have you seen my pants?" I asked Charlie, who was stepping unsteadily into his own khaki shorts.

Charlie rubbed his forehead. "I'm going to go out to the kitchen and see if I can find some coffee. I don't remember you having any pants."

"Very funny," I said to his back as he walked out. Then it hit me, with the same sudden anxiety that comes in those dreams where you're late to a final exam and realize you're in your underwear. I had no pants. Charlie and I had decided, on a whim, to escape the sweltering city and head to my friend Patricia's beach house. I'd thrown on a bathing suit, T-shirt, and some flip-flops, then grabbed a towel and off we'd gone in the Zipcar. We hadn't planned to stay over . . . or drink those margaritas.

Across the room I spotted my blue bikini hanging limply on the back of a chair and made my way toward it. Clutching the chair, I teetered on one leg, stepping into the bottoms, which were, to my surprise, still a tad damp, then I fastened the unpleasantly clammy top around my back. I retrieved my bright pink T-shirt from the floor and pulled it over my head, realizing too late it was on inside out. I saw my sunscreen on the chair and threw it in my bag just as my phone trilled excitedly on the nightstand again. I grabbed it, thinking how royally screwed I'd be if I'd left it there.

"Hey," Laurie said, "what did you find out?"

"It sounds like something is happening. My detective said he's on his way to the scene."

"Dataminr says there could be nine people inside."

"Jesus. Okay, I'm getting dressed and heading over there."

"Hurry up," Laurie said. "We're pulling up now."

Of course she is. Of course Best News Network, or BNN as everyone called it, was arriving while Newschannel 13 was still dicking around looking for a crew. Laurie and BNN were always three steps ahead of everyone else.

"Is Gabe there? Which stations are there?" I asked. "Is WNBC there? Laurie?"

She'd hung up.

I threw my phone in my bag and headed to the kitchen, where Patricia was standing at the sink filling a kettle with water.

"I'm sorry, did we wake you? We've gotta go," I told her.

"I know. I heard. If you can wait five minutes, I'm making coffee."

"I really can't," I said. "Charlie, you and I can hit a drive-through when we get there, okay?" I was trying to sound accommodating, but my voice came out too loud and urgent.

Patricia turned from the sink and stopped. "Is that what you're wearing?"

"I don't have anything else!" I said, my chest getting tighter. "It was so hot when we left the city."

"But shouldn't you put on some . . . shorts?"

"I didn't bring any!" I practically yelled, circling the sofa now, looking for my purse. "I thought we'd just be at the beach!"

She screwed up her mouth. "I'd give you some of mine, but you'd swim in them."

"Let me try 'em," I said, sending Patricia into her room, from which she emerged twenty seconds later holding out a pair of faded blue cotton shorts. I stepped into them, zipped them up, snapped the top snap, then watched them fall directly down to my ankles. "Yeah, that's not gonna work," I said. "Shit! I can't go to an armed standoff at a federal post office with no pants."

"What is the proper attire for an armed standoff?" Patricia asked seriously. People were always asking me about my TV clothes, where I got them, how much they cost, how I knew which colors to wear to which stories.

"I mean, there's no handbook for a hostage situation per se," I said, in a ridiculous attempt to try to actually answer her question. "But I'd say pants. For starters."

"I can drive around and find you something," Charlie offered. "As soon as I find coffee."

"Has anyone seen my flip-flops?" I asked, scanning the carpet until I spied them under the sofa. "Oh, thank God," I said, holding one up and waving its pinkness at Patricia, "though, may I add, these are not appropriate footwear for an armed standoff. Let's go," I said to Charlie, who was already grabbing the car keys from the counter. "The assignment desk needs me there in ten minutes!"

The radio reports in the car were a jumble of urgent bulletins that I tried to commit to memory in order to repeat them for my phoner: SWAT teams arriving, police setting up a perimeter. Post office opened at eight. First reports twenty-three minutes later. Unclear how many inside. Gunman's identity not yet known. Unknown number of injuries or fatalities . . .

I found a white cocktail napkin in my bag, a cling-on from last night, and jotted notes as Charlie drove. "The cops have *got* to know the gunman's name by now," I told him.

Now I was excited. This was exactly the kind of story I'd been waiting for: something big, the kind that would require insight and depth and tenacity and good sources. A story I could own. One that Jeff Davis couldn't bigfoot. A story that would get attention, and maybe get me out of Newschannel 13, Land of Car Crashes and Water Main Breaks.

Man, how many water main breaks had I covered? There was that horrible one in Midtown last winter, where I stood in the middle of the street, a deluge gurgling around my rubber boots, sending ice-cold blood from my toes to my brain and giving me the dreaded mouth freeze that makes reporters sound drunk. Then that other one in North Jersey in February, where I was stuck for five hours and had to cancel on Charlie for dinner.

I thought about Laurie's life at BNN, that coveted wonderland of high salaries and rich resources, a haven of Ivy League—educated producers and brand-name anchors—so far from my little world of local news with its budget cuts and worn-out equipment. BNN seemed an almost mythical place: A deep-pocketed national *network*, with good lighting, great bookers, greenrooms with goodies, and cameramen who don't make reporters carry the tripod. A paradise of professional makeup artists and wardrobe mavens who transform correspondents into brightly hued television creatures. Working at a network was like living in a shining castle on a hill, with gold statuettes lining the lobby shelves, and big scoops just waiting to be broken. Dammit. Laurie was probably working over some sheriff's deputy at the post office right now, getting an exclusive interview. If only Charlie would step on it, maybe I could beat the other local reporters there. And maybe this one could be my ticket off the local news bus and onto the network luxury liner.

"I have to find out the gunman's identity and backstory," I told Charlie as I turned up the radio, hoping for some new nugget.

"I'm going to guess he's the same as a lot of these guys," Charlie said. "Unhinged, mentally unstable, susceptible to suggestion, then something sets him off."

I wrote that down: *Unhinged, susceptible to suggestion, set off by something.* I liked how Charlie phrased that—plus I was desperate for something to say on the phoner. I rolled down my window, taking in big gulps of air. The sun was up, revealing a baby blue sky. I had to admit, it was perfect. I couldn't ask for a better day for an armed standoff. Being outside for twelve hours of live shots would be a breeze. I watched the trees out the window passing too slowly and felt my right foot pressing down on an imaginary accelerator. "Hit the gas, would you!!" I almost yelled at Charlie, though I couldn't very well expect my mild-mannered boyfriend to have the same pedal-to-the-metal excitement for a developing calamity that those of us in news did. Charlie was different—he got excited by a well-written thought piece in the *Nation*. His students loved him for being an approachable, open-door professor. And I loved that he was a globally minded do-gooder rather than a jaded news guy who got off on ambulance chasing and talking about his last kick-ass assignment that always somehow took place in a war zone. I'd first spotted Charlie a year ago, one night last summer. I'd just moved back to New York and Laurie convinced me to abandon all the cardboard boxes in my fourth-floor walk-up so we could celebrate my new reporting job in the number one market and my escape from the crappy Roanoke station where I'd been trapped for two years.

A few of Laurie's coworkers from BNN were already gathered at a craft beer bar in the East Village when we walked in, but my attention was drawn to the cute, slightly tousled guy reading the *New York Times* alone at a table. Reading an actual paper? How old school. It made him look more interesting than the TV guys on their iPhones. When Charlie stood up to get a beer, my eyes followed him to the bar and then back to his table for one. It was clear he wasn't one of those slick city guys who was trying too hard. In fact, he didn't seem to be trying at all. He didn't appear to own an iron—and it was possible he'd misplaced his comb. Later that night as we chatted at the bar and he described his recent trip to Argentina, I was transfixed. I wanted to hear more. About his trip . . . and him. Charlie Sterling. His name had such a nice ring to it, I couldn't help trying it on for size. Amanda Sterling. Of course, I wouldn't use that on the air. I already had a little name recognition as Gallo—even if it was just on New York's smallest station.

Mom was relieved that my new boyfriend was an associate professor at NYU, rather than a drummer in a rock band. Mom was all for career success, of course—she was over the moon when I'd gotten a scholarship to journalism school—but lately she'd begun mentioning, not so subtly, how wonderful it was that women today could "have it all," which I knew was code for have a successful career *and* produce some grandchildren.

The flashing blue lights of police cruisers told me we'd found the right corner, and I pointed Charlie to the middle of the block and a small brick building with three crisp American flags waving in front. And there, across the street, sat a sole hulking satellite truck, vibrating loudly, with BNN written in big royal blue letters on its side. I could already imagine Laurie inside that truck, notepad in hand, prepping Gabe "America's Premier Newsman" Wellborn to go live. Those two were unbeatable. I looked around for their live shot setup but didn't see a tripod, or even a cameraman pulling cables. Was the story already over? Maybe the gunman was already in custody. For a second, my heart sank. Maybe the hostage situation was resolved and this wasn't my moment after all. I put my hand to my breastbone to slow the beating.

I marched up to the BNN sat truck, Charlie right behind me, and was about to climb its metal mesh stairs when the door swung open with a loud creak and Laurie blew out, shouting over her shoulder, "If they won't let us shoot through the window, just spray the scene!"

"Hey!" I said.

"Hey," she answered, then asked, "Who do I have to fuck around here to get some B-roll?"

That made me laugh and realize the whole thing must be over. Laurie's fotog would probably just shoot some video wallpaper to be used in a reporter package later when the evening anchor recapped top stories.

"Is it over?" I asked. "Did they get the guy?"

"No, he's still in there. Nine hostages, they think."

"Oh, good," I accidentally said. "Who is he?"

"Don't know. The cops aren't saying. There's a presser at eleven, but that's too late. I gotta start getting elements for a package now. Where's your crew?" she asked, looking down at Charlie and me from the stairs.

"The desk hadn't even found a fotog yet when I called. I have to do a phoner as soon as I get some details."

She nodded at my legs. "And just out of curiosity, where are your pants?"

"I don't have any! I thought we were just going to the beach!"

"Well, okay then!" she said, like I had won that point. "By the way, I'm starving. If this thing is wrapped up by lunchtime, I hear there's a great burger place down the road. Anyway, come into the truck. I've got to start crashing this piece."

I stared up at Laurie swinging into breaking news mode and remembered the first time I ever saw her: the first day of my very first TV job as a desk assistant at BNN seven years ago. I felt so lucky to have scored such a plum job right out of college, at a network no less! That first day, as I fidgeted with the rest of the desk assistants, clutching our pens and notepads, looking around for clues on where to stand and what to do, I noticed a young woman, game face on, already hard at work, sitting at a Beta machine logging a stack of tapes. Her long red hair was pulled up in a messy bun with a pencil stuck through the middle holding it in place. I heard one of the guys on the desk say, "You're kicking ass, Laurie." It took me a week to realize she'd started the same day as the rest of us but had gotten there earlier and was already running the joint.

We were just twenty-two years old, but somehow Laurie wasn't intimidated by Gabe Wellborn, and she didn't audibly chortle, like one kid did, when Gabe told us to refer to him as "America's Premier Newsman." Our first month at BNN, while I tried to cajole cameramen into shooting stand-ups for my résumé tape, Laurie convinced a famous money manager turned Ponzi-scheme swindler to give Gabe an exclusive one-on-one interview. From that moment, she was Gabe's right hand.

Weirdly, Laurie never wanted to be on camera. She had all the right ingredients—tenacity, brains, great looks—yet she only wanted to make Gabe look good. I didn't get it. Why wouldn't she want her own face and voice recognized by millions?

"On camera? Oh, God, no," she'd said when I asked her about it once. "All that hair and makeup stuff. Everybody's eyes on you. Having to eat rice cakes to fit into clothes. No, thanks." I was pretty sure Laurie knew I didn't eat rice cakes, but I didn't press the point because explaining why I wanted recognition and stardom and the adulation of strangers made me feel shallow and in need of a shrink. Of course, Laurie *was* famous, in the business, among other producers, who considered her a powerhouse. And she didn't seem to mind when viewers sent fan mail to Gabe about a stellar piece or great interview he'd done, though it was Laurie who made those happen. I didn't get it, but I admired it.

"Is Gabe here yet?" I asked her now, as she stood on the stairs of the sat truck.

"God, no. He's at some golf tournament in Virginia. I called him, but he said he's not coming back unless a lot of people are killed."

"Gross," Charlie said.

"Yeah, they're going to send some other correspondent. Gabe doesn't go to mass shootings anymore unless the body count is more than ten." Laurie rolled her eyes, but I could tell she was proud that Gabe was such a big star he could call the shots, so to speak. "Remember when six people were shot at that office building last month?" she asked. "Gabe said, 'Not good enough!'" She imitated Gabe's authoritative voice and raised a hand like he was Julius Caesar or someone.

I shook my head and let out a chuckle at Gabe saying out loud what my news director would only whisper: that mass shootings had become so commonplace, unless it was another Virginia Tech or Newtown, maybe they weren't worth the cost of hopping on an airplane to cover them.

"That's disturbing," Charlie said, and I quickly forced my smile to go flat. *Oh, that's right, normal people don't find newsroom humor funny. And they don't root for breaking news to be big and bloody.* Even on a typical day, Laurie had a tendency to treat covering tragedy as a routine part of her job description, like morning conference calls or last-minute travel.

"I'm going to go look for some coffee," Charlie said. "Do you want some breakfast?"

"I'd love that," I told him. "And if you see a Walmart or something, can you grab me some pants?"

That's when the sound of three gunshots sliced through the air. *Bang! Bang, bang!* I involuntarily ducked and screamed. "Oh, my God! What was that?"

"Goddammit!" Laurie yelled into the truck, "Petey, get our shot up now!"

I turned to see a line of four guys in black SWAT gear with guns drawn run toward the building.

"I need everyone to clear the area," a police officer barked, using his arm to push us back off the sidewalk.

"We're journalists!" Laurie yelled at him. "BNN and Newschannel 13!" Even in the anxiety of that moment, I loved Laurie for putting us together like that, as if Newschannel 13 were in the same category as the network.

"I need to see your credentials or you need to clear the scene," he said, eyeing my bare legs.

I rooted around in my purse for the lanyard string that held my ID and office key, holding it up for him, forgoing an explanation for my lack of pants.

"I'll head out," Charlie told the cop, and again, I felt a ping of pride at Laurie's and my privileged positions.

"We need to secure this area. All live shots have to be behind this line," the cop said, stringing yellow tape from one street pole to the next. Another squad of police cruisers raced past us to the corner, and I spotted Detective Pultro in the crowd, conferring with another officer.

"Detective!" I yelled and started jogging toward him. "Detective Pultro!"

He saw me and looked annoyed, then turned away.

"Detective! Just one second," I yelled, using my hand to summon him toward me.

He held up a finger to the other cop like he'd be back in one second.

"Make it fast, Amanda," he told me.

"What's happening in there? Has anyone been hurt?" I asked, using a euphemism for killed because it was too upsetting to think people were lying dead yards away from us.

"Don't know yet. Our guys aren't inside. We've got eyes on the guy from outside. But we don't know who's shot."

"Who's the gunman?"

"I told you on the phone we haven't confirmed that yet."

"I know, but surely you've got something. Have you run all the plates in the parking lot?"

He exhaled. "Amanda, you know you gotta go through my PIO."

"I know, I know," I said. "I was just thinking maybe you have something I could work with. And, well, I was also thinking how great it is to have Lester Kravec behind bars."

He gave me a look and his lips tightened. "Yes, Kravec was a very bad guy."

It seemed like he was about to walk away, so I went on. "You know, it's so rare to be able to feature one of those cold fugitive cases on the news. News directors only want fresh stories. I mean, obviously I was able to convince mine to cover the Kravec case, even though it was fifteen years old, because I knew how important it was." That's when I saw the inverted V on his sleeve and remembered. "And it was really great that you got promoted to Detective Sergeant after Kravec was captured, I mean after all your hard work, you know, staying on the case all those years. But mostly it was great that we got Kravec." I smiled at him.

"You're a pain in the ass, you know that?" he said.

"So are you," I told him.

He turned his head away from me, like he was looking down the street and said, "Richard Betts."

"B-E-T-S?" I asked.

"Two *t*'s."

"What else?"

"Fifty-seven years old. Pennsylvania plates. You might check Facebook," he said.

"Thank you. You're the best," I told him.

"You're still a pain in the ass," he told me, then turned and walked briskly back to the cluster of cops. I ran back to the BNN truck and up the precarious steps, ripping open the door. "I got some info," I told Laurie. Just then, I heard a loud rumble from down the road and saw another satellite truck rounding the corner, a yellow-lettered logo on the side.

"Shit! That's ABC," I said.

"Fuck!" Laurie said, "I need my fucking talent to get here. I will not let ABC beat us."

"Can you pull something up on your laptop?" I asked her. "I've got to do this phoner."

"I saw you working your cop over there," she said, and I got an

unexpected ego tingle from Laurie's lingo. She was the person famous for working sources, not me. "What'd he give you?"

"He gave me a name and said to check Facebook."

"That's it?" she said, and I realized what a rookie I was compared
to her. Laurie would have gotten more.

"When are they sending you a reporter?" I asked, looking around,
half expecting some big-time BNN correspondent to suddenly pop out
of the edit bay, microphone in hand, and elbow me out of the way to do
a live shot before my phoner. But all I saw were two coffee-stained Styrofoam cups on a tabletop and a half-eaten box of Little Debbie do-
nuts, its lid still open. Laurie's fotog had telltale white powder on the
front of his T-shirt and incriminating crumbs on his console.

"Petey, you know my friend Amanda. Newschannel 13's finest,"
Laurie said, taking a seat on a rolling chair and starting to type into
her laptop. "What's the name?"

"Richard Betts. Two *t*'s."

"Shit, there's a hundred of them," she said, looking at the screen.

"Look for one from Pennsylvania." I told her.

"Here's one," she said. "He has some sort of blog post. Says, 'Let's go
ahead and invite as many Rapefugees in, then kill them. The Government = THE DEVIL.'"

I started reading over her shoulder. The text ran down the page
with no paragraph breaks but plenty of ALL CAPS, misspellings,
and grammatical oddities. WAKE UP SINNERS U CANT SAVE YOUR-
SELF U WILL DIE AND WORMS SHALL EAT YOUR FLESH, NOW YOUR
SOUL IS GOING SOMEWHERE. TIME FOR REVOLUTION.

"Oh, my God. Does it say how old he is?" I asked.

"Fifty-seven."

"I think that's him," I said and leaned closer. "Look at the next
part. TURN ON THE TV AND LISTEN. GOVERNMENT DESTROYS. WEL-
COMED FOREIGNORS, GAVE THEM OUR JOBS, AND THEY TAKE OUR
FREEDOM TO PROTECT OURSELVES FROM THEM. AMERICA FIRST.
LEAD THE WORLD OUT OF SODOM AND SIN. THE EMPIRE WON'T BE
DESTROYED. WE'RE NOT GOING ANYWHERE FOLLOW US!"

I stared at the oxymoronic brilliance of that last sentence, then
looked up from the laptop at Laurie. "I've got to call the PIO and get

her to confirm all this. We need a second source. And I need to get on the air! I need a crew. And a truck! I gotta break this story!"

Laurie was still scrolling down his blog post, when she stopped and looked straight up at me.

"Petey, set up for a live shot," she ordered.

"But we don't have a correspondent yet," he said.

"We do now," Laurie said.

"What?" Petey asked, turning toward me and pointing with his thumb. "We can't put a reporter from Newschannel 13 on our air."

"You'd rather have ABC beat us?" Laurie said. "Set it up."

My head started swimming. This was the moment I'd been waiting for, but it was even *bigger*. If Laurie put me on BNN, people not just in New York but around the country would wake up, turn on their TVs, and I would be on their screens, the first to tell them the news.

"Oh, my God," I said, covering my mouth with my hand, eyes popping at Laurie. "Can we do this?"

"I don't see why not," she said, pressing numbers on her cell phone. "I'll tell our desk I just hired you as a one-day stringer. They'll be psyched if we get on before ABC. Call your desk. Tell them you're the first reporter here and you need to be the first on the air. Give them our coordinates. They can pull it off the bird. Petey, get off your ass."

"She can't go on air like that," Petey said, cocking his head at my bare legs, flip-flops, bed head, and hangover, which I was pretty sure was now visible.

"He's right," I admitted. "I need your shirt, Laur."

Laurie gave a quick nod and started unbuttoning her wrinkled white blouse, then stopped. "Turn around, Petey. You can't handle seeing a set of tatas like these."

"Shit," Petey muttered, turning away to face the monitors on his edit bay.

Laurie's shirt reeked of stale cigarette smoke.

"Your shirt stinks," I told her.

"Late night," she mumbled, pulling my pink T-shirt over her head.

"Do you have another notepad?" I asked.

"Wow. A reporter without a notepad, a laptop, a sat truck, a shirt, or pants," Laurie said. "You must be a helluva reporter."

"Hey, I got the gunman's name!" I reminded her.

"So," she said, theatrically putting her first finger to her lower lip and tapping, "what will you owe me for all this?"

"My life!" I said fast, my heart pounding.

"Not very creative," she said.

"My firstborn," I tried, grabbing the notepad from her.

"A baby?" Laurie pulled her chin in toward her neck and looked like she might throw up. "No, thanks."

Then I got it. I knew the right answer. "My Peabody, when I win it for breaking news coverage."

At that, Laurie touched her first finger to her nose and pointed the other one at me. "Now you're talking."

That was our Everest. The elusive Peabody, the apex of awards that forevermore signaled we were at the top of the journalism mount. In a field that says you're only as good as your last story, where news directors forget the killer package or awesome live shot they complimented you on just yesterday, the Peabody was forever, the credential of top-notch news chops that no one could ever take away. For me, it would be a golden calling card that would make network doors fly open. And for Laurie, well, I guess it would stand triumphant on her shelf, in front of her collection of Emmys, announcing her place as the best producer at BNN.

"And in lieu of that," I said, in case I couldn't deliver, "how about a lifetime supply of Moscow Mules?"

"That'll work," she said.

"Come on," I said to Petey, jumping up and swinging open the door. "And listen, do *NOT* shoot me from the waist down. When I say, 'as you can see,' you zoom into the building, but you do *NOT* pull out to a wide shot. Got it?"

"You're awfully demanding for someone with no pants," Petey grumbled, then grabbed the tripod.

"Amanda, can you hear us?"

"Yes!" I yelled. I was on the sidewalk, twenty yards from the squad of officers and flashing police cars at the corner, where five minutes ago I'd gotten the PIO to confirm that the Richard Betts I found was the same one in the post office.

"We can't see you," the voice in my ear said.

"I'm here! I'm here," I said, waving my arms at the sat truck half a block away.

"This is Tony in New York. We need you in front of the camera right now. We got your shot up and we're coming to you out of this break!"

Tony's voice was crunchy with static, but at least I knew the IFB Petey had put in my ear was working.

I started jogging back to the camera, my arm twisted around my back, holding the battery pack firmly between my shoulder blades to keep it from falling off my bathing suit strap, now serving as a bra. "You're going to say I'm from Newschannel 13, right?" I asked. "That was the deal, okay?"

"Yup, yup. It's in the copy."

For a second, I considered running into the truck to find my purse and apply some powder to my sweaty face, but there was no time. I raced up to the camera, bent over to look into the lens, using it as a mirror, and was horrified by the sight of my own unkempt reflection. I stuck the stick microphone under my armpit, attempting to smooth down my humid beach hair with both hands.

"We're coming to you in ten!" Tony said in my ear. "Ted Forest is your anchor."

I heard the familiar sound effect for BNN's breaking news. "From BNN headquarters in New York," the anchor said. "We have breaking news out of Long Island. A gunman is engaged in a standoff with police at a post office in Smithtown, and there are hostages inside. Newschannel 13's Amanda Gallo was the first reporter on the scene. Amanda, what can you tell us?"

"Ted, I was standing at this spot twenty minutes ago when the sound of three gunshots burst from the building behind me. Police still don't know if anyone inside was injured or killed. But as you can see, there is a battalion of police officers, a SWAT team, and a dozen emergency vehicles surrounding this scene. Hostage negotiators are in contact with the gunman, trying to end the standoff. According to my sources, the gunman is fifty-seven-year-old Richard Betts from Pennsylvania, an apparently unhinged zealot. Police say his online postings suggest a festering anger that today exploded."

Chapter 2

The Impossible Dream

My sour stomach was surging from the stop-and-go motion of the Newschannel 13 crew car as we inched along in lunchtime traffic. I wanted to take a nap but Doug, my fotog, had the AC cranked, and even with his windbreaker draped across me, I had goose bumps.

"I can't take this crap," Doug said, hitting the dial to change from a pop station to classic rock. I could tell Doug had gone overboard last night celebrating the end of our grueling assignment, and now those Long Island Iced Teas weren't mixing well with the Long Island Expressway. Doug had one hand on the wheel and the other on his cell phone, using his thumb to text. Just then the car to our right swooped over, cutting us off. I saw its back bumper zoom in for a close-up and Doug jammed on the brakes.

"Hey, buddy! Pick a lane and commit to it!" Doug yelled, which struck me as comically philosophical when a simple honk of the horn would have sufficed. "Sorry," Doug said to me, checking his rearview mirror. "I just want to get home to see the kids. Been a long week."

Doug always drove, regardless of how long we'd been working or how tired he claimed not to be. "Oh, good, looks like it's just a bad accident ahead," he said. "For this traffic, somebody better be dead."

Ah, more news humor.

I'd been on camera for twelve hours straight when police finally crashed an armored vehicle through the glass doors of the post office to rescue the hostages. By then, the gunman had killed three people, including a police officer, and injured five others. I turned my head as the bodies were carried out. *Stay focused, stay focused*, I told myself, trying to swallow the heat that always burned in my throat the seconds before tears fell. *Do not get emotional.* I heard my journalism professor's voice in my head. *This is not about you. You're here to give the facts.* We stayed on location for three days, knocking on the doors of victims, interviewing officials, and getting Betts's backstory; it made for long days of standing in the sweltering August sun, from the five A.M. morning show through the ten P.M. evening news. Some nights I was so tired, I fell face first onto the hotel bed without washing off my drugstore makeup or taking off the shirts Charlie had picked up for me, on sale at the Gap nearby.

I stared out the window of the SUV at the passing landscape and wished I weren't on the road so much and could spend more time with Charlie. I couldn't count the times I'd lurched along some highway like this, covering random stories in the tristate area: how to start a small business in Danbury, a life-saving medical breakthrough at a hospital in Princeton. Last July, I'd spent two days at the Jersey Shore covering a beached whale. And last month Doug and I drove all the way to Montauk so I could prove once and for all which ice cream parlor had the most delicious peach ice cream in a blind taste test. All this and I didn't even have a contract with Newschannel 13. I just kept working my ass off, hoping they'd offer me one, or better yet, someone else would.

A muffled ringing was coming from somewhere deep in my purse. I smiled. Maybe Charlie was out of class early. I unearthed my phone, unnerved to see "Jake Raddle" on the caller ID.

"Oh, no," I said. "It's my agent. You don't think he saw those stupid photos online, do you?"

"If so, he probably loved it," Doug said, grinning over at me and reciting from memory, "Reporter Leaps Lauer Without Pants."

I felt sick thinking of that stupid homemade website, with pictures of me right next to Matt Lauer's live shot, holding my microphone, wearing a deadly serious expression, but no pants. Sure, I secretly liked that the website said I was first on the scene, but I hated that it didn't explain *why* I wasn't wearing pants. I didn't know who the asshole was who took the pics and posted them; maybe a competitor from another station, or some neighborhood kid. Either way, the link was retweeted thousands of times. My own personal pantsgate.

"Hi, Jake," I said into the phone.

"Well, hello there, my little shooting star," Jake responded, with the particularly slippery voice he used when impressed, usually with himself. Jake was short and squat and wore a reptilian leer. He lived in a New York City penthouse and had a taste for hand-sewn European shirts, along with an insatiable appetite for finding talent who had "it," as he called it. Jake loved to wine and dine up-and-coming reporters at fancy restaurants to give them a taste of their glorious future under his representation. There's nothing that seduces quite like shrimp cocktail and sizzling steak when you've been eating canned tuna and popcorn for a couple of years. Jake's own expanding waistline seemed to be a tribute to those tax-deductible business dinners. I'd signed Jake's contract right there and then, on the white tablecloth of the Four Seasons, after I'd devoured the steak, before the strawberries and whipped cream arrived.

But ever since getting me out of Roanoke, Jake had proved almost impossible to reach. He acted like Newschannel 13 with its one satellite truck and bare-bones budget was a great gig because it was in New York City. And since they hadn't given me a contract, they could dump me at any time.

"Where have you been?" I asked him. "I've been leaving you messages. I hope you recorded all my coverage of the post office story. I got the exclusive with the wife of the police officer who was killed. You need to add that to my résumé link, then I need you to—"

"You won't be needing that old résumé tape much longer," Jake interrupted.

"Why's that?" I asked.

"I've arranged an interview for you . . . for the biggest break of your life," he slithered.

"What? What is it?"

"I'll tell you. My tireless pursuit of bigger opportunities for you has finally paid off. I've secured an interview for you with Benji Diggs. Yes, that Benji Diggs."

"No way!" I squealed, a shiver of excitement shooting up my spine. There was no bigger broadcaster than world-famous Benji Diggs. At just forty years old, Diggs was named "the Master of Mass

Media" by *Time* magazine, and *Vanity Fair* called him "A one-man media empire!" At least once a month, a cover story on Benji Diggs appeared in some magazine, his Midas media touch the subject of expansive profiles. *Variety* proclaimed, "With Diggs's multimedia platform and countless charity events, he's taken the mantle from Merv Griffin and Dick Clark, even eclipsing Oprah."

Diggs was famous for a lot of things: broadcasting a daily radio show, publishing a couple of media/marketing best sellers, putting on an annual charity ball that brought in millions for cancer research. But his biggest feat was creating successful TV shows, including the longest-running reality show in history, *The Impossible Dream!*

It was appointment viewing. Every week *The Impossible Dream!* found contestants who would admit to a secret lifelong dream— maybe it was to be an astronaut, or a rock star. Whatever their fantasy, Benji Diggs gave them a shot at it by creating seemingly impossible challenges, mental and physical, that, if completed, would advance contestants to the next level. At the end of the season, the person who'd made it to the top would get their wish fulfilled by Benji Diggs, who would emerge from behind a hidden door and announce, "You dared to dream . . . and now the dream is yours!" Diggs would then pop them on a rocket ship or the Rolling Stones' tour bus or whatever.

"He wants me to be on *The Impossible Dream!*?" I whispered into my phone, covering my mouth so Doug wouldn't hear.

"Oh, goodness, no," Jake laughed. "Diggs is starting a new cable news network. It's been top secret, though, of course, I've known about it all along. And it's better than CBS or NBC or even BNN because it'll be on twenty-four hours a day," Jake explained. "It's cable! You'd have endless face time!"

Endless face time . . . Take that, Jeff Davis! "So what is it?" I asked. "And why start *another* cable news network?"

Jake laughed as though that were a preposterous question. "Because this one will be different. First of all, it's not going to be conservative like Fox or liberal like MSNBC. It's going to be straight down the middle—without any bias. It'll give *both* sides. That's why he's calling it the FAIR News Network."

"Isn't that already called CNN?"

"Oh, good grief, Amanda," Jake snorted into the phone. "CNN covers breaking news around the world. That's different. If you want to know what's happening in Syria, you turn on CNN. Bo-ring. FAIR will be the news that the country has been clamoring for. It won't just cover conflicts, it will *solve* them. I tell you, I am sooo sick and tired of all of the division. So much yelling and anger, I could scream. Now imagine a kinder, gentler cable news network where, for the first time, both sides will be brought together, not to yell at each other, but to talk it out."

"Hmm," I said.

"It's truly groundbreaking. But that's what makes Benji Diggs such a genius. Anyway, he loved your coverage of the hostage thing. Apparently you got the police side *and* you gave the gunman's mind-set. I don't know, I didn't see it, but he wants to meet with you today at three."

My eyes darted to the clock on the dashboard. It was 12:30. We were probably two hours outside the city, give or take.

"Yes, that'll work," I said, rolling the dice that I'd be able to dash to my apartment and shower in the space of half an hour.

"I mean, this is it, Amanda. If this interview goes well, you could jump to the next level. The national level. He's offering a national correspondent title, it would be a three-year deal, no outs, twice what you're making now. Oh, and a generous clothing allowance."

I tried to imagine what twice my Newschannel 13 salary would look like on a bank deposit slip . . . plus he'd said the magic words to cast a spell on any struggling newsgal.

"Clothing allowance," I murmured. "Oh, my God." I reached up to push my greasy hair out of my face, and was assaulted by the smell of my own blouse—the pale blue cotton blend with cap sleeves Charlie had brought for me on that very first day, along with, finally, some khaki pants, which I'd worn in live shot after live shot, hour after hour, sweat dripping down my back. The blouse now carried a rank combo of sweat and Hampton Inn bedspread.

"You'll have your own designated team, a cameraman and producer," Jake went on, "and you'll cover stories all over the country. You would need to start almost immediately."

"You had me at clothing allowance!" I giggled.

"Thank heavens I had the foresight to keep you off contract at Newschannel 13. You're free to leave anytime! All part of my master plan for you."

Sure it was. "So what do I need to know?"

"You need to know that Benji Diggs is taking over the world. At this rate he'll be president someday. This is *IT*, Amanda. Don't screw it up." Then, as a helpful afterthought, he added, "Oh, and remember to wear pants this time."

"Very fu—" I heard him hang up.

"What's up?" Doug asked, turning to look at me as I put the phone back in my bag.

"Benji Diggs wants to meet me!" I said before I could stop myself.

"No way!" Doug said.

"Yeah. He's starting a new network. A news network."

"Really?" Doug asked. "What is it?"

"It's called FAIR News," I gushed. "And it's about to change the world."

Chapter 3

Left and Right

After a thirty-second shower, the fastest surveying ever of my closet's scant options, a failed attempt at hailing three passing taxis, and a last-ditch bicycle-drawn rickshaw ride, I arrived at a towering skyscraper in Midtown and stood in front of the future FAIR News Network headquarters. It felt special knowing something big was going on in there that the general public wasn't aware of yet. I glanced up and saw its glass panels catch the summer sun and send off blinding rays that gleamed like lasers. I stood on the sidewalk for a split second admiring the light show before marching inside, signing in, and taking the elevator to the third floor.

Opening a set of glass doors, I walked into what I guessed was a waiting room but could have been a sports bar. Pop music played through ceiling speakers and there were four big TV monitors built into one wall projecting CNN, Fox, MSNBC, and BNN all at once, creating a news din that three young women at desks were ignoring. The women were not seated at their desks; rather they were walking on moving treadmills while typing on keyboards raised to elbow height. In the middle of the room sat a quiet foosball table, next to a mesh bin holding, from what I could see, a collection of Nerf footballs, a kickball, softballs, tennis balls, rackets, a lacrosse stick, and a Frisbee. And in the corner of the room, right next to the entrance, was an open box, three feet tall and big enough to climb into, brimming with small multicolored rubber balls.

"Oh, hi!" one of the young women said, turning from her computer and leaping off her treadmill. She wore a turquoise sundress that was, to my mind, too short for the office, and a pair of platform heels, too high, I felt, for speedwalking on a treadmill. "Amanda, right?"

"Yes," I answered. "I'm looking for Benji Diggs. Is this the break room?"

"LOL!" she said. "This *is* Benji's office. I'm Melissa, his assistant. Benji says it's important to keep the creative juices flowing. And," she giggled, "Benji always says it takes balls to start a news network. So we have balls! Did you see our ball pit?" she asked, extending her arm to the supersized playpen of multicolored balls. "You can jump in there and roll around. It's like an awesome body massage. Want to try it?"

I looked over at the red, blue, green, and yellow balls sitting idly in their pen. "Maybe on my way out."

"Benji is just finishing up a phone call," she said. Then, putting her hand to the side of her mouth dramatically and lowering her voice, she confided with obvious pride, "He's on with Ryan Seacrest. You know they're besties, right?"

"I don't think I did know that," I said, slowly feeling the panic rise as I realized I hadn't had time to research him online. Luckily his office held some clues. I moved toward a wall covered in framed photos of Diggs throughout his career: a half dozen or so 2 x 3-foot color posters of Diggs joshing around with his reality show competitors. There was Diggs, arm in arm with Tom Bergeron, pretending to be "Dancing with the Stars." In the next, Diggs was shadowboxing Blake Shelton in front of a neon red *The Voice* sign. Then, an extra-large photo of Benji Diggs and Ryan Seacrest on a red carpet, both in sunglasses, smiling out at the crowd surrounding them, each with an arm raised, as if in victory. In the middle of the wall was a black-and-white photo, blown up to its grainiest proportions, of a probably six-year-old Benji Diggs sitting at a soundboard wearing oversized earphones that almost swallowed his head.

I walked farther along the wall and, wait, what's this? I stopped in front of a photo of Benji Diggs and the famous actor Victor Fluke together on the set of Fluke's long-running hit TV show *Home of the Brave.* The photo had to be at least fifteen years old, because Fluke still had his mustache and trademark cowboy hat. I'd forgotten how handsome he was in his heyday, like Tom Selleck in his *Magnum, P.I.* prime. Fluke played the part of the beloved patriarch Sam Stockton, the character we'd all grown up wishing was our dad. After Stockton was finally (and tragically) killed off, Fluke went on to star in a series of amusing aftershave commercials featuring a character called "The World's Most Successful Man."

I smiled, remembering my favorite one. In it, Fluke was riding a horse and, at the same time, shooting a bow and arrow at a target. The commercial was hilarious because Fluke was actually shooting the bow backward, behind his back, while the horse was in full gallop. Oh, and Fluke was blindfolded. Come to think of it, so was the horse. But Fluke made a bull's-eye, of course. Then the announcer said, "There must be something the World's Most Successful Man can't do. But no one can remember what that might be." I shook my head at the absurdity of that guy now considering a run for president. *Impossible.*

I paced around, trying to rehearse the lines I'd practiced in my head on the ride over: Hello, Mr. Diggs. *Shit. Too formal.* Hi, Benji! *Better.* If you've by chance seen that silly link to my inappropriate attire at the post office shooting, *ha, ha, ha, so silly!* let me assure you of my solid journalism credentials. I went to college on an academic scholarship, majored in broadcast journalism, graduated with honors. Got my first job as a desk assistant with Gabe Wellborn, America's Premier Newsman, helping to produce his award-winning nightly newscast (I should probably omit that my most pressing job duty was "producing" tomato juice for Gabe's lunch). I got my first on-air job in teeny Salisbury, Maryland, then jumped to Roanoke, Virginia, and now Newschannel 13. I made a mental note to tell Diggs that years ago I'd read his memoir on his rise from paperboy to radio host to media mogul. At that, my stomach made a noise so loud that I was sure Melissa heard it. *I shouldn't have had that Filet-O-Fish sandwich.*

"Hey, you!" I heard a man's voice say, and until that very moment I hadn't realized how familiar that voice was to me: a smooth, broadcast baritone, ubiquitous yet unique. I thought for a second the TV was talking to me, until I heard footsteps and turned to see Benji Diggs, fit and tan in a slim-cut navy suit with just two buttons, which screamed custom made. His trousers were an inch or two shorter than I was used to, which I worried was a dry cleaning error until I saw he had eschewed socks and had unusually handsome ankles. His caramel-colored shoes were a shade lighter than I'd ever seen on a man, with a patina I'd only spotted in ads for Italian footwear. I had to force my eyes up as his feet strode out from his office and moved across the waiting room toward me.

Shorter than I'd expected, Benji was roughly my height in heels, and slight. I should have known. Television personalities were always smaller in person than they appeared on screen. In college, my journalism professor claimed I'd be successful on TV, not only because I worked harder than my classmates, but because I had what he deemed the winning combination: big head, small body. Something in common, Benji Diggs and me. I turned toward Benji, extending my right hand, which he breezed by.

"I've watched you so much this past week," he said, opening his arms wide, "I feel like I already know you." And then Benji Diggs pulled me into a tight embrace.

"Oh, okay," I said into his shoulder.

"Let me have a look at you," he said, taking a step back but holding my hands tightly, like we were long lost friends who'd just reunited. "You're much better looking in person," he said, keeping his eyes locked on mine for about three beats too long, as if drinking me in. "The camera is not doing you justice. But not to worry!" he said, launching his first finger into the air. "We will fix that! Follow me!" He turned and took double-speed strides back to his office. "Let's really get to know each other."

"Um, sure," I said, breaking into a jog behind him.

"Come in," he said, turning to face me and walking backward. "Make yourself at home. What would you like? Sparkling water? A cappuccino? I can have Melissa run out and get us these awesome green juices. There's one with kale and green apple and celery. I'm off carbs so I live on these things. You want one?"

"Oh, no, thanks."

"Yeah, I don't blame you. They're horrible." Benji made a sweeping gesture with his arm, then sat down and patted the spot next to him on his black-and-white cowhide sofa that looked exactly like the one I'd just seen on the cover of *Architectural Digest*.

"So," he said.

"So," I repeated after about two seconds, unsure if that was my cue or his windup.

"So let me tell you what we're doing here," he said, locking his hands together and stopping to take a big inhale, as though this were the first time he'd ever confessed this to anyone. "We're changing the face of cable news. I mean, it's that simple, yet that monumental. Okay?"

"Okay," I agreed.

"Right now, you've got Fox for conservatives and MSNBC for liberals and CNN for news junkies—and then, of course, the big networks, ABC, NBC, BNN, and CBS, which are dying a slow, painful death in front of all our eyes. Now, why would anyone in their right mind want to add another news network to that?" He paused and looked at me.

"Um . . . because we need more," I said, without the right conviction.

"No! Because we need less!" he exclaimed. "All that cable news has done is divide this country in half. You've got liberals and conservatives, red and blue, black and white, right and wrong, okay? Now what if . . . what if"—he paused dramatically to let his hypothetical hang midair—"what if, there could be one news network that would have all of those in one place? What if the point were not to divide the country, but to bring everyone together? Because, you know, the other networks want you to think there are only polar extremes. But maybe there's a whole unexplored world in the middle where both sides can coexist. You know?"

"Yes," I said, nodding but not really knowing.

"Now imagine this: What if you had one-stop shopping for news consumers? What if Republicans *and* Democrats, midwesterners *and* northeasterners, old *and* young, could *all* watch the same news network?" He stopped and looked at me, his eyes so lit up they glinted.

"I can't really imagine that," I admitted, struggling with what to do with my hands before deciding to just sit on them.

"Look, the election is a little more than a year from now. And history tells us there is no better ratings driver than a presidential race, so the timing here is perfect. We're going to get all these polarized groups that hate each other out of their echo chambers and into one room to hear each other for the first time. And why stop there? Maybe FAIR News can help them come up with solutions. Let's dissolve the left-right paradigm. Enough of this binary model."

Uh-oh. The double whammy of "paradigm" and "binary" almost disconnected my neurotransmitters and put my brain into sleep mode. Those two words taken individually always had a soporific effect on me—but at the same time? I feared a blackout coming on and forced my eyelids extra open to show how interested I was in whatever it was he'd just said.

"Look, I'm just spitballing here. My point is, TV news has the power to polarize—and God knows others have made a fortune doing that—but it also has the power to bring people together. And that's what I want to do. Let's create a solution-oriented model." He put his hands together and interwove them to show me how easily it could be done.

"Well, that would be incredible," I admitted. I liked the sound of Benji's vision. Just last week, I had been telling Charlie how I longed for a time when the news was just the news, meaning purveyor of useful information, rather than a lightning rod of controversy. Back when Mom and I watched at the breakfast table, after the final fight when she'd told Dad to get out. Back then the news wasn't open for debate. That seemed a more peaceful time—before cable news created crazy conversations and drove a wedge into the world.

"You know, I was just saying this last week," I told Benji, leaning forward toward him on the sofa. "It's impossible to watch the news without seeing some loudmouth Bill O'Reilly type getting into a shouting match with some Rachel Maddow wannabe. I mean, when I was growing up, my mom and I would watch the news every morning to learn about the world. But now the news has turned into a mortal combat cage match."

"Mortal combat cage match! I like that!" Benji said. "We should name a show that. Ironically, of course, because at FAIR News we won't make guests fight each other. We'll make them *hear* each other. More like Mind-Blowing Fairness Forum. I'm just thinking out loud."

"That sounds wonderful," I said, but even I could hear my skepticism.

"It's possible," Benji said. "Do you know that Walter Cronkite had a hundred and twenty-five million viewers for the first moonwalk? One hundred and twenty-five million! Think about how many more TVs there are today, yet no one brings in those numbers. I mean Fox gets, what? A million or two a day? And they trumpet that like it's a huge success. What if we could get fifty million throughout the day? A hundred million? The sky's the limit with this because we'll have something for everyone. Now, I know, I know, 'millennials don't watch TV,'" he said, rolling his eyes and making air quotes with his fingers. "'Kids are glued to their iPhones.' That's fine. They don't have to sit down and actually watch TV. We'll give them content streaming on their devices; we'll be a newsroom without walls, blah, blah, blah. The point is, we'll get the twenty-five to fifty-four-year-old demo, *and* even early twentysomethings will come to us, because again, we're the *only* ones who'll give you all the information in one place, all sides. It's so retro it's revolutionary!"

"Wow, that's pretty ambitious," I said, unsure whether to challenge his prediction of millions in this new niche-targeted world.

"Look, I've run the numbers," he said, reading my mind, "and I see the path to get there. Add up all the morning shows and all the evening newscasts and all of cable and you get some pretty impressive numbers. I believe we can even bring some of the cord cutters back for big news. Hey! Do you know where the word 'broadcast' comes from?"

I scratched my head, trying to channel Professor Jordan from my Journalism 101 class.

"It's an old farming practice," he went on, "of casting out seeds broadly, scattering them to take root. I mean, how great is that? Let's get back to that notion of seeds and ideas being planted."

"I love that," I told him, and I did. I was starting to see why Benji Diggs was such a visionary.

"You gotta think big. You can't accomplish what I have in my career and not think big and dream bigger. No one thought *The Impossible Dream!* would last even one season. But look at it! It's been on almost twenty years. I can't believe it myself. I look at that twenty-two-year-old kid in those photos and I can't believe that's me. But it's time to do it again. It's time for the next Big Bold Benji Diggs Dream."

"That's exciting," I said, wondering if at any point we'd get around to talking about my role in the Benji Bonanza.

"And that's where you come in," Benji said, taking my hand. "This vision sounds simple, but it's not—and not everyone will understand what we're trying to do here. But I think you do."

"I think I do," I said quickly.

"Good, because this is going to require a different kind of journalist, one who's more evolved. Believe it or not, I wouldn't hire Walter Cronkite now."

"No?"

"I mean, number one, he's dead."

"Right."

"Number two, he'd be bad for the demo. You can't have an old guy with a comb-over competing with David Muir, who looks like Adonis, okay? But more important, no one wants their anchor or reporter to broadcast down from on high, devoid of feeling and emotion. They want to see broadcasters as human. And I think you have a human quality."

"Oh, thank you."

"I saw that interview you did with that cop's wife. You teared up there, didn't you?"

Oh, no. How unprofessional. "Well, see, we'd been working for fourteen hours and it was extremely hot," I explained, so Benji would think he'd seen sweat, not sadness.

"Stop," he said, reaching out his finger and putting it to my lips. "It's okay," he whispered, squeezing my hand as though I were the grieving widow. "This is not your grandfather's journalism class, where you have to be 'objective' about a tragedy. You showed that you feel things. And that really works."

"Oh, uh, okay," I said, trying nonchalantly to extract my hand from his grip so I could shoo away the specter of Professor Jordan sitting on my shoulder. *Journalists are conduits of information. A good reporter never lets her own emotions get in the way of the story.* Of course, I'd already taken some liberties on that front. You can't have a blind taste test of the best peach ice cream and be objective. *Okay, Professor Jordan?*

"The news is terrible and people want to know you feel that. I mean, you're in their bedrooms every morning and at their dinner table every night. It's okay for them to feel your sadness. Aren't we all sad about the news?" He looked at me with moist eyes and I decided not to mention that I found news exciting.

"So," he said, straightening up and clapping his hands together, "we've got our work cut out for us. We're launching next month. I predict combining our first year with the presidential race will boost the numbers enough to put FAIR News on the map."

"Sounds smart," I agreed. "And that reminds me. I saw that photo of you and Victor Fluke out on your wall—"

"Yeah, I love that photo. That's when I met Fluke. When he did a guest spot on *The Impossible Dream!* That was one of our highest-rated episodes ever."

"Yeah?" I said, wanting more. "So what do you think? Do you think he'll actually run?"

"I don't think so," Benji said. "I haven't talked to him in a long time, but I know the guy doesn't know shit from Shinola about politics. He loved being a TV star. I think he's pretending he might run, to get back in the limelight. And it's working. He's getting some press. But no, I don't think he'll really do it. He likes his beach house in Malibu and his sports car too much. I don't see him going to the Iowa State Fair and eating deep-fried butter, or whatever the hell they eat there." At that Benji cringed, like no amount of kale would unclog that thought. "But listen, back to us. A TV start-up is not for the faint of heart! This job will take stamina. And I get the impression you don't let anything stop you. Hey," he said, locking onto my eyes, "did you really go on the air without pants?"

I stiffened. "Okay, now see, I can explain—"

"Not necessary," he interrupted. "It's fantastic! I did some checking. You had about two thousand Twitter followers before that. You know how many you have now?"

I didn't. Ever since the pantsless photos went viral I'd taken a Twitter vacation.

"You have 5,138! *That's* the power of what can happen overnight when you put something out there that people are interested in." Benji laughed, and I attempted a laugh, too, though I couldn't tell if he was kidding.

"So whaddya say?" Benji boomed. "Do you want to be part of this experiment in radical fairness? Do you want to be on the front lines of this bold plan to bring the country together?"

I liked what Benji was saying about uniting the country, of course, though I had no earthly idea how he planned to do it. Mostly, I just couldn't stop thinking about the six-figure salary that was coming my way, not to mention the clothing allowance. Money talks, and I liked what this salary was saying about paying my rent and helping Mom out, too. So, like every tough assignment I'd ever been given, I figured I'd work out the details later—the old "we'll fix it in the edit room" strategy that so many of us in TV news relied on when a script wasn't quite perfect, but the clock was ticking.

"Yes," I said, slapping my palms on my knees.

"That's terrific!" Benji said, clapping his hands together. "I'll call your agent today and make an offer. It's time for you to experience a Big Benji Diggs Production. Let's get you out of that Newschannel 13 hellhole. Jesus, their set looks like something my three-year-old glued together in preschool. Hey, let me show you a picture!" Benji reached to grab a sleek silver frame off the coffee table. His toddler, I assumed.

"You have two children, right?" I said, trying to show interest in what I was discovering was a major point of fascination to Benji Diggs: himself.

"Four, actually," he said, handing me another photo in another frame of four adorably dressed kids. "A seventeen-year-old, a fifteen-year-old, a three-year-old, and a one-year-old."

"How'd that happen?" I asked, immediately hearing how inappropriate it was to inquire about Benji Diggs's family planning process.

"Different wives," he said. "I married the first one right out of college, then got divorced. It was sad, she's a great lady. We were just too young. Anyway, I married my current wife and had these two little beauties. God, having kids is sooo amazing!" he said, staring at his own family's photo. "Do you have any kids?"

"Nope," I said, thinking that was a weird question. He must know that the rigors of field reporting made having a baby impossible for a single twenty-nine-year-old. But someday . . . if this FAIR News thing worked out . . . and I could work my way up to anchoring . . . and spend more time with Charlie . . . and get married . . . I almost didn't want to let myself dream that far ahead.

"Oh, you've *got* to do it. I mean, it's such a life changer. I love it. And I'm gonna keep doing it until I get a boy," he said, turning to place the frames back on the table. "I was very close to my mother growing up, still am." Benji stopped and I could have sworn his throat caught. He looked at me with soupy eyes. "I wish that for you. There's nothing like it. And how great would it be to have girls *and* boys?"

"Both sides," I said and smiled. "Problem solved."

"Yes!" he said, holding his hands out at me, palms wide open. "That's it! You've got it."

Chapter 4

Backstory

"Then he offered me the job!" I was on the phone telling Mom all about Benji and FAIR News and the offer.

"Well, sweetheart, it sounds like it's all coming together and all your hard work is paying off. Maybe now that Harriet Tubman is on the twenty-dollar bill, you can be next."

I smiled. There wasn't much Mom couldn't connect to the subject of women's equality. "They *should* put a journalist on the hundred!" I said. "Can you believe I'm going to be on national TV! I mean, this is *it*. My dream is coming true. Benji's right—there is no impossible dream!"

"I remember that day you first came up with your dream," Mom said before uttering the two words that said it all. "Suzy Berenson."

"Suzy Berenson," I repeated.

I remembered the moment, too. I was sitting at the breakfast table in a funk. I was fifteen years old—old enough to realize that my original childhood dream of "being a star" probably wasn't going to be possible with my feeble talents. I'd attempted a few avenues. First up: dancer. Ballet, tap, and jazz classes—none of them worked. I never developed the skill to stand out in a recital. Next: musician. That didn't pan out either. I took piano lessons but wasn't driven enough to practice regularly. Singer. Out of the question. The distressed facial expression of my music teacher when I opened my mouth was hard to miss. Even friends would slap their hands over their ears as I attempted to belt out "Tomorrow" like Annie.

Actress. Seemed like a logical fit. Mom had gotten me into children's community theater at seven years old, and I liked being on stage. But while I spent a lot of time daydreaming about getting the lead role, I always ended up being cast as a flower (nonspeaking, garden variety). The lead always went to Betsy, the little girl with the hovering mother who would brush Betsy's long blond hair while dutifully going over her lines.

I couldn't help but notice that being the star looked good. Betsy got more attention and more opportunity than the rest of us. Somebody was going to put her in a commercial. After Mom and Dad got divorced, Mom tried to keep everything the same at home, but I knew money was tight and figured if I was a star we'd never have to worry about bills again. Mom didn't want me worrying; she told me to just follow my dream. "You don't get to pick your parents, sweetheart, you only get to pick your path," she told me.

Once we were on our own, Mom and I developed a morning ritual—over breakfast we'd watch *The Morning Show with Suzy Berenson* on the old TV that took up half our kitchen counter. Suzy Berenson delivered all the news, uplifting or devastating, in her soothing, measured way. Nelson Mandela becoming president of South Africa, Princess Diana's car crash—Suzy brought them into our kitchen. One morning I was home sick from school and heard Mom gasp and cover her mouth. I looked up in time to see ashy gray smoke floating from an explosion that sliced through a federal building in Oklahoma City. The news, even when it was bad, gave Mom and me something to focus on other than Dad's absence.

Then, on one fateful morning, sitting at the breakfast table, staring at the TV as I had a thousand times, something was ignited. There was Suzy Berenson in her TV studio, interviewing a family whose baby desperately needed a heart transplant. I was gripped, praying a heart would come through before it was too late. Leaning ever so slightly forward, Suzy nodded with compassion, asking about their pain. And then something amazing happened. Right in the middle of the segment, a hospital called. They'd found a heart for the baby! The family burst into tears of joy, as did I in the kitchen, then they got up right there in the studio and left for the hospital. All on live TV! And that's when it hit me. *Television news is powerful! It can save lives. And, hey, I like asking questions and solving problems, too. Wait, does that job pay money?* So, at fifteen, TV news became my North Star, lighting a path to a bigger, brighter future.

On the first day of college, at freshman orientation, I sat in an auditorium among two hundred budding broadcast journalism students. The dean admonished all of us idealistic freshmen to be realistic. "This is a highly competitive business," she warned. "I know all of you want to be network news anchors, but look around this room. Only two of you will ever make it to a network." I turned around in my seat to see who the other person was.

I focused on standing out in my journalism classes so I would be chosen as a reporter for the campus TV station. Professor Jordan taught us that journalism was a public service—we were to be "watchdogs" of government and institutions and authority figures. We had access to powerful people that others didn't. He had three principles we were to live by. He wrote them on the board:

1. Be objective: check your personal biases and emotions at the door. The story is not about you.
2. Be truthful: double-check your facts and the credibility of your sources. A journalist is only as good as her sources. Get two of them and make sure they're rock solid.
3. Never burn a source: they're your lifeblood. Ask yourself if you'd be willing to go to jail to protect a confidential source. If not, don't use that info. No surprises for your sources.

Professor Jordan had a whole bunch of other helpful TV tips, too: avoid clichés, don't bury the lede, and never end a report with the tired tag "Time will tell." He taught us to think of our script as a winding country road, some parts uphill, some down, some shaded, some sunny. I didn't really get that, but I got an A because I worked my ass off and handed everything in on time.

I focused on my future with the zeal some kids used to party. On Thursday nights as my dorm threw yet another kegger, I'd be in the studio editing field tapes for Friday's newscast. I was too busy to indulge in the usual antics like frat parties or crushes on professors.

"I think Professor Davidson likes you," a classmate said with an insinuating smile one day as we walked out of our U.S. History class.

It was true, Professor Davidson had directed much of that morning's lecture toward me.

"He invited me to lunch," I confessed to her.

"Ooh, are you going to sleep with him?" she asked, lifting her eyebrows in anticipation.

"I can't," I told her. "I have a two P.M. media law class."

I never knew what people meant by a runner's high—that euphoric release of endorphins that tells you everything in the world will be all right—until the first time I went out on campus on a cold day with a camera and microphone and I felt it. My toes were numb, my nose was running, the metal mic was almost too cold to hold. Still, I felt the hot rush through my veins as I practiced talking into the camera for the first time.

"In three, two, one . . . wait! What was I saying? Let me redo that. Okay, in three, two, one . . . hold on! Can we rewind that last one, so I can look at it again?"

I flubbed take after take of my stand-ups until my poor classmate, shivering behind the camera, said, "I think you're just going to have to stick with one of these even if it sucks."

I did suck. But somehow that didn't matter; the TV drug had hit my bloodstream and I felt its intoxication immediately. I would bring important campus issues to light. With a camera, I could get the university president to talk to me. I had pull now. I had power—and attention: students thanked me for revealing the lousy cafeteria conditions and the dorm's rat infestation problem. I wanted to do even bigger, better stories. So when I graduated and got my first job, working for Gabe Wellborn (for crying out loud!), America's Premier Newsman, it looked like I was on the fast track to dream fulfillment.

"I feel like everything has been leading up to this moment," I told Mom on the phone. "From Campus TV to FAIR News."

"Maybe you'll have the chance to interview Virginia Wynn," Mom said. "Wouldn't that be thrilling? I think she has a real shot at becoming president. Two powerful women talking."

Oh, boy. It was going to be a long year if Mom tried to turn every one of my assignments into a campaign commercial for her favorite candidate, Virginia Wynn, the heavily favored Democrat. "Yes, Mom," I said with resignation, "that would be exciting."

. . . . .

The day after Benji made the offer, Charlie and I went out to cele-brate at a charming little trattoria we'd discovered in the West Vil-lage. Flush with the promise of my new contract, we splurged on the forty-five dollar prix fixe *and* a bottle of wine. I couldn't stop smiling.

"A clothing allowance!" I squealed.

"You'll be able to buy pants," Charlie said, clinking my glass.

"Maybe I shouldn't. Pants free is my signature look." I winked.

"Seriously, what else did Diggs say about what you'll be doing?"

I loved that Charlie was hanging on every word from my Benji meeting, though it seemed funny that he'd only refer to Benji as Diggs, as if the name Benji was just too goofy to call a grown man.

"He said FAIR News will be a place for viewers to get all the infor-mation, not just the left-right paradigm that's so pervasive on cable news." I hoped my use of "paradigm" *and* "pervasive" might make Benji's plan sound more strategic.

"What does that mean?" Charlie asked, tearing another hunk of bread from the loaf and dunking it in the last of the spicy olive oil.

"It means Benji wants to go back to a time when the news gave people real information. And it was information they could use to solve problems, rather than the partisan echo chamber where viewers just hear their own warped worldview." I impressed myself with that one. Hearing my own explanation was the first time I really got it.

"Huh?" Charlie said.

I got more emphatic. "Benji wants to bring the country together. Did you know that 125 million people watched Walter Cronkite cover the first moonwalk? Benji thinks TV news can bring both sides together again."

"I think that rocket has left the launchpad," Charlie said, taking another bite of the Bolognese. "People look for confirmation bias, not real information. Do you know that in 2004, scientists did MRIs on George Bush and John Kerry supporters and found that their brain centers only lit up when they thought the other candidate was lying, not their own candidate? Even when they read the exact same statement."

That was interesting, though I thought Charlie might be missing the point. "But I like Benji's idea of bringing both sides together to hear each other. Maybe that's what those Bush and Kerry supporters needed. I want to do that."

Charlie gave a thoughtful pause. "Maybe you should focus on human interest stories. Like that interview you did with the cop's wife. That was terrific."

"Thank you. Benji mentioned that one, too. He thought I was showing good emotion. He thinks reporters don't always need to be objective." I brought my thumb to my mouth to nibble on my nail.

"No," Charlie said. "It's the opposite. You're great because you don't overly emote. You could be the next Barbara Walters or Diane Sawyer, but even better because you don't contort your face into that TV pity look. You're less saccharine."

"I think that might be your wine talking," I said, flattered that Charlie thought I was already in the same league as the two titans of the teary interview art form, though I didn't know what to make of his perception. This wasn't the first time two viewers saw two completely different things in my facial expressions. Some viewers saw sympathy, or sadness, while others saw contempt and discomfort— all during the same interview. I was beginning to see my neutral "news face" as a Rorschach test.

"I wish you could hear Benji talk," I told him. "He's inspiring."

"I'm sure he is," Charlie said in a way that made me think he was not at all sure. "But look, I think Diggs is right about the time for objectivity being over. The media shouldn't be focused on objectivity. It should be focused on truth."

I bit my lip. Was objectivity officially out the window? Professor Jordan popped up on my shoulder and wagged his finger at me. *Not now, professor!*

"Anyway, I'm excited for you," Charlie said, smiling at me. "I knew it was only a matter of time for you to make your mark." He signaled for the check. "Come on, let's get out of here."

"Yeah, I have a big day tomorrow. I have to tell Newschannel 13 that they won't have Amanda Gallo to kick around anymore. Tomorrow I begin the transition from lowly local reporter to national news correspondent. I plan to become insufferable!"

Charlie reached across the table for my hands. "Don't change too much, okay? I love you just like this."

Chapter 5

Jump Cut

My new office at FAIR was on the sixteenth floor, aka "the talent floor." It was a self-important, haughty term that I loved more than I should. No longer was I referred to as a "field reporter" as I had been in Roanoke and at Newschannel 13. Now I was "talent," with all its glamorous and indispensable connotations. The sixteenth floor also housed a big pod of producers' desks in the middle of a huge open space, surrounded by the anchors' and reporters' offices on all four sides. "Talent" offices had windows with natural light, and doors that shut and locked. Producers, on the other hand, had to toil in the public square, under fluorescent bulbs, unable to make personal calls or take a bite of their sandwiches in private.

I liked walking around the sixteenth floor, reading the nameplates of other "talent," particularly the famous anchors Benji Diggs had stolen from the competition. I'd peek into their offices as I passed. Some offices were tiny, smaller than a dorm room, with barely the space to cram a desk, chair, and clothing rack. Others were broad and handsome, with leather-bound books in custom-made shelves. It took me a few weeks to realize that office size directly correlated to contract size. Mine was small. But I liked it. I'd tacked some old snapshots onto a corkboard: me holding a microphone to a police officer's mouth, me blindfolded for my ice cream taste test, and my now favorite shot—me, in my old red puffy parka standing in a snowbank, covering yet another blizzard. *Ha! All yours, Jeff Davis!*

I loved my new reporting assignments, each one more interesting than the last, and each a fresh opportunity to show Benji how much I *got* the concept of what we were doing at FAIR.

"Yes, yes!" Benji would say to the conference room filled with a dozen producers and reporters, pointing up to the huge screen on which one of my packages had just been projected.

"This is exactly what I'm looking for," he declared after screening my piece on the death penalty. "See what Amanda did here?" he asked the crowd. "She got that great interview with the cop's daughter, who lost her dad and wants that scumbag murderer to get the electric chair. And so, you're like, 'Yeah, yeah, kill him!' Then she interviews the Board of Prisons woman, who explains how much more the death penalty costs taxpayers, and you're like, 'Now hold on a second.' Then she interviews that sociologist, who asks, 'Why is the government murdering someone to prove how wrong it is to murder someone? How's that civilized?' And you're like, 'Hey, I never thought of that.' See? *All* sides have a point."

Everyone would nod, like they always did when Benji spoke, though I feared that afterward they'd give me the hairy eyeball in the hallway. But they didn't. They complimented my death penalty piece, and my piece on the automated cars that studies showed had fewer accidents but might be more dangerous because they were more prone to hacking. And of course, they really liked that perennial favorite I had reprised for FAIR News—the blindfolded taste test of the best peach ice cream in Montauk. That one was evergreen. I could stick it in the can until Memorial Day and it would still be a crowd-pleaser then.

I didn't think any of these pieces would win me a Peabody, but my chances were better at FAIR than they'd ever been. And for the first time I felt like I might actually be in Laurie's league of doing stories that got the attention of awards committees.

Charlie took issue with a couple of my pieces, particularly the one I did on gun control. The angle was Hollywood celebrities who railed against guns while having round-the-clock armed guards to protect their own families. Charlie thought the answer was obvious: crack down on gun sales and you'd have less violence and less need for bodyguards. I argued that the story was about hypocrisy. A different set of rules for the elite. After our first official fight, he reluctantly conceded that maybe my angle had some merit, and a few days later he offered an olive branch in the form of a red T-shirt that said

"Devil's Advocate" across the front. I found the shirt way too corny to ever wear, until I realized that, paired with some hideous red spandex workout pants, a red headband with pointy ears attached, pumps, a pitchfork, and a sensible black blazer one might wear in a law firm, the "Devil's Advocate" shirt made the perfect Halloween costume.

I was so busy covering medical breakthroughs, technology innovations, and other human interest stories that some days I could almost forget that there was a surreal primary season under way. In late September, a couple of weeks after I arrived at FAIR, Victor Fluke threw his hat in the ring, figuratively and literally. In a made-for-TV event in Fort Worth, Texas, Fluke rode around a football stadium atop a bucking bronco, then with great fanfare tossed his old Sam Stockton cowboy hat into a ring of fire. I had to admit, it was awesome.

"This is re-donk-u-lous," Laurie said, as she, Charlie, and I stood in front of my TV screen, arms folded across our chests, watching the spectacle. Somehow Fluke managed to tame the bronco into an obedient mare in the space of a couple of minutes, then he dismounted and made his way to a microphone, chaps and all. He gave a salute to the crowd and launched into a malapropalooza of promises.

"I love this great country," Fluke boomed. "That's why I'm jumping into this race with both boots. You all probably remember me as Sam Stockton, may he rest in peace, and then as the World's Most Successful Man. And if you see fit to elect me president, I'll make America the Most Successful Country. Yee-haw!"

The crowd cheered.

"I have Six Secrets of Success that I'm ready to share with all of you. Listen up! Number one: you've got to think positive to grow rich!"

"Wait a second, isn't that a book?" Charlie asked. "By Napoleon Hill, I think?"

"Napoleon," Laurie repeated. "Bad omen."

"With my winning formula, in a few months we'll pay down the national deficient!" Fluke said.

"He means deficit," said Charlie.

"Number two: maintain strong values, like traditional marriage and families. When I'm president, we'll bring down the divorce rate. Divorce will have the same stigmata as drunk driving."

"Stigmata?" I said.

"Just like what Mothers for Drunk Driving did to save lives, we'll do to save marriages."

Laurie snorted. "He means Mothers *Against* Drunk Driving."

"Number three: total self-awareness. Because the secret to your success is already inside of you. As your president, I'll show you how to bring it out."

"What next?" Laurie asked. "Promising to give everyone courage and a heart?"

"If you love this country, let's make it the Home of the Brave again!" Fluke said, with a fist raise. "Let there be a Bronco in every backyard!" With that he threw a leg over his horse, saddled back up, and rode off.

Laurie hit the mute button. "Well, that was fun. Now back to planet Earth. I give it twenty-four hours till he drops out."

"Too bad," I said. "Having him in the race would be entertaining. It would shake up politics as usual. Give new meaning to the horse race. Think of it!"

Charlie wasn't laughing. He narrowed his eyes at the TV. "Hmm," was all he said.

Chapter 6

Hair and Makeup

The brisk snip of the scissors was snapping next to my ear, but the chair was swiveled around so I couldn't see what Angie, FAIR's top stylist, was doing. I'd been sitting for so long my feet had fallen asleep.

"How's it going?" I asked.

"Almost done," she said. "Wait till you see this new cut and ya new culah!"

"What 'culah' is it exactly?" I asked, hoping Angie didn't mind my poking fun at her Bronx accent. I was nervous. She hadn't let me take a peek during the hour and a half she'd spent painting dollops of bleach up and down my mousy brown strands, then letting them marinate in tin foil before washing out the dye in the sink.

"Ya *blond*, baby. Much blonder. I threw in lots of chunky highlights. Benji will love it!" Angie had been at *Good Morning America* for years, until Benji convinced her to come to FAIR six months ago for the launch. "Ya got sooo much hair here. God bless. It's thicker than Stephanopoulos's," she marveled. "Now we gotta make this mop pop. Benji wants all you talent to have great hay-yer." Hair was so important that Angie gave it two syllables. "That should be our motto," she said, "FAIR: The Best Hay-yer in News!"

"Powerful," I told her, then went back to chewing my lip, praying that Angie-from-the-Block's own big hair was no harbinger of what I was about to have on my head, and wondering why Benji had ordered this makeover for me now, when I'd already been on the air for six months. It seemed a little late. "Can I see it?"

"Not yet. Let me blow it out so you can get the full effect." She turned on the blow-dryer, its deafening buzz roaring in my ear. "You hear about that new business reporter who's fucking one of the Third Floor?" Angie shouted, using the shorthand term we all used to refer to every executive under Benji, all of whom were housed on the third floor.

"What?" I shouted back, though I'd heard her. I just had a hard time believing that one of the Third Floor would be bedding a new reporter.

"Believe it!" she yelled—and I had to admit, the hair and makeup artists at every TV station always had the juiciest and most reliable gossip. "The guy's apparently an animal in bed." Angie made a growling noise.

"Eewww," I responded, trying to imagine which of the Third Floor was most tigerlike, but they all blurred into one big bureaucratic blob.

"Oh, yeah," Angie went on, "they do it in his office!"

"No way," I said, unable to imagine any of the corporate types having sex in his office, or anywhere for that matter. They were all so buttoned up, I imagined them showering in their business suits. "Where are you getting your information?"

"I never reveal a source. I'm extremely discreet," she yelled. "So you want to be an anchor?" Angie asked, switching gears again.

"Um, yeah, sure," I said softly and nonchalantly, not wanting to admit to Angie how much I hoped for that someday.

"Well, a little birdie thinks that could be in the cards," she said coyly.

"Really?" I asked, connecting with her eyes in the mirror. "Who's that?"

"Just word on the street." Angie turned off the dryer, and the din died down. "All right, ya ready to see ya new 'do'?"

"I guess so," I said, clutching the side of the chair as she twirled it around. And when it stopped, I gasped. There in the mirror was a beautiful, stylish prom queen with smooth, shiny blond hair bouncing down her shoulder blades. It took me a second to recognize the glamour girl as me.

"Oh, my God," I said, getting up and moving closer to the mirror, checking for an optical illusion.

"Gawr-geous, right?" Angie smacked her hairbrush with satisfaction.

"Amanda, is that you?" I asked my reflection. I looked so differ-ent. So much better. I was suddenly part of the pretty-girl posse from high school, one of the cheerleaders who knew how to use a flat iron. Gone was the wavy brown mess that swelled on my head like a chia pet in any drop of humidity. I couldn't wait to show Charlie. I felt bad that the poor guy had been enduring the old Amanda all this time.

"Thank you, Angie!" I said, grabbing her shoulders in gratitude.

"Hold on, Blondie, ya not done yet. Head down the hall. Jess is waiting for ya in makeup."

"I do my own makeup," I told her. "I don't really need Jess."

"Yeah, well, Benji wants to see what you'll look like with the Jess treatment."

"Why's that?" I asked, casting my eyes sideways at her, skeptical as to whether Angie had actually talked to Benji or was making this all up as a power play.

"He wants to see how some reporters look with hair and makeup, that's all," she said. "Stop fighting it."

Heading down the hallway, I thought I'd figured it out—maybe I'd be tagging my reports in the studio sometimes, rather than in the field. Even that would be super exciting. Being any part of Benji's vision was thrilling. I walked through the next curtain, behind which stood a stunning black woman with flawless skin and warm caramel eyes. Her space was like a Broadway dressing room; a leather chair faced a massive vanity mirror framed by bright bulbous lights. On the coun-ter was an open makeup case filled with bottles of sparkly potions designed to make the skin glitter. Jess sat me down, then with a flour-ish snapped open a black cape and draped it over me as though I were part of a magic trick that would make Amanda disappear.

"Ah!" Jess shrieked, her makeup brush suspended in midair. "What are those?! Sugar, you have caterpillars for eyebrows. I have *got* to do some surgery." She grabbed her tweezers and commenced a surgical strike.

"Ow!" I yelped.

For the next few painful minutes, Jess plucked and pulled at my brows, yanking them out by the clump. When satisfied with the pruning, she ran her thumbs gently over my lids as if to dissolve the pain portion of her performance and prepare her subject for the next act. I watched Jess pick up a thin brush with bristles the size of a candle's flame, then dip it in a pot of sparkly purple powder.

"Close, please," she instructed, dusting the eye shadow gently across my lids. Just as I was relaxing into her spalike treatment, I heard the sound of a loud generator turn on and my eyes sprang open in time to catch Jess holding a black cord like a tiny garden hose. She began spraying a fine beige mist over my cheeks and forehead. I shut my eyes tight again, imagining all the time Michelangelo could have saved if he'd had one of these contraptions in the Sistine Chapel.

"Now let that dry," Jess said, grabbing another thin brush and dipping it in a gooey pot of pink, then painting my lips with gobs of gloss. "To make them plump and peachy," she explained. It felt like I'd taken a big bite of a heavily frosted cupcake without a napkin handy.

"Head up. Look down. But don't close," Jess said, and while I contemplated the pat-your-head-rub-your-stomach nature of that instruction, she reached again for the tweezers and began affixing fluttery false lashes, dipped in glue, onto my eyelids one at a time. I tried not to blink, though I had the sensation of butterflies alighting on my lids.

"Bangin'!" Jess proclaimed with a final flourish of her makeup wand.

I opened my eyes and looked into the mirror. Amanda hadn't disappeared—to the contrary, she'd come alive, in full Technicolor. In the space of twenty-five minutes, I morphed from mere mortal to sexy siren. I turned my head left and then right, marveling at my sudden bone structure. "I have cheekbones," I said.

"You do now," Jess said, reaching around to pat her own shoulder.

"You're a miracle worker! I wish I had somewhere fancy to go all dolled up like this," I told her, getting up from the chair to leave.

"Wait!" Jess said. "Let me see your legs."

"Heh?"

"Viewers are going to see your legs on set," she said. "They need to look good."

"I'm not on set much," I told her.

"You never know," she said casually. "In this business you gotta be ready for anything."

"Tell me about it," I said, deciding against sharing my previous pants mishap.

Jess bent down and pulled up my pant leg. "Oh, man," she said. "Your legs are like a ghost's."

I was about to tell her that a ghost doesn't have legs when she pushed me back into her chair and hiked my pants above my knees. "Benji does not like white legs! We have to bronze those babies up."

Jess poured a different, darker liquid into her magic spray machine, then bent over and began shellacking my calves up one side and down the other. In seconds, my sallow skin turned golden brown. *I gotta remember this contraption before my next beach trip!*

"Give that five minutes to dry and you're good to go," Jess said. "Now get upstairs, girl! You can't be late for Benji."

Man, Benji's sure taking an active role at every level of the network. You'd think he'd have more pressing things to worry about than the color of my legs under my pants. His attention to detail is amazing—no wonder he's such a success story. I pranced down the hallway toward the elevator with a new spring in my step, or maybe it was a swagger. Anyone could pop out of the greenroom on the left and I'd be ready. Chris Hemsworth? Ryan Reynolds? Bring 'em on. This must be what beautiful women feel like—as though doors will swing open and opportunities will fall in their laps. I held my head higher, the old weight lifted, my new blond highlights bouncing buoyantly. *Look at me! It's impossible to catch me from a bad angle.*

"Amanda?" It was Emily Galen, the unusually timid field producer I'd worked with on a few pieces, walking down the hallway toward me with wide eyes and her mouth agape.

"Yes, it's me. The stylists went to town, I know." I smiled, basking in her gaze.

"I just can't believe how . . . well . . . great you look," she blinked at my face, unable to turn away, making me feel naked despite the mask of makeup.

Wait a second. Was it that incredible that I looked so good? I felt a blush sweep my face. "Yup, it's amazing what these hair and makeup magicians can do," I said. "Spinning hay into gold."

"No! No. It's not that," Emily said, trying to backpedal. "I was just wondering why you're in hair and makeup? Are you shooting something?" She whispered the last part. Even though Emily had left ABC months ago, her paranoia lingered. Like most network producers, she still carried the dog-eat-dog terror of someone stabbing her in the back, stealing her idea, or taking her job. But unlike the effect it had on Laurie, the *Lord of the Flies* news world didn't make Emily more assertive, it made her scared of her own shadow.

"I think Benji just wanted to give me a little make-over," I told her. "He's very engaged with his correspondents."

"Oh, he must have *big* plans for you." Emily looked over her shoulder. "Benji is a genius. I'm sure he'll want to grow you." She leaned closer and whispered, "I hear he's having problems with the morning show. You should tell him you want to be the host of that."

I felt almost sorry for Emily and her naïveté. No one goes from reporter at Newschannel 13 to national morning show anchor in the space of six months. It took Suzy Berenson years of top-ten market reporting before she got her big break at *The Morning Show* on BNN.

"Thanks for the tip," I told Emily, crossing my fingers as if her suggestion were rooted in reality. "I'll keep you posted."

"Hey you! Come on in," Benji called. "Wait. Let me check you out." Benji stood in the threshold of his office, arms crossed, taking in the sight of the new me, head to toe. "Wow. You look terrific. I knew we had something to work with in there."

I tried not to wince at his unvarnished assessment.

"You've got great hair," he noted. "Great hair makes for great TV. How many extensions did they put in there?"

"Extensions? Hair extensions?" I asked, touching my own head to see if Angie had snuck some in without my knowing. "None . . . I think . . ."

"Whoa! That's all your hair? Jesus! You win! That's amazing. Who did you?"

"Did me? Oh, did my hair? Angie. And Jess did the makeup," I said, suddenly self-conscious to have Benji eyeballing me so intensely.

"They're the best. You know I stole Angie from ABC, right? She'll have you looking as good as Kelly Ripa soon," he said, as though it were perfectly fine to say someone wasn't as pretty as someone else. "Oh, word of warning, do not go to Roberta. Have you met him?"

"You mean, the tall Asian . . . Cher impersonator . . . person?"

"Yeah, that's him, though on Tuesdays he's Beyoncé. Stunning, right?"

"Oh, yes, very striking."

"I mean, hot," Benji said, moving his hand back and forth fast like he'd felt an open flame. "Unfortunately, he can't do makeup to save his life, which is very weird for a dude who pretends to be a chick, right?"

"Um, yeah."

"I was psyched to find Roberta," Benji went on. "FAIR's got to have at least one bi-curious, homoflexible drag queen on staff. I mean, it's perfect, really. But do *NOT* let him touch your face."

Benji sat down and patted the couch. "So let's talk about how everything is going."

"Let's," I agreed.

"Your pieces in the field have been terrific. But I have a problem and I'm thinking you can help."

"Of course," I said, hoping against hope that Emily and Angie might have been right and this might be about anchoring the morning show, though it was more likely Benji needed me to swap offices with someone or something.

"So I'm having issues with the morning show. I need to retool it and rebrand it. What do you think of the name *Wake Up, USA!* Great, right? It's with an exclamation point," he exclaimed, "which I think will really set it apart."

"Oh, yes, great," I said, realizing how little I knew about TV and how much Benji had to teach me since I would have called that cheesy.

Benji took a deep breath and pressed his lips together like he was about to deliver some very bad news. "The show has not been working.

It hasn't taken off like I'd hoped. None of the anchor teams I've tried are gelling."

"Oh, I'm sorry," I said, trying not to smile.

"Yeah, it sucks. I mean some of these pairs should work together, they really should. I got Rob Lahr from CBS. Super guy. Great on TV. Also a bit of an asshole. Handsome as hell. Oh, and he's straight. You know how hard that combo is to find on TV? I mean, men in makeup? Most of the time you just want to punch them in their pretty lips."

I smiled at Benji's own pretty lips, a perfect flesh color that department store makeup counter clerks were always trying to recreate by mixing pinks and browns on their personal palettes. Someone should patent Benji's lip color, I thought. *Media Maven Mauve, maybe.*

"Now, occasionally you get a male anchor who's a real man you'd want to have a beer with, but it's rare. Anyway, Rob Lahr's got it. But he's not clicking with any of the women. I tried a bunch. You know Kerry Shaw?"

"Yes, of course. Came from WABC?"

"Yup. Fantastic prompter reader. The best I've ever seen. But dumb. Heaven help her if that prompter goes down. If you asked her, 'Kerry, what was that story about you were just reading?' She'd say, 'What story?' So that didn't work. Then I tried Margot Hamilton. I don't know if you've met her. I found her in Seattle. She's gorgeous. Black hair, green eyes. She looks like a fucking Disney princess. She really wants the slot. Anyway, I've tried those two together for the past couple of months. I thought it would be Lois Lane and Clark Kent . . . and . . . ppppbhhh." Benji put his tongue between his lips and made a farting sound. "Nothing's working. I couldn't figure out why, so I focus-grouped a couple of their shows and people haaated them." He shook his head in disgust.

"What's the problem?" I asked, so I could immediately fix it in myself.

"Well, with Margot, it turns out she's beautiful, but she's too damn nice. She's sooo sweet. She's just not—" He stopped and looked off to the left, struggling to find the right word.

"Relatable?" I offered.

"Hot," he said. "She's just not hot enough. No one in the focus groups found her sexy. And that's a big problem."

I sat stunned on the sofa, trying to find the right response but feeling a little sick. Newsrooms were notoriously sexist, but I wasn't used to the head of the company being so overt.

"Oh, hey," Benji said, taking my hand, "I didn't mean to offend you. I just get the impression I can talk to you honestly. I think you get it. And I think you like to understand the problem. So listen," he went on, taking a big breath, "we're a little more than six months from the election. I never thought this would be the scenario, but with Victor Fluke and Virginia Wynn going head-to-head, things are getting real. These next six months are crucial, and I can't have a shitty morning show. And that's where you come in."

"O . . . kay . . ." I said slowly, trying not to get ahead of myself, praying that he might somehow be considering me, rather than asking me to be part of the next focus group.

"I want to test you with Rob—"

"Great!" I blurted before he was done. I wanted to jump up and click my heels in the air. Wait until I called Mom, and Laurie and Charlie!

"I have a hunch this could work," Benji said, nodding at me.

"Yes, okay! Great!"

Benji folded his arms and looked at me. "Did you ever see *Gone with the Wind*?"

"Um, yes, I mean, years ago."

"You remind me of Scarlett O'Hara."

"Petulant and demanding?" I asked.

"Ha! That's a good one. See, you're funny. That's good. No. I mean, you're not beautiful. But somehow when you're on the air, I want to watch what you'll do next. That stand-up you did at the Harley Company, where you jumped on the bike and drove off? Great reporter involvement. And the one from that ostrich farm with all of them pecking you? Terrific. But my favorite was that blind ice cream taste test. Was the peach ice cream really that good?"

"Oh, it was," I assured him.

"I thought so! Shit, I wish I wasn't off dairy! Anyway, I can't quite explain your presence, cause there's a bunch of girls prettier than you, but somehow you've got 'it.'"

Hearing Benji Diggs say I had "it" flooded every one of my cells with a rush of liquid gold.

"Hey, do you know the secret to being a TV star?"

"No, what?" I asked, leaning in.

"Anchors have to be aspirational. This is particularly true for women. Maybe it's sexist, I don't know, but I know it's true. You watch Rachel Maddow and you want to be smart like her. You see Diane Sawyer and you think she's so sophisticated, even when she's undercover, sleeping in some jail cell. Oprah makes us feel, hey, she's one of us, maybe I could be that rich someday. And the High Priestess of the Mornings, Suzy Berenson, you know what makes her so popular?"

"No, *what*?" I begged, practically falling into him.

"She's smart *and* sexy. Women want to have lunch with her and men want to date her. That's it. And that's what I'm looking for here. And that's what I think you might have—star quality."

It took every ounce of muscle control to keep from screaming that Benji Diggs had just used my name in the same sentence as Suzy Berenson and star.

"So whaddya say?" he said.

"I say yes!" I said, clapping my hands like I was applauding his decision.

"Fantastic! Now we gotta work fast. I need to test you with Rob on Friday. It's just a chemistry test, okay, but I'm hoping it works. And also, please keep this quiet. Don't tell any of the other ladies yet, especially not Margot. She's sooo damn nice, it's torture. So I need you to keep this on the DL."

"Yes, of course."

"Now just remember on Friday for this test, whatever the topic, I want to hear both sides. We're trying to find solutions here."

"Okay. But what will the topics be?"

"Anything and everything," he said, cracking his knuckles. "But the point is, the one-sided world of partisan news channels is over.

For the next six months—or six decades if FAIR News actually takes off—we're here to help the country end these dangerous divisions. FAIR News is going to be the big tent that brings everyone together. Now, if we could get a little more press, get our message out, and help people understand what we're doing here, we'd have a shot. I've got the *New York Times* coming in next week to spend a day. *Vanity Fair*'s been shadowing me all week. It's happening. Slowly. But it's happening."

"Yes! It's happening!" I agreed, though at that moment I was talking about my own life.

Benji nodded at me. "So. I'm working on getting Virginia Wynn and Victor Fluke to agree to come on FAIR. How awesome would it be to get them together in studio? But I gotta tell ya, it's very hard to get their people to agree. Neither one of them is doing interviews. They think all the fighting and calling each other names on the stump is working for them. Anyway, my dream is to get them on the morning show—together or apart."

"Definitely. Good idea," I said, hoping the more I acted as if it were my show, the likelier it would be.

Benji picked up the phone. "Hey, Melissa, need you to call Meg. Have her get Amanda fitted for wardrobe ASAP," he nodded into the receiver. "Good. Tell Meg I'm thinking something sort of sassy."

I bit my lip. He hung up.

"And let's get you some real shoes" Benji said, looking at my feet with a mix of disgust and amusement. "Viewers, men and women, pay attention to shoes. I mean, good shoes. Not . . . those."

I involuntarily moved my feet under his sofa, wishing desperately that I owned a fancier pair than these scuffed Nine West pumps.

Benji stared sympathetically into my eyes and nodded gently. "There's a hole in your sole."

"My soul?"

"Yes, the sole of your left shoe. It looks beat up. That'd be bad on camera. You've gotta have new soles on TV."

"No soul in TV?" I'd always heard network news could be soulless. I couldn't believe Benji was admitting it.

"New," he clarified. "You need nice shoes if you're going to be a role model."

"A sole model," I said.

"Ha! That's good. Hey, save that for the air. Remember, we're creating a new paradigm. And you're gonna be great!" Benji slapped my knee and got up. "Cause you're down to earth, and smart and funny. You've got something for everyone. I mean, really, who doesn't want the girl next door in their bedroom every morning?"

"What are those?" Charlie asked, walking into my apartment and looking at me with nervous eyes. He put down his bag and moved tentatively in my direction, as if approaching something flammable. "What's on your eyes?"

"Oh, they're fake eyelashes," I said to his cheek, now two inches from mine. "The makeup artist put them on."

He put his fingers to my lashes and touched them in wonderment, like a child feeling a snowflake for the first time. "Do they come off?"

"I assume so," I said, backing away before he accidentally poked my eyeball. "But how about my hair? Doesn't it look fabulous?"

Charlie took one of my highlighted strands and rubbed it between his thumb and forefinger. "Does that wash out, too?"

"No, it grows out. Unfortunately," I answered, annoyed and feeling almost as self-conscious as I had in the office when Benji was eyeing me.

"It's . . . interesting," Charlie said. "It's a little"—he paused and I could tell he was struggling for something diplomatic—"overdone. It's not natural looking."

"Well, it's not for real life. It's for TV." I was bursting with my big news and waiting for an opening so I could break it.

"I don't think you need all that makeup," Charlie said.

"Well, I do if I'm going to be an anchor!" I exclaimed. "Benji wants me to audition for an anchor slot on the morning show!"

"Oh, wow, really?" Charlie's face lit up. "That's terrific! How did that happen?"

"Well, I guess none of the women he's tried are working," I said, deciding to omit the lack of hotness part. "So I'm going to audition for it on Friday!" I surprised myself by attempting a sudden pirouette.

"Wow, that's great!" Charlie said, coming over to hug me. "Tell me about this show. What is it?"

"Come on, let's talk while we eat. I'm starving," I said, moving to the counter to unwrap the takeout from Curry in a Hurry. "It's going to be called *Wake Up, USA!* and it sounds great. We'll be talking about anything and everything in the news. And the point is to cover both sides of every issue, you know, have a real conversation. Here, let's split this mulligatawny," I said, handing him a Styrofoam bowl.

"Right, both sides," Charlie nodded, diving into a samosa. "How does that work?"

"Okay, well," I started uncertainly. "Benji's idea, as you know, is to stop all the partisan rancor of other cable morning shows. We're going to give viewers real information and try to mend the rift."

"Hmm," Charlie said, as though trying to get his mind around that. "But what does that sound like?"

"Well, Benji's plan is to get Fluke and Wynn on the show, maybe even together! How great would that be?"

"I don't think that's a good idea," Charlie said. "That elevates Fluke too much. A circus clown sharing the stage with an accomplished senator? That makes Victor Fluke look legitimate." Even saying Fluke's name caused Charlie to look like he might cough up a kebab. "Remember, Amanda, Benji Diggs is not a journalist. He's a reality show star and a media-meister. And I'm not sure his utopian vision for some sort of all-for-one, feel-good news network is realistic during this campaign. You know, I was thinking the other day about what Benji told you when you joined about the Walter Cronkite era and the big tent of TV news back then. He seems to have glossed over the Vietnam War. Not exactly a heyday of unity."

Charlie's passion for history and politics always wowed me. It was one of the first things that attracted me the night we met, when he detailed his Argentina trip and the history of Juan Perón's crackdown on newspapers and free speech. But tonight it was a buzzkill.

"This is a morning show," I told Charlie, trying to revive his original excitement about my shot. "Morning shows are supposed to make you feel good, send you out the door with a spring in your step." I made a super-corny attaboy gesture with my arm.

"You're right. And you're on your way," Charlie said, mimicking my mood and relaxing into the grinning Charlie I knew and loved. "Look out, Suzy Berenson! Here comes Amanda Gallo!"

Chapter 7

Jewel Tones

"So you're shooting a pilot on Friday and you need some outfits," Meg said, taking sips of her venti black coffee, summing up her task but not looking at me. It was ten A.M. sharp and I was standing next to her in front of a huge showroom on the sixteenth floor of FAIR, staring out at rows and rows of the most delicious designer clothes I'd ever seen. "The Third Floor should have told me about this pilot sooner," she said, sighing with impatience. "You haven't given me much time."

"It's just a chemistry test, really. I only need one outfit," I said with regret as I looked out at all the clothes, ripe for the plucking.

"Oh, no," she said, turning toward me for the first time, alarmed. "One outfit will never do. Benji likes options."

Meg was FAIR's wardrobe stylist and arbiter of all on-air appearance. Uberthin and clad head to toe in black, Meg had ironclad rules: no prints, no patterns, no bows, no big jewelry, no neutrals. Only bold colors.

"Go ahead," she said, nudging me toward a rack of candy-colored cashmere. "Grab your favorites."

I stood paralyzed by the possibilities. The rack next to the cashmere was filled with the latest billowy blouses and sharp suits from Theory. The rack next to that was all Calvin Klein dresses. Beyond that Max Mara, Michael Kors, Carmen Marc Valvo, Nicole Miller, DVF, Tahari, on and on, spread out like a field of intoxicating poppies.

"Don't just stand there," she said.

Walking forward as if in a dream, I began roaming the rows, letting my fingers brush against plush sweaters and silky tops. I waded into a sea of sleeveless sheaths and skinny pencil skirts. Rich leather jackets in deep browns and merlots bobbed by my field of vision.

As a child, I'd had a fantasy of being locked in the Paramus Mall after closing and having my pick of everthing without Mom having to pay for it. Not that my taste was very extravagant. I would have settled for jeans that weren't two inches too short and a sweater without moth holes in it.

"This isn't a museum," Meg called from somewhere in the maze of clothing. "You need to pull some pieces!"

"I don't know where to start. It all looks so . . . beautiful." I was starting to feel woozy.

"Just pick whatever you like," Meg said, coming down the row toward me with a clipboard. "I've been told to spare no expense on you."

"Oh, my gosh. Really?" I said, then ran my hand over some soft, brushed wool pants in a camel color. "These are nice."

"No pants in the anchor chair," Meg snapped. "Ever!"

"Oh? Really? Why's that?"

"Viewers like to see legs. Just ask Suzy Berenson. She's got the best legs in the business and she never misses a chance to show them off."

Good to know! Hey, if it works for Suzy, I'll give it a shot.

"What do you call this color?" I asked, stroking a soft, greenish blouse.

"It's chartreuse," Meg said. "That would be hideous on your skin tone. You need emerald. Think jewel tones."

"Oops, all right. Look at this one. It's gorgeous." I pointed to a charcoal Tahari cotton dress. "Would I look good in gray?"

"No gray allowed on the morning show. Too funereal," Meg said, practically slapping it out of my hands.

"I like this!" I said, turning to a burnt orange Theory blouse.

"No orange! Benji Diggs hates orange! Orange is *never* to be seen on air. It's a mistake to even have it here!" She grabbed the offending shirt from the rack and thrust it at one of her helpers.

"Maybe you should pick some clothes for me," I concluded.

"Oh, for crying out loud. Hand me that pen," Meg commanded an assistant. "Begin gathering! I want to see Amanda in that red ruched Alice and Olivia. And grab the asymmetrical Derek Lam in magenta.

That could be stunning. I love the lavender Black Halo and the white light cashmere Calvin Klein. *Très* elegant! And lots and lots of purple. Benji loves purple." Assistants scurried around as Meg jotted down ideas on her clipboard, then spun toward me. "Take off your clothes."

"I beg your pardon?"

"I'll need to have all these pieces tailored to fit you perfectly by the pilot on Friday," she said, exasperated. "You never know which one Benji will like best. Now step out of those pants. And where did you get those anyway? They're three seasons old. Throw them out."

"Are you kidding?" I choked. "I don't throw out clothes," I said, unbuttoning my shirt and handing it to Meg.

"Obviously," she sniffed, taking my shirt with just two fingers, like it was a dirty diaper.

Waste not, want not. That was Mom's motto throughout my adolescence and I'd applied it to my own wardrobe ever since. I stood in my underwear as Meg and her assistants slipped dress after dress over my head and off again.

"Look at this body!" Meg said, staring at me. "Who knew you had such boobs! Why have you been hiding them? We've got to show these off more."

I screwed up my mouth at Meg. I couldn't imagine Suzy Berenson enduring this treatment. Suzy looked so polished and professional every morning. Was it possible someone was focused on how best to showcase her tits?

"Hand me a clip!" Meg ordered her assistant, then began cinching a royal blue Rolando Santana dress around my waist until it felt like a corset. "Now, let's rearrange these," Megs said, reaching inside my bra, cupping my left breast and hoisting it into a more prominent position.

"Hey!" I shrieked.

"That's better. Now hand me the pins." Meg tacked the dress four inches above my knee.

I caught my concerned reflection in the full-length mirror, tugging at the hem. "Is this a dress or a scarf?" I asked her.

"Listen, Benji has research showing that ratings rise one tenth of a point for every inch higher the skirt. There's a correlation."

Wow. Duly noted. See, these are the things they never tell you in local news.

"Be thankful you're not at NBC," Meg went on. "They just did away with their clothing allowance. Can you imagine?"

I shook my head in horror. Meg took the pen from her assistant and cross-checked the items hanging on the shiny steel rack with what she'd written on her clipboard. "Excellent collection, if I do say so myself. I'll pair these outfits with shoes and have them waiting for you in your office by Friday."

"Did you say shoes?" I asked, my eyebrows lifting at the prospect of shedding my holey soles.

Meg shook her head at my old pumps. "I'll handle it. I don't have time for another sartorial tutorial."

"Thank you so much, Meg! I don't know what I would have worn if left to my own devices."

"I don't want to think about it," she said, shuddering slightly. "But no worries, now you will look smashing." Meg blew me an air kiss and swished out the door.

Pushing aside a half-eaten sandwich, I pulled my keyboard toward me and typed in the secret code Melissa had provided to watch air checks of FAIR's morning show. To be honest, I'd tried to tune in before but always switched right over to Suzy Berenson. She was a tough habit to break. I hit play. Cue the cheerful morning music.

"Good Wednesday morning to all of you," Margot Hamilton began in her sweet singsong. I stared at her perfectly symmetrical features, flawless skin, and raven hair. A perfect Snow White. She even looked good in HD. "I'm Margot Hamilton. Thank you so much for spending your valuable time with us this morning. We appreciate it."

"And I'm Rob Lahr. Our top story this morning . . ."

I hit pause and stared at her coanchor, Rob Lahr, the chiseled anchorman with coiffed chestnut-colored hair and lapis blue eyes. Upon googling him, I'd discovered he had a penchant for dating starlets. A trove of online photos captured him at various galas, an arm around a different babe at every one.

Rob and Margot were sitting next to each other on a sofa, but they

didn't seem to be in the same room or zip code for that matter. They
each read into their own camera. Why wasn't the director taking a
wide two-shot? That would certainly give the show a warmer feel.
On my notepad under "Suggestions," I wrote down "more two-shots"
and "more cross talk needed."

"Wait until you hear this next story," Margot said before dropping her voice to the grave register. "There is an apartment complex
in Cleveland where one brave veteran cannot hang his U.S. Marine
Corps flag." Margot tried to look outraged, but mostly she just looked
pretty.

"Let's unpack this, Margot," Rob continued, not looking at her.
"See, the managers at this condo association say this veteran has to
take down his flag that he's flown every day since returning from
Iraq, because it doesn't comply with building code. The veteran says
he's tried to call the condo association but no response."

I hit pause. Arguments with a condo board were the kinds of stories I tracked for "5 on Your Side" in Roanoke: small local stories
that made a big impact on a few people. I'd make a couple of phone
calls, poke around the condo office with a camera, and bingo, that
flag was back up. I could do this in my sleep. I hit play again.

"Now, let's look at all sides of this flag flap," Margot suggested.
"You could say that rules are rules," she went on. "And of course,
rules are rules. But you could also say this is the kind of political correctness run amok that just makes you shake your head." She shook
her head.

"You could also say that it's a slippery slope," Rob added. "And if
the condo association let him fly his flag, then they might have to let
somebody fly their Tea Party flag, and somebody else fly their gay pride
flag—"

"And what if somebody has an ISIS flag?" Margot interjected. "I
mean, where does it stop?"

"Now, from the get-go," Rob said, "this Marine has said he's just
trying to honor military service and he's not asking for special treatment." At that, I snorted out loud. For years Laurie claimed that anytime anyone used the term "special treatment," it was code for oral
sex, as in "the governor demanded special treatment from the mayor,"

or "the warden doesn't believe prisoners should get special treatment." I stared at Rob Lahr's mouth for a second, then shook my head
to clear the connotation.

"We want to know what *you* think about this," Rob said. "Email
us and we'll read your comments later. Right back after this commercial."

"That's great, guys!" a woman's voice boomed over loudspeakers
in the studio, and I realized I wasn't watching an air check but the
in-house feed, which was even better. I could see what they did
during commercials. "When we're back from break, let's do the
'women nagging' talking point," the loudspeaker voice said.

"Roger that," Rob said, shuffling a couple of papers on the coffee
table in front of him. Margot smoothed her perfect hair.

"You guys ready?" I heard one of the crew ask. "In five, four,
three . . ."

"Welcome back," Rob said, grinning a big TV grin. "We have an
interesting new study to unpack this morning. Listen up, all you
husbands out there. The University of Cincinnati just released research that found nagging from your wife is just as toxic to a marriage as infidelity! Finally, men have some hard research to back up
our belief that we should be left alone in our man caves."

Oh, brother, I sighed. Nothing like a little sexism with your corn-
flakes. I waited for Margot to shoot down the premise.

"That's ridiculous," Margot started. "What about the wife's point
of view? Do you really think asking your husband to pick up his
dirty socks is as bad in a marriage as cheating on him? Do you? Do
you really think that?" She was staring at Rob as she badgered him
for an answer. It sounded like Margot was actually nagging Rob.
Wait, is this a bit they're doing? I couldn't tell. Neither one was smiling. Maybe they're about to do something clever here. I waited for
it . . . and . . . nope.

"I assure you," she went on, smiling sweetly now, "my husband
would much rather I tell him to mow the lawn than I start having an
affair!"

Something told me that Margot's husband, a wildly wealthy hedge
fund manager, hadn't mowed a lawn in a couple of decades.

"You sure about that?" Rob muttered under his breath. My eyes widened. Oh, I get it. He doesn't like her. That's why this all feels painfully awkward. I clicked the off button. Benji is so right—this show desperately needs some personality. "More fun, some laughs," I wrote down. This, I thought, will be easy.

Chapter 8

Chemistry Test

"So, this is all a big secret, right?" Angie shouted over the hair dryer.

"Yes," I whispered.

"Don't let Margot know ya doing this," she shouted. "It'd break that poor girl's heart. God bless."

"Shhhhh!" I tried.

"Yeah, yeah, I got it. Ya secret's safe with me. So ya married?" Angie yelled.

"No," I said, nervously tapping my feet on the footrest of her chair. The chemistry test with Rob was in half an hour and I had no idea what to expect. I didn't like taking tests, chemistry or otherwise, with no notes, no prep, no nothing.

"Ya got a boyfriend?"

"I do."

"Is he in the biz?" she asked, tugging hard at my damp hair.

"No, he's an associate professor of history at NYU."

"A smarty-pants, huh? Ya met Rob yet?"

"Not yet," I said softly, trying to set an example for Angie to turn it down. For all I knew Rob was getting makeup in the next stall.

"Stay away from him," she warned.

"Oh?" I asked, connecting with her eyes in the mirror.

"Yeah," she said. "He's a big pussy hound. Ya read *The Inside Scoop* last week? Says he was spotted 'canoodling' with that girl, oh, what's her name? She was in that movie. You know who I'm talking about, right? Blond. Big boobs."

"Sorry, that doesn't narrow it down," I said, reaching into my bag to check my phone, half expecting to learn the chemistry test was cancelled. Or maybe that I had dreamt it.

"Don't matter. It'll be someone new next week. Love-em-leave-em Lahr, they call him. He's a contagious bachelor."

"I think you mean chronic."

"I mean the kind that gets under ya skin and stays there, like a bad rash. Be careful."

My hands were tingling as I approached the studio, partly from nerves and partly from the pile of dresses draped over my left arm, cutting off my circulation. Meg insisted I bring them all, in every possible color, so the director could decide what looked best on camera.

I was ten minutes early but I wanted to steal a peek at the studio, to see where I would sit and which camera I would look at, before the producer showed up. I pushed open the black swinging door with the Studio A sign, expecting it to be dark and empty, but I was wrong and a half dozen heads spun in my direction. *Shit!* There were Margot and Rob sitting on the sofa. I froze as the door slammed behind me.

A balding guy in his fifties, dressed in stonewashed jeans and an ill-fitting bright blue sweatshirt, raced over from the side of the stage to body block me from moving any farther, dramatically putting his first finger to his lips, silently shushing me as though he were Charlie Chaplin. I took three steps back into the darkness and looked around, trying to figure out how to reopen the door quietly and get the hell out of there without disrupting whatever this was.

The set seemed much smaller in real life than it did on screen. The sofa was a semicircle of beige, the walls a bright red, blue, or purple, depending, it appeared, on the subject matter. I hadn't noticed when I'd watched on the computer that the saturation levels morphed from muted to supercharged from sentence to sentence.

I stood in the wings, torn now between wanting to flee and wanting to watch what was happening, and hoping the unlit area made me invisible. One, two, three, four, five . . . I counted the cameras, my palms getting moist. Three big cameras were on heavy bases with wheels. Another camera was on the end of a crane, floating overhead for a bird's-eye view, and the fifth camera was balanced on the shoulder of one of the crew, shooting what looked like an array of desserts on a table, away from the main set, for a food segment. I looked at all the crew guys, particularly the one behind Camera 1, with his baseball cap pulled down over his eyes and a paperback book propped open under his viewfinder. I couldn't tell whether he was reading or sleeping.

Around the studio were a half dozen monitors, huge flat-screen TVs projecting the on-set action in real time. One was divided into four screens showing what Fox, CNN, MSNBC, and BNN were broadcasting at that very moment. Then I spotted the teleprompters hidden in the cameras and felt a lump forming in my throat. This might be a good time to mention to someone that I'm not really proficient at prompter reading. I filled in on the anchor desk in Roanoke a couple of times but that was different. That wasn't national. That wasn't a Benji Diggs production with millions of people watching.

"That's a wrap, guys," came that woman's voice over the loudspeakers. "Great job. I'll talk to Benji and let you know what's next."

"We're clear!" the mime in the sweatshirt shouted to the sedated crew.

I knew that was my cue to exit before I was forced to explain what I was doing there, but as I turned to slink out I heard my name.

"Amanda!" Margot was zipping up to me, her heels clicking against the floor. "Hey! I've been wanting to meet you," she said.

I stood paralyzed, staring at her beautiful face, at her pert features and beautiful green eyes, and all I could think was Benji was right—it was a crime that she sucked on TV.

"Oh, my gosh, your packages are sooo great!" she gushed. "I loved that one you did on the ostrich farm where they were pecking at you. We used that on the show. Sooo cute!"

"Oh, thanks," I said, trying to back away before she noticed I was holding a week's worth of dresses in my arms.

"And that story you did on the death penalty. Gosh, such a sad story," she said, putting her hand to her chest to comfort herself. "Oh, my gosh."

"Yes, yes," I agreed. "Very sad."

"I mean, I don't know how you do it, how you keep it together out there. Being in the field must be sooo tough. I know I couldn't do it." She stopped then, like maybe she was looking for a real response.

"Um, I guess, you know, I try to remove myself from the emotion and just think of it as a good story and stick to the facts."

"So what are you doing here? Taping an on-set intro for one of your stories?"

"Um, yeah, I think so . . ." I said, feeling as guilty as a mistress invited to dinner by her lover's wife. "What are you all doing in here? You end at nine usually, right?"

"Oh, yeah, usually. Benji just wanted us to do a couple of practice runs. He's rebranding the show, new name, new slogan. You know, trying to build the audience. I mean everything's going really, really well," she nodded at me with enthusiasm, "but it never hurts to try to get more viewers. Benji's really excited about our show."

"He is?"

"Oh, shoot, I didn't realize it was so late. I've *got* to get a gel manicure before lunch! Let's grab coffee next week," she said, squeezing my free arm then heading for the studio door.

I stood disoriented, looking around again, then spotted the mime ambling in my direction. "You must be Amanda," he said. "I'm Larry, the floor director. Sorry I ambushed you over there."

"I'm sorry I interrupted," I said. "No one told me you all were shooting something."

"Yeah, well, I've noticed they don't clue everyone in around here," he said, nodding toward the door through which Margot had just exited, then he leaned closer. "I understand you're doing a chemistry test today. Come, let me introduce you to this motley crew."

Larry led me toward a crop of cameramen scattered around one end of the studio. "Hey, guys," he said to get their attention, "I want to introduce you to Amanda. She's our next chemistry test." *Next chemistry test?* I looked to the guys' faces for clues as to how many of these they'd done, but they looked indifferent, like they'd rather be at home rewatching *Caddyshack.*

"So, that's Jeremy behind Camera One," Larry said, pointing to the sleepy guy with the baseball cap and the book, who gave me a somnolent nod.

"And that's Rocco behind Camera Two there. That'll be your camera, so you'll have to be extra nice to him." A sixtyish, super-skinny guy with salt-and-pepper hair pulled back in a ponytail offered up a grin. "Don't worry," he said, "I gotcha covered."

"Over there, that's Casanova on Camera Three," Larry said, gesturing to a cute, twentysomething black guy with his hair pulled into a man bun. "He's our resident heartbreaker. He can't help it, that's his real name." At that, Casanova gave a courtly bow in my direction. I reflexively bowed back.

"And this here is Anthony Panzullo on the handheld." A jolly looking, round-faced, midforties, mustachioed guy gave me a quick nod before tucking back into his egg and cheese on a bulky roll.

"Panzullo doesn't like to get too much exercise, so try not to move too much," Rocco said, not to me but to the guys, causing them to guffaw.

"Why, I oughta!" Panzullo countered in a Three Stooges voice.

"Oh, a wise guy, eh?" Rocco responded.

I looked around the big room, overwhelmed and anxious. "How many guys work on the show?" I asked Larry, trying to make small talk.

"About half." Larry smiled, eliciting groans from the crew.

"So what do I need to know, other than never slam open the studio door in the middle of a show?"

"Well, let's see," Larry said. "You should follow me for all your time cues. You know the hand signals, right? You know what this means?" he asked, circling his first finger around and around near his head.

"You're crazy?" I ventured.

"Ha! No, it means wrap it up in thirty seconds. You know what this means?" he asked, making a fist and shaking it sideways.

"You're gonna punch someone?"

"Maybe!" he laughed. "No, it means you've got fifteen seconds to a hard break. That means the commercial is going to cut you off so wrap fast. Got it?"

"I guess so," I said, feeling my throat tighten again.

"You're gonna fit in fine around here, I can tell. Remember, just have fun with it. Morning shows can be fun," he said without further explanation.

"Don't listen to anything he says," a deep voice advised from my right. Rob Lahr waltzed up next to Larry and slung an arm over his shoulder, then pretended to punch Larry in the gut with his other hand. "Larry's like my work wife, the way he nags me to keep the desk clean."

"You should be so lucky," Larry chided.

"Ah, touché," Rob said.

"Be careful of this guy, Amanda," Larry said.

"Nothing to fear here. I'm a big pussycat." Rob flashed me a smile. "You ready to do this? I'm gonna hit the head for a second. Don't worry, this'll be a blast." Rob turned his right hand into a gun and cocked his finger in my direction with a clicking noise, then strode out of the studio without looking back.

I tried not to roll my eyes. *What a frat boy.* I knew dozens of those guys in college. Big-man-on-campus types, too handsome for their own good and accustomed to getting their way with women. *Such a cliché.*

"Amanda? There you are." A woman, around my age, pretty, with long dark hair, light-brown skin, and a serious navy blue suit, was approaching. "Hi! I'm Fatima. I'm the executive producer on the show. I'll be in the control room for your test today. I see you've met some of the crew. Any questions?"

"Well"—I didn't want to admit I had a million—"just how does it work?"

"Oh, here," she said, handing me a couple of articles. "Basically you and Rob will talk about some stories in the news. I found a flag story out of South Carolina for you two to discuss. It's really just to see you two interacting together."

"Oh, the story about the Marine who was fighting the condo association? I saw that . . . I mean, I read about that one," I said quickly, realizing she might not appreciate me spying on Rob and Margot.

"No, no, I found a better one," Fatima said. "This is about a Confederate flag at a condo."

"Oh," I said, bringing my nail to my mouth. "Okay, that's different. Let me read through it."

"Don't worry about the facts," Fatima said. "We just want to see how you do with Rob." She leaned in to speak. "He can be a little . . .

um . . . prickly . . . but try to play along. I've seen your stuff from the field. This will be easy for you." She nodded encouragingly. "We've tried a few anchor combos on the show, but Benji's most excited about this one with you."

"He is?" I said, feeling the jolt that came from hearing Benji's name connected to me. "I'm excited to give it a shot."

"I'll be in your ear telling you when to wrap or stretch and other info. Larry here will keep you honest with time cues." She patted him on the back. "But word of warning: Larry's got an endless supply of bad puns. He thinks he's a real card."

Larry's face lit up. "Yeah, I should be dealt with! Come on, let's get you mic'd up. You need any of these dresses?" he asked, removing the load from my arms.

"I didn't know which color was best to wear," I explained.

"That magenta you have on looks great," Fatima said.

"Isn't that purple?" Larry asked. "Or is it a pigment of my imagination?"

"Oh, here we go," Rob said, shaking his head as he sauntered back into the studio. "Larry's found a new victim. You ready to do this?" he asked, punching a fist into his own hand, I assumed, to ramp back up. "Let's try to give this one some juice. I'm getting a little tired of playing the Dating Game. At work, that is." He gave a wink.

I took a seat on the sofa, my heart pounding. This was it. This was my shot at the next level.

"Hi, there," a guy said from behind the sofa. "I'm Bruce. Can I put this on your bra?" Before I could answer, Bruce had unzipped my dress to my waist, grabbed my bra strap, and attached a square black battery the same size as an ice pack—and just as cold—between my shoulder blades.

"Wow!" I gasped.

"Here's an earpiece," he said, handing one end to me, then plugging the other into an IFB pack and putting that, too, on my bra.

"Places, everyone!" Larry yelled to the crew. "We're going to do this live to tape. Control room says they're ready. So let's give it a shot in thirty seconds! You need anything, Amanda?" Larry asked.

"Maybe CPR," I said, only half joking. It was possible my racing heart could explode.

"How about mouth-to-mouth?" Rob suggested, putting his warm hand on my bare knee and squeezing. "Let's have some fun with this one. Mix it up a bit."

"Okay," I nodded nervously.

"Let's try this," Larry yelled, "In five, four, three, two . . ."

I heard an upbeat sting sound in my ear, signaling a morning show was starting.

"And good morning, everyone," Rob said into Camera 2. "Welcome to *Wake Up, USA!* We begin with a controversy that's cropped up at a condo association in South Carolina, where one man is in trouble for hanging a Confederate flag from his balcony. What do you think about this, Amanda?"

Hearing Rob's question, I froze. What did I think? No one had ever asked me to offer my opinion on camera. A shot of discomfort raced up my neck to my throat. "I, um, well . . ." I started. "It's not what I think, it's what his neighbors think. And it's safe to assume they don't like having a symbol of racism and hatred hanging in their condo complex."

"Maybe they don't mind," Rob said with what looked like a half grin on his face, like he had something up his sleeve.

"Of course they do," I told him, my body recoiling from his on the couch. "That flag represents one of the worst chapters in our history. I'm sure his neighbors don't want to be reminded of that every day."

"That's not what the polls say," Rob said, reaching across the table for a piece of paper on which I saw a bar graph, colored in yellow, red, and blue. "Many Americans believe the Confederate flag honors their grandfathers, who were killed for the cause of states' rights. Let me read for our viewers the latest CNN/ORC poll, which is completely different from what you're saying, Amanda. Fifty-seven percent of the country sees the flag as a symbol of southern pride," he read. "Only thirty-three percent see it as a symbol of slavery."

Shit. I felt my stomach churning and caught my own face in one of the monitors, wearing an expression of defensive disgust, which I could see was not a good look.

"Let me see that," I said, grabbing it out of his hands. "Wait a second. You're selectively reading the results. It says here that seventy-five percent of blacks see it as a symbol of slavery and racism." I shook the paper back at him. "So a majority of African Americans see it in a negative light!"

"But it's a minority of the country," Rob said. "So why not go with the majority? Or do you believe if anyone is offended, it needs to come down? Some people would call that political correctness."

"It's not politically correct to try to avoid being offensive," I told him.

"Actually, that's exactly what it is," he said.

I didn't know what was happening, but I knew the chemistry test was derailing. Rob was being more aggressive with me than he had been with Margot and not leaving any room for bonding. I could feel my face getting flushed and my shot at anchoring going up in flames.

"Do you think it's okay to offend seventy-five percent of blacks in this country? Because if so, how about hanging, oh, I don't know, a KKK flag in the condo?" I asked, too sarcastically. "Is that okay?"

"Nobody's suggesting that. Let's avoid the hypothetical game." Rob laughed and I wanted to slap him. I couldn't believe this was it, and in the space of five minutes I'd somehow blown my chance at becoming the next Suzy Berenson.

"I have an idea," I said, my cheeks burning, but knowing Benji wanted us to find solutions. "How about everyone just hangs an American flag? Maybe that could solve the problem."

Rob gave an audible snort. "Oh, well played. Yes, life is easier when no one stirs the pot."

"So what's your suggestion, Captain Obvious?" Shit! Now, I was resorting to schoolyard taunts. I felt like screaming.

"My suggestion?" Rob said, turning back to the camera. "My suggestion is to go to WakeUpUSA.com and send us your thoughts. We'll read the best on the air."

"We're clear," Larry yelled to the crew. I sat stunned on the sofa, fuming and hoping to hear Fatima's voice over the loudspeakers suggesting we give it another shot. But there was only silence. I put my hands up to my cheeks to try to absorb the burning. Then suddenly, the sound of a loud bang as the studio door flew open, slamming against the wall and Benji burst in.

"*THAT*," he yelled, "was fantastic! Better than I could have imagined! Oh, my God, you two," he said, wagging his finger at us and laughing. "Did you guys practice that or something?"

"What?" I asked.

"That's exactly what I was looking for," he said, taking a seat on the table between us, facing us and putting one hand on each of our legs. "You had bickering. You had good-natured needling, and you had solutions. It was perfect. I was riveted in the control room. There was more diversity of thought in those two minutes than any anchor team has had in twenty years. You crushed it! The best part was that what you said was true *and* it felt equal, so no one watching would come away feeling like their side didn't get a fair shake. You did it. We have a morning show! We will launch *Wake Up, USA!* with Rob and Amanda!"

"So . . ." I said, my brain casting about wildly, "it's okay if we disagree, and you want every story to be true and both sides to be equal?"

"Yes, yes. I want true and equal. Wait! That's it!" he said, startling me by leaping up on top of the table, à la Tom Cruise on Oprah's sofa. "True and Equal!! That's it!" He flung his arms overhead like we'd made a touchdown. "FAIR News will be True and Equal!"

Chapter 9

The Rundown

6:15 P.M. Sunday night. I checked my cell phone, then put it down, then picked it up again. Still nothing, other than a bloodied cuticle on my right thumb, which I hadn't realized I'd been gnawing on. Why hadn't Fatima sent the rundown yet? *Wake Up, USA!* was launching tomorrow! Over the weekend I'd spent every second trying to absorb every newspaper article on every topic until they'd become a mind-boggling blur. *I must do well. This is what I've been working toward since I was fifteen. My entire future hangs on this.*

We'd had one dress rehearsal, yesterday, which, it turned out, was just for staging, blocking, and lighting. Fatima said there was no point in a complete editorial run-through, since the stories would be different by Monday. But I couldn't report on something with no prep. Dammit! I should call someone and explain that having me anchor the show is a terrible mistake. *Breathe. Breathe.*

6:17 P.M. The show was starting in less than twelve hours. *Shit!* I stared at the clock, trying to backtime my morning: Hair and makeup at 4:00 A.M. Car at 3:45. Alarm set for 3:00. Bedtime at . . . *Ow!* I'd just torn another hunk of skin from my thumb.

"Still no word?" Charlie asked.

"Is it possible this thing isn't working?" I asked, picking up my phone and shaking it. "Why hasn't she sent anything?"

My phone rang and I answered it as if waiting for test results. "Hello?"

"Hello, Pumpkin." It was Mom, her tone excited and soothing all at once. "Did you get that link I emailed you? 'The Distinguished Early Graduates at Vassar'? Turns out there were many more than just Virginia Wynn. I also cut it out of the paper if you want me to send it to you. Maybe you could feature some of those women on your show."

"Maybe," I said, pulling my phone from my ear to see if the rundown had come yet.

"Okay, sweetie, I'm sure you're busy. I'm just calling to say break a leg tomorrow. I have my alarm set and I've alerted Aunt Marie and Uncle Henry and all the neighbors. And the Wynn volunteers who worked at the polling place with me, they'll all be getting up to watch you. Everyone's very excited."

"Wow, that's quite a cheering section. I hope they're all Nielsen families."

"Are you ready? Do you know what topics you'll be covering?"

"Well, not really," I said, picking at my nail. "The producer hasn't sent the rundown yet, so I don't know which stories we're doing and I'm getting anxious." I cradled the phone between my shoulder and ear so I could shut the blinds against the light streaming through my window. "Plus it's still sunny out, so that makes it a little tough to get ready for bed."

"Yes, I can imagine. But I know you'll do wonderfully. I'm going to bed soon, too. I want to get up bright and early to watch you. I'm so proud of you. Oh, and tell Charlie I said hi."

"Okay, Mom. I love you." The buzzer sounded.

"That's the food," Charlie called, making his way to the door.

I looked down at my cell again. "Oh, the rundown's here!"

TO: Amanda
FROM: Fatima
RE: Rundown

Hi! Here you go. Benji has an awesome idea for the launch. He wants to focus on climate change since no other network touches that story. We've booked a bunch of guests on it, so I'd say study up most on that. The producers will send research packets. (Below you'll see which segments you have and which Rob does.) And we nailed a huge get for the 8B—Arthur Dove! If you have any questions, we can talk when you get in. (I've GOT to go to sleep. Exhausted.) Tomorrow we launch the most groundbreaking morning show in history! Woo-hoo!! See ya at 4!

Arthur Dove. *Holy shit!* My eyes raced up and down the guests and topics:

Guests booked so far:

6:15—Haley Josephs, climatologist. Is climate change naturally occurring or man-made? (Rob and Amanda)

6:35—Congresswoman Kelly Carpenter on her new book, *The Danger of Denial: How Deniers Fuel the Fire.* (Amanda)

6:50—Melting ice means new business opportunities in Alaska; new fishing and shipping lanes opening. Maybe global warming is *good* for the economy! Entrepreneur Tim Keim on set. (Rob and Amanda)

7:10—New *Wall Street Journal* Op-Ed, "No Need to Panic," by two Princeton professors and climate scientists. They say the Earth is getting *colder*, not *warmer*. Both guests live in studio. (Amanda)

7:35—But last summer was the hottest on record! Is global warming happening faster than imagined? Guest TBD. (Rob)

8:10—Arthur Dove, Victor Fluke's chief strategist, spells out Fluke's position on climate change and news of the day. (Rob and Amanda)

8:20—If big polluters like China and India won't use green technology, why should the U.S.? Senator Bob Lewis. (Rob)

8:35—Piglet and puppy race (in studio). Who will win the Piglet-Puppy Challenge for Charity? (Rob and Amanda)

8:50—Gisele Bündchen releases new yoga DVD. (Amanda)

I sat blinking at the rundown.

"How's it looking?" Charlie called from the kitchen, emerging seconds later, plastic container in hand, to check on me. "Amanda?"

"Oh, my God," I said, handing him the phone. Charlie put down the container and I put a hand to my forehead, rubbing it in anticipation of a headache. "How am I supposed to study all these topics in the next hour?"

"Whoa," Charlie said. "This is all over the place. Does FAIR News believe in climate change or not? And why would they have that flamethrower Arthur Dove on?"

"Cause he's the GOP nominee's top adviser," I said, taking the phone back, hoping maybe the rundown had magically morphed into more recognizable morning fare, like, say, a Brownie Bake-Off, or Summer's Hot Swimsuit Styles. "We do have Gisele Bündchen," I said, mostly to myself.

Charlie sat down next to me. "This makes no sense. Why would the producers put climate deniers on TV?"

"Benji wants us to show both sides of every story." My head was getting hot from anxiety.

"But climate deniers have no side," Charlie said. "They reject science. They deny that the ice caps are collapsing and that hurricanes are increasing. They think all the wildfires and superstorms are some kind of crazy coincidence."

"How am I gonna get my mind around all of this?"

"Just read the UN's climate change report," Charlie suggested.

"Tonight?"

"Don't worry," Charlie said, seeing my expression. "This will be easy. You have facts on your side."

I picked up my phone and started typing.

TO: Fatima
FROM: Amanda
RE: Rundown
Hey, sorry to bug you. It seems like there's an awful lot here. Not sure where to begin.

I hit send and immediately regretted it, fearing she'd see me as being one of the three most-mocked anchor types: high maintenance, lazy, or dumb.

"Come on," Charlie called from the kitchen. "Food's getting cold. Let's eat."

"Eat? My stomach is in knots. I've *got* to start doing some research. Then I think I have to go to bed."

"You sure? You won't have to go to bed at seven every night, right?"

"I don't know. I hope not."

"All right, I guess I'll head home after I watch a bit of the game. Break a leg tomorrow."

And I thought field reporting with the unpredictability of breaking news cut into my time with Charlie. Anchoring was supposed to be easier on your life. I started gnawing my thumb again. Climbing onto the bed and popping open my laptop, I was relieved to find a response from Fatima.

TO: Amanda
FROM: Fatima
RE: Rundown
No worries! The segment producers will send you packets of research that'll explain everything as soon they finish them tonight or in the morning. Night-night!

I stared at the computer screen, trying to take deep breaths. I clicked on the rundown and examined it, this time more slowly. It felt like I was preparing for a final exam but I'd missed every class— and the test would be a three-hour oral report in front of a million people. Maybe I shouldn't have sent that email telling everyone I know to tune in. *You can do this, Amanda. Just take it segment by segment. Take a deep breath.* The thought of sitting next to Arthur Dove on a sofa sent a shiver across my shoulders. He was the strategist behind some of the most extreme political campaigns in recent memory, or, as Laurie called him, Satan Incarnate. *I wonder how evil he'll be in person.*

I typed in "UN Report on Climate Change." Days and days worth of research and studies popped up and I started scribbling. Mountain ice caps melting . . . sea ice in the Arctic collapsing . . . heat waves intensifying . . . coral reefs dying . . . Antarctic ice coring data showing CO_2 levels higher now than in past 650,000 years . . . I put my hands to my head to press on my temples.

An email popped up.

TO: Amanda
FROM: Topher
RE: 8:10 segment: Arthur Dove
Hey Amanda, psyched for the big show relaunch tomorrow! I'm producing your 8B segment but I wasn't able to get a preinterview

with Dove. I did find a new statement on the Fluke website that says warmists are standing in the way of success with regulations and trying to shut down industry. Also, says global warming is a hoax. So you should start with that. Cool? See ya tomorrow.

I stared at his email, then looked around the room, like maybe Fatima had installed a hidden camera somewhere to catch my incredulous face. Or maybe Topher was playing a prank on the new anchor: tell her you scored a huge interview with a Big Get who makes outlandish claims, then don't give her any more info. I looked at the clock. 8:00 P.M. I rubbed my temples again as I heard Benji's voice: *Give all sides. True and equal. So does that mean letting the deniers have their say or challenging them? I had no idea.*

I shut off the computer, padded to my bag, put my notes in, then climbed under the covers and reached for the light switch. I could hear the muffled sound of the game Charlie was watching on TV in the other room. I lay in my undark room with the sun shining through the gaps in the curtains. I shut my eyes tighter. *Now sleep,* I commanded myself. *Sleep!* I was wide awake.

Chapter 10

Cold Open

A nerve-jangling chirping was piercing my eardrum, like someone's parakeet had become trapped in my bedroom and was whistling for help. Don't people realize it's 3:15 in the morning? I fixed my eyes on my bedside clock. *Oh, my God! It's 3:15 in the morning!* I threw off the covers and staggered to the shower. The hot water raining down, I went over my mental checklist:

- Apply self-tanner on legs.
- Bring sneakers. Get Gisele Bündchen to show me some yoga moves.
- Don't forget this is a morning show. Be light, funny.
- Try not to faint on air. Or throw up. Or sneeze.
- Don't read too fast. "Don't race the prompter home," as I'd been told I did in Roanoke.
- This may be my one and only shot. If nothing else, enjoy it.

I sifted through my narrow closet, yanking down some old brown sweatpants and a baggy beige sweatshirt. I slipped a pair of beat-up clogs onto my bare feet and pulled my wet hair into a ponytail. I stared at my dark reflection in the mirror on the closet door, marking this momentous morning that would change the course of my life. I looked like a homeless person. A homeless person with awesome highlights.

Grabbing my bag, I shut the door softly, tiptoeing along the silent hallway then down the four flights of stairs.

"Going out for a walk at this hour?" the overnight super asked, giving me a quizzical look.

"Actually, going to work. I'm hosting a new morning show, *Wake Up, USA!* on FAIR News." It sounded strange to say it out loud.

"Oh, yeah? I'll be sure to turn it on. Looks like that's your car." He motioned to a black Lincoln idling out front. Inside, the driver was sleeping, his seat reclined. I rapped gently on the window.

"Gallo?" he asked, straightening up in a jiffy.

"Yup."

"Going to FAIR News?"

"That's right."

"You always go to work at this time?"

"I do now," I said, realizing this was the first day of my new life.

He hit the gas and we sped off through Midtown's mostly deserted streets, save for a few scantily clad women on a corner and some raucous college kids clustered outside a strip club. We pulled up to the studio and I climbed out, heading for the unmarked talent-only door; no guests or visitors or even producers were allowed to set foot through its special threshold.

Before I could fish out my passcard, the door swung open. "Good morning, Ms. Gallo," said a guard with "Stanley" on his name tag. "Here, let me help you with that bag. It looks heavy."

I spotted Angie across the hall, just coming through the main entrance, struggling to pull open a set of heavy glass doors while wrestling her unwieldy roller bag up three stairs. One wheel was stuck on the first step. She gave a violent tug, causing the suitcase to pop open like a jack-in-the-box and spill its contents down the stairs.

"Motherscratcher!" she yelled. The guard didn't budge.

"Oh!" I scrambled toward her and crouched down on the stairs. "Let me give you a hand." She had a salon's worth of stuff in there: a blow-dryer, curling iron, backup blow-dryer, flat iron. There were more combs and brushes than I'd ever seen at once: fat round ones, thin metal ones plus scissors, hair gel, mousse, Moroccan oil, dry shampoo, brush-on highlights, leave-in lowlights, and a half dozen hair spray canisters.

"No, no," she said, shooing me away. "You gotta go get dressed! I'll meet you in my room in five. This is ya big day, girl!"

I stood up too fast, my stomach doing a flip. I helped her steady her suitcase, then darted to the elevator, my heart pounding. *God, don't let me be this nervous throughout the whole show.* I tried taking the deep breaths I'd learned in yoga class but realized they didn't work when jogging down a hallway. *There's no* namaste *in news,* I thought, smiling at my own joke. *Remember that line for Gisele Bündchen!*

I keyed into my office and spotted what might have been a mirage. Draped over my chair was the outfit Meg had selected for my debut: a stunning sleeveless cranberry-colored crepe Rolando Santana dress, plus a gold pendant necklace she'd hung around the top of the hanger, and matching earrings she'd left on my desk. Two ruby-soled pumps sat at the foot of my chair. I threw off my brown sweat suit and kicked my clogs in a corner, then hopped around the office trying to zip myself into the dress.

4:15 A.M. "Excuse me, Amanda?" a tentative voice said from behind where I sat in the hair chair. In the mirror's reflection, I could see a dark-haired girl approaching. "I'm Jada. I'm the PA this morning. I have some articles and research packets here for you."

Jada was teeny: five foot nothing, even in ridiculously high heels. She carried a massive stack of newspapers and articles, half the length of her torso, then dropped the load into my lap. "Fatima will be picking the talking points from these articles."

"Talking points?" I asked into the reflection.

"That's where you and Rob will talk about things in the news."

"Oh," I said, picking at my cuticle again. "Fatima didn't mention those."

"I'll be across the hall in the greenroom if you need anything," Jada said. "Anything at all."

I stared down at the mound of material and began digging through it, article by article, reading the headlines.

- Virginia Wynn Releases Her Top Priorities if Elected. #1 Gun Control.
- Texas Pastor Organizes Rally in Dallas to Make Texas an "Open Carry" State. Encourages Fluke Supporters to Bring Firearms to Church.

- Study Shows American Marriage Rate Falling. Victor Fluke Writes Op-Ed on Decay of Traditional Marriage.
- Victor Fluke Prepares to Share His Fourth Secret of Success on Campaign Website.

Fuck. That's a lot of Fluke. For a second, I felt Charlie looking aghast over my shoulder until I remembered he was in his apartment in bed. *Does balance in the show mean having the same number of segments for both candidates or showing both sides of every segment? I've got to ask Fatima about that.* I checked my watch and reached for a highlighter in my purse.

"Sit back," Angie commanded.

"But I need to start studying."

"Beauty before brains, doll." She smiled, but she was serious and wielding a 600-watt weapon.

The highlighter slipped in my sweaty palm. I rearranged the five-pound stack on my lap to keep my feet from falling asleep. "I really have to go soon."

"Not so fast. Relax. I gotta give ya my signature sexy bang swoop, right he-yah in the front."

"I . . . I . . . actually . . . don't have—" I stopped, catching my own stunning head in the mirror. "I didn't know my hair could do that."

"Whatitellya?" Angie said, making it sound like one word. "Now ya done." She put down the dryer like she was resting her case.

I lifted the tower of papers from my lap and reached for my bag, trying to keep the sneakers from spilling out, then looked at the clock. 4:30 A.M. I dashed out and rounded the corner into the kitchen, almost bumping into a deliveryman wheeling a cart of fragrant warm bagels, oversized fruit muffins, and shiny glazed doughnuts. "Who are those for?" I asked him, actually licking my lips.

"Anyone," he shrugged. "Want one?"

My eyes danced over a yellow, softball-sized corn muffin studded with cranberries, then moved to a blueberry one, then one loaded with chocolate chips, until they landed on a reasonably sized cinnamon-raisin bagel that seemed to represent a responsible breakfast choice. I reached in and grabbed it, feeling its fresh-from-the-oven warmth in my hand. What I would have given for someone to hand me a free bagel and cream cheese when I worked for Gabe Wellborn.

Back then, I made $250 a week. By the last day of the month, after paying for groceries, rent on my group house, gas, and the loan on my used car, I had one dollar left to my name. Literally. And a hot pretzel from the street vendor was exactly one buck. I would buy a pretzel in the morning, then ration it throughout the day—one arm for breakfast, the other for lunch, and the middle twist for dinner. Mustard doubled as a different food group. *You're gonna make it after all*, I sang softly, the way Mom used to.

Stuffing a chunk of the cinnamon-raisin bagel in my mouth, I darted into the greenroom looking for Fatima or anyone who could tell me what to do next, then I stopped in my tracks. Sitting right there on the couch was Arthur Dove, looking exactly like, well, the infamous Arthur Dove.

He had a fleshy dough face, like a biscuit that hadn't been baked, making him look younger than his fifty-plus years, though his wispy blond comb-over gave it away. I'd seen him on TV dozens of times, ferrying Victor Fluke to the next campaign stop, but only now did I realize Dove's features were the opposite of menacing: they were squishy, round, and pale, except for the dark sunken sockets around his eyes that made him look like a lifelong smoker or insomniac.

Here in the greenroom, his pallor hadn't gotten any rosier, but his demeanor had. He looked almost amused, sitting there next to Gisele Bündchen, surrounded by scampering and snorting piglets and puppies. For a second I felt my body hovering over the scene, trying to compute how on earth I would sum it up for Charlie.

"Amanda." It was Arthur Dove saying my name. And now he was smiling at me—a warm, genial smile. And now he was standing, like any courtly southern gentleman would do, and stretching out his hand to shake mine.

"Pleasure to meet you. T minus sixty!" he said in an enthusiastic Texas drawl. "I'm excited to be part of this historic re-launch. Whenever anyone asks me in the future, where were you on the day *Wake Up, USA!* started, I will say, 'I was right there in the greenroom, with a pack of piglets.' Oh, by the way, I remember the first time I saw you on TV. It was at that post office shooting and, boy, you were just terrific. Man, that Richard Betts was one unhinged fellow. But you were cool as a cucumber."

A moist mound of bagel had come to rest on my tongue, which I now strained to swallow without chewing. "Thank you," I mumbled.

"I'm just chattin' with my new friend here, Gisele Bündchen," Dove continued, smiling as if we were all in on the same joke. "She says she's gonna show me some Down Dog."

"Hi." Gisele gave me a sultry wave from her perch on the sofa.

Dove went on, "Gisele and I were debatin' where to find the best ribs. Texas or Kansas City? Care to weigh in? Not that either of you girls looks like you've ever eaten a single rib in your lives."

"Um . . ." I struggled to get my bearings, then held up my bagel with the bite taken out. "I'm actually not that picky. Any style would do around now."

"Well, I'll tell you what. The next time I come in to your fine studio, I'll bring you a big ole rack of Texas ribs and then you can see their sublime righteousness for yourself."

"Sounds good," I said, half hoping I would never see Dove again and half hoping if I did, he'd bring some of those ribs. I was also hoping there wasn't a big ole brown raisin stuck on my tooth. "So I'm actually trying to find the producers."

"That's right. You've got a show to prepare for," Dove said, slapping his own hand. "Let me know if I can answer any questions. Can I get you some coffee to wash down that bagel?" he asked, springing toward me.

"Oh, no thanks," I said, backing away. *Wait till I tell Charlie! Arthur Dove is my new manservant!* A miniature dachshund let out a loud yap under my foot.

"Here, let me help you carry that stuff," Jada said, appearing out of the chaos and standing next to me.

"Oh, thank God. Where is Fatima? I have a lot of questions." My stomach was starting to seize up.

"We should probably get you into makeup," Jada said, leading me by the arm away from Dove and down the hall.

I slid back the curtain to Jess's stall, then stopped cold. There in her chair was Margot.

"Oh," I said, startled.

"Morning," Margot said, not looking up from her cell phone.

"I . . . I . . . need to get into makeup," I said to my own reflection. "I thought this was my time slot."

"Nope," Margot said. "Didn't Benji tell you? This is my slot now. Now that I'm doing the five A.M. show, *Wake Up Now!*"

"Oh, okay," I said, looking to Jess for some direction.

Jess looked back with eyes like coffee-filled saucers. "Maybe you could come back in half an hour?"

"I really can't," I said. "I need to start prepping for the show."

"Good idea," Margot said, still looking down at her phone. "Anchoring a show is very hard, particularly for someone who's not an anchor. People think anyone can be an anchor, but they can't."

I stood paralyzed, staring at the top of her perfect head.

"Not that it matters anyway," she went on, "because I have my own show now, which my agent says is really, really good for me."

"That's great," I said.

"Yes, it *IS* great," she said, not looking at me. "Oh, that reminds me, Roberta is waiting for you. He'll be doing your makeup from now on."

"Oh, no," I said, bringing my hand to my mouth and meeting Jess's eyes.

"Sorry," she mouthed, then one more word: "Benji."

Just then, Roberta swooped into the stall. Six feet tall in skinny jeans and strappy gold heels, his long black Cher-hair was ironed smooth and his fingernails were painted in gold and black zebra stripes. "I've got you, babe," he said with an impeccable Cher affect, kissing me on both cheeks French style. "I've been waiting for you! We've got to get started. We're going to glam you up for the debut!" Roberta grabbed my hand and dragged me away from Jess and down the hall to his own stall.

"Here, lie down, relax," he said, plopping me in a chair, then reaching for a lever and reclining the seat until I was lying back, almost flat, looking up into his nostrils. The view seemed strangely familiar, until I realized I recognized it from my semiannual teeth cleaning.

"I'd kind of like to see what you're doing," I told him.

"What, you don't trust me?" he trilled. "I've done the biggest names on the runway. You'll be gorge!"

I was starting to sweat. Not only could I not see my face, I couldn't read my notes. Shutting my eyes tight, I tried to slow my breath and meditate through what felt like Roberta sponging cold clay onto my cheeks. After an unbearably long time, he popped me upright again.

"Voila!"

I almost screamed. Whatever he'd used on my face had turned my skin a chalky gray. Plus he'd applied bright red lipstick and extra-long fake lashes, giving me the look of a hooker with bubonic plague.

"Um, oh boy," I said, my throat starting to close. "I look a little . . . gray."

"Right," he agreed, "I had to use a base with cool tones because those studio lights cast crazy warmth. They're awful. I honestly cannot believe a place with this much money has such crazy-ass lighting. Luckily, I know how to correct with blue tones to keep you from looking orange on air. *That* would be awful."

"Amanda, I need to bring you downstairs now." Jada poked her head through the curtain. "I'll grab all your stuff and . . . Ooh," she said.

"Yeah, let's go," I said.

"Work it, girl," Roberta called.

"Where's the closest bathroom?" I asked Jada when we were out of earshot. "I need to wipe all this off."

"I really have to bring you downstairs first. The producers are waiting for you." Scuffing along the linoleum to the elevator, I could see Jada's yellow plastic heels were a size too big for her. Blisters were forming on the backs of her ankles.

"So, Jada, what time did you get here?" I asked when the elevator doors closed.

"Two A.M. I couldn't even sleep I was so excited. I think I'm going to get a chance to produce some of your segments. I want to be a reporter someday, and then an anchor. Just like you." She paused to look up at me before scurrying forward again.

People think I'm an anchor, I thought. *I'm an anchor.*

"Here we are," she said, halting at a nondescript pod of six desks in the middle of the newsroom, one of thirty identical pods in rows.

"Hi," I said to the back of four producers' heads, all staring into computer screens.

"Oh, Amanda, hi!" Fatima said, glancing over her shoulder at me. "Insane morning here. Our graphics editor overslept, so I'm trying to find a replacement. But we may not have graphics for the show. And I'm down a producer cause Margot needed one. And we lost our Salt Lake City satellite, so I'm going to have to find a way to fill the 7:35 segment. Grab a desk. I'm sorry I don't have time to talk."

"Um, okay. I do have a couple questions, though," I said, clutching my notes to my chest and gripping my pen.

"Make it fast," she said.

"Um, okay, well, Topher's research packet didn't give me any stats on global warming. This is dense stuff and I'm worried that some of our guests, like the Princeton professors, are saying things for which there's no evidence."

"Oh, don't worry about that, it's really simple. Just always give the other side of whatever anyone is saying. That way we make sure everything is T and E, okay?"

"I'm sorry?"

"'True and Equal,' our motto, remember? This is going to be great. I can feel it!" Fatima glanced at her computer screen. "Crap!" she said, jumping up. "I've gotta run to the graphics department. They just produced a map that's missing Maryland! I'll see you on the set."

I sat down at a computer in the corner, which I could tell had previously been occupied by someone not in peak health. Pushing aside a box of tissues, an empty packet of aspirin, and a crumpled bag of potato chips, I pulled the keyboard to me. On the wall, someone had hung a small wooden sign, like the kind you get at a souvenir store: NEVER LET THE FACTS GET IN THE WAY OF A GOOD STORY. Funny, I thought, as I reached for a stapler and started trying to sort through all the material without the distraction of the dryer.

"Good morning, Team Fun." I turned to see Rob breezing into the pod, unencumbered by any papers. "Is everyone ready to make some TV magic? Has the *New York Post* been delivered yet?" he asked. "Oh, hey, Amanda. You feeling okay?"

"Uh, you know, I'm a tad nervous," I admitted.

"You're not gonna yak, are you?" he asked, taking a few steps back. "Are you fluish? Cause you look sort of . . . bluish."

"What?" I asked, putting a hand to my own face to feel for a temperature before remembering I was made up like an undead anchor from the underworld. "Oh, right. I think I got some bad makeup. Does it look bad?"

"Not if you're auditioning for *Zombie Apocalypse*," Rob said, then pointed to my massive paper mountain. "What's that? Your senior thesis?"

"Aren't these the clippings we're supposed to study?"

Rob snorted, turning to the producers. "People, the rainforest is being depleted. Amanda doesn't want to be responsible for the death of more trees." He leaned up against my desk and bent down to speak sotto voce. "Don't overthink this. We give both sides, we have a few laughs. This isn't brain surgery."

"Yeah, okay," I said, wishing I had a drop of his cocksureness.

"Now if you'll all excuse me," Rob announced, straightening up. "I've got to go to my office and pick the perfect tie to complement Amanda's vibrant outfit and corpselike complexion. See you in a few." He slapped me on the back and strode out.

Chapter 11

The A Block

5:50 A.M. "Can I take you to the set now?" Jada asked. I'd lost track of time, trying to absorb more climate change stats. "We have ten minutes until the show starts."

"Ten minutes!" My heart started racing around my chest. This was the moment I'd dreamt of, well . . . all my life. Jogging after Jada, I thought of Mom and me at the breakfast table with Suzy Berenson. I was about to be that voice for people waking up around the country.

Jada's heels skidded along the polished floor, and I followed her fast shuffle onto the elevator. The doors opened one flight up, revealing the hallway filled with a dozen people, guests and their handlers spilling out of the greenroom. There was Arthur Dove again, standing by the coffee maker this time. He nodded at me and raised his paper cup in a cheerful salute.

"Knock 'em dead, Amanda!"

Man, Dove is so friendly. Maybe we've been wrong about him. I gave a nod and speedwalked down the hall, clutching my research packets against me. When I got to the studio door, I pushed it open and a wall of people turned their anxious faces to me, all speaking in a chorus.

"Take a seat on the sofa, Amanda," Larry instructed.

"Amanda, I've got your microphone and IFB here," Bruce said, holding up a battery pack in each hand. "Do you have your earpiece?"

"Amanda, I need to spray ya. Ya got one hair sticking straight up like Alfalfa," Angie said, releasing a cloud of noxious hairspray over the crowd.

Then Jess caught sight of me. "Oh, hell, no! *Hell, no,*" she said.

"Girl, what happened to your face? Roberta should be arrested. I cannot fix this in the next five minutes." She dabbed at my face with one of her sponges.

Underneath the voices, I could hear Elvis Costello coming from an iPhone on the set and it seemed perfect. What *is* so funny about peace, love, and understanding?

Rob sang and tapped his pen on the desk like a drumstick.

"I didn't realize there'd be a serenade," I said, hoping no one could detect my trembling hands.

"This is Rob's morning ritual," Larry said. "He plays this before every show. It turns him from cynical to agreeable in one easy step."

"Hey, Larry, see this?" Rob called, holding up his middle finger. "It doesn't mean thumbs-up."

"Does it mean we're going to be number one in cable news?" Larry asked.

"Touché," Rob said.

I sat down on the sofa, and three pairs of hands began molesting me from all sides. Angie tugged, teased, and sprayed. Jess wiped my blood-red lips with a Wet-Nap, then reapplied gobs of pink gloss. Bruce unzipped my dress to the waist, attached two battery packs to my bra, then zipped me back up faster than I could say, "What the—!"

Two small hands poked through the hive. "Here are your news scripts if you need them. You read the news at the top and bottom of each hour," Jada explained.

"One minute till airtime! Kill the music, Rob," Larry yelled. "Clear the set, everyone!"

I stood up to leave.

"Not you, Amanda," Larry said.

"Oh, right," I grimaced.

This is it, I told myself. *This is the moment.*

"Have a great show, everyone! We're live in five, four, three, two . . .!" Larry pointed at Camera 1, a musical sting sounded, and Rob began.

"Good morning, everyone. And welcome to the launch of *Wake Up, USA!* Starting today, we're bringing you something different in morning news. This show is for those of you who've tuned out network morning shows because they're too light. And the rest of you who've tuned out other cable news channels because they're too one sided. Welcome to your new home. I'm Rob Lahr."

Larry pointed to me to read into Camera 2.

"And I'm Amanda Gallo," I said, surprised to see my own name in the teleprompter. "We're going to bring you both sides of every story. So you get all the information in one place—away from the polarization and vitriol—to a new place where we can start to solve problems.

"And to prove how different we are, we begin with an important topic that the other morning shows won't touch because they think it's too complicated and controversial. It's climate change." I caught a glimpse of my face in the monitor. Whatever Jess had done had helped. I didn't look great, but I didn't look ghoulish.

"That's right, Amanda," Rob said, nodding at me. "We'll have Congresswoman Carpenter on this hour to help us unpack it. She's just written a new book called *The Danger of Denial*. And later we'll have two scientists here who say the Earth is not getting warmer, it's getting *colder*! Again, you'll never hear all of that in one place."

Larry waved at me and pointed to Camera 2. My mouth had become so dry it was hard to unstick my tongue from its roof. "Also, we'll have the senior adviser to Victor Fluke here. Arthur Dove will explain Fluke's position on global warming. And in our third hour, Gisele Bündchen will be here to show us how she stays in shape."

"You've got my attention," Rob said to me. "You ready for this wild ride?"

"I'll fasten my seat belt," I told him. "*Wake Up, USA!* starts right now!"

The music to the open sounded and adrenaline flooded my body. Ah yes, I know this sensation, this current of electricity coursing up my spine, the same rush as a roller coaster. The closest thing to euphoria I'd ever known.

8:10 A.M. We were in commercial break. Two hours in and my racing heart had slowed to a steady gallop. The nerve endings in my numb fingers were tingling once again. The sensation in my body, no longer Daytona 500, now Pacific Coast Highway; I was cruising on all cylinders and taking in the scenery.

"Good morning, all!" Arthur Dove said, he and his exuberance entering the studio. "This show is looking good! And you two are cookin' with gas. How ya feeling, Amanda?" he said. "This guy taking care of you?" Dove slapped Rob's back.

"So far, so good," I said, not knowing exactly what Rob "taking care of me" would look like.

"Good, cause I don't want to have to come back here and give him what for. You hear me, Rob?"

"Don't worry," Rob said, "she's in good hands."

"Quiet everyone! We're back in five, four, three, two . . ." Larry yelled.

"Welcome back," I started. "Presidential candidate Victor Fluke has held lots of rallies but not been interviewed by the press in three months or spelled out any specifics on his platform. This week Fluke posted a statement on the campaign website saying he has a plan to 'Make Every American Successful.' Fluke's adviser, Arthur Dove, joins us now to explain."

"Howdy," Dove said, turning up the Texas. "I'm pleased as punch to be with y'all this morning on your maiden voyage. But I do have to clarify something you just said, Amanda."

Uh-oh, had I gotten the statement wrong? Wait, was it posted on a different website?

"See, Amanda, you said Victor Fluke hasn't spelled out his plan but that's not true. Mr. Fluke has spoken to lots of real people about his plan to make them successful. We prefer to take our message directly to the voters rather than the misleading media. But hey, I'm here today to give FAIR News a shot."

"And we appreciate you being here," Rob said.

"We don't hate the media," Dove said. "We just don't like the media bias. For instance, the misleading media isn't reporting the fact that Virginia Wynn stole the primaries from her Democratic opponents."

Huh? I almost said to his non sequitur. "Based on what information?" I asked, as soon as I got over being stunned that he would make that bald accusation on national television.

"Let's unpack that," Rob followed. "How did she steal the primaries?"

Rob's question made me grip the sofa—it treated Dove's outrageous claim as if it were true.

"Oh, man, we've got a mountain of evidence," Dove said. "First of all, we know the Wynn campaign registered illegals in Texas, and Arizona, and who knows how many other states."

"What's your evidence?" I asked.

"Victor Fluke and I have spent the past three months studying all the procedures and results in twelve primaries that Virginia supposedly won. We've interviewed dozens of eyewitnesses and heard a whole bunch of stories that made what little hair I have left stand on end."

"Mr. Dove, you're making very serious accusations here," I said. "But again, what's your evidence?"

"All right, Amanda, you want evidence. Let's see, where should I start? In Hawaii, for example, the organizers ran out of ballots, so Wynn operatives created more from Post-its and scraps of paper. In that state, she ended up with more votes than participants. I'm no math whiz, but that don't add up.

"Or take Nevada," Dove went on. "Do you know Wynn supporters there flushed some ballots down the toilets? Now, last time I checked with the FEC, that ain't allowed. And how 'bout Florida? State election officials received two thousand complaints of voter fraud, many from folks who say they saw busloads of foreigners just idling in the parking lots of voting sites. We're working on getting sworn affidavits. And how 'bout the reports of campaign 'volunteers' registering the names of so-called voters who happen to share the same names as the entire starting lineup of the Dallas Cowboys? As we say in Texas, somethin's fishy, and it ain't a tuna boat."

"That does sound suspicious," Rob agreed.

That sounds like something we should have known if the segment producer had done his job! Jesus!

"Listen, here's the point," Dove went on. "Victor Fluke wants everyday Americans to be successful, not illegal aliens and foreign sponges. So, on Election Day, let's put Americans first."

I was hoping Rob would dive in at that point with some ammunition to fight Dove's fraud claims, but he didn't. "Let's talk about the issues," I said. "Does Victor Fluke believe in global warming?"

"Amanda, I heard your other guest last hour, Democrat Congresswoman Carpenter, talkin' about global warming and I had to laugh. Virginia Wynn and her cronies are trying to buffalo the folks into buying their green energy agenda. But the public doesn't buy it," Dove said. "Victor Fluke and his supporters know that the temperature goes up and it goes down. And weather is not connected to drivin' or drillin'. Victor Fluke knows that the U.S. needs to get off our dependence on foreign oil and that drilling in ANWR would be like sticking a needle in a whale—it wouldn't hurt a thing. Meanwhile, Wynn wants to give her friends in green energy taxpayer money that won't do a damn thing to change the weather. She's taking away regular Americans' freedom to be successful in the fuel industry."

"But Mr. Dove," I said, "Ninety-seven percent of scientists say climate change is real and it's dangerous."

"You know, Amanda, ninety-seven percent of doctors used to think leeching was a good way to treat scarlet fever. Sometimes science gets it wrong. And everyone should be wary of the so-called science since we know scientists are cooking the books on this stuff. Everyone remembers what happened when the researchers at East Anglia University didn't find any evidence of global warming: they buried their findings and made stuff up."

"But the Arctic ice caps and glaciers are melting. That's hard evidence," I said. "That's not cooking the books."

"Well, hold on, Amanda. See now you're cherry-picking. The ice in Antarctica is *increasing*. NASA scientists found it hit a record high recently. More ice than they've ever measured before. And new data shows the snow-capped peaks of the Himalayas have lost no ice over the last decade, which, of course, blows up the projections of the UN climate change panel. They predicted the Himalayan glaciers would melt by 2035, when, in fact, for the past eight years the ice increased. So you see, temperatures go up, they go down. All cyclical." Dove smiled at me. "Talk about an inconvenient truth."

My face was flush with heat, imagining Charlie in his apartment furiously scribbling citations to science articles and Mom and all her friends harrumphing at the TV. I had no idea if anything Dove was saying was true and I was scared shitless to debate on national TV what sounded like real facts and stats—as opposed to what I had: one highlighted paragraph, a vague memory of what Congresswoman Carpenter had said two hours ago, and a long-held hunch.

"So, sounds like both sides have a point," Rob said, interrupting my staring contest with Dove.

Larry held up a piece of white cardboard with black letters on it and shook it at me: thirty seconds.

Dove piped up again, directly to me. "Anyway, listen, y'all, this is exactly why Victor Fluke is running. It's time to share his secrets of success with America."

"Wrap," Fatima said in our ears. "Twenty seconds to black. Read the tease."

Larry was swirling one finger fast in the air and pointing the other one at me to read into Camera 2 before the commercial cut us off.

"And coming up," I read, "Gisele Bündchen is here to help us make our booty extra hot." *Tell me I didn't just say that.*

"And we're clear!" Larry yelled.

Dove stood up and slapped Rob's back. "I'm serious, Amanda, don't take any guff from this guy. And listen, here's my only advice to you: Don't believe everything you read. Have a good day, y'all."

Dove strode out and I turned to Rob. "What the hell was that?"

"What was what?" he asked.

"Why didn't you help me shoot down his bullshit?"

"I didn't want to get caught in the crossfire!" Rob said. "And that was some fine TV you were making there."

"What does that mean?"

"That back and forth was great."

"Great TV? We let him say whatever he wanted!"

Rob smirked and I had a bad feeling Prickly Rob from the chemistry test was about to make a comeback. "We're supposed to give both sides."

"We're supposed to give viewers real info and try to find solutions," I told him. "We didn't do either!"

"You don't think we solved the existential crisis of climate change there?" Rob asked with a blithe smile, like he might wink at me next.

"Rob, everything he was saying was wrong."

"How do you know? Are you a climatologist?"

"No, but I know he's full of shit."

"How?"

"Because everyone knows global warming is real."

"You ever read the East Anglia stuff?"

Fuck. I didn't even know what that meant. I gave Rob a heavy sigh to let him know I was done debating this, then turned and began busying myself by reading viewer comments. On the screen, the show's Twitter feed was up and in line after line I saw my name.

The liberal agenda of @AmandaGallo is disgusting! She makes me sick.

My stomach contracted like I'd been punched, and my eyes moved down to the next.

Everyone knows #climatechangeBS is made up by global warmists on the left. Tell @AmandaGallo to do her homework next time! #f'ingidiot.

Do my homework? Fuck you, you troll. You try doing a segment in front of a million people with Topher's research packet. I clicked on the next one.

Hey @AmandaGallo, Good job with Congresswoman Carpenter. And I like your dangle.

I didn't know what that meant and I didn't want to know, but I checked my nose anyway, and then my bra, to make sure nothing was hanging before reading the next one.

@FAIRNews. Please get rid of @AmandaGallo. She's a progressive imbecile! She's not even pretty. Send her to @MSNBC where she belongs. @MargotHamilton is so much better!

I closed the laptop fast.

8:45 A.M. Fifteen minutes left in the show. My head had that empty, woozy feeling that follows a big brain drain. After the climate change debates, came the piglet and puppy race that resulted in a slew of piglets getting loose in the studio, and scampering around as the crew chased them and Larry yelled things like "I smell bacon!" and "This segment is going to the dogs!" It was all a little dizzying. I bit into my third dry bagel and took another swig of now cold, bitter greenroom coffee.

"Amanda, your next segment is in the demo area," Larry called, studying his rundown. "It's with Gisele Bündchen."

"Right now? Shit! Do I have time to change?"

"Sure," Larry said. "You've got ninety seconds."

I leaped off the sofa and sprinted down the hall to Angie's room, yanking down the zipper on my dress while trying to hold my mic pack on my bra. I stepped out of the dress, leaving it in a puddle on the floor, then hopped around, tugging on yoga pants and a T-shirt. I sprinted back to the studio barefoot, where I was surprised to find Gisele Bündchen clad in a hot pink Lycra tank top and tight gray yoga pants, already stretched in an inverted V shape, her volleyball butt pointed high to the ceiling. The floor crew was huddled around her, not blinking.

"You know, Gisele, I've always thought yoga could be great for my back," Panzullo said, rubbing his own shoulder. "It gets really sore from carrying this heavy camera all day."

"Have you tried Thai massage?" she asked.

"Thigh massage?" he replied.

"You've been here for a couple hours, huh, Gisele?" Casanova asked. "You must be hungry. Can I grab you a bagel or something?"

"Oh, no, thanks. I don't eat bread," Gisele said, moving onto all fours and arching her back like a cat. "I'm gluten free."

I felt Larry sidle up next to me. "She's a gluten for punishment," he whispered.

We came back from commercial, and for the next three minutes Gisele guided me through a series of stretches and lunges, all of which struck me as sexually suggestive. I couldn't see the monitor, but it seemed like Panzullo was shooting us directly from behind, exposing our rear ends to the world. I tried using my head to signal him to move to the left but his lens stayed trained on Gisele's ass.

"I'm not sure this is my angle," I called out, upside down, looking through my own legs.

"Oh, trust me," Rob called back, "it is."

"Okay, wrap it up," Fatima directed in my ear. I straightened up, light-headed, and looked into the camera. "More *Wake Up, USA!* in just two minutes."

"Great job, Gisele!" all the guys said in unison.

"Amanda, head back to the sofa," Fatima instructed. "We have one minute left. Let me know if you have any viewer tweets or Facebook posts you'd like to read. Maybe something on global warming?"

"Yeah, here's a good viewer email," Rob said, pointing to his computer screen as I took my seat.

TO: WakeUpUSA
FROM: GladI8her
RE: Amanda's thighs
Amanda, spread your hot, juicy thighs! Keep going! Don't stop now. I'm not done jerking off.

Dozens of emails with my name on them, most with dirty subject lines, spanned the page. "Oh, gross!" I said, feeling that last bagel working its way back up.

"GladI8her . . . hmm," Rob mused out loud. "Coliseum reference, I assume? He must be a history buff. Anyway, he's sent about a dozen emails with the same 'juicy thigh' theme. I think he found your sexercise very, um, stimulating. Hey! Should we turn one of these into a full-screen graphic? We could call it Favorite Viewer Email."

"Rob, knock it off," Fatima said. "Just tease tomorrow's show."

"Roger that," Rob said.

"We're back in ten, nine, eight . . ." Larry shouted. "Rob, stop reading email and look up! Don't blow the landing!"

"Blow this," Rob shouted back at him, then smiled as the red light on Camera 3 turned on. "And that's our show today. Thanks so much for joining us on our premier. But before we go, I just want to read one email here. We've gotten a lot like this." I jerked my head toward Rob and he looked back, his left dimple flaring. "It reads, 'Dear *Wake Up, USA!*, what a refreshing show. Thanks for bringing us both sides of the story.'"

I exhaled.

Rob smiled at me. "Amanda, excited to come back for more?"

"Not as excited as you are," I accidentally said, then we cut to commercial and the show ended.

"That's a wrap!" Larry yelled.

"Great first show everyone," Fatima said. "Let's have a pitch meeting in the Think Tank in ten."

I stood up, feeling like I'd just run a marathon: winded, stiff legged, with that woozy post-adrenaline sensation, exhausted but euphoric. Rob strolled off the set and Larry offered his hand to help me step down. "Great job today," he said. "You're off to a good start." Then, more softly, "I know Rob's not easy."

"Yeah, he's sort of a—" I stopped, deciding to bite my tongue.

"Dick?" Larry suggested.

"Yeah, that's the word."

"Well, you handle him better than any of the other women here. For what that's worth."

"Thanks, Larry." I gathered my notes and started out of the studio, wondering when I'd see Benji and what he thought. And Mom. And Laurie. And Charlie!

I stole into the now empty greenroom and sat down in the corner.

"Hi, Mom!" I said when she picked up.

"Oh, sweetheart! I'm so glad you're calling. You were absolutely terrific!"

"Really? You think so?"

"Oh, yes. And those topics you had were not easy. And, oh my, Arthur Dove. I don't know how you managed to keep a straight face."

"I know. I know."

"Well, you did a great job, even though some of your guests were not exactly"—she paused and I waited to hear her analysis—"fact based. I don't know what these deniers are thinking."

"I know," I said, my stomach starting to churn for not challenging them more. "I've got to talk to the producers about getting better info. In fact, I better go."

"I'll look forward to hearing much more."

I hung up and looked at the clock on the wall, calculating that Charlie might have a few minutes before his 9:30 class. I dialed his number.

"So?" I asked when he didn't immediately offer. "What did you think?"

"I thought you were great . . ."

I heard a "but" coming. "But what?"

"But the Arthur Dove segment was wildly irresponsible. I think in the future, you know, when you're more comfortable, you'll be able to challenge your guests more. And your producers should book less insane guests. You know?"

Charlie was right, but that wasn't what I wanted to hear. "Yeah," I said, then I went silent and Charlie shifted tone. "But, hey, you did really well, babe. I'll see you later?"

"Yup." I sat holding my phone, then dialed Laurie's cell.

"I can't talk," she said upon answering.

"Did you watch my debut?" I asked.

"Oh, shit. No, I couldn't."

"Wow, thanks."

"Sorry, I've been on a stakeout all night."

"Yeah, no problem," I said. "I'm only *anchoring a national morning show*!"

"How'd it go?"

"Uh, I can't really tell. I need you to watch and let me know. Charlie didn't love it."

"Has Charlie ever seen a morning show?" Laurie asked.

I had to think about that one. "I mean, the TV's been on *near* him sometimes in the morning. Does that count?"

"I don't know if I'd use Charlie as my one-man focus group," she said. "He finds C-SPAN compelling. I'll watch some clips online. And I'll try to swing by tonight."

Chapter 12

Pitches

I hadn't had occasion yet to be in the room that Benji had coined "the Think Tank," but I'd walked by its glass walls for the past few months, staring in at show meetings, wondering what exciting decisions were being made in there. The space was really just a long conference table and chairs, surrounded on all sides by glass, in the middle of the newsroom.

Pushing open its door, I stepped in toward Fatima and a half dozen bleary-eyed twentysomethings, most of their faces smeared with a maroon goo. In the middle of the table sat a deep rectangular aluminum tray filled with racks of ribs slathered in barbeque sauce. Next to the tray, two paper plates were stacked high with bright yellow corn bread squares. The producers looked like a pack of hungry hyenas surrounding a fresh kill.

Rob sauntered in right behind me, pointing to the bin. "What's that, the rest of the piglets?"

"Arthur Dove sent these ribs over. He said he wanted Amanda to try them," Fatima explained.

"Yay, Arthur Dove," someone mumbled with her mouth full.

I felt a little sick that Dove was doting on me. But I also felt hungry. So I sat down and pulled up a rib.

"Oh, and did you see his tweet?" Fatima asked, wiping her hands and reaching for her phone. "Here, let me read it: 'Hope you caught my conversation with @AmandaGallo and @RobLahr on @WakeUpUSA! Super smart show. #bothsides.' Hashtag both sides," she repeated. "How great is that? You guys need to check your Twitter accounts. I bet they went up by thousands today."

People munched agreement. And I scratched my head. Maybe the segment looked better on TV than I remembered it. Or maybe Dove was a master media manipulator.

One of the producers, notably abstaining from the ribs orgy, sat bolt upright and cracked his knuckles. His buzz cut and ripped biceps made him look like a lost ROTC cadet. In front of him stood a water bottle filled with bright yellow liquid.

"How long are you going to go without food?" the redheaded girl next to him asked, sucking her sauce-covered fingers.

"They say two weeks is optimal," the ROTC-wannabe answered.

"Dude, that's fucking idiotic," said a guy dressed in black, sitting on the left side of the table. My eyes lingered on his dyed goth-black hair, his multiple ear piercings, and the scorpion tattoo on his forearm.

"What are you guys talking about?" I asked in what I hoped would be a team-building way, before I went ballistic on their shitty producing.

"Topher's doing a juice cleanse," the redheaded girl told me, pointing to the buff kid.

"Why?" I asked.

"Because he's manorexic," she answered.

"No," Topher said. "Because it's *great* for you!"

"Says who? Your spiritual leader, Rush Limbaugh?" the goth guy asked. "He doesn't look like he's been doing much of a cleanse . . . unless it's a cheeseburger cleanse."

"Mmmm, cheeseburger," another guy said.

"It works!" Topher insisted. "A lot of people do it. It's lemon juice, maple syrup, and cayenne pepper. It's basically lemonade." He shook up the mixture in his bottle.

"It looks like a urine sample," the goth guy remarked. "Dude, you know you're just going to lose muscle mass." Strange, I thought, for someone clad in black who didn't look like he'd ever set foot inside a gym.

"Hey, here's a pitch idea," the goth guy said to Fatima. "Morons who do juice cleanses."

"I like it," Fatima said. "Rob, Amanda, why don't you guys do one and we'll follow your progress?"

"Are you kidding?" Rob said, gesturing toward me with his thumb. "This one eats like a trucker at a Cracker Barrel buffet. She wouldn't survive a cleanse."

"Can it be a bagel cleanse?" I asked, self-conscious, suddenly aware that Rob must have been counting how many I'd inhaled.

"I think it would be cool to put all the wacky fad diets to the test: juice cleanses, grapefruit diets, Caveman diet, HCG diet," the red-head suggested.

"Great idea, Tiffany," Fatima said, pointing a pen at her. "We'll get one doctor who says these diets work and another who says they don't. How about Dr. Bob on that tomorrow?"

"Wouldn't it be better to book a doctor who's not obese?" Tiffany asked.

"Right," Fatima nodded. "Let's get, um . . . who's that blond doctor they use on Fox with the big boobs? What's her name?"

"I don't know, but book her," Rob said.

"I have another medical pitch," said a pretty black girl sitting at one end of the table.

"Go ahead," said Fatima.

"There's a report that finds many more kids today are being diagnosed with ADD and being prescribed medicine than ten years ago. But some doctors say the kids are overmedicated and maybe they just need to focus better."

"I like that it has both sides, but is it new?" Fatima wondered. "Rob, what do you think?"

"Sorry, I wasn't paying attention. What?"

"Oh, my God. Next pitch."

"I have a good one," Topher said. "Fake astronauts just returned from a fake mission to Mars."

"Is this fake news?" Fatima asked.

"No, this fake story is real," he said. "They actually simulated a journey to Mars for 520 days. Basically ever since Obama killed the space program, people have to take fake space trips."

"I like it," Fatima remarked. "Try to find a NASA guy who says we need to revive the space program and then some budget hawk who says, no, it's not worth the money." She turned to me. "Amanda, do you have anything?"

I hadn't brought any pitch ideas but thought back to the articles I'd glanced at in the *New York Times* before the show. "Well, I read this morning that Bono thinks AIDS can be completely eradicated in the next five years. He's come up with a way to distribute antiviral drugs throughout Africa that will—"

"What's the other side?" Fatima interrupted.

"What?" I asked.

"I mean, I like the story, but what's the other side? Everyone thinks curing AIDS is good, right?"

"Well, yes, it's a major medical breakthrough. I don't know if there is any other side."

"We need another side," Fatima said. "Remember, guys, this is our brand. True and Equal. Every guest segment has to have two sides, okay, and preferably stories that don't already have solutions. Also we need a couple of interesting headlines for our news blocks. We've got twelve more hours of TV to produce this week. So let's hear some more pitches, bitches."

"Wait," I said. "Can we talk about today's show for a second? A little postmortem?"

"Sure," Fatima said, not looking up from her laptop.

"Okay, I think we're going to need a lot more research and information for our guest segments. We can't have guests on who make wild claims and don't provide any evidence." I needed to say that in a group setting so no one felt singled out. Plus I could indirectly show Rob how wrongheaded he'd been on set about Dove.

"Oh, my God," Tiffany said, pointing at her iPhone. "Do you see all the pickup we're getting from the Dove stuff about the voter fraud? I keep getting Google alerts. *Washington Post*, Politico. It's trending on Twitter. They're all citing *Wake Up*. Wait, wait, here's another one. *New York Times*. It says, 'FAIR's new morning show wasted no time making a splash in the crowded cable field. On *Wake Up, USA!* Arthur Dove accused Senator Virginia Wynn of voter fraud in the primaries and told anchors Amanda Gallo and Rob Lahr of Victor Fluke's plans to make every American a success story.'"

"That's fucking awesome!" Fatima said. "We're already breaking news! Guys, this is great. We need to do another segment tomorrow on the Wynn voter fraud stuff."

I didn't want to feel as excited as I did hearing my name in the

New York Times, but after being in the witness protection program known as Newschannel 13, it felt amazing to be in the middle of the action. Rob turned to me for a high five and I reluctantly offered one up.

"Hold on a second," I said. "Yes, it's fantastic that we're already getting attention, but we had nothing to counter Dove's claims. Thousands of complaints of voter fraud? Eyewitnesses who saw illegal aliens voting? I mean, this is nuts. We need to confirm these things or he can't say them."

"But *we* didn't say them," Topher said. "We can't help what a guest says."

"No, but we can correct him," I said, "and try to stop him from making inflammatory claims with no evidence."

"She's got a point, Topher," Fatima said. "Why don't you start trying to find these eyewitnesses to voting scams. See if there really are affidavits."

"Hey," Morgan said, "is Fluke doing any TV?"

"Complete radio silence," Topher said.

"Dove liked us. Maybe we can get Fluke to come in," Fatima said to Topher. "Start working on that. Call Dove again, become his best friend."

"Copy that," Topher said.

"Okay, guys, let's talk about tomorrow. Benji called the control room during the show. He thought the global warming theme really worked. So let's come up with another hot-button topic for tomorrow."

"Maybe we should do something on abortion," Jada suggested from the corner. "That guy who's suing his ex-girlfriend to stop her from getting an abortion. He's says it's his baby, too, and he has rights."

"Ooh, that is good," Fatima said.

"Ugh," Rob said. "Abortion—not morning TV."

"Have there been any court rulings on that issue?" I wondered.

"I'll check Wikipedia," Topher said.

"Is the guy talking to the press?" Fatima asked.

"Doesn't look like it," Jada said.

"So try to get the guy and the girlfriend. And if they won't do it, get a pro-life nut and a pro-choice type. Perfect T and E. This'll be good." She folded her laptop. "Let's hear it for a great first show, guys!"

Everyone clapped, but I was still annoyed. The producers started filing out and I tapped Topher on the back. "Hey, do you have a second?"

"Sure, what's up?" he asked, grabbing his bright yellow concoction and turning his wide face toward me.

"I wanted to talk about the segment you produced. With Dove."

"Yeah, great job with that, by the way," he said. "You got a few fireworks there."

I cocked my head at him. "I don't think so, Topher. I didn't know what he was talking about with voter fraud—or climate change for that matter. You didn't put any research in the packet."

"Oh, I emailed you. Dove wasn't available for a preinterview."

"I know. But *you* still have to provide facts. You have to search for anything he's ever said on these issues from other sources and fact-check those comments. Plus he was sitting in the greenroom for two hours. You could have preinterviewed him then."

"That's a good idea," he said, like that brilliant thought had never crossed his mind.

"Here's the deal," I said, pressing my head toward his to impress the notion into his skull, "I need to know beforehand about his claims of busloads of immigrants and flushed ballots and illegal registration. We can't be blindsided on the air like that. It makes us look bad and it only confuses the viewers."

"Yeah, but you challenged him, so we're covered on T and E."

I stared at him for a second, waiting for the punch line. "Topher, that's not good enough. We need facts. You didn't get a statement from local poll watchers or the election commission. We didn't confirm that there are active investigations or real signed affidavits. You need to produce these segments." I scanned his open face for a glimmer of understanding.

He looked at me blankly. "But we didn't say any of that. He did."

"I know. But we need to give the viewers real information, not wild claims from our guests, okay? I can't believe you haven't gotten into trouble before now."

"Oh, I have," he said brightly. "I used to work at Channel Eight in Hartford. Remember when they reported that Admiral Fanning of the Joint Chiefs had seen a UFO?"

"No," I said slowly.

"Well, that was wrong, apparently. That turned out to be fake news from a satire website. But, you know, it looked really real."

"I rest my case," I said, gathering my bags. "So when you're producing for me, please send facts."

"You got it," he said, offering a fist bump to seal the deal.

"Hi, Amanda!" Melissa jumped off her treadmill and bounded toward me as I approached Benji's office. "You were a-*maze*-balls today. We all came in early for the launch and watched the show up here on that huge monitor. You were *so* good with Dove! And I loved the Gisele Bündchen segment. What was she like? Was she nice? And you *looked* beautiful."

"Oh, thank you," I said. I didn't want to be so flattered by comments on my looks, but I was, and I was relieved that Melissa couldn't detect the Roberta makeup disaster.

"Benji's waiting for you!" Melissa clapped her hands together, quickly but quietly, in excited silent applause.

"Come here, you superstar!" Benji called from the threshold of his office. "How ya feeling?"

"Great," I lied, realizing today might not be the day to share my concerns over the amateurish producing.

"You should be! I think we truly made morning show history." Benji grabbed the remote off his desk to mute the monitors in his office playing the other networks, then said "Jesus!" and gestured up at the screen. "What is Jane wearing?"

I glanced up to see Jane, the nine-to-eleven anchor, looking stern and clad in chartreuse.

"Come on!" Benji yelled at the TV. "Lime green? What is Meg doing to me? Melissa!" he yelled out his door. "Call Meg and tell her to burn that dress Jane's wearing." He shook his head at me and sat down. "Anyway, great, great show today. I mean, groundbreaking. Did you see all the pickup you're getting? It's better than I could have hoped for. Great idea having Dove on today. What a way to launch!"

"Yeah," I said, trying to match his enthusiasm. "But do you think we should be worried that he made lots of wild claims about voter fraud?"

"He sure as hell made news! But yeah, you should check out what he was saying. That'd be a great coup for you. Get to the bottom of it. That would totally put you on the map. I mean, that's star stuff."

I liked the sound of that. *Yeah, I don't need Topher. I'll get to the bottom of stuff and break stories myself!* "You're right. I'll do that."

"And I don't think any other network has ever devoted its morning show to climate change," he went on. "Oh, and I loved the Gisele Bündchen thing you did. How hot was she in person?"

"Oh, very attractive. But, on the climate change issue," I said, balling up my hand and pressing my knuckles to my chin, "you know, I worry we might have left the viewers a tad confused. I mean, we never really gave a definitive answer on whether the Earth is warming or cooling or whether it's cyclical or man-made or what to do about it."

"Oh, well, come on," he said, giving me a what-do-you-expect look, "don't beat yourself up over that. You've got, what, six minutes tops for those segments? You're not going to solve global warming in six minutes. And by the way, our research shows that viewers in the morning only watch in five-minute chunks. So really you're just planting a seed. You know, again, broadcasting." He smiled because we both got the reference.

"But what I really liked about what you did," he went on, "is that you had on those two kooks, those two deniers, but you didn't call them kooks or deniers, you let them have their say. And that way, you get the normal news watchers *and* you get that twenty-five percent of the country that's in denial. And hey, you had that congresswoman on who thinks they're dangerous, so maybe they all learned a little something about each other today."

I turned to stare out Benji's giant window looking over Midtown, pondering that one.

"Look here," Benji said, leaping up and snatching a sheet of paper off his desk. "This will blow your mind. This is a map of the U.S. from the last presidential race broken down by political party."

He handed me the paper, showing the country covered in big red splotches and some bright blue dots up and down the coasts and sprinkled in the middle. "This is a red versus blue country. But most of it is red, by the way, which I know is like completely crazy, right? And there's not a single network that caters to all these people until now. At FAIR News, we don't think red versus blue, we think purple. We're the Purple Party. We're not dividing people. We're bringing them together."

I nodded.

"I mean, who doesn't like purple?" he asked. "In fact, has Meg given you some purple dresses? You should make that your signature color. You know what would be great? What if you died your hair that purple color that you see around now?"

"Wait, really?"

"You know, the color all the millennials are doing on their hair. I saw Kelly Ripa with it the other day. It could be great for the demo. Think about it. Oh, that reminds me, you looked like hell this morning."

"What?"

"What did Jess do to your face?"

"Oh!" I said, a feeling of chagrin creeping up my cheeks. Leave it to Benji to tell me the truth. "I had to go to Roberta. Jess was too busy doing Margot. She said you insisted on it."

"Oh, right. Margot," he said, then shook his head. "God. That girl is sooo fucking nice. Do you know what she said when I told her that you were getting the morning slot, not her?"

"No, what?"

"She said, 'Well, if that's God's will, then I'm sure that's the right plan.' She thinks Jesus Christ made the decision! Anyway, I had to throw her a bone, so I said she could go to Jess. Can't you go after her?"

"Well, no, I need to be downstairs with the producers, prepping."

"So go before."

"Jess doesn't come in until four."

"Oh. That's a problem. I can't pay her any overtime. We gotta bring this show in on budget. Well, I'm sure you'll figure it out," he said, standing and signaling our time had run out.

Chapter 13

Good Get

"You know what I think would be a good segment for you?" Charlie said. "There's a great piece in the *Economist* on the cultural underpinnings of the EU's bloated bureaucracy. You know, all the precursors to Brexit. I was thinking that could be good material for your show. You could go to the Council on Foreign Relations and get different voices on how Europe got to this point."

I pressed my fingers to my lips, trying to nod thoughtfully, to keep myself from smiling at how adorable Charlie was being. I could tell he felt bad about criticizing the show and was trying to transition to helpful-suggestion mode. He wasn't going to criticize *Wake Up, USA!* He was going to turn it into PBS.

"Or," he went on, "you could find a history professor. I mean, not me, of course, I don't want to be on camera, but at Yale or somewhere, who could give you all the historical reference points for what's happening with Fluke. All of his Successful Man crap. There are similarities with 1968 and George Wallace and the race-baiting, immigrant-hating stuff. You could even go back to Alexander Hamilton and examine that era. Anyway, that would be a provocative piece."

I bit my upper lip to keep from laughing and turned to my right to look at Laurie, seated at my tiny kitchen table.

"Provocative," Laurie repeated, looking at me like she, too, was about to burst out laughing at Charlie's idea of good TV. "And maybe the *New York Review of Books* has something really juicy coming out on the Constitutional Convention of 1787," she said. And then we couldn't contain ourselves and started giggling.

"What?" Charlie said.

"I'm pretty sure nothing in the *Economist* has ever found its way onto cable news," I said. "In fact, Rob Lahr told me this morning to ignore all my newspaper clippings. He only reads Page Six in the *New York Post*. Probably to spot himself. He prepares for the show by studying Mediaite."

"He sounds like a Nobel Laureate," Charlie said. "You want more wine, Laur?"

She nodded and he poured, then looked my way. I waved away his offer. My new job, I realized with some regret, would forever-more make a weeknight glass of wine impossible.

"Look, I'll be honest," Charlie said. "*You* were great, babe, but I don't understand why FAIR News would give a megaphone to Arthur Dove. And your climate change guests were complete crackpots."

"Actually, they're not," I started. "One of those deniers is a pro-fessor at Princeton and the other the president of the National Acad-emy of Sciences. So they're legit. Do you know that twenty-six percent of the country doesn't believe in global warming?"

"That's exactly the danger of doing segments like the ones you did this morning!" he said, growing exercised. "You feed the ignorance."

Charlie's reaction gave me a sinking feeling. I liked Benji's better. "But see, that's the point," I said. "FAIR News isn't going to pretend that a quarter of the country doesn't exist. We're going to talk to them."

"Amanda, they sounded like imbeciles," Charlie said. "They were making stuff up."

"Well, no. Here's the crazy part. Everything they said—and the stuff Dove said about global warming—was actually true. I looked it up after the show. According to NASA, the ice *did* increase in the Antarctic and the Himalayas. Oh, and by the way, scientists at East Anglia University *did* put out bogus research. See, this is the stuff the deniers hang their hats on. I never understood why they reject science until now. I mean, obviously they're wrong. They don't do deep enough research. But they're not making it up."

I said it slowly, waiting for lightning to strike me at the table or for Laurie to call me out for conspiring with Dove the Devil. But Lau-rie was looking down, checking her phone.

"Amanda, as the great Senator Daniel Patrick Moynihan said, 'Ev-eryone is entitled to his own opinion but not to his own facts.'"

"But that's the problem," I told Charlie. "Dove *did* come with his-own facts. That's what the Internet has done. It's given everyone their own facts."

"As Nietzsche said, 'There are no facts, only interpretations,'" Laurie declared.

"Who are you?" I asked her.

"I have an app," she said. "It sends me a daily philosophy factoid."

"Well, there you have it," I told Charlie, gesturing at Laurie. "There are no facts, only factoids. Anyway, tomorrow's going to be an interesting show. Benji thinks we should do it on abortion. There's this woman who wants an abortion, but her ex-boyfriend is suing to stop her because he wants the kid. We booked the VP of NARAL. And I gotta hand it to this young producer, Jada. She convinced the boyfriend to come on even though he'd never done any TV."

"That is a good get," Laurie said, without looking up.

"I guess I don't understand your business," Charlie said, putting his glass down on the table. "I mean, why give this antiabortion guy airtime? It's not his choice."

"Because it's good TV," Laurie said.

"But you're going to have to dismantle his argument," Charlie told me. "You should do a background check on the guy. I bet he's a shill for one of these shadow antiabortion operations that stages undercover stings at clinics."

"He doesn't sound like it," I said. "I read up on him. He's a fifth grade teacher. He has a son from a previous marriage, coaches Little League. In the deposition, it sounds like he really wants the kid. I don't think this is political for him. This is personal." I was starting to feel strangely defensive—like Charlie thought he knew this story and subject better than me. "And it's interesting. I've never thought of it this way," I went on. "Why are the father's needs overruled by the mother's? You know? He wants this child."

"Because it's a woman's body," Charlie said.

"Right. Of course. But it's his kid, too."

"But, babe, if you got pregnant, should I be the one to make the decision whether you have it?"

"Wow," Laurie said, looking up with wide eyes like we'd just woken her. "Didn't think you'd go there."

I paused. "Well, when you put it that way." I knew we could leave

it at that. But something felt unfinished. Was that the lens I was supposed to apply to news stories: my own life? Because if so, I did have
experience with the subject of pregnancy and its prevention. I could
still summon the memory of the redbrick exterior of the clinic. In
high school, I would routinely steer nervous friends into its parking
lot, assuring them they had nothing to worry about; the clinic
wouldn't call their parents to tell them their daughters wanted birth
control. Usually everything went perfectly and we'd bound out of the
building an hour later, brown bag filled with pills in our hands. Mission accomplished. But one day was different: that horrible rainy
morning when I skipped school and secretly headed to my friend
Dani's street to find her waiting on the corner. She'd snuck away
from the bus stop. We drove silently into Planned Parenthood's
parking lot again. I guided her into the empty waiting room. We
didn't really talk. I knew all I needed to about how she'd gotten into
this situation—her strict Korean parents had found her pills and
thrown them out, grounded her, and screamed at her, threatening to
send her far away to an all-girls school.

The nurse came and ushered Dani behind a closed door while I
stared at the same page of a fashion magazine in the waiting room,
trying not to imagine what was happening. When Dani reappeared
an hour later, she was limp, seemingly drugged or just emotionally
crushed, I couldn't tell. I never for a second, before or after that, thought
abortion should be illegal, but I did think it was harder on everyone
than both sides let on. And I loved Planned Parenthood for doling out
all that free birth control to try to keep Dani's situation from happening. I shook my head and snapped back to my kitchen table with Charlie, who I knew didn't have any real-life experience with this.

"I mean, aren't I supposed to give both sides of the abortion debate and let the viewers decide?" I said.

"You're supposed to look at the facts. And the fact is that abortion
is legal and the Supreme Court has ruled it's the woman's decision.
And I don't think you should provide any fodder to change that."

"I just think the father has a right to tell his side," I said. "I mean,
I've never really thought about the guy's feelings. Wouldn't you want
to be part of the decision?"

"Yeah, of course," Charlie said. "But ultimately, it's not my decision."

"Are we still on the abortion topic?" Laurie asked, looking up.

I scratched my head and looked away.

"Sorry," she said. "I'm working on something. I might be sitting on a Fluke bombshell."

"Sounds uncomfortable," I muttered.

"Fluke bombshell?" Charlie asked, perking up and rubbing his hands together. "What is it?"

"No story before it's time, my friends. I need to vet it with legal before I can bust this wide open." Sometimes when Laurie got excited, she sounded like Nancy Drew.

"Just give us a little something, Laur," Charlie chided her in that way that people not in the news business sometimes did. As if things like exclusives, and confidentiality, and off-the-record agreements were just things we made up to feel important. "Give us a clue."

"Well," Laurie said, "let's just say Victor Fluke's Put Americans First bullshit is bullshit."

"That's a news flash?" Charlie said with a testiness that was new.

"No, but what I have is. And that's *all* I can say."

"If you told me he murdered someone, I wouldn't be surprised," Charlie said.

I felt my phone vibrate. "Oh, good, here's the rundown!" I said. "Oh, my God." I scrolled up and down twice to make sure my eyes weren't playing tricks on me and I was reading it correctly. "Victor Fluke is on tomorrow."

Chapter 14

The Dangle

4:00 A.M. "Hey, cutie," Roberta whispered, sticking his head in the greenroom, interrupting my studying.

"You scared me," I said. I'd come in early, hoping to get into Jess's makeup chair before Margot could get there. But Jess wasn't in yet and now here was Roberta in a massive blond wig with Pre-Raphaelite waves. Oh, right, it was Beyoncé Tuesday.

"My goodness, look at you! Without any makeup you look like you're twelve years old." Roberta put his hand to his mouth to cover a coquettish smile. "Oh, my gosh, you're so pretty. Come on, let's get you started. It's going to take Jess fifteen minutes to set up anyway. And I'm all ready for you."

Thus began a process I feared might last forever: Roberta would do my makeup at 4:00 A.M. and Jess would undo it at 5:00.

5:55 A.M. Larry checked his watch. "You're cutting it a little close to air, Amanda," he said as I blew past him like a tornado of notes on my way to the sofa.

"I know, I know. Sorry," I said, dropping my papers on the table, where I could claw at them when needed in a few minutes.

"You look lovely this morning, Amanda," said Casanova, coming out from behind Camera 3 and grabbing my hand, then spinning me, waltz style. To the left of Casanova, I caught a blurred glimpse of myself in a monitor. My body looked lumpy.

"Larry, can I see myself in Camera Two for a second?" I frowned. "I think this dress Meg picked out may be giving me a muffin top. Or maybe it's from actual muffins." I didn't mention I'd just inhaled a chocolate one.

Larry pressed a button on the control pack he wore on his belt. "Camera Two for Amanda, please."

With a flash, my body was full frame on four huge monitors, an unflattering belly pouf projected around the studio. *Ooooph, maybe the camera does add fifteen pounds.* And then I said something I never thought I'd say. "Does this dress make me look fat?"

The crew guys exchanged nervous glances, like their spidey senses were tingling.

"I don't know," Rob said. "Take it off and let me have a look."

"Watch it, Rob," Casanova said.

I sat and tried to pat down the belly bulge, then gave up to log on to the laptop. "Shit," I said to no one in particular, feeling my stomach start to churn. I needed more information. I'd fallen asleep last night before I'd researched all of Fluke's past inflammatory statements on abortion. Just then my stomach gave a long, loud growl.

Rob looked up. "Was that you?"

"Sorry. I think that last muffin is wearing off," I said. "I'm ravenous. When do you eat on this shift?"

"Eat?" Rob said. "I take a Five-Hour ENERGY shot and power through."

"I can have one of the crew get you breakfast, Amanda," Larry offered. "If that would egg-cite you."

"Oh, for Chrissakes, Larry," Rob snapped.

"The yolks on you, Rob," Larry said. "Now kill the music and have a great show, everyone! We're live in five, four, three, two . . ." Larry pointed to Camera 2 for me to start but, yikes! I wasn't ready.

"Hello, everyone! Top of the muffin to you," I heard myself say. I froze. Rocco laughed, then cleared his throat as cover. "I mean morning!" I said. "Good morning, everyone." I put my hand to my mouth.

"You never know what to expect when you *Wake Up, USA!*" Rob said. "And today is no different. We have a huge guest joining us in our seven o'clock hour. After three months of media silence, Victor Fluke will be on our program live."

6:20 A.M. My hands were tingling again, this time from nerves. Topher's research packet on the abortion case sucked. He hadn't been able to book the woman wanting the abortion, just her attorney. But he booked her too late, he said, for a preinterview. So I had no idea what to expect.

"Welcome back," I said to Camera 1. "I want to bring in Donna McLeod, the attorney for the woman being sued by her ex-boyfriend to prevent her from having an abortion. Ms. McLeod, as you know, the ex-boyfriend Kevin Pearl has a sad story. He lost his wife in a car accident six years ago. He says he's always wanted another child and he is willing to raise this child on his own, completely absolving your client of any parental responsibilities. What's your response?"

"Amanda, your viewers should know that this case has been taken up by an extremist antiabortion group. That's who is funding this lawsuit. They'll use any excuse to criminalize abortion. And this is another of their blatant manipulations."

I blanched at her answer. Once again, I was hearing important info for the first time. Plus, the attorney was giving the facts, but her delivery was impersonal and off-putting. She wasn't connecting the case to the real person.

"Ms. McLeod, we just interviewed Mr. Pearl. He says he is not interested in outlawing abortion. This is not political to him. He's simply fighting for his rights as a father. Should fathers have any rights?"

I waited for her to explain that yes, in this world of gender equality fathers should have rights and we should certainly talk about those, but at the end of the day, it's the woman's body and the way our laws work, that's who ultimately makes the decision.

"As I've said, Amanda, this story is being used by extremists who are trying to deprive women of access to health care. That's what this is about."

She was sticking to her talking points like glue, missing the sensitivity quotient that would let viewers know she heard the father. I sat trying to figure out how to elicit the human side, when Rob jumped in.

"So let's unpack this," Rob said. "You're saying if a woman wants to have a child and the man doesn't, tough luck—the man is on the hook financially for that child for eighteen years. But if the *man* wants a child, and is happy to financially support and raise the child, but the *woman* does not, tough luck again for the guy, that baby should be aborted. How's that fair?"

Donna didn't say Rob's name as she had mine in her response. "I'm not going to dignify this frivolous lawsuit," she said. "Obviously, abortion is legal and it's the woman's right to choose."

"So what kind of message is that for men?" Rob asked.

"We recommend that anyone not wanting a child use birth control," she said.

She was right, of course, but her advice seemed a tad tardy for this situation.

"That's not a satisfying solution for the father in this case," I said, trying to give her one more chance.

"Wrap," Fatima said, before the attorney had a chance to respond.

"We'll see what Victor Fluke thinks of this issue," Rob interjected, "when he joins us in the next hour."

We hit the commercial break and Rob clicked on his computer screen.

"Holy shit!" he said. "Do you see all these tweets?"

"No," I said, chewing the inside of my cheek at what was about to be unleashed. Somehow I'd inadvertently tag-teamed with Rob to make the attorney and the woman look bad. It wasn't my intention to come off as antiabortion, but I had a terrible feeling that's what had happened.

"I'll read some," Rob said, looking over his shoulder at me. "Here's one: @AmandaGallo just busted the abortion bitch @FAIRNews. #banabortion."

"That's not what happened," I said, feeling sick with interviewer's remorse. Maybe I challenged her too much.

"Here's another," Rob said, "from @helentucker. '@Amanda Gallo hates women. Her conservative agenda is obvious. She should be ashamed of herself. There's a special place in hell for her.'"

Rob raised an eyebrow at me. "Hmmm. I think Helen may be off her meds."

If I'd had a gun, I'd have shot the laptop. "That's enough," I told him. "I don't want to hear anymore. I have to get ready for the Fluke interview."

"Wait, here's a good one," Rob went on. "'Send the right-wing @AmandaGallo to Fox News where she belongs. #womenshealth #supportPP.'"

Rob laughed like this was all hilarious.

"Larry, how much time do we have in this break?" I asked.

Larry checked his watch. "You've got three minutes."

"Wait, wait," Rob said. "You'll like this next one. I promise. It's from @Michiganmomma. '@AmandaGallo cracks me up. #topofthe muffin. She even makes that tool next to her seem nicer.'"

"I do like that one," I admitted.

"Last one, last one," Rob said. "It's from your boy @Frankin Fresno. This guy tweets a lot. Big fan. '@AmandaGallo. You're killing it. Love the dangle. Keep up the good work.'"

Against my better judgment, I asked, "What the hell is a dangle?"

"You know, a dangle." Rob pointed down at my nude pump, which I was surprised to see hanging from my heel. "You let your shoe dangle off your foot. You know you do that, right?"

My hollow stomach groaned again. "No, Rob," I snapped. "I'm not focused on my foot. I'm focused on the show, like you should be. Fluke is coming up!"

Rob put his hands up in a defensive position. "Hey, I'm not the one playing footsie with the viewers. Try it on Fluke. Your dangle might disarm him."

"Good one," I said, stone-faced.

"Maybe your foot will be his Kryptonite."

"Maybe it's his Achilles' heel," I said, then stuck my tongue out at Rob.

"Oh, touché!" Rob said, lighting up.

My God, this was ridiculous. Rob's sophomoric nature was rubbing off on me. I straightened up and started digging for my Fluke notes, growing even more anxious when I saw how little I'd written down last night before falling asleep.

"Amanda, your breakfast is here," Larry called out.

I grabbed the container out of Larry's hands. "How much time?"

Larry checked his stopwatch. "Ninety seconds."

"I can do it in eighty." I needed to get some real food in my stomach to quell the nervous, nauseous feeling, even if it was cold eggs and dry toast. I popped open the plastic top, and tore into the plastic wrap for the fork and knife, when I noticed Rob wearing a curdled expression.

"What's that smell?" he asked.

"It's called eggs," I said.

"Really? Cause it smells like ass. I thought maybe Jeremy had shit his pants."

Jeremy looked up from his book behind Camera 1. "What did I do?"

"We're back in thirty seconds," Larry yelled. "Clear the table of all drinks and food!"

"You know, Rob, you can really be an ass—a child sometimes." I was about to say asshole, but I knew my mic was hot. "Too bad some of us aren't fueled by Red Bull and ego." I tossed my uneaten cold eggs in the garbage.

7:50 A.M. I was starving and grouchy. I had a whole six minutes to kill while Rob interviewed a soldier fighting for a bill to get IVF funding for military families, which was being blocked by conservatives in state legislatures. Now seemed like a good time to run to the greenroom and grab another muffin. I stood up, my legs stiff from sitting, just as the soldier in a wheelchair glided into the studio, followed by four young children and his wife. The soldier stopped at the six-inch riser of the set, unable to go any farther.

"Here, let's make this easy," Larry said, guiding the soldier's wheelchair back to the flat demo area where Larry positioned the kids in descending height to the left of the soldier and the wife to the right. I tiptoed behind Rocco's camera, trying to avoid the family on my way to the kitchen.

"Amanda?" the wife called. "Is there any way we could get a picture with you?" Her round cheeks reddened. "I know how busy you are."

"Oh, okay, sure," I said, slightly annoyed that she was cutting into my muffin time. I sized up the family in a split second: southern, from some state I always had a hard time identifying on a map,

Tennessee probably. The mom's age was tough to pin, could be thirty-two or forty-two; the baby weight was still plumping her face. Her flat blond hair was shoulder length with standard-issue bangs. She could use some highlights, I thought. The three boys, with blond crew cuts, stood quietly and in a line. The little girl on the end was wearing a pink dress and eyeglasses held on by a thick rubber band stretched around the back of her head, that stayed put as she gazed up at the studio lights.

"Here," Larry offered, taking the camera from the mom's shaky hands, "let me snap one of all of you."

The mom crouched down to the same level as the wheelchair and I did the same, the soft padding of her arm touching mine and trembling as the flash went off.

"There you go," I said, springing up. I never knew what to say to these families whose life experience seemed so foreign to mine. This was probably their first time in New York, I assumed. The wife was as far from a Jersey girl as I was from a Georgia peach.

"Thank you, Amanda," the wife quivered. "You don't know how much this means to us. My goodness, you're even prettier in person."

"Oh, thanks," I said.

"Thank you for doing this story. Ronnie and I wouldn't have been able to have these two without IVF, you know, after he got injured. But most people can't afford it. And these lawmakers who want personhood amendments don't understand that they would outlaw IVF, because, you know, they forbid doctors from performing any procedure that destroys or discards embryos. We're very grateful that FAIR wants to hear all sides of the abortion debate." She reached out and hugged me.

"Oh, okay, thank you," I stammered, realizing with a pang of chagrin that maybe she and I had more in common than I'd thought. Maybe I'd been way too quick to judge.

"Hey, buddy." Rob had moved from the desk to the demo area and was patting the soldier on the back. "I see you brought the whole crew today." Rob sounded like he was talking to an old college pal. "And thank you for your service, man. We couldn't do any of this without you."

Thank you for your service? Thank you for your service. Rob's words played in my head as I walked out of the studio. I would never have thought to say it.

I meandered slowly toward the muffins wondering if my time was already up, but Larry wasn't calling me back. Right before the kitchen, I stopped to stare at a bustling pack of people in front of the coffee machine. There, sticking straight out of the top of the pack, a half foot above the rest, was Victor Fluke's head. All strong, angular features, Fluke looked like he was waiting for someone to add him to Mount Rushmore. I stood frozen, unsure whether to approach or turn and run.

"Just a second, gentlemen," I heard him say as he swept his arm to part the pack, "I want to say hello to someone." Two young guys in blue suits and blank expressions flanking Fluke folded out like swinging doors, taking the exact same split-legged stance, arms down and right hands gripping their left wrists.

In person, Fluke was more handsome than I remembered: tall and broad shouldered, with roguish dark hair. "Amanda Gallo," he said, then smiled a winning smile and extended his right hand. "I'm Victor Fluke."

It felt weird to have someone so famous introduce himself—like a ridiculous gesture of false modesty—but I resisted the impulse to snort and say, "Duh! Of course you are!" I wanted to stand still and study him, to try to determine who he was more like: the celebrated showman P. T. Barnum or a standard-issue bullshit artist. But, as if by magnetic force, I moved toward Fluke.

"You do a terrific job," he said. "I'm a big fan."

"Is that right?" I replied, sarcastic and satisfied that I'd just busted him in a bald-faced lie because *you don't watch the main-stream media, right? Plus, I just started on this show yesterday, you dummy, so you can't be a big fan. Ha! Gotcha!*

"Yes, whenever I came to New York I always watched Newschannel 13, frankly because I liked watching you. I mean, it's not a great channel otherwise." He gave me a comical head tilt that said, *You know what I mean.* "At the risk of sounding a little obsessed, I've always enjoyed your stories. I remember you did a blind ice cream taste test, oh, probably a year or so ago. You probably don't even re-member it. But I enjoyed that one." He took a deep breath before piv-oting to a look of concern. "And then, of course, I watched your coverage of that horrible standoff at the post office. What an awful situation that was. Anyway, I was very excited when you got this big break at FAIR News."

"Thank you," I said softly. *God, was I wrong about everyone?*

I stood frozen, blinking at him. His voice was deep and gravelly, almost hypnotic. And all of a sudden I was thirteen, sitting on the sofa watching *Home of the Brave* while Mom made dinner and every so often would glance over at the screen and shake her head. "Sam Stockton . . ."

"So, Amanda, as you know, I haven't done much media lately, but when Arthur told me that I could sit down and talk to you, well, I figured that's a damn good reason to break my mortuarium."

"Moratorium," I said, spellbound.

"Right. I know how intelligent and honest and, well, pardon the expression, fair you are. So here I am." He turned his hands sky-ward like he was just a humble man, here for some mercy.

"Hey there, girl!" It was Arthur Dove coming out of the green-room. "I'm sure glad we could make this happen today. I was telling Mr. Fluke what a warm welcome you gave me yesterday. You know, we don't like doin' too many interviews, what with all the liberal gotcha questions, but I told Mr. Fluke FAIR News is different and you're in good hands with Amanda."

"Mr. Dove," I said, forcing my eyes onto Arthur Dove's doughy face so I could break the spell of Fluke's gaze.

"Please, call me Arthur. I think we've reached that point in our relationship." He smiled at me.

"Arthur," I said, though I wouldn't have called this a relation-ship. "Those eyewitnesses to voter fraud you told us about yesterday, could you provide some contact info? I'm having a hard time finding any and I'd like to talk to them."

"I can do you one better," he said. "How 'bout we get 'em on your show? Give you a scoop."

"Amanda!" Larry yelled down the hall. "Need you back in the studio. You've got less than two minutes!"

I turned back to Fluke. "Sounds like they're ready for us." I said, almost cringing when I heard myself use the word "us."

"Well, then, let's go share some secrets of success with the American people," Fluke said, smiling and extending his arm gallantly, as though we were headed out the door on a romantic date. "Take it easy on me," he said with a mischievous grin. "I'm a little rusty."

My hands were visibly shaking as I slid onto the sofa to Rob's left. Rob stood up and extended a hearty handshake to Fluke. "Mr. Fluke, nice to see you've come out of hiding."

Fluke laughed and patted Rob on the back. "Gotta get you back out on the golf course, Lahr."

"You must be looking to lose more money," Rob grinned.

Oh, great. Leave it to Rob to have a secret bromance with the World's Most Successful Man.

Fluke took a seat to Rob's right and I saw Dove standing in the darkened wings, arms folded, watching.

"In five, four, three . . ." Larry motioned for Rob to begin reading to Camera 2.

"Welcome back, everyone. It's been almost three months since Victor Fluke has given an interview to the press. But this morning, in a *Wake Up, USA!* exclusive, Mr. Fluke joins us live in studio."

"Great to be with you both. It's a real honor."

"So," Rob started, "you say you want to share your secrets of success with every American. How about you start now? What are they?"

"It's very simple," Fluke said, turning to the camera. "I want every American to be as successful as me, the World's Most Successful Man. It starts with the can-do spirit of our forefathers, who built this great country, and I don't want us to surrender that. Because see, we're Ameri-*cans*.

"See, that's why everyone in the world wants to be American. America is more than a country, it's a movement and a mind-set, and it's the only country on the planet that was founded on an idea. The idea of freedom. And we've got to protect that and cherish it and keep it for Ameri-*cans* rather than hand it over to outsiders. Or as I like to call them, Ameri-*can'ts*."

Dove nodded as Fluke spoke, and I couldn't help noticing how as Fluke's message grew more populist, his malaprops went missing.

"The American people are angry at the Ameri-*can'ts* who take advantage of our generosity. And they're tired of Washington telling Ameri-*cans* to share the spoils of our great nation with people who don't deserve them. My team and I have spent these past months listening to these good folks and, believe me, they're angry at foreigners taking their jobs and at politicians like Virginia cheating the system."

"Mr. Fluke, there's no evidence Senator Wynn cheated. You're making accusations that no news outlet has been able to confirm."

"That's because the media's in the bag for Wynn. But look, I get it, Amanda, you're a journalist, and you're an excellent journalist, by the way, and your job is to find the facts."

Fluke's flattery had the unwanted visceral effect of making my body turn ever so slightly in his direction.

"People want the truth. That's what my campaign is about. People in this country still believe in American values of hard work, faith, and truth, and when I'm elected, I'm going to share my success with everyone."

I looked at Fluke's strong features, and for the first time, I got it. This guy is magnetic, and what he says is exactly what his supporters want to hear. I want to know the secrets to success, too! And for a moment I forgot it was all founded on a TV commercial.

"So, Mr. Fluke," Rob said, "let's talk about your top issues."

"Well, I just watched your terrific interview with that proabortion attorney. Look, I want Planned Parenthood defunded and *Roe v. Wade* overturned. And when I'm president I'll install Supreme Court justices who will do that.

"And wasn't it interesting?" Fluke went on. "That attorney could not give you a single straight answer about fathers' rights. She tried to dodge every one of your questions. But you really pressed her, Amanda. And I think you proved that the abortionists want to kill babies at any cost—even when there's a loving parent begging for them to live. That's why we're going to defund down Planned Parenthood."

Fluke said everything like it was a fact, plus he made it sound like we were on the same team. I could practically hear Charlie screaming at the TV.

"If we take away their money, they won't be able to perform abortions. Right now they're an abortion factory. And they're proud of it."

I wanted to scream. "Mr. Fluke, those are very incendiary words. It's not an abortion factory. It's an abortion provider for women with no other place to go."

"Call it what you want, Amanda. Abortion is ninety percent of what they do."

Jesus, that is *a lot. But, wait, that's not right!* I stared down at my scribbled notes.

"Abortion is not ninety percent of what they do. It's three percent." I said. "That's right on their website."

"Well, I don't know what they say, but I know a woman who used to work there in Houston and she told me that it's their main business. She also said that if you can get a fifteen-year-old hooked on abortion early, she'll come back for four or five more. It becomes their birth control. It's tragic, really." Fluke shook his head.

"Wrap," Fatima said. "Thirty seconds to break." Larry's hands were swirling.

"Hooked on abortion?" I said. "Mr. Fluke, that doesn't make sense."

"And this is why I'm calling on my devoted followers to picket outside of every clinic until we can shut the organization down for good."

"That sounds like a recipe for violence, Mr. Fluke," I told him.

"Wrap!" Fatima screamed in my ear. Larry made a bigger circle with his hand.

"Oh, absolutely not," Fluke said. "I would hate for there to be any violence. But we do want the freedom to express our position."

"Wrap!" Fatima said in our earpieces. "Three seconds to black!!"

"Thank you, Mr. Fluke, for being here," Rob said. "More *Wake Up* in three minutes."

"We're clear!" Larry yelled.

"Thanks, everyone," Fluke said to the crew, then stepped off the set. "Real pleasure to be on with you."

"Have a good day, y'all," Arthur Dove said, raising a hand to the crew. "And keep up the good work, Amanda."

I narrowed my eyes to watch Fluke's gait, confident and determined, stride in the darkness toward the studio door, surrounded by his flunkies, then whipped my head toward Rob. "You did it again!"

"What?"

"You didn't say anything! You didn't challenge Fluke on his insane statements!"

"Yeah," Rob said, shaking his head. "I don't love that topic. I don't think it buys us anything. Abortion over breakfast? Not appetizing."

"So you sit it out and let Fluke spout craziness?"

"I'm sure a lot of viewers feel the way he does."

"They might *feel* that way, but he's flat fucking wrong! He's getting his information from some friend of his! Some disgruntled former worker. Abortion is three percent of their services, not ninety!"

"And where are you getting your information?" Rob asked.

"I studied it online last night!"

Rob nodded. "Ah, the Internet. Well, then, it must be right."

"Plus, he said women 'get hooked on abortion'! That's insane."

"He said a worker there told him that," Rob said.

"Look," I said, lowering my voice and leaning toward Rob's ear, "I brought a friend there once." I let my words sink in for a few beats so he would know I had firsthand experience. "I assure you, it was not an abortion factory."

Rob nodded again, mulling that. "So, your friend's experience who went there once is more accurate than Fluke's friend who worked there?"

Yes, I wanted to say. "Rob, admit it. You didn't dive in because you didn't do your homework. You don't know anything about the topic."

"Okay, Amanda," Rob said, putting his pen down and turning to me with purpose. "You want the facts? Planned Parenthood does 330,000 abortions a year. And you know how many adoption referrals they made last year? 2,300." Rob exhaled sharply. It seemed like he might say more but he turned back to his laptop.

I stared at him, trying to figure out what this new, serious Rob had done with my superficial cohost. "How do you know that?" I asked, before wishing I hadn't.

Rob sighed and looked straight ahead for a second. "My sister and brother-in-law have been trying to have a kid for years. Now they're waiting to adopt a baby. You know, there's just not enough out there. It's tearing them up."

"I'm sorry to hear that," I said. It hadn't occurred to me that this could be personal for Rob. It also hadn't occurred to me that Rob was a living, breathing human being, with a life outside of the studio and cocktail parties. Until now, I thought he might have been created in a top-of-the-line anchorman factory, bringing well-crafted newsmen to a network near you. Even hearing he had a sister surprised me because I didn't know newsbots had siblings. I wonder what he knows of my life? Does my life ever cross his mind?

"And also," he went on with new energy, "I do think guys get a raw deal with this stuff. We're the bad guys if we don't want the kid. We're the bad guys if we do want the kid. One of my buddies got his girlfriend pregnant; he's on the hook for the kid now, through college. I don't know. The whole thing bums me out, to tell you the truth."

"So that means you check out for the whole show?"

"It's turnoff TV. I told Fatima that. You're never going to change anyone's mind on abortion. People's feelings are too strong. Good thing we had Fluke or this would tank in the ratings."

"Great job with Fluke, guys," Fatima said in our ears. "It's already getting pickup. Big Politico headline. Fluke—Back with a Vengeance."

"Cool," Rob said with renewed vigor, back to his old instant-gratification self. "Let's check Facebook."

"Let's not," I said.

Too late. Rob was already reading posts on my open laptop. He couldn't help himself, I realized. He thrived on it.

"Look at this one," he said, turning my laptop toward me. "Deborah Culpepper uses a butterfly as her avatar. Isn't that sweet?" Rob affected a feminine voice to channel Deborah. "'Shameful! Just shameful, taking the side of the abortionists against Fluke. You know what, Amanda? You'll answer for this to a higher power than any of this crony bull crap media you work for. To think I liked you at Newschannel 13. Now you are despised. Remember that. Not even God will forgive you.'"

Rob started tapping at the keyboard. "Deb, kiss my sweet ass." He hit send.

"Hey!" I shrieked. "That's my account!"

"Oh, look, here's a tweet from your boy Frank in Fresno. 'Good job pushing back on that big bobblehead Fluke. Keep it up!'"

"What, no dangle talk?" I asked.

"No, he did. He direct messaged me to ask what your shoes smell like. But I took a pass on checking that out."

"That crosses the line even for you?"

"Even I have limits."

8:55 A.M. Time for the kicker to end the show and send people out the door chuckling. It was all I could do to still speak. The brain burn of coming face-to-face with Fluke had fried my mind.

"And we leave you with this Catch of the Day. You've gotta see this video of two surfers in California." Rob was in full salesman mode, making it sound like the most thrilling moment ever captured on video. "You can see a guy and a girl sitting on their surfboards, just sort of paddling around, when all of a sudden, holy smokes! Out of nowhere a *whale* leaps out of the water in a full breach."

"They do not look like they were expecting that," I said, because I had nothing else.

"No, that was a whale of a surprise. Kinda like what happens on our show every morning. We'll see you here tomorrow when you *Wake Up, USA!*"

"And we're clear!" Larry yelled.

Rocco stretched his arms over his head and turned his torso to and fro to work out the kinks of the past three hours. As I gathered my notes, Larry walked over to the sofa, touched my shoulder, and handed me a folded piece of paper on which he'd scribbled a message.

All's whale that ends whale.

I offered him a half smile and tucked it into my folder. I reached down to get my papers and glanced over at Rob, whose face was bent in close to his computer screen.

"Jackpot!!" he exclaimed, pulling his right fist down like he'd just hit triple cherries on a one-armed bandit.

"What happened?" I said.

"My Google Alert for Amanda Gallo is going berserk," he said.

"Oh, no," I said.

He turned the screen to me. Link after link of websites, lit up in light blue, all with my name on them.

"Check it out," Rob said. "You're everywhere. Here's the Daily Caller. Wow, look at this! Time.com, Forbes. You're on fire."

My eyes scanned up and down the screen.

"Victor Fluke Returns to the Airways and Schools Amanda Gallo!"
—Breitbart

"Victor Fluke Shuts Down Leftist Anchor."—The Blaze

The next headline was from some website called PoliticalNews:

"Victor Fluke Is Back on TV and He Just DESTROYED Amanda
Gallo for Her Lies in a BRUTAL WAY!"
(Watch here)

The site had captured a freeze-frame of my face midblink and blown up wide, making me look like a clueless cartoon character. The headline was so over the top with outrage that I couldn't help but reach over Rob and click on it. "FAIR Anchor Amanda Gallo tried to embarrass Victor Fluke on air, but Fluke was in no mood to accept it!" That was the first sentence and I didn't need to see more. A wave of nausea was already working its way across my stomach.

"I don't like this," I said.

"What do you mean?" Rob said, like that was preposterous.

"Be real, Rob," I said. "It sucks to get so much hate directed at you."

"Are you kidding? Any morning show would kill for this kind of buzz. The *Today* show wishes it were this relevant. It's fucking awesome."

"It's not fucking awesome," I said. "And Fluke didn't *school* me."

"Trust me," Rob said, "this is good for the show. We want them talking about us. Benji's going to love it."

Chapter 15

Split Screen

"I love it," Benji said. He was pacing around his office squeezing a stress ball. "I mean, getting Fluke on was a huge coup. We gotta get him to come back as often as possible. He hates the other networks at the moment, so we're in the perfect position to use the hell out of him. What you did this morning was exactly what I had in mind when I came up with this concept of FAIR News. You got that pro-choice attorney lady, you got that tearjerker dad, and you had the icing on top, Victor Fluke. I mean, does it get any more FAIR than that? No one else is doing this. The entire conversation in one place."

"Well, yeah," I said. "We gave both sides, but we never really got to the bottom of any of it. I mean, Fluke said abortion is ninety percent of what Planned Parenthood does. They say it's three percent. You know, what's the truth?"

"I guess that depends on who you ask," Benji said.

"But we should find the answers," I said.

"Look," Benji said, tossing the ball back and forth between his hands. "It's probably somewhere in the middle. That's what the other cable news outlets don't get. Life is not black and white."

"Yeah," I said, agreeing but feeling unsatisfied.

"Do you know what *Good Morning America* was doing while you were doing the abortion stuff?" he asked.

I shook my head.

"They were interviewing the castoffs from *Dancing with the Stars*! I mean, they have given up on news. If people want to know what's going on in the country, they're going to have to tune in to us."

"Yeah," I said again, this time with more gusto.

"Listen, I just got the overnights from yesterday. You want to take a guess at the number we did?"

I raised my eyebrows, ready for a big surprise.

"Through the fucking roof. Now, I don't think we can assume that every day will be like that. I'm sure there was some curiosity sampling. But I'm telling you, Amanda, it's looking very good. We're onto something here. Viewers are loving it."

A feeling of euphoria swept over my doubts. Who was I to argue with the viewers? Plus I loved hearing Benji say "we," and that what "we" were doing was working. "Wow, that's wonderful," I said, then paused wanting more of his wisdom but worried I might ruin the mood.

"What?" he asked.

"Well, it's interesting, because the feedback on social media is, um, not overwhelmingly positive, I'd say."

"What are they saying?"

"Um, it depends. When I was challenging the woman's attorney, they said I was a right-wing, antiabortion woman hater. And when I was challenging Fluke, they said I was a left-wing, liberal baby killer. Those were the more pleasant ones."

Benji snorted. "Then you must be doing something right! And you know what? Fuck them. These are losers in their mothers' basements who think they have power because they can log on to the Internet. See, everyone is still trying to put you into some box. You must be a liberal or a conservative because that's all they've ever known. Cable news has trained them into thinking that everyone is one extreme or the other. FAIR News is total cognitive dissonance for them. And it's going to take a while to deprogram them from the cable cult that's been brainwashing them."

"Yes, yes, yes," I said. I was so glad that Benji was reminding me of all this. We were doing something groundbreaking. Of course it felt uncomfortable.

"Anyway, who cares what they say as long as they're watching? Did you see all the pickup your Fluke interview got?"

I nodded.

"And hey, did you see the tweet Fluke sent out about you?"

"No."

"Oh, it was great! Let me read it. 'Thanks to @AmandaGallo and

@WakeUpUSA for a terrific interview. A great journalist.' Your Twitter followers went up by four thousand. You're at ten thousand! You can't buy that kind of publicity. You're doing it, Amanda. It's working."

It turned out it wasn't just losers in their basements watching *Wake Up, USA!*, it was also members of Congress.

I had just walked into my apartment, surprised to find Charlie already there with the TV on. "Have you seen this?" Charlie asked, pointing across the room. He sounded appalled, like he was about to show me something valuable that our dog had destroyed. Except we didn't have a dog. I followed his finger point to the TV screen.

"And that's exactly what I'm saying," Senator Kathy Burns was saying into the microphone at a press conference. "As a mother and grandmother, I find abortion morally reprehensible and vile. I applaud FAIR News for highlighting the long-overlooked issue of fathers' rights. And as I said, anyone who saw the father's story on *Wake Up, USA!* this morning knows it raised a number of questions that taxpayers deserve answers to. That is why I am joining with Victor Fluke today, calling for my colleagues in the Senate to vote to defund this organization." Charlie hit mute.

I didn't know my hands were over my mouth until I tried to speak. "Oh, no."

"Oh, yes," Charlie said. "They're using your segment to argue for defunding Planned Parenthood."

I fell on the sofa next to him, feeling the weight of that. That must be the reason for three voice mail messages from Mom.

"Look, obviously you're not responsible for Senator Burns deciding this is her cause celeb. But it sounds like your show did crank it up again."

My buzzer sounded.

"That's Laurie," I said.

Laurie came in, dropped her bag, kicked off her shoes, walked to the fridge, grabbed a beer, and collapsed on the couch before acknowledging us. She acted like my roommate who happened to live in a different apartment across town.

She looked at me. "Why do you look like your dog died?"

"I don't have a dog," I told her, though I thought Laurie might be a mind reader.

"You look like something happened."

"Something did happen," Charlie told her, motioning to the TV. "Kathy Burns is citing Amanda's show as the reason to hold hearings to defund Planned Parenthood."

"Hmm," Laurie said. "I don't think they have the votes."

"The point is," I said, turning toward Laurie, "are you responsible for what people do with the information you and Gabe put out there?"

"Of course not," Laurie said. "Our job is to provide the information. How people use it is not our fault."

"Yes!" I said, pointing at Laurie for Charlie, as though she were Exhibit A in my case for exoneration.

"I got Kenny the Rat, you know from the Winter Hill Gang, to talk a couple of weeks ago when nobody thought he would. That's my job. And I can't be responsible for what happens next."

"Yeah?" I said, sensing there was more. "Wait, not the one who was killed in that car explosion last week?"

"Well . . ." She took a swig of her beer. "That one was unfortunate."

"Jesus, Laurie."

"Look," she said, "I'm here for one beer. I don't have time to dissect the challenges of a free press. I gotta get back to work. Gabe and I are getting closer to breaking that big Fluke story. If the fucking lawyers would get their asses in gear, we could report it."

"So what is it?" Charlie asked.

Laurie let out a long exhale, then grabbed her big black bag like she'd just robbed a bank and it was full of loot. "We got this letter. Obviously, do not breathe a word of this. I shouldn't even be talking about it."

"Of course," I said, pulling the big wicker chest I used as a coffee table closer, so she could lay out whatever was in her bag.

"These will reveal the real Victor Fluke, underneath the character in this dramedy we're all living. Consider this your private preview." She reached into her bag and pulled out a thin manila folder.

"What is it?" Charlie asked.

"It's a letter from Fluke's former nanny. She says that for years Fluke and his wife used a housekeeper from Haiti, who they paid off the books and who . . . wait for it," she said, holding up her hand, "wait for it . . . was an illegal alien. Ta-da!"

Charlie nodded. "That's pretty good."

"But beyond a letter from a nanny, whaddya have?" I asked.

"Glad you asked," Laurie said. "It gets better."

"This nanny, who in the past two weeks has become my new best friend—sorry Amanda."

I nodded with understanding. Temporary best friends were part of Laurie's M.O.

"So, my new best friend, um," she looked down at the letter, "Emilia, right, *Emilia,* says the Haitian housekeeper left under sort of suspicious circumstances *and* that she heard that Fluke bought the housekeeper a *house* somewhere to get rid of her but keep her in the U.S."

"When was this?" I asked.

"About fifteen years ago."

"This is good, Laurie," Charlie said, more upbeat than I'd seen him in weeks. "Maybe this will be the silver bullet that stops Fluke."

"Really?" I asked, looking at both their excited faces with skepticism, not because I doubted the story but because having met the guy in person it seemed like one fifteen-year-old silver bullet might not be enough to kill off Sam Stockton's evil twin. "Won't Fluke just say he didn't know she was here illegally or he got rid of her the second he found out? Or he'll say he's 'evolved' since then." I shrugged. "I don't think this is enough to scare away the legion of Successful Man-iacs."

"Well, obviously there's more to the story than meets the eye. Who buys a house for their maid?" Charlie said.

"Where's the house?" I asked.

"Emilia is a little unclear on that. She heard it was in New Mexico, in some small town. I've been digging through real estate records but I haven't found anything yet."

"Maybe he didn't buy it in his own name," Charlie said.

"Right," Laurie said. "And I can't find anything in the housekeeper's name . . . yet. But Emilia is pretty certain about this. And she's dying to go on camera and tell the story. She hates Victor Fluke. But BNN's lawyers are slow rolling this. They say I need a second source. It's making me crazy."

"I don't blame them," I said. "I mean, maybe the nanny has an ax to grind against Fluke. Maybe she had a beef with his wife. Why's she just coming forward now, after fifteen years? I don't know. I'm dubious."

"*Cherchez la femme*," Charlie said, nodding at both of us.

"Huh?" I said.

"Did you ever read Alexandre Dumas, *The Mohicans of Paris*?" he asked.

I looked over at Laurie and readied myself for another Charlie Treatise on Historical Fiction. "Um, no."

"Well, the phrase is French obviously. And it literally means 'look for the woman.' At the root of every mystery is a woman. So basically, you find the woman, you find the story," he said. "Find that house-keeper."

"Ah, *cherchez la femme*," I said to Laurie in my best French accent. "*Cherchez la femme*."

Chapter 16

The Demo

I was late for the pitch meeting, having been held up by the studio crew trying to cajole me into going to what they described as their Wednesday morning "staff meeting" in "Studio M," which I learned was code for a postshow boozefest at McLoone's, the Irish bar across the street. Their offer was about as tempting as a root canal. What I really wanted was a nap. But I played along, telling them in as non-committal a way as possible that I might show.

In the Think Tank, the usual assemblage of segment producers and production assistants sat around the conference table, some doodling on pads, all looking exhausted. Rob was leaning back in a chair, typing into his cell phone. Goth guy Morgan was just winding up for a pitch.

"So here's a very interesting science story that I think would be great. Scientists in the Galapagos are now studying sea turtles because they never get sick, ever."

Silence.

"How do they know they never get sick?" Tiffany asked after a delay.

"Well, first of all, they live to a ridiculously old age—like 150 years. And scientists think if they can unlock the secret to their longevity, it can translate to us." He looked around victoriously.

Fatima glanced up from her laptop. "When do we get to the very interesting part?"

"That's just it!" Morgan said. "We could figure out how to live to be 150."

"Is it by eating seaweed and walking very slowly?" Tiffany asked. "Because I can do that."

"You of all people should like this," Morgan told her. "You majored in zoology!"

"Psychology," she said.

"Whatever. It's a great story."

Fatima wasn't feeling it. "Next pitch. Jada?"

"There's a story out of Oklahoma about a man who was saved from choking to death by the airbag in his car."

"Interesting," Fatima said. "How?"

"He was choking on a raisin and he drove off the road and hit a telephone pole and the airbag deployed and dislodged the raisin."

"Is there video?" Fatima asked.

"I'm not sure. I'll check."

"Okay, next. Amanda, do you have anything?"

"Hold on." I was stuck on the raisin story, my lifelong fear of choking getting the best of me. "How was he choking on a raisin? I mean, that's so much smaller than his windpipe."

"You can choke on anything," Topher said authoritatively. "You can even choke on water."

"You can?" I asked, trying to hide my panic.

Fatima looked up from typing. "Maybe it was a *golden* raisin. You know how big *those* are?"

"Yeah, they *are* big," I said, making a mental note to throw out the ones sitting on a shelf in my kitchen.

"Maybe it was a craisin," Morgan offered.

Rob looked up from his iPhone for the first time. "Wait, what does this have to do with a turtle?"

Morgan jumped in. "Has Fluke weighed in? Was the raisin grown in America?"

"You're all losers," Fatima said. "I have a show to produce. Does anyone have anything?"

"Yeah, I have a great outrage story," Topher began. "The FBI is sanitizing their handbook to make it more PC and not offend Muslims."

"How so?" I asked, wary of anything Topher thought was great.

"They're taking out any phrases that might be offensive to Muslims," he repeated.

"Ooh, that *is* good," Fatima said, beginning to type into her laptop. "That definitely has two sides."

"Such as?" I pressed Topher.

"I'm sure it's things like 'terrorist' or 'radical Islam.' You know, all the words that Virginia Wynn doesn't use so she doesn't offend terrorists," Topher said.

"Don't you mean offend Muslims? Or do you use the two terms interchangeably?" I asked. "Besides, what's your source?"

"Senator Davis wrote a letter to the FBI telling them to change something like eight hundred pages."

"We should book a debate between some liberal Islamic imam and Aisha Muhammad. She's great because she's Muslim," Fatima said, thinking out loud.

"And hot," Morgan chimed in.

"Giddyup," Rob said.

"Plus," Topher said, "she thinks radical Islam is going to blow up the world and she's not afraid to say it."

"Shouldn't we first see what text was expunged?" I asked, annoyed. "Maybe we could find the letter, for starters?"

"Good point, Amanda. What does the letter say?" Fatima asked Topher, shifting her eyes to mine and nodding like we were on the same page.

"I don't know, but I bet there's a bunch of PC stuff in there. Probably," he said.

"Good God, Topher. You sound like a dumb shit," Fatima said. "Do your homework next time. Cause my Pakistani grandma's getting sick of the media hating on Muslims, okay? Next pitch. What's your name, sweetie?"

A terrified-looking intern looked up. "Sally," she whispered.

"And you have a pitch? Go ahead," Fatima guided her.

"Yes, a conservative watchdog group says they've found the voter registration list where Wynn volunteers registered fake names, like the Dallas Cowboys and Mickey Mouse and Bugs Bunny. The FEC says it's looking into it."

"Oh, that's great! That's what Fluke was talking about. We should do a bunch of segments on that tomorrow," Fatima said, starting to type.

"Isn't that kind of small ball?" Rob asked.

"Not if her volunteers are committing voter fraud," Fatima said. "That's a scandal."

"But if it's one rogue volunteer and one registration list, that doesn't rise to the level of scandal," I said, trying to build on Rob's skepticism.

"We've got nothing else for tomorrow," Fatima said.

Jesus, Laurie, hurry up with that Fluke housekeeper story, would ya, before we go down a Bugs Bunny rabbit hole.

"I have another one," Morgan began. "So, the Centers for Medicare and Medicaid Services just released a report—"

"Stop right there," Fatima said. "You're really starting a pitch with a report about Medicare?"

"Yeah, I thought we could have the HHS secretary on to discuss—"

Morgan was interrupted by loud snoring coming from Rob. "Oh, sorry, I nodded off for a second."

Even I had unconsciously picked up a paper and started perusing the Style section.

"You've *GOT* to think about the demo, people," Fatima explained. "We can't be pitching stories for sixty-five-year-olds."

"But that's who watches cable news," Morgan said.

"Yes, but we don't *want* them. We certainly shouldn't be giving them a reason to watch," Fatima emphasized.

"Yeah, haven't they suffered enough?" Tiffany asked.

"Tiffany, go," Fatima said, moving on.

"Okay, fashion pitch. Models are wearing pajamas out at night."

"Which models are those?" Rob said.

"A lot of them," Tiffany said. "The pictures are all over online. I can get a pair for Amanda to model."

"What now?" I said, putting down the newspaper and deciding to pay more attention starting then.

"Good, get Amanda a pair and, oh, that reminds me," Fatima said. "Production called. They know it's six months away, but they want us to start thinking of costume ideas for Halloween. Benji thinks FAIR might get a few tickets to the White House Halloween Party, and he wants us to hit it out of the park. How awesome would that be? So production wants to get a jump on some concepts and not wait till the last minute—and we can definitely come up with much better ideas than they have. They want Amanda and Rob to go as a Rubik's Cube."

The White House! Oh, my God! I was so excited by the idea of going to a party at the White House that I hadn't absorbed the rest of it, until one of the interns asked, "What's a Rubik's Cube?"

"It's lame, that's what," Rob said.

"How about they go as Beyoncé and Jay Z?" somebody said.

"I know!" Tiffany said. "Kim and Kanye! Kimye."

"That's so last Halloween," another intern said. "How 'bout Kylie and Kendall Jenner?"

"Aren't those both girls?" Rob asked.

"Oh! How about Caitlyn Jenner!" Morgan suggested. "That would be perfect for you, Rob."

"The hell?" Rob said.

"I mean because she has such a deep voice."

"*I know, right?*" Tiffany said. "It's like she's not even *trying* to be a woman."

"How about Woodward and Bernstein?" I said.

"What's our costume? Carrying pens?" Rob said. "Rubik's Cube is starting to make sense."

"Oh, wow! Look at this!" Fatima said, pointing at her laptop. "We just got the early overnights from yesterday. Wow, wow wow! It looks like the seven A.M. was huge!"

Rob sat up. "We had Fluke at the top of the seven."

"Holy crap!" Fatima said. "It looks like we beat CNN and MSNBC! Oh, my God! We beat Fox! Oh wait, here's an email from Benji." She nodded her head while reading. "He says to book Fluke again for tomorrow. And see what days he can do next week, too. He wants Fluke on as often as possible. Topher, get on that!"

"Aye, aye, Captain," Topher said.

"What topic are we booking him on?" I asked, wondering if anybody had any inkling of the story Laurie was sitting on.

"Who cares?" Fatima said. "Just book him. Get him to commit to as many days as possible."

I walked out of the Think Tank in search of a phone. Pushing aside an old cookie wrapper, I sat on the edge of a desk in the newsroom, making sure no one was close enough to overhear.

"Hey." Laurie's voice was scratchy.

"Shit. Did I wake you?"

"Yes."

"It's funny that my work day is over before you wake up," I told her.

"Um-hmm."

"So what's the deal? Did you get any more scoop on the house-keeper?"

"Um, yeah. I talked to a gardener guy who thinks he remembers the name of the town where Fluke bought the house. I'm going to try to dig through some property records today."

"Cool," I said, "cause my producers are planning a Fluke fest and it would be great if I could confront him with the info you have. I mean, after you break it, of course. Are you getting close?"

There was silence on the other end and I thought Laurie was deep in thought, until I realized she'd fallen asleep.

"Laur!"

"Yeah, yeah," she mumbled. "I'm trying. Call me later."

Chapter 17

Studio M

I couldn't believe what time it was when I walked through the door of McLoone's. How could I already have had an hour of hair and makeup, anchored a three-hour show, changed clothes, sat through a pitch meeting, and now be at a bar and it only be 10:15 A.M.? I also couldn't believe it had been a month since *Wake Up, USA!* started. In the past month, it felt like I'd covered a lifetime of topics—so many I already couldn't remember some of them. I knew we'd tackled gun control this morning and Virginia Wynn's proposal to expand background checks, but I couldn't tell you who our 7:35 guest had been if there'd been a gun to my head.

It was in this bleary-brained state that I decided it was a good idea to finally go to McLoone's for drinks with the crew. They'd asked me several times, but mostly I was here because I knew that the *only* way to be successful on any show is to ingratiate yourself with the guys who mic you, light you, cue you, shoot you, and tell you if your dress is bunching or your underwear is showing. They also pot down your mic when you're peeing—or they don't, if you piss them off. Plus I was too tired to navigate the subway and go home. So here I was.

I waited in the doorway for a minute until my eyes adjusted to the dim saloon lighting. The darkness made it easier to pretend this was a perfectly normal time for an after-work drink. McLoone's smelled like sour beer mixed with Windex, coming from the guy with the mop and bucket over in the corner trying to wipe away last night's stench.

"Hey, hey, hey!" I heard someone say and saw Panzullo hoist his arm with a beer mug attached. "Look who it is! I told you she'd show, guys! Welcome to Studio M!"

I nodded like, "Yeah, that's right," acting like it had been my plan all along to pop over, since they'd clearly been betting against me.

"Gallo in the house!" Jeremy said, with more energy than I'd ever seen him exert behind Camera 1. He was still wearing his baseball cap, but now he was wide awake under it.

"Yup, I'm here," I said, smiling, trying to match their festivity. "Get the party started."

"Yay-uh!" Rocco cheered, then hopped off his barstool, presenting it to me as if it were a golden throne. "Have a seat right here, Amanda," he said, using his hand to dust off imaginary dirt. "What are you drinking, my dear?" In this mode, Rocco didn't seem so much like a ponytailed ex-hippie as he did one of my uncles on Christmas, making sure I'd had enough to eat.

"Um, well, I guess . . . hmm, what are you guys having?" I looked around for inspiration at the drinks lined up on the bar: mugs of beers, rocks glasses filled with various colored liquids, and empty shot glasses. I bit my lip. I didn't want a straight cup of booze at this hour . . . or really anything other than my bed.

"How 'bout a Bloody Mary?" I asked, thinking that might at least come with a celery stalk, which could pass for a breakfast item.

"Right away," Casanova said, stepping up to the bar. "Hey, Lou," he called to the guy at the other end of the bar. "One of your extra special Bloody Marys, please."

The guys all stood around smiling at me and I thought, *Huh, I guess they're excited about how well the show is doing*, until I realized that I was the only girl in the joint and something more biological was at work here.

"So guys," I said, looking around, trying to get them to turn their attention from me, "do they have food here?"

"Yes, of course!" Casanova grabbed a plastic menu off the bar and presented it to me.

"Let's get Amanda whatever she wants," Larry suggested. "We *relish* the fact that you *mustard* the strength to come."

"*Oy, gevalt,*" Jeremy said, then slapped the back of Larry's head.

"We just ordered a whole bunch of apps," Panzullo told me. "We got mozz sticks and buffalo wings coming. They have nachos. You want nachos?"

I'd been thinking eggs, but I said, "Hell, yeah, I want nachos!" 'cause I knew they'd like that.

"Yay-uh!" Rocco roared.

"Girl after my own heart," Panzullo said.

"Time for another round of shots, Lou!" Rocco called down the bar. "Six lemon drops, please!"

"Oh, boy," I muttered. The last thing I needed was to be drunk by 10:30, hung over by lunchtime, and out cold before the rundown came out.

"You ready for a shot, Amanda?" Casanova asked, holding out a sloppy shot glass, dripping with vodka and sticky sugar.

"Absolutely," I said.

"*Salute!*" Rocco said, and we all hoisted our glass and downed the shots.

"You know what Rocco considers a balanced diet?" Jeremy asked me.

"No, what?" I said.

"A drink in each hand."

"Ay!" Rocco said. "You know what's wrong with Jeremy?"

"No, what?" I said.

"He's got too much blood in his alcohol system."

The guys groaned and Larry stepped up to the circle as if it were open mic night.

"Hey, Amanda, Panzullo here is an alcoholic. You know how you can help?"

"Buy him a drink," I said.

"Hey!" Larry said. "You knew that one?"

"I've seen the T-shirt," I said.

The guys laughed and Panzullo surprised me by bending over and kissing the top of my head. "See guys, I told you she was cool. Amanda can hang."

"I knew she was cool from that first chemistry test," Jeremy said. "You're so much better than Margot. *Oh, Margot*," he said, like the name alone caused him pain. "She's such a bitch."

I frowned. "No, she's not. She's super sweet."

"Nope," Jeremy said. "She pretends to be sweet on air, but off camera she's a raging bitch. She never talks to us during her show. If you say hi to her in the hallway, she doesn't even respond. She just walks right by."

He was right. Margot never said hello in the hallway. She was always talking into her phone, but not talking *to* someone—more like dictating thoughts.

"You know she's writing a book," Rocco said.

"On *what*?" I asked.

"Something about female power. You know, women's lib."

I chortled at Rocco's description. "You sure you're not confusing her with Gloria Steinem?"

"That's who she thinks she is. But Margot's a big phony," Rocco said. "She acts like she loves Victor Fluke when he's here, and then, when she talks to Wynn, she's all for women and women's rights."

"What do you mean 'when she talks to Wynn'?" I asked, my throat getting tight.

"Oh, you know, she's always trying to get an interview with Wynn," Jeremy said. "Even on the set, Margot's always calling the press people and begging them. They're probably sick of her, too."

The aftertaste of the lemon drop soured in my mouth. *Dammit!* I'd accepted the bookers' claims that Wynn had refused to come on our show, probably because we were doing Fluke so much, and I hadn't even considered trying to get her myself. *God, I'm so stupid!* Margot was craftier than I'd given her credit for. I felt sick at the prospect of her getting Wynn. *I'm such an idiot! Maybe if I call Wynn's press office today, I can get her to come on our show first. Or maybe Margot's already annoyed them so much they won't take any more calls from FAIR.*

"I better go soon, guys," I said.

"It's only ten thirty," Panzullo said. "Besides, Rob might show."

"Nah, he said he had plans," Larry said, then looked at me. "So, how's it going with him?"

"Um," I started, unsure of how honest to be. "I think he can be . . . a little"—I knew this next part was dicey. I didn't want the crew to turn on me, but I was just buzzed enough to blurt out—"douchey."

"Hey, now," Rocco said in a deep voice, like he'd turned into Barry White.

"Don't worry," Larry said. "Rob will grow on you." He paused and I waited. "Like a fungus."

I nodded and figured I'd probably gone far enough, when Jeremy looked at me and asked, "Have you noticed that Rob says certain things over and over?"

"Yes!" I yelled too enthusiastically.

"It's almost like he has verbal tics, or something," Jeremy said.

"Like 'roger that,' which he says all the time!" I said.

"Or how about 'let's unpack this'?" Jeremy said. "That one kills me."

"And 'from the get-go,'" I said.

"Don't forget 'touché!'" Rocco added.

"We should turn them into a drinking game," I suggested.

"There you go," Jeremy said.

"Every time he says one of them during the show, one of us has to chug our coffee," I told them.

"Yay-uh!" Rocco said.

"That's a plan," Panzullo said.

At that moment, Michael Jackson's "Don't Stop 'Til You Get Enough" came on the sound system, and Rocco, Panzullo, and Jeremy all started chanting "Ca-sa-no-va, Ca-sa-no-va, Ca-sa-no-va!"

"This is just for you," Casanova said to me. He jumped up from his stool, went to the middle of the wood floor, and executed a perfect moonwalk. We all clapped.

"Wanna dance, Amanda?" he called.

"I better get going, guys," I said glumly, as if I were disappointed that I had to be so responsible.

"Come on, just one dance," Casanova asked.

"You know the Sprinkler," Jeremy said, demonstrating it to me with one arm in front of him, fake spraying us with water. "Or the Butter Churn," he said, stirring his hands and giving a circular hip motion.

"I've got a better one," I said, hopping off my barstool and skipping over to Casanova on the floor. I knew this was my finale, so I thrust my left arm in front of me and threw my right one in the air, circling it as if I were a cowgirl with a rope and was about to lasso the crew. I made a giddyup motion with my legs like I was a horse. "You know what I call this move?" I shouted to them. "It's the Fluke! I'm roping 'em all in."

The guys cheered and pumped their fists. I took a bow, then sauntered back to my barstool and grabbed my bags. "Okay, guys, on that note: Gallo out!"

Casanova came over and gave me a kiss on the cheek. "You're the best, Amanda," he said.

"You, too," I called over my shoulder, then gave one last victory lasso with my arm and staggered out the door to the bright, sunny street.

PART II

Devil's Advocate

Chapter 18

Rubik's Cube

By the fourth month of anchoring the show, I could see an unhealthy pattern emerging in my sleep cycle. After the pitch meetings, I was too tired to begin the trek home. So I'd chug a cup of coffee for energy, then stagger out of the building to the subway. When I got home, I'd be too wired to nap, so I'd take a melatonin to fall asleep. *Isn't this what killed Michael Jackson? Is melatonin a gateway drug to propofol?* I wondered as I wandered from the cafeteria, coffee in hand, back to my office.

That's when I noticed Fatima, Rob, Topher, and Tiffany standing in the hallway, engaged in a peculiar scene. They were surrounded by three PAs holding tape measures and scissors. Fatima was hoisting a three-foot-long bright green cardboard box with smaller orange squares attached to its sides, attempting to lower it over Rob's head.

"What's happening?" I asked.

"Oh, good, you're here," Fatima said. "Did you get my email? Production wants us to try on a possible costume for the White House Halloween Party."

"It's only August," I reminded her.

"I know. They think this is the last slow news week we'll have before the election kicks into overdrive, and they want to get this done." Fatima stood on her tiptoes, and Rob ducked his head into the box so she could slide it down his torso.

"I thought we'd agreed on Bill and Hillary Clinton," I said. "I got the perfect pantsuit."

"Production didn't like that," she told me. "They suggested Batman and Robin but Rob won't wear tights."

"Violation of man law," Rob said from inside the box. "Though feel free to wear a leotard, Amanda."

"So we're going with a *Saturday Night Live* theme?" I asked.

"What? No. What do you mean?" Fatima asked, annoyed.

"Oh, sorry, I just figured this was Dick in a Box," I said before realizing it was outloud.

"Oh, snap!" Fatima snorted. The PAs' eyes darted from me to the towering case covering Rob.

"Yeah, hysterical," came the muffled voice from the box. Then suddenly a loud *THWOP!* as Rob punched through the cardboard with his fist. He worked his hand through the hole and held up his middle finger in my general direction.

"Perfect!" Fatima said. "We needed an arm hole there. Quick, Tiffany, grab the scissors and cut it into a circle."

"Watch it!" Rob yelled from inside. "That's my arm!"

"Seriously, what is this?" I asked again.

"It's Rubik's Cube," Fatima explained. "Half the box will fit on Rob and the other half on you, then you two click together. Hopefully. Now, if you could try this other box on, we'll see if you and Rob fit together."

"Like oil and water," I said.

Fatima grabbed my coffee and placed it on a table, then took my waist, pointing me forward, and reached for a big blue and yellow rectangle of cardboard, crisscrossed in black electrical tape in a tic-tac-toe pattern designed to look like individual squares. Fatima positioned the box over my shoulders with suspenders made of duct tape.

"Ooh, this looks good," she said. "It's working. Now, let me see if Rob can fit into this part of your box."

"That sounds dirty," Rob said, peeking through the newly cut armhole.

"My God, you're a pig," I said.

"Come on, guys," Fatima said. "This will only take a minute. Now, Amanda, you stand right here, like so." She grabbed the cardboard around my waist and moved me into position to Rob's left. "And Rob, you slide over here," she said, tugging Rob toward me until the sides of our boxes were flush against each other. "Now, you'll need to be able to walk around stuck together. Can you walk like that?"

"I doubt it," I said, trying to stabilize the unwieldy, heavy cardboard weighing down my shoulders.

"This is ridiculous," Rob announced. "Where's the hole for my head? Can we be done?"

Rob took a step to the left and began trying to wriggle out of his box just as I took a step to my right to see if I was mobile. Our thick cardboard shells bounced off each other, sending us teetering precariously. For two long seconds, Rob looked like the Leaning Tower of Pisa. Then, in slow motion, he lost his footing and toppled toward me. Like dominoes, we fell to the ground, Rob's box on top of mine.

"Oh, my God," Fatima shrieked, half laughing. "Are you guys okay?"

I couldn't speak, the weight of Rob and the boxes knocking the wind out of me.

"Holy crap, Topher, help me get their boxes off!" Fatima yelled. Topher yanked Rob's box over his head, allowing Rob to regain use of his arms. I felt Rob's legs pressing on mine, trying to untangle our limbs, then Topher tore the box off me.

"God, I'm sorry Amanda," Rob said. "Are you all right?"

"Um, I think so," I mustered.

"Jesus, guys." Rob kneeled, then put his arms around me and pulled me up to a sitting position. "You turned Amanda and me into a human pretzel." Keeping his arms tight around my body, Rob used both hands to hoist me to a standing position alongside him, our bodies still pressed together.

"Oh, thanks," I said, dazed. I must have been knocked in the head, because for a fleeting moment it seemed like Rob looked at me sweetly, like he was worried about me, then he took his hands off me.

"All right, we're done," Rob announced. "I think you got what you needed, plus a fantastic YouTube moment if anyone had their iPhone on them." Rob brushed himself off, turned, and walked away down the hall.

Chapter 19

Solid Sources

Charlie and I strolled along the sidewalk in the fuzzy postbrunch idyll of an August Sunday, trying to ignore the headlines blaring out of newsstands about the presidential race that continued to heat up. After the intensity of my workweeks, with the voices on each side getting louder and angrier, I spent weekends in a dreamlike fog—until it was time to kick my brain into high gear again on Sunday nights. I lolled past the boutiques in SoHo, which were already segueing from sundresses and sandals to sweaters and vests, and paused in front of one to admire a pair of gorgeous over-the-knee black suede boots—the kind that even Meg couldn't justify buying for our work wardrobes. Someday soon, when Jake renegotiates my contract at an anchor salary, whatever that is, I might buy those boots. Or I might not. Maybe I'll save my money to upgrade my apartment, someplace with an elevator and a view. *You're gonna make it after all.* I sang it in my head. Boy, was Mom happy lately. "Finally, a progressive female presidential candidate who shares my vision!" she'd say. "All she has to do is win."

My phone was already ringing when I got to my desk after the show Monday morning.

"I found the housekeeper," Laurie said.

"Oh, my God. Tell me!"

"Her name is Martina Harrow and Fluke bought her a very nice home in Arizona."

"How'd you figure it out?"

"Well, it took awhile. Turns out the house was bought sixteen years ago, so the timeline matches. There's no evidence of a mortgage. It was bought in cash, and the purchaser used an LLC, which was named 'Successful Man, Inc.' and registered to the address of Fluke's office in Bel Air! How fucking dumb is this guy?"

"Oh, my God! So did you get her to talk?"

"Uh, not yet. She's hung up on me three times. But I'll get her."

"What's your plan?"

"BNN's lawyers say between the nanny and these real estate records, we can go with it. So we're crashing something together for tonight. I gotta go."

"Listen, Laur, after you guys break it, do you think I could get those real estate records from you? I could hit Fluke with them when he comes on this week."

"Of course," she said. "You're the only network that has access to Fluke. You gotta nail him."

"Done," I said.

That night, Laurie and Gabe broke the housekeeper story, though they didn't use her name and didn't get her on camera, and the next morning I walked into the *Wake Up* pod, where Fatima and a bunch of PAs were hunched over a monitor, watching video that I assumed was BNN's report.

"What's the deal?" I asked, tapping Fatima on the shoulder.

"Oh, hey, Amanda," she said, keeping her eyes glued to the screen. "Have you seen this stuff? It's amazing."

"I know!" I said. "I think BNN is trying to get the housekeeper to talk!"

"What?" Fatima said, turning toward me. "Oh, you mean that BNN stuff? Yeah, we can't touch that. But check this out. This is Fluke's North Carolina SUCCESS! rally last night that got really violent. Somebody pepper-sprayed the crowd."

"And this old lady got a snout full," Morgan said, hitting pause on the monitor at the moment a white-haired woman had raised her hand to her head, eyes squeezed shut and mouth open, her face contorted in pain.

"It's great video!" Fatima said. "So we'll play this at the top and bottom of every hour."

I stared at her. "What do you mean we can't touch the house-keeper story? That's huge news."

"But we don't have anything on it. Benji called and he doesn't want it in the show," Fatima told me. "He doesn't want to use BNN's reporting."

"I don't understand," I said. "Obviously BNN wouldn't air some-thing unless they had rock-solid sources. Why can't we attribute the reporting to BNN?"

"Because that's not what we do. We don't just repeat accusations in some endless media echo chamber. We're changing cable news to be fair again."

At that, I stole a look at the side of Fatima's head to see if she was wearing earphones with Benji feeding lines directly into her brain and out her mouth.

"Look," she went on, "we have to wait until we have something on the housekeeper ourselves. Until then, Benji doesn't want either of you asking Fluke about it when he comes on. Got it?"

"Roger that," Rob said from next to me, though I hadn't noticed he'd come into the pod.

"What if I could get some documents proving the allegations?" I asked. "Like the property records proving Fluke bought her a house?"

"Well, that would be amazing," Fatima said. "Can you do that?"

"I think so," I said. "Give me a few hours."

"Psst," I said in a stage whisper from behind a tree on the edge of Central Park.

"Oh, brother," Laurie said, walking toward me, shaking her head.

I had sunglasses on, and for full effect, I'd also decided to wear a baseball cap pulled down low on my head, and a scarf pulled up high over my mouth.

"You look absurd," she told me.

"I was considering a fake mustache, but can you believe they don't carry them at CVS?"

"Very cloak and dagger," she said. "Why not a trench coat?"

"Dammit! I should have."

"Listen," she said, "here they are. Obviously, I'd be royally screwed if anyone knew I gave these to you." She handed me a brown paper bag from Fairway Market.

"Yes, of course," I said. "*Fair*-way. I get it. I like it!"

"I thought you would. Now, if anyone asks, you cannot say where you got these documents."

"What documents?" I said.

"Good. Call me at nine tonight, after you watch our next install-ment of Maidgate, Creole edition. *Cherchez le femme.*"

"Laur, I go to sleep at eight," I told her. "Did you get the house-keeper to talk yet?"

"No, but her lawyer called to threaten me with a cease and desist if I keep calling her, which I plan to ignore. Anyway, tonight we have an exclusive with Emilia the nanny, who says Fluke and the house-keeper were having an affair."

"Of course they were!" I said, slapping my hands together. "The actor and the French maid—okay, Haitian maid—having a torrid af-fair. This guy is a walking Hollywood movie script. I'll try to stay up to watch. And then you can watch me break the cable news exclu-sive tomorrow morning."

"I don't get up that early," Laurie said.

"Whatever," I told her, then I held up the brown paper bag. "Thank you, thank you, thank you. I owe you one."

"One? Frankly, I've lost count. Call me later."

Chapter 20

Fair Way

4:00 A.M. "I got the documents," I said, tapping Fatima on the shoulder again, this time with the evidence. Fatima was hunched over her keyboard, typing numbers into the rundown. "I emailed you last night about them," I told her. "But I never heard back from you."

"Crap, sorry," she said. "I went to bed at six."

I reached into the Fairway bag and pulled out the papers, like I was presenting the Hope Diamond on a silver platter.

Rob strolled into the pod. "What are those?"

"I got the Fluke documents," I told him. "It's all right here. The letter from the nanny that says Fluke was employing the housekeeper illegally, plus the property records showing his LLC bought a house for her in cash. Plus, if you watched Gabe Wellborn's report last night, you know the nanny thinks Fluke was having an affair with the housekeeper under his wife's nose. Everything's in there. All the salacious details."

"Holy crap!" Fatima said, riffling through them. "This is incredible stuff. How'd you get these?"

"Um, let's just say I know people who pester people." I gave a smug I'm-so-connected shrug.

"This is good," Rob said, pointing at the papers. "We've got to lead with this."

Whoa. Something gets Rob's attention? I'd given up on him being a real news partner, though hearing him praise my scoop made me think a latent journalist might be trapped inside him.

"So shit! This changes the whole rundown." Fatima drummed her fingers on the desk, thinking. "I have to let the Third Floor know I'm going to blow up the show to lead with this. Why don't you two go get into hair and makeup? I'll find you and let you know how we're going to handle it. I can't believe you got these! I can't believe we have them first in cable news!"

"Well played," Rob said to me as I walked out. "I look forward to unpacking this."

"Amanda," Fatima called after me. "You rock!"

5:57 A.M. "Come on, man!" Rob sounded ticked off as I rushed into the studio late. He was in the middle of the sofa, face pinched, hand shielding his vision. "I'm getting an eyeful of ass!"

Jeremy looked up from his book over to Rocco in front of Camera 2. "Jesus, Rocco! You moonlighting as a plumber?"

I followed his line of sight right to the top of Rocco's butt crack peeking out of his jeans as he bent over, adjusting the brightness on his camera monitor.

Rob recoiled again, pressing his back into the cushion of the sofa. "Get a belt, man! No one sees this much crack at 6:00 A.M.—except maybe Charlie Sheen."

"It *is* the crack of dawn," Larry pointed out. "Okay, people, places. We're live on the air in thirty seconds. You ready, Amanda?"

"Not really," I said, trying to get my Fluke documents situated in front of me. "I don't see my headline scripts anywhere. I need to proofread them before I say them on the air."

"I'll print them for you," Larry said. "It'll take a few minutes. Places! We're in the cold open in ten, nine, eight . . ."

The FAIR News Break bonged. "Welcome to *Wake Up, USA!* We've got a huge show for you this morning," Rob read into Camera 3. "Victor Fluke will be here to talk about our top story: why he says it's time to make traditional marriage the law of the land again. And on the other side, we'll have liberal columnist Karen Burke here with her take on how gay couples raise better children."

My head shot up and I almost screamed, *What? That's not the top story!* Larry signaled for me to read into Camera 2.

"But first, we have a news alert," I read, surprised to hear my own words about breaking news. I needed those news scripts! "Police are asking for the public's help this morning to find a beloved school principal. Principal James Hardon has not been seen since last week." I paused. That didn't sound right. Hardon. Did I just say hard-on on TV? *Shit!* I knew I needed to swallow the second syllable and pronounce it like "Harden," but that's not how it was written in the prompter.

"Principal HARD-on," I tried again, this time emphasizing the first syllable, which somehow made it worse. "Sorry, Principal Hard-ON has gone missing." *Dammit! I did it again.*

The crew was starting to titter, which I feared my mic might be picking up. Somehow I had to get unstuck and move on to the next sentence. "Um . . . police say he hasn't been seen for days. If you see James Hard-on"—*Goddammit!*—"please call your local authorities."

I could see Larry's face bursting, then he said, loud enough to be broadcast, "And if you see him for more than four hours, call your doctor!"

Panzullo doubled over and grabbed his gut.

"Don't worry, Amanda," Rob said, patting my knee. "I'm sure he'll pop up."

I knew the Twittersphere would have a field day with that one, but mostly I needed to know what happened to our lead Fluke story. I waited for Rob to read, then whisper-yelled into my mic. "Fatima!"

"What's up?" she said.

"The Fluke housekeeper story belongs at the top of the A block!"

"Ohhhh, riiight," she said, like I was reminding her of something from weeks ago. "Sorry, didn't Topher come find you? Third Floor says we can't use those documents you got. They said they don't know where you got them. And I didn't realize they're copies. They're not the originals. So, you know, Third Floor doesn't want to be Dan Rathered."

"But I can vouch for their authenticity!" I hissed into the mic as Rob was finishing and Larry was pointing at me to read.

"We'll talk about it after the show," Fatima said in my ear. "You've got the next headline!"

7:00 A.M. Top of the A block. This was the moment I was supposed to be breaking my big cable news Fluke scoop. But instead, here was Fluke on the sofa spouting his same tired line about one of his favorite topics.

"Traditional marriage is the foundation of this country. And if we give that up, we give up the stability of our homes, and our families and communities fail. When I'm elected, we're going to get back to success."

And there it was: the perfect opening. I took a deep breath. "I guess I'm wondering, Mr. Fluke, if you think that all heterosexual couples have done a good job of protecting the solemn oath of fidelity that's the underpinning of marriage."

Fluke stared at me. "I'm sorry, I don't understand your question."

"Which one do you think provides more stability," I went on, my heart thumping, "gay marriage with commitment or traditional marriage with infidelity?" I decided not to voice my next question: "And how does your undocumented girlfriend feel about this?" Instead I said, "Perhaps you'd like to respond to BNN's reporting."

Fluke raised one eyebrow almost imperceptibly, more of a twitch, really. But I saw it. And he saw me see it.

"I haven't seen it and I prefer not to deal in hypotheticals, Amanda."

Is that right, Mr. Maid-Lover? What does your wife think about the foundation of the house you bought for your Haitian housekeeper? The voices in my head were drowning out whatever Fluke said next, and before I knew it, Rob had wrapped the segment and read the tease.

"We're clear!" Larry yelled.

Fluke walked over to the dark part of the studio, where Dove was waiting.

"Here's lookin' at you, Amanda," Dove said, this time not smiling but pointing at me, then turning and exiting the studio. I watched the studio door close, and when it did, I yelled. "That sucked! We cannot do that!" Everyone looked at me.

"We can't ignore the biggest story of the day! Look at the Quad Box! CNN, BNN, everyone else is talking about the housekeeper story and we're the only ones who have Fluke on and WE'RE NOT TOUCHING IT!"

"Don't worry," Rob told me. "We'll still win this quarter hour. We had Fluke."

"I don't care who wins the hour!" I yelled. "We look like idiots. We're Fluke stooges!"

There was silence in the studio until Larry said, "We got Fluked."

"Uh, Fatima," Rob said, tapping his microphone and pointing to the Quad Box, "it looks like BNN is busting the break. What's happening?"

"Unclear," Fatima said, her voice nervous. "Let me check. We're shuffling the order of some things. Stand by."

I turned to the silent monitor playing the other four channels. A bold red BNN breaking news graphic splashed on the screen, interrupting a commercial, then wiped to Gabe Wellborn sitting at the anchor desk. *Jesus, this must be big. Gabe is never up this early.* "What's he saying?" I yelled.

"It looks like something's up with Fluke. Turn up REM 15," Fatima shouted to someone in the control room. "Um, I think it's a press conference . . . Turn up the volume on BNN. It looks like it's . . . no, it's the lawyers for the housekeeper . . . announcing a press conference at noon. Shit! Let me call the assignment desk. Amanda, need you to put those pajamas on now."

"What?" Surely I'd misheard her.

"I had to shuffle some things. We lost our eight thirty, that constitutional law expert. The driver never showed up to bring him to the studio. So I need you to model those pajamas now."

"What pajamas?" I asked, looking at Larry, who, I was sure, would deliver the punch line that was missing here. But he was checking his stopwatch.

"Amanda, you've got two minutes to put on some pajamas," Larry said matter-of-factly, like that was a regular request.

"What the fuck?" I said to the crew, then turned to Rob. "We need to cover the breaking news! We're not going to do a pajama segment while everyone else is on a Fluke presser, right? Right?" My stomach felt like I was about to go over the tippy-top of a roller coaster. "Fatima! Fatima!"

"Fatima, need some guidance out here," Rob said.

"Guys, the presser's not until noon," Fatima said. "We've got a hole in the show now! I'm plugging in the models-wearing-pajamas-out-to-nightclubs story."

"Sounds like the control room is in a bind," Rob said to me. "They've got nothing else to go to."

"Nothing else?" I yelled. "We are sitting on the Fluke documents! The biggest story of the day, the week, the year! What do you mean?"

"I told you, Amanda," Fatima said in my ear. "We do *NOT* have our lawyers' permission to go with those. Do *NOT* get out ahead of this. I'm telling you, I have a hole in the show here. The presser isn't happening until noon. We're not going to sit around and talk about an upcoming presser for six minutes. I'm putting the pajama segment in."

I knew that adage, "Don't get ahead of the story." Professor Jordan told us that Peter Jennings had preached it, as had Ted Koppel, and Tom Brokaw, and anyone who'd ever watched one of their colleagues be 100 percent certain of a scoop, only to have it blow up in their face like a GM pickup truck. And hearing Fatima say the lawyers were aware of my documents made me feel better. Maybe I could use them tomorrow.

"Need you to move, Amanda!" Fatima yelled.

"Here," Larry said, handing me a bag from Macy's. "One of the interns dropped these off during the last break. You've got less than two minutes left in commercial."

I opened the bag and saw a pair of red satin pajamas, price tag still attached.

"You've got ninety seconds," Larry said, checking his stopwatch again. "Make a decision."

"I'll help you," Rob said.

"How?" I shrieked.

"Not sure yet."

"Now!" Fatima yelled.

I jumped off the sofa, bag in hand, and raced down the hallway to Angie's hair room. "Unzip me!"

"One minute back, Amanda!" Larry yelled down the hall.

"What in God's name ya doing?" Angie asked.

"Putting on pajamas," I said, hopping around her stall. "Models are wearing them out at night. They're a fashion trend."

"Oh, yeah? And that's more important than Fluke having an affair with an illegal immigrant?" She pointed the hairbrush, bristle side out, at Gabe Wellborn on the TV monitor next to her mirror. The echo of Gabe's voice sounded down the hallway from all the TVs in the makeup corridor tuned to BNN's breaking news. "Whatever ya do, don't mess up the hay-yer," Angie called without turning around, as I dashed out into the hallway, now clad in red pajamas and high heels.

"Amanda, need you back in the studio! You've got thirty seconds!" Larry yelled down the hall to me.

I stopped short. Was I really supposed to go back into the studio and sit there next to Rob, joshing around, pretending not to know the news? I couldn't do it. I felt the walls of the hallway closing in. I couldn't breathe. My mind emptied except for one single, powerful instinct: I need air.

"I gotta get out," I muttered to myself.

"What?" Larry yelled back. "I think I heard her say she's going out. Amanda? Amanda? Panzullo, Camera Four, follow her!!"

I ran toward the side doors. Stanley the guard grabbed his key.

"You gotta go handheld, Panzullo!" Larry's voice was loud in my IFB. "Audio! Bruce, give her a stick mic! Her lav won't work out there."

Stanley pushed the thick glass door open and the heavy August air enveloped me. I felt the pores on the back of my neck open to the heat under the satin collar. Panzullo came chugging through the door after me, breathing hard, with one hand on the camera, the other holding up his pants.

"I need to go back to the gym," he said.

"Amanda, where are you?" Fatima yelled into my ear.

"I'm outside," I said, calm now as I stood still in the heat, watching the chaos of the morning commute buzz around me. *All these people going their separate ways, unaffected by any breaking news. Maybe the documents aren't so life changing.*

"Love it!" Fatima yelled in my ear. "Let's bong in with a FAIR News Break! We'll have our own breaking news!" I could hear Fatima off mic, issuing orders to the line producer. "Give me a split screen!"

"We're back in five, four, three, two, one." Larry was counting down Rob in the studio.

A taxi honked. I looked around and realized, with a jolt of

anxiety, I had no plan. I felt the satin sleeves starting to cling to my moist skin. The ominous bong of the breaking news sound effect clanged in my ear, bringing me back to the reality that I was now on live television . . . in pajamas.

Rob's voice, deep with newsman gravity, said, "Folks, we have some breaking news. Amanda Gallo appears to have left the building. Now what makes this particularly newsworthy is that she's wearing pajamas. Amanda, can you hear me?"

I turned to look into the lens. "I can, Rob."

"Amanda, I can't help but notice, you're wearing a fetching pair of red pajamas."

"You're nothing if not observant, Rob," I said, walking backward on the sidewalk as Panzullo walked the camera toward me.

"Care to explain yourself?" Rob asked.

"Well, I'm conducting a little experiment here on the streets of New York City," I said, surprising myself by opening my arm like Vanna White, to reveal a throng of pedestrians on the corner waiting for the light to change. "Apparently, fashion models in New York have begun wearing their pajamas out to nightclubs."

"Interesting," Rob said. "Now what does that have to do with you being in the middle of Midtown Manhattan in broad daylight?"

"Again, insightful of you, Rob, to point out that minor discrepancy. See . . ." I stopped. I had no idea what to say or do next. I could hear the sound of dead air as I waited for something to come to me. "So . . ."

"I know your plan," Rob said, jumping in, "was to see how this fashion trend would go over with regular New Yorkers."

"Yes," I said, "that's right." *Of course. Turn this into a man-on-the-street segment. That's the answer. Thank you, Rob. Thank you.*

"And I see a group of businessmen right over your left shoulder," Rob said, steering me to the next beat. "Why don't you ask them what they think of your outfit?"

I turned to find the targets Rob had identified, right where he'd promised. *Thank you, Rob.* I darted up to the group of standard-issue young businessmen. Panzullo jogged behind me. "Hello, gentlemen."

"Hi," they said, eyeing me up and down.

"I'm just wondering if you notice anything unusual about my outfit?"

"It looks like you're wearing pajamas," one offered.

"That's right. This is a new trend," I said, staring at their matching navy blue Brooks Brothers suits. "You guys look like slaves to fashion. What do you think of this?"

"It's a little weird," the tallest one said. "But it could work. I guess."

"How about you?" I asked the next guy.

"It's good," he said.

I bit my lip. These guys were not exactly lighting the screen on fire.

"Hey, Amanda," Rob chimed in.

"Yes?"

"I see some taxis stopped at the light behind you. Why don't you ask them?"

Yes, of course! Keep the action moving. The secret to live TV. I vowed to buy Rob a case of Red Bull to show my gratitude, but first I jogged to the taxi line.

Using the stick mic, I rapped on a driver's window. "Excuse me, sir," I said, as Panzullo pushed in for a close-up. The driver looked up at me with an expression of sheer panic, shook his head vigorously, then stepped on the gas and zoomed away. Through my earpiece, I could hear Rocco and Larry inside laughing.

"I'm gonna guess he's not crazy about the pajamas," Rob concluded.

"Yeah," I said. "I guess not."

"Either that, or he's wanted by the authorities. But listen, Amanda, we all give you a big round of applause here in the studio. We think you look terrific."

"Thanks for that, Rob," I said, grateful for his instinct to wrap the segment on that note. I'd never been part of any team before—sports, anchor, or otherwise—but suddenly I knew what it felt like to have a teammate carry me.

"All right, you trendsetter," Rob said. "Come back in and cool off. We'll have some lemonade waiting for you."

"Thanks, Rob," I said.

"And coming up tomorrow," Rob went on, "horror and bloodshed in Syria as government goons mow down their own people. And Victor Fluke will be here to talk about why he thinks refugees are so dangerous. Tune in then."

I handed the stick mic back to Panzullo, then put my hands to my flushed face. I was light-headed.

"That was brilliant, Amanda!" Fatima said in my ear.

"Rob saved it," I told her.

I made my way back to the side door, dizzy and disoriented. Stanley held the door open and a wall of air-conditioning slapped my hot skin. *God, I hope Virginia Wynn wasn't watching that.* I had a sneaking suspicion the pajama bit might submarine the pitch I'd been making to her press office, trying to convince them that I was a real journalist and *Wake Up, USA!* was a real news program. The good news was that Margot hadn't secured a sit-down with Wynn yet either, though she was probably pulling a clip of me in my pajamas right now and sending it to the Wynn people.

I stood temporarily blinded in the hallway, my eyes adjusting to the fluorescent lighting. As the pixels came into focus, there was Arthur Dove, standing in the corridor staring at me, smirking.

"I gotta hand it to ya, Amanda," he said. "Not everyone could pull off pajamas on national TV in front of a million people." He held up his hand for a high five. I instinctively raised my hand, and as our palms touched, it dawned on me I was high-fiving Arthur Dove . . . in my pajamas. *What's happening to my life?* I wondered.

"Mr. Fluke did not enjoy the segment today as much as usual. He felt some of it was unnecessary, if you're picking up what I'm putting down. I'd hate for Mr. Fluke to start declining your invitations to be on *Wake Up.* That wouldn't be in any of our interests."

"So what about BNN's story about Mr. Fluke employing an undocumented housekeeper?" I asked him.

"God, Amanda, you can't fall for phony stories. It's nothing."

His response was so definitive that for a second I was relieved I hadn't run with the documents. Then I remembered that some people don't look uncomfortable when lying.

"Anyway, Mr. Fluke wanted me to give you this," Dove said, handing me an envelope, sealed.

I wanted to ask Dove more questions, but the envelope caught me off guard. Plus I was in still in my pajamas.

"We'll see you soon, Amanda," Dove said, moving past me toward the door. "Don't forget, we've got a lot of followers and we all want the same thing: success."

When he was gone, I opened the envelope.

Amanda,
If you want to keep winning, don't be susceptible to rumor and insinuation.
> *—Victor Fluke*

"No, I don't understand," I said to Fatima across the table at the pitch meeting. "Why didn't the lawyers let us show the documents?"

"They want to make sure they're not fake," she said. "And that they weren't planted by the Wynn people, you know, to smear Fluke."

"They weren't," I told her, though I didn't really know Emilia or her motivation for sending the letter to Laurie months ago and didn't want to admit that.

"I believe you, Amanda," she said. "But on a story this big, we have to be one hundred percent buttoned-up. The lawyers said we don't have to be first, we have to be right."

"What if the housekeeper comes forward and confirms the story at the presser at noon?"

"Then we run with it," Fatima said. "Then we're golden. That's what we need—her story. That's what we stand for at FAIR. Both sides. We don't just give one side. We have to make sure we're totally T and E. In the meantime, Topher, see if Fluke can do tomorrow or Monday. And see what other days he's available next week. That way, if she comes forward today or tomorrow or over the weekend, we have him and we're covered."

"Hey, are you seeing this?" Tiffany asked. "Arthur Dove just tweeted something about Amanda." She stopped. "Uh-oh."

"What is it?" I asked, looking around the room.

"It says '@AmandaGallo tries gotcha journalism. Epic fail!! @WakeUpUSA falls for fake news.'"

"Shit," Fatima said, and everyone stared at me with a mix of pity and terror.

"It's not playing gotcha to ask Fluke legitimate questions!" I told the table. "That's our job! It's malpractice for us to ignore it."

"You better send him an apology," Topher said. "We need him to come back tomorrow—and every day through the election."

"Are you kidding!" I said. "Victor Fluke does not dictate our editorial decisions!"

"I get that," Topher said. "But we need him. We're winning. And we don't win without him."

Chapter 21

Ratings Gold

I knocked on Rob's office door, not knowing if he'd still be at work.

"Come in," he said.

I turned the knob and got my first glimpse inside Rob's world—his uncluttered desk, his bookshelves filled with hardcovers, his walls covered with framed 8 x 10 glossies of him with an array of celebrities and politicians, arm in arm, grinning ear to ear, including one of Rob and Fluke, both wearing visors and carrying golf clubs.

Rob was bent over, putting some gym clothes into a bag, and I considered backing out of the room before he stood up.

"Oh, hey," he said, looking up.

"You have a second?"

"Sure, have a seat." He gestured to the chair across from his desk. It was funny to see Rob in casual mode. His suit and tie were gone; his white dress shirt hung untucked over old jeans. His brown hair was looser than on set, like he'd just run his hand through it.

"So I wanted to thank you for your help with that pajama segment today. I couldn't have gotten through it without you."

"Sure you could have. I just goosed it a little. But you were great out there. It was pretty hilarious. You should go back and watch it. BuzzFeed picked it up."

That was the moment I would have said thank you again, then politely left, if that's really what I'd come for. But instead I sat there biting my lip.

"So what's up?" he asked.

"Well," I started, then realized I should have practiced this part—or at least given more thought to what I wanted out of Rob. "I've been thinking about the show . . . and what our mission is." I screwed up my mouth, trying to find the words. "Because I don't think we're getting it right."

Rob leaned back in his chair, putting his arms behind his head. "What's the problem?"

"Well, for starters, we're letting Fluke come on all the time and say whatever the fuck he wants *and* we're treating him with kid gloves *and* we're not even using the evidence we have of his huge fucking hypocrisy." I hadn't meant to get worked up, but there it was.

"But it's working," Rob said. "No one thought we'd be killing it so soon after launch. What Benji's done is nothing short of a miracle. And let's face it, most of it is the Fluke factor."

"It's working for ratings, but it's not working for the viewers."

"If we're getting good ratings, it's working for the viewers. By definition. Good ratings mean we're giving viewers what they're interested in."

"Virginia Wynn would get good ratings, too, but the bookers never book her."

"They try, but she won't come on. And don't kid yourself. She's no ratings machine. MSNBC just did an hour on her gun-control measures and it tanked."

I felt strangely relieved to hear that Wynn hadn't generated big ratings, in case I lost out to Margot for a Wynn sit-down. "Still, I don't think we should be giving Fluke such a regular platform to spout his nonsense."

"You think it's nonsense. But that's your opinion."

"No, it's not. Half of the things he says are wrong. He says the people can overturn the Supreme Court. He makes up abortion statistics. And now this housekeeper story proves he's a huge hypocrite on marriage and immigration and taxes and everything!"

"None of that's proven yet," Rob said.

"Look, I get it. You're a Fluke fan," I said.

"I think he's a complete tool," Rob said.

I cocked my head at him. "Really?" I said, jutting my head in the direction of the photo. "You play golf with him."

"That picture was from years ago. Back when he was the World's Most Successful Man . . . before he became the World's Most Unlikely

Nominee. Besides, I play golf with a lot of people. Doesn't mean I like them."

"But you like his ideas," I concluded. "You're conservative, right?"

"Wrong again," Rob said. "You're battin' a thousand, huh?"

"Come on, Rob, you never challenge our conservative guests."

"That's because you always do. You always take the liberal side. So you force me to take the other side."

"No, I don't," I said, suddenly self-conscious.

"Yeah. You do."

Shit. Was that right? "So you're not a conservative?"

"My family were all firefighters, my dad, his brothers, all my cousins. I guess you'd call them Reagan Democrats. I don't know. I don't love labels."

"So why aren't you a fireman?" I asked, trying to get Rob to admit that he liked all the trappings of being a newsman more than doing something altruistic.

"Uh, well, I wanted to be one. But after my dad died in a fire, my mom refused to let me go to the academy."

"Oh, wow. I'm sorry. I had no idea."

"Thank you," Rob nodded, like he'd had to say that a thousand times.

"But, um, why news?" I said, trying to change the subject.

"Well, I know it sounds funny, but I've always thought of this job as being kind of like a fireman. You know, an alarm goes off, or in our case, news breaks, and it doesn't matter if you're at home with your family or asleep or whatever, you spring into action. It's the same adrenaline rush. I like being where the action is. You know, in the heat of it all."

"Hmm," I said. "That makes sense. But, you know, beyond the rush, we're supposed to shed light, not misinformation. Don't you think we're doing way too much Fluke?"

"I don't think there's any such thing. The fact that so many people are watching our show tells you that there's a big appetite out there for what Fluke has to say. There's nothing more democratic than TV. It gives viewers the ultimate power. They vote every morning with their remotes. They vote every *minute*, actually. And our viewers are voting to see Fluke. He's ratings gold."

"But journalism shouldn't be about ratings."

Rob snorted. "I don't know where you've worked, but everywhere I have, that's *all* it's about. And by the way, that's not a bad thing. If you don't have ratings, that means you don't have viewers. And if you don't have viewers, you don't have advertisers. And if you don't have revenue, you don't have a channel for very long. And then it doesn't matter how great your journalism is, no one will ever see it. Look at Al Jazeera. They had a good idea: covering the Middle East better than anyone else. No ratings. Shut down after two years. Look at Piers Morgan—passionate about gun control. That's important journalism, right? His ratings tanked. Show canceled."

"Don't you think we look stupid doing a pajama segment while everyone else is doing the housekeeper story?"

"I think it's smart to counterprogram. Let's wait till we see the numbers. I bet the pajamas rate."

"I think we *have* to cover the housekeeper. It's our duty."

"Listen, maybe this will help," he said. "Think about your audience. Think about what *they* want, not what *you* think they should want. And they've been pretty clear. They want more Fluke. Every time he's on, the ratings spike. That tells you something about what's going on in this country—and we're smart to pay attention."

I stared past Rob, taking it in and trying not to get confused by all the competing agendas: Mom wanted more Wynn, Charlie wanted no Fluke, Rob wanted good ratings, and what did I want, besides those black suede boots in the store window? I wanted a successful career and to make a difference in people's lives and to follow in Suzy Berenson's footsteps. And I could argue that I was achieving all those things, so really, what more did I want?

"Listen, I'd love to hang out and bat this around more, but I gotta go," Rob said, standing up. "I have a date."

"At ten thirty A.M.?"

"This one won't leave me alone," he grinned and shook his head. "She needs more of the Lahr love."

"How can you function at this hour? I can barely talk."

"Who said there'd be any talking?" He grabbed his keys off the desk. "Listen, you'll figure this all out. If it's any consolation, the viewers seem to really like you, particularly Frank in Fresno. He's says he's hoping for a double dangle tomorrow." Rob patted me on the back and walked out.

11:58 A.M. I stared at the giant TV monitor on my office wall. BNN had broken into regular programming, and now Gabe and two pundits were stretching to kill time, waiting for the presser to start.

"Folks, we're awaiting a press conference in this developing story on Victor Fluke's former housekeeper." Gabe was using his America's Premier Newsman cadence, which made it sound like he might announce that bin Laden had just been killed all over again. "We've been given a two-minute warning that the press conference is about to start, regarding allegations of wrongdoing by Victor Fluke in what's come to be called Maidgate. Will this derail his presidential campaign?"

BNN cut from the anchor desk to a reporter scrum around an empty podium, and I leaned forward in my chair, wishing I were home on the couch with Charlie and some popcorn.

Look! There's Laurie! It was funny. Even though I was on TV, somehow seeing Laurie on TV was very exciting. Like a celebrity sighting. I watched her milling around next to the pack of cameramen adjusting microphones on the rim of the podium. Laurie looked impatient, like the lawyers were keeping her personally waiting.

Gabe reappeared, now in a split screen. "As you know, this story has developed quickly since our investigative report revealed that presidential candidate Victor Fluke may have employed an undocumented immigrant from Haiti sixteen years ago and then bought her a house in the U.S. using a shell company. So lots of questions that, thus far, Mr. Fluke has not answered. We're not sure what to expect from the attorneys for the housekeeper at this press conference, but here they are now."

A small group of serious-faced lawyers in business suits stepped to the podium. The tallest one, a middle-aged, sandy-haired man, leaned down toward the microphones.

"Good afternoon, everyone. We can make this quick. Ever since the media decided to dredge up a decades-old rumor, my client has lived in fear of being hounded and harassed. Let me make my client's position very clear: she does not want to speak about the circumstances of her employment sixteen years ago or about Victor Fluke. She does not want her identity revealed. She respectfully requests you all stop attempting to contact her and leave her alone. She will not have any further comments. Thank you very much. Good day."

"Did she have a relationship with Victor Fluke?" one reporter yelled.

"Was she in the country illegally?" another shouted.

My eyes searched for Laurie. I knew she'd yell a follow-up question. But she didn't. Instead, she grabbed her bag and walked out of the frame.

Charlie was reading at the desk when I walked into his apartment.

"Hi. What are you up to? How was class?" I asked in an effort to deflect attention from my day.

"Just looking over these essays," Charlie said, pushing his glasses up on the bridge of his nose. "It's going to be a challenging semester. I told the students to write reports over the summer using source attribution, and this one kid is starting every paragraph with the phrase 'According to me.'"

I laughed. "That's funny. Sounds like some of my guests."

"How'd it go today?" he asked, putting down his pen. "Did you bust the Fluke case wide open?"

"I couldn't," I sighed. "They wouldn't let me use the documents."

"What? Why not?"

"They said they didn't know where I got them and I didn't want to reveal they were from Laurie."

"Isn't it more likely your producers are trying to protect Fluke?"

"They say we need the other side. You know, the woman's side. We can't just repeat some rumor."

"That's bullshit," Charlie said, his ire rising.

"I thought so, too, at first, but I think they're trying to be careful, particularly now that the housekeeper won't talk. And when I think about it, Laurie is operating off a letter from a possibly disgruntled nanny. And maybe Virginia Wynn's people did plant the story to bring down Fluke."

"Interesting conspiracy theory," Charlie said. "If only there was someone connected to the story you could ask about her sources."

"Very funny," I said. "I texted her."

My cell phone rang on the coffee table.

"Hey, got your text," Laurie whispered into the phone. "I can't talk. I'm on a stakeout. I'm trying to ambush the attorney. I gotta be ready to spring if he comes out. Did you use the documents today?"

"They wouldn't let me."

"Why not?"

"Well, they had questions about where I got them, which, of course, I didn't reveal. Plus they say we need the housekeeper to talk."

"Get in line," Laurie said.

"I know. From that press conference, it sounds impossible."

"Nothing's impossible," Laurie said. "Hold on, is that him?" I could hear Laurie conferring with her cameraman. "No, wait, that's a woman. Shit, we need to get closer."

"So what's your plan since the housekeeper doesn't want to be identified?" I asked.

"I have her name. I have her number. I'm trying to convince her attorney to let her talk to Gabe, but I gotta ambush him cause he's not returning my calls."

I heard a clicking on her end, and Laurie said, "That's Gabe calling."

"He probably wants some tomato juice."

"Stand by," Laurie said, clicking over, then back a second later. "I gotta go. I'm working on it. Somebody at FAIR News should be working on this, too. I'm sure Benji has pull with the attorneys on this case. Get him to set something up for you to meet with them."

"That's a good idea," I said, wishing I'd thought of that.

"Jesus, why do you even pay that asshole agent of yours? Just send me ten percent of your paycheck. Wait, that's the attorney!" Laurie yelled. "There he goes! Follow him!" I heard a scramble of movement and equipment. "Shit! I shouldn't have been on the phone. I gotta go trail him." The sound went dead on the other end.

"What'd she say?" Charlie asked.

"Not much," I said, bringing the phone to rest on the coffee table again. "She's chasing the lawyer down the street."

Chapter 22

Man on the Street

Laurie didn't get the housekeeper, but by late September she had started fooling around with the attorney. She seemed to like the guy, though I was pretty sure that if she ever did get the housekeeper to talk, the affair might come to a hasty halt. Laurie and I had a name for relationships that sprang up in TV news when reporters, producers, and their sources were on assignment, on location, away from home, bonding with each other during long days of live shots and late drunken dinners. We called them "locationships." In Laurie and the attorney's case, this was more like a scoopship, or a sourceship, or a tipship, or something. I couldn't quite tell.

While Laurie worked over her source, I stewed about Margot having finally secured the first FAIR News sit-down with Virginia Wynn. I was so bummed about her campaign people picking Margot over me that I'd almost convinced myself we were justified in having Fluke on *Wake Up, USA!* all the time to teach Wynn's people a lesson. *Hey, if she won't come on, then she can't blame us for booking the other biggest newsmaker,* I thought indignantly, even though our Fluke fixation pre-dated Wynn's denial of my request.

"I can't wait to watch the Virginia Wynn gun-control special on Thursday," Mom said. "Now is that something that in the future you might be able to be involved in?"

"I tried, Mom. I tried."

"But why does Margot get to interview her? *You* should be doing that."

"I don't know," I sighed. "Wynn's people decided to go with Margot, not me."

"Maybe it's because your show has Fluke on all the time. It's no wonder Wynn wouldn't want to come on."

"Well, my show is the highest-rated cable morning show. So if she wants to reach a lot of voters, she should do our show," I said, leaving out the part that we only got sky-high ratings the mornings Fluke came on.

When I hung up, I sat stewing again, torn about whether to even watch Margot's special, then an email popped up from Fatima that gave me new purpose.

TO: Amanda
FROM: Fatima
RE: This week
Hey, want to send you to a Fluke rally in New Hampshire on Thursday night. Thousands of people are expected to turn out. Want you to do a piece on these Fluke followers, who they are and what they want.
Some people got hurt at last week's rally, so you'll be in perfect position to get all the color if there's more violence.

Perfect. With any luck something dramatic *will* happen and my live reporting will preempt Margot's taped Wynn special. Being an anchor in the studio was fantastic; but the field was where the action was, where you got the real juice of the story. I'd show Margot.

So off we drove to Manchester, New Hampshire. Fluke had rented the civic center, predicting an overflow crowd and, sure enough, as the crew and I rolled up in the SUV, we saw a huge line of people stretching three city blocks.

"Shit," I said, stepping out of the crew car into a surprisingly chilly night. "It wasn't cold in New York."

I exhaled a stream of air out my nose, which I could tell was about to start running. *Now I remember: working in the field, out in the elements, is much harder than the studio.* At that moment, starting to shiver and fishing around for a tissue in my purse, I decided I would slap the next anchor I heard complaining about anything. The worst was an anchor like Margot who had never been a field reporter and felt free to complain about her shift, or the dress Meg had picked out, or her bad hair day—all while sitting in the warm comfort of the makeup chair. I'd been out of the crew car approximately sixty seconds and my hands were already freezing.

"Did you bring a hat?" my fotog, Gary, asked, pulling on his own unsightly orange striped one.

"No," I said. "I wasn't expecting it to be this cold in September."

"Major tactical error," the sound guy said. "This is New Hampshire. It snows year-round. Anyway, grab the stick mic. Let's go get some MOS."

"I thought we were going to shoot *inside* the civic center," I mumbled, pausing to scan the street for BNN's live truck, where I knew I could find Laurie. While waiting for the housekeeper to come around, Laurie was busy going from Fluke rally to Fluke rally, doing investigative pieces on what the Fluke followers were planning to do if he lost. Spotting BNN's truck halfway down the block, I was relieved. If I got too cold outside, I could retreat in there to warm up.

I reached back into the crew car for my pen and notepad, then stuffed my left hand deep into my coat pocket for warmth and felt something woolly. *Oh, thank God,* my gloves were still in my coat from March. *See? I* am *actually prepared.* I sighed out steam, then reached into the right-hand pocket for the other one and felt only emptiness. *Shit!*

"Um, can you guys wait one second? I have to give my friend at BNN something," I lied. "It'll only take a minute." I darted off to Laurie's truck, running up the stairs and yanking open the heavy door.

"Oh, hey," she said, looking up from her laptop. "When did you get here?"

"Like a second ago," I told her. "I didn't know it would be so cold. Do you have some gloves I could borrow?"

"You didn't bring gloves?" she said, like I was a hopeless case.

"Well, I did. But only one. And I have to go do MOS."

"I can't give up my gloves," she said. "I found a National Guard guy who's planning to take over some recruiting station if Fluke doesn't win. It's crazy. So I gotta get him on camera before he comes to his senses. Besides," she said, looking at me like she knew me better than I knew myself, "isn't forgetting a vital piece of clothing kinda what you're known for? Isn't that sort of *your thing*?"

"Oh, that's funny," I told her. "But no, that's my *old* thing. Haven't you heard? My new thing is *the dangle.*"

"I don't like how that sounds," she said.

"I'll explain later," I told her, opening the door and feeling the sting of cold on my way out.

"Ready, Amanda?" my fotog asked when I ran up. The sound guy reached into the equipment cage in the back of the car and handed me the stick mic, which felt as cold as a monkey bar on a playground in December. "Ready," I said.

We marched up to the line of supporters, some with signs, some just shifting back and forth on their feet, trying to stay warm. I began the familiar process of trying to suss out who would give me a good man-on-the-street sound bite based on body language. Someone who saw the camera and turned his back = bad. Someone who made eye contact = good. One sixtyish guy with a SUCCESSFUL MAN baseball cap watched me without looking away. He, I decided, would be the lucky winner of my MOS sweepstakes.

"Hi, sir, we're from FAIR News," I started. "Can I ask you a couple of questions about what you're doing out here?"

"Did you say FAIR News?" He looked around at the others in the line like he was gearing up for something. "Well, then step right up! How can we help you?" Everyone around him laughed and nodded, then spread out into a semicircle to let me in.

"That was easy," I said. "Sometimes getting people to go on camera can be like pulling teeth."

"Oh, we won't talk to the lamestream media," one smiling woman told me. "But we love FAIR News. And we sure love watching you every morning."

"My husband has a little crush on you," another woman gushed. "Isn't that right, Bill?" she asked, turning to a tall gray-haired man next to her who shrugged with schoolboy embarrassment, then nodded and said, "Yup, she's right." The others cracked up.

"I'm Susan, by the way," the wife said.

"Hi Susan, I'm Amanda," I said.

"Oh, we know who you are. You're the only morning show we watch," Susan said, "because we love you and we love seeing Mr. Fluke on your show. You're the only ones who take Mr. Fluke seriously. The other networks act like he's a joke. But he's not a joke."

Hearing that, a weird sensation came over me, pride mixed with disgust, attraction, and revulsion. These people loved me—and they loved Victor Fluke. And they thought I took him seriously. And maybe that was a good thing.

"Can we get a picture with you?" one of the guys asked.

"Yes, of course," I said. "But let me ask you some questions first." I looked over my shoulder at Gary, who already had his camera hoisted on his shoulder in the ready position. He gave me the go nod.

"Tell me your name," I said to the first guy, in the SUCCESSFUL MAN cap.

"I'm Tom Keller. K-E-L-L-E-R."

"Okay, Tom, why are you standing out here in the cold?"

"Well, because we want to protect our Second Amendment rights. And we need Mr. Fluke's help."

"What can he do?"

"Well, he can stop Virginia Wynn from abolishing the Second Amendment, for one."

"Virginia Wynn does not want to abolish the Second Amendment," I told him.

"Well, not yet," Tom said. "But if she wins this election she will. First it's these proposals she's laying out. Next it will be taking away all our guns."

"Here, let me get in on this," Susan said, standing to Tom's right and pushing her head closer to my microphone. "Virginia Wynn wants all these new laws but Victor Fluke knows there are already twenty thousand gun laws on the books!"

"But they're not working," I told her. "The number of mass shootings and school shootings has gone up. Don't you want to stop those?"

"Hell, yeah, we do," Tom said. "Every time some deranged lunatic shoots up a theater, it hurts our cause. But if a crazy person started mowing down people with his Chevy Bronco, we wouldn't be taking away everyone's cars or holding automobile manufacturers responsible."

"Why should regular people be able to buy AK-47s?" I asked.

"Cause they're a heck of a lot of fun!" Bill laughed and so did the rest.

"But no self-respecting hunter needs an AK-47 that can fire a hundred rounds."

"No one *needs* a sports car either," Bill said. "But in America you have the freedom to buy one. And cars are not even protected in the Constitution the way guns are."

"Oh, hey, Amanda," Tom in the hat said, "here comes my wife. Over here, honey!" He waved across the street to someone. "I knew she wouldn't want to miss this."

I lowered the mic for a second and turned to await Tom's wife, already imagining another gray-haired Granite Stater, so when I saw her, I gasped. "Oh, my God, you're black!" I almost said.

"Hey, honey!" Tom said, putting his arm around her. "Amanda, this is my wife, Joyce. She's another one of your big fans."

"I raced right over," Joyce said, "when Tom texted me that FAIR News was here. This is exciting for us."

"And are you a fan of Victor Fluke's, too?" I asked, thinking there might be a reason why she'd stayed home.

"Absolutely," she said. "I love what he says—the only way to stop a bad guy with a gun is with a good guy with a gun."

"Well, then, let me ask you," I said to Joyce, lifting the mic to her mouth. "There are something like 270 million guns in this country. Is Senator Wynn right when she says we need to get a lot of those off the streets?"

"Actually, guns make us safer," Joyce told me. "Firearm ownership is at an all-time high and violent crime is down. Do you know that someone tried to break into our house last year?" Joyce said, looking at me with new urgency. "And it took the police fifteen minutes to get there!"

"Oh, my gosh," I said. "What did you do?"

Joyce looked over at Tom. "I introduced him to my friend Sig Sauer," he said. "Shot a couple rounds out the window. And funny enough, that guy never came back."

"That'd do it!" Susan said. The other friends gave hearty laughs. "Sixty-two thousand violent crimes a year are stopped by regular people like Tom having guns and fighting off the bad guys," Susan told me. "Virginia Wynn never tells you that statistic."

Wow, this is tougher than I thought. They have an answer to every-thing.

"What about the gun-show loophole?" I asked, thinking this would be my last question. These people were like one-stop shopping for sound bites; we could go after they shot this one down. "What's your problem with closing that?"

"I don't have a problem with closing that," Tom said. Bill and Susan moved their heads back and forth for a second, as if deciding whether to disagree, then shook their heads in agreement.

"Wait, what?" I said.

"Why should there be one bar for everyone, but then a door next to that bar for people at gun shows to walk through?"

He'd lost me. Was that a metaphor or was there really a door next to a bar at a gun show that people kept walking through? "Can you say that again?"

"They should close the gun-show loophole," Bill said. "If we have to fill out background checks, everyone should have to."

Whoa, what? This was getting more interesting. "How about the forty percent of sales that are private, person-to-person transfers to a friend or relative? Should those require background checks?" I knew that'd fire them back up.

Tom reluctantly nodded. "I'm fine with that, I guess. Background checks for everyone."

Is anyone else hearing this? I turned to look at my cameraman to make sure he was rolling on this moment of consensus with Virginia Wynn.

"So beyond closing the loophole," I pressed, energized by the un-expected agreement, "how about keeping guns out of the hands of the mentally ill?"

"Oh, yes," Joyce said. "I'd like to see HIPAA laws changed so that if someone's a danger to themselves or others, that can be added to the gun database."

"Do you realize," I started, "that those measures you just agreed to are the *very things* Wynn is calling for in her gun-control plan?" I was already imagining the eye-opening piece I would send back to Fatima that would reveal that everyone's on the same page, they just don't know it. I bet Benji will play that across the network for days.

"Well, now, hold on," Tom said. "Those are the only things she's *admitting* to, but we know she'll do a bait and switch if she's elected."

"What if she promised *only those things*, nothing else?" I asked. "Then would you support her plan?"

"I don't trust her," Susan said.

That's when I had another stroke of genius. Wynn should reach out to these people, have her own rally here, so she could hear their distrust. Or better yet, I could moderate a "Gun Town Hall Meeting" on FAIR News. I'd get these Fluke folks who want gun rights and Wynn supporters who want gun control and they could all talk to each other. *Benji will go bonkers. Try that, Margot!*

"How about Wynn's no-fly, no-buy proposal?" I pressed, drunk on my problem-solving power. "Stop people on the terrorist watch list from buying a gun. That's a no-brainer, right?*"

I can smell the Peabody!

"Oh, no," Tom said. "I wouldn't agree to that."

"Wait, what?" I frowned. "You're comfortable with a terror suspect being able to buy a gun?"

"Well, no, but I'm less comfortable with someone the FBI claims is suspicious being denied their due process and constitutional right to own a gun just because the FBI doesn't like them. If they're guilty of something, adjudicate them. If not, leave 'em alone. Don't take away their constitutional rights. That's how this country works."

Whelp, I guess I won't be needing that Peabody acceptance speech. But hey, three points of agreement are a start!

"Listen," Susan said to me, as if I hadn't been, "we're here to see Victor Fluke because he understands us. That's why he's going to win this election. And that's why he's the most successful man in the world!"

Susan said it with such conviction that for a second I thought it was an original thought. "Wait," I said. "You know that title is from a *commercial for aftershave,* right?"

"Yes, I know that!" she said. "But he really *is* that successful. He's strong, and decisive, and a natural-born winner."

"Those were the words in the commercial!" I told her, and then we all started laughing, because it was all so absurd—for me, anyway.

"One last question," I said. "Any of you worried about violence here tonight?"

"We've got concealed carry here in New Hampshire," Tom laughed. "So we don't worry about any left-wing agitators bothering us."

"I hope Susan isn't packing heat," I told them.

"Look out, Amanda!" she said, and then we all laughed again.

"Okay, let me get the spelling of all your names," I said, reaching into my pocket for my pen.

"Sweetie, where's your other glove?" Joyce asked me, taking my now red hand in hers and rubbing it. "Oh, my gosh, you're freezing. Here, take my gloves! And you need a hat, too. Tom, give her your hat," she instructed.

"Oh, thanks," I said, waving off her offer of putting on Tom's SUCCESS-FUL MAN cap. "The crew and I are heading inside in a sec. I'll be fine."

"Do you all have a place to stay?" Tom asked. "Cause we've got room, if you don't have a place."

"Oh, thanks, you guys," I said, smiling at the nice and slightly ridiculous offer. "We're going to race back to New York after this."

"Can I get your business card?" Bill asked. "I'd like to have it as a keepsake."

"He'll cherish that," Susan said, and I knew she was being sincere. I was starting to like these people. In fact, the idea of staying at Tom and Joyce's place seemed sort of pleasant. I imagined Charlie and me, up for a weekend, playing cards with them in their den, then enjoying Tom's special blueberry pancakes in the morning.

"Here, take our number," Joyce said, taking a pen from her purse and writing on a piece of scrap paper before pressing it into my hand. "In case you ever need anything."

I laughed. "Thanks. We'll see you guys inside."

The crew and I fought our way through the crowd in the stadium. And every time we hit a logjam of people, Gary would yell, "Excuse us! First Amendment emergency!" When that line got old, he'd try, "Freedom of speech, coming through!" So I was laughing all the way to the corner spot where we locked down the camera on a good shot of the podium. I leaned against a wall, rubbing my cold hand until it could hold a pen again.

Then Fluke walked onstage, and the crowd went nuts.

I spotted Tom, Susan, Bill, and Joyce in the crowd nodding vigorously at each other and clapping. They saw me and waved, and I waved back, like we were old high school pals at an Aerosmith concert. Watching my newfound New Hampshire friends applauding so unabashedly made me listen more closely to Fluke's Laws of Success.

"I've studied successful individuals, like myself, who've amassed personal fortunes. Number one, don't be susceptible to negativity. Be susceptible to success. Be Ameri-*cans*."

He's right. There is something satisfying about the power of positive thinking, I caught myself thinking, until that thought was interrupted by a loud bunch of protestors right near Tom and Joyce, carrying big handwritten signs.

"FLUKE'S SUCCESS IS A SCAM!"

"FLUKE WINS, WE ALL LOSE!"

One sign kept it simple with "FUCK FLUKE!"

I tapped Gary's arm and pointed. "We should get some of those protestors after this is over."

"Reject all negative people," Fluke was booming into the microphone. "Stamp out negativity!"

At that exact moment, I heard a howl come from the crowd. "Fuck you, Fluke!" one of the protestors yelled. I looked over in time to see the crowd start to sway and tussle and some of the protestors push some of the supporters, including Tom and Joyce. I watched Tom put his hands up in a defensive block, right before one of the protestors decked him in the head.

"Oh, my God!" I said. "They hit Tom. We have to get over there."

"Hold on," Gary said. "I gotta get off the sticks and go handheld!"

I kept my eyes trained on the spot where the fight was breaking out and saw another fist fly. I couldn't see it connect, but Joyce reeled backward and fell to the ground. I involuntarily screamed and started rushing toward them. Even through the din, I could hear Tom yelling, "Don't touch my wife! Back it up!" That's when I saw Tom reach down to his lower leg and come up with a gun.

"Oh, my God! No!" I screamed, then watched Tom clock one of the protestors in the side of the head with his gun.

"Squash the negativity!" Fluke yelled from the podium.

A full fracas had erupted. In the blur of bodies, I saw blood coming from Tom's head and the head of the protestor he hit. I watched Joyce try to get up, then get elbowed down again.

"Are you getting this?" I yelled to Gary.

"Yes," he told me.

"Joyce!" I yelled when we got closer. "Tom!" But they couldn't hear me. Security guards were already on them, dragging them out.

By the time the crew and I got outside, ambulances were taking people away and the cops were trying to clear the scene. Fatima emailed that she'd watched the rally live and decided it was so good, we should do the show from New Hampshire in the morning. She'd booked us at the local Comfort Inn and was sending a live truck. I read her text and told Gary and the sound guy that we'd be spending the night, then I climbed in the back of the SUV.

"Coming up here was sure worth it," Gary said, starting the car. "We got some great video."

I didn't respond because I was having a hard time catching my breath, then I put my cold hands to my eyes and did something I had never done on a story before—I started to cry.

"What's wrong?" Gary asked, alarmed.

"God, Gary, I thought somebody was going to be killed in there."

"Who?"

"Joyce and Tom! Or anyone! I thought Tom was going to shoot that guy. None of this should be happening. The country has gone mad. There's so much anger, and they don't even realize that they agree with each other on some things. This election has made people crazy. And it's got to stop."

"Do you want to go to grab a bite?" Gary asked, putting the car in drive. "Or do you want to go to the hotel and get some sleep?"

"I want to go to the hospital," I said. "I want to make sure they're okay."

The next morning, at 6:02 A.M., I stood in the cold in front of the now dark, quiet stadium with one glove on, waiting to give my account of what happened.

"Amanda, get ready. We're coming to you in ten seconds," Fatima said. I heard the loud breaking news bong through my IFB and then Rob's voice.

"Let's go live to Manchester, New Hampshire, and our own Amanda Gallo, who was at the scene of the melee last night and witnessed the violence. Amanda?"

"That's right, Rob. More than ten thousand people filled this civic center behind me for a chance to hear Victor Fluke. He was about ten minutes into his standard stump speech on how to be successful when we heard shouting coming from the floor and I saw a violent fistfight break out."

"And this morning, Amanda, there are some questions about who started that fight. Did you see that part?"

"Yes, I did. It was . . ." At that point I paused, because for a second my foggy 6:00 A.M. brain had scrambled who were the protestors and who were supporters. Joyce and Tom were supporters of Fluke, of course, but protestors of Wynn's gun plan, so what was the other side called? Then my connectors clicked and I knew how to clear up the confusion. "The group that started the fight were left-wing agitators who had come to shut down the rally."

"Now, Amanda, I'm sure you've heard some of the reporting on the other networks that it was the Fluke supporters who started the fight. In fact, there's video of one of them pistol-whipping a protestor in the head."

"No, no, Rob," I corrected. "That protestor, the one who got hit in the head, he started it. He threw the first punch, and, in fact, the Fluke supporter who hit him was trying to protect his wife, who had been hit and knocked to the ground by the protestors."

"And do you have video of that moment?" Rob asked, dutifully and perfectly, as though he'd thought of that question himself and not as though I'd coached him in the commercial break preceding my live shot. The second I'd reviewed the video in the crew car last night, I realized, in horror, that Gary hadn't gotten the money shot of the protestor hitting Tom. And that that was going to be a big fucking problem. I wanted to get out in front of it by explaining how Gary had missed it by running with the camera in his hand for a few seconds, rather than on his shoulder, thereby recording lots of shuffling of feet but not the actual fistfight. By the time Gary got the camera on his shoulder, Tom was clocking the guy in the head. *That,* Gary caught on tape.

"Yes, Rob, we got video of the fight, but not the initial moments of it breaking out because our camera was locked down on Victor Fluke. But I can tell you that it was the protestors who started it by yelling obscenities and becoming violent with the Fluke supporters. And yes, one of the supporters did hit a protestor in the head with a gun, as you can see from the video on your screen right now. But given how many people in New Hampshire carry guns, it's lucky that that protestor was only pistol-whipped and that this melee didn't spiral into something much worse."

I did six live shots that morning, at the top and bottom of every hour, while Rob covered the rest of the show from the studio in New York, and by the time I got back in the car to head home, the blogosphere had blown up with reports of the Fluke supporters starting the fight and my reporting being wrong.

Huffington Post: FAIR NEWS ANCHOR BLAMES "LEFT-WING AGITATORS" FOR MELEE

Salon: AMANDA GALLO CLAIMS VIOLENT FLUKE SUPPORTERS WERE VICTIMS

Stupid mainstream media, I heard myself think. Luckily, I had a four-hour car ride back to New York, during which I could compose a strongly worded email to every single blogger and hater to tell them they weren't there and had no fucking idea what they were talking about. Then I stopped and put my phone down, looked out the window, and thought about the anchorman at Newschannel 13 who wrote back to a critical online viewer comment with the salutation, "Hey Fuckface," and was packing up his desk the next day.

I toggled back to Twitter and found three dozen more hateful messages, along with one toward the top from good ole Frank in Fresno that against all logic made me feel better.

@AmandaGallo. Your coverage of the rally was excellent. I believe you.

God, I must be desperate to seek solace from a foot fetishist. I dialed Charlie.

"What *happened*?" he said, in the same tone he would have used had I been in a terrible car accident.

"Well, there was this fight that broke out," I started.

"No, I know," he interrupted. "I mean, how did you get the story wrong?"

"I didn't get it wrong!" I said. "I saw what happened."

"Then why didn't any of the other stations see that?"

"I don't know, but my crew saw it. Right, guys?" I yelled to the front seat. "Didn't you see the protestors punch Tom?"

"I saw the fight," Gary said into the rearview mirror. "But I didn't see who started it."

"Same," my sound guy said.

"But you saw Joyce get knocked down, right?"

"Yeah, I saw that part," Gary said.

"My crew saw most of it," I told Charlie, wishing I could rewind real life and show it to everyone. "The protestors started it."

"I can't really talk now," Charlie said. "I just stepped out of class to take your call. But I'll see you tonight, 'kay?"

"Yeah," I said. I hung up and for a minute considered sending Charlie the message from Frank in Fresno to show him that *somebody* believed me.

At home I took a long nap, and when I woke up in the late afternoon, the light looked softer and things seemed calmer. I was alone; my apartment was quiet. It almost seemed like I'd dreamt the fight and the angry aftermath. And I was pretty sure I could keep that sanguine feeling, so long as I never logged back onto Twitter. I walked around my apartment in a pleasant, slow-moving fog, enjoying the Friday night freedom from deadlines and second-by-second countdowns, and by the time I got out of the shower, got dressed, and got in a taxi, I was surprised to see it was already close to 8:00 P.M.

Charlie and I had decided, via text, to order dinner in and watch a movie, which seemed like the perfect mindless antidote to my overthinking workweek. Laurie said she might swing by for a beer.

"Hi," Charlie said. "What took you so long? I'm starving."

"Sorry, I guess I was wiped out by the past twenty-four hours. It was all pretty intense. Want to do Curry in a Hurry?" I asked, walking to the kitchen drawer where he kept the takeout menus.

"Sure," Charlie said, "I know what I want." Then, "Amanda?" His voice sounded strange. "Amanda?"

"Yes?" I walked back into the living room and looked at him, but he didn't look back. His eyes were trained on the TV, and I heard my own voice coming from the screen. I turned to see a clip of me from this morning playing in an over-the-shoulder graphic, while the MS-NBC anchor shook his head and looked like he might start laughing.

"You heard that right, folks. Over at FAIR News, aka the Fluke Always Is Right network, their morning anchor Amanda Gallo had an entirely different take on the violence at the Fluke rally. She blamed 'left-wing agitators.'"

The show froze my face midthought, then did a slow-motion push in with my eyes at half-mast, my mouth gaping wide, giving me the look of an imbecile.

"Oh, no," I whispered, my hand flying up to my mouth.

"Gallo even went so far as to say that one protestor was 'lucky' to be pistol-whipped and that something much worse should have happened to him. Honestly, folks, the so-called journalists at FAIR News will stop at nothing to protect Fluke and his followers."

I peeled my hand from my mouth. "That's not what I said."

"Wait, I want to hear the rest," Charlie said, shushing me.

"Whatever Benji Diggs is doing at FAIR News, it seems pretty clear it has nothing to do with news and everything to do with positioning the impresario for his next big gig. Maybe it's chairman of the FCC or television czar or ambassador to Cannes, who knows what he's angling for if Fluke wins? But Amanda Gallo and her Ken Doll of a cohost seem to be in on the scheme."

I grabbed the remote from Charlie's hand and pressed the channel down button fast, finding Anderson Cooper staring back at us.

"And now for the RidicuList," he said. "Amanda Gallo at FAIR News is right at the top. She claims to have seen something at last night's Fluke rally that somehow escaped the rest of the press corps."

"Oh, my God!" I screamed.

"Now, just for a little background, let me remind everyone that Gallo is the same '*news anchor*,'" he used his fingers for air quotes, "who recently spent the first two minutes of her morning show making lewd jokes with her floor crew about erections as though they were at a frat party."

"You were joking about erections?" Charlie asked.

"Oh, God, no. I messed up a prompter read," I said, bringing my fingers to my head to massage my temples, and taking fast breaths, trying to remember exactly what I'd said about Principal Hardon—but it was all a muddled mess.

My phone rang and my eyes darted to the caller ID. *Oh, thank God.* "Mom, I'm so glad it's you."

"Honey, I'm not sure if you're watching the news," she said.

"I am."

"So what do you think happened there?" she asked.

"Mom, I know what happened. The protestors started it."

"But did you get a second source?" Mom asked absurdly. I could tell she was quoting some journalism rule I must have mentioned to her years ago.

"You don't need a second source when you witness something with your own eyes, Mom!"

"Was Laurie there, too?" she asked, and I heard the subtext. If *Laurie* saw it, then it was legit. *She* worked at BNN.

"Mom, I saw it. I don't need Laurie to see it."

"No, of course not," she said. "But BNN had video showing that the Fluke supporters were the violent ones. Either way, why are you focusing on Fluke? Why aren't you covering Virginia Wynn's gun control plan?"

"I had a different angle, okay, Mom? Look, I'm at Charlie's. I gotta go. Let's talk later this weekend." I put the phone down and reached for the remote to turn off the TV. Then we sat in silence.

"Amanda," Charlie said softly, like one might when doing an intervention on an alcoholic. "I think you've given this enough of a shot. It's pretty clear that the morning show experiment isn't working and it's actually hurting your career."

"What does that mean?"

"Look, I heard what your mom just said and she has a point. FAIR News is different than BNN. And you are getting a reputation for being in the tank for Fluke. And that's not a good thing for your future, regardless of who wins this election."

"I'm not in the tank for Fluke," I said. "But I do think his supporters deserve a chance to be heard."

"But they're idiots," Charlie told me.

"They're not idiots," I said. "They actually make some good points. And they're half of this country."

"Yeah, the uneducated racist half."

"That's not true, Charlie. You can't generalize like that. I've talked to them. They're not racists."

"Oh, right. They're Ameri-*cans*, i.e., peasants with pitchforks."

"So what are you saying?" I asked, crossing my arms across my chest.

"I think you've got to get out of there."

I stared at him, trying to absorb it. "Quit my job? I'm a national morning anchor. Do you have any idea how many people would pay to be in my shoes?"

"Sure, but as Harry Truman said, it's never good to be the piano player in a whorehouse." Charlie attempted a half smile, but I stayed frowning, then he said more gently, "Amanda, I know this is your dream, but there's got to be a different way to fulfill it."

My head was starting to feel light and woozy. "Charlie, I can't quit even if I wanted to," I told him. "I'm under contract. That means I can't get another TV job for two more years."

"Maybe you don't have to work in TV. Maybe you could, I don't know, do something in print journalism or teach or something. Do something that gives back to society."

"You don't think broadcast journalism is important to society? Are you kidding? This is my life. This is what I do! I've worked for this since I was fifteen. I'm not going to throw it away because Anderson Cooper thinks I'm ridiculous."

Charlie shook his head. "It's more than just this rally. It's all the crazy segments you're doing. This militant balance that Diggs demands. It's a fraudulent idea of fairness. Ban abortion, no don't. Ban gay marriage—or maybe not. Maybe food stamps are bad, maybe they're good. Cut taxes for the rich, no don't! You really feel comfortable peddling this kind of misinformation?"

"No, I don't feel comfortable!" I said. "And maybe that's the point. Maybe it's a useful exercise for a journalist to be *uncomfortable* with her subject matter sometimes. Yes, we put on opposing opinions, and I'm forced to really listen to all of them and think about them. Television news is not a university lecture hall with a professor pontificating while everyone has to dutifully take notes!" I had a feeling that one might hit a little close to home, but Charlie was pissing me off with his holier-than-thou crap.

"Amanda, be honest, your show is a bullhorn for Victor Fluke because that's what gets ratings. That's not journalism. It's television. If Victor Fluke wins, you and your show will in large part be responsible. You gave him a platform and access to millions of people that he wouldn't have had. Can you live with that?"

"I don't see it that way, Charlie. We didn't create him, we covered him. And if we hadn't, somebody else would have. You assume putting him on TV has a positive effect on his campaign. Maybe it's the opposite. Maybe it exposes how little he knows. Maybe seeing Fluke on our show galvanizes Wynn supporters and motivates people to vote against him. You don't know what people do with the information. Besides, don't you want to hear from his supporters? Find out what they want? Why they're angry? I've met them. They think the media treats him like a joke. And to them, he's not a joke. He gives them hope. You know, I learned something at that rally. Fluke's supporters are not as extreme as we think. There's room for compromise. But we've got to get together to find it. That's what I'm trying to show."

I was drained and done with my soapbox. "Listen, Charlie, is there any way you could just be supportive? So much of my life is intense, I don't want to have to fight you, too."

Charlie sighed. "Do you realize this is all we talk about, your job? Beyond that, I'm not sure how to get your attention."

I was tempted to dispute that, but he was right. I couldn't remember the last dinner conversation we'd had that wasn't FAIR News focused. And it had been a long time since I'd had the energy to join him and his friends for their Freestyle Frisbee in Central Park.

I heard a quick knock on the door. The knob turned, and Laurie waltzed in. "Hey, hey," she said. "What's wrong?" she said, seeing me.

"Did you see the protestors start the fight at the rally?" I asked her without saying hello.

"No," she said. "I was outside with that National Guard guy. But I saw all the Twitter insanity about what you reported."

"And?" I asked.

"I'm sure the protestors started it in one part of the stadium and the Fluke supporters started it in another part." She shrugged at me. "This too shall pass."

I looked at the TV screen, which was now off, and tried to imagine my discomfort passing. That didn't seem likely as long as Fluke was around. God, what happens if Fluke wins? What happens if he loses? Either scenario was starting to seem inconceivable.

"Any progress getting the housekeeper to talk?" I asked.

"Still working on it," she said.

Chapter 23

Pot Luck

I reached up to ring the buzzer at Karen Burke's apartment. Karen was one of the liberal pundits we used on the show. She was always reasonable and somehow maintained her sense of humor through all the debates with Fluke surrogates. I enjoyed her appearances, particularly because she tended to make eye contact only with me, even when Rob asked a question. "If you keep looking at Amanda, I'm gonna have to cockblock you, Burke," Rob told her the last time she was on, which cracked Karen up. During a commercial break, she invited me to swing by her potluck party on Saturday. So here we were in Brooklyn, on her brownstone steps, holding the foil-covered cornbread Charlie had baked and cradling a bottle of red.

"Well, hello there!" Karen said, pulling open the door and revealing a couple dozen guests clad in varying shades of boho neutral. I sensed hemp. Karen was wearing what looked like men's pleated pants and a plain white T-shirt covered by a baggy suit jacket, like an overgrown four-year-old playing dress up in her dad's clothes.

"I was hoping you'd show!" she said.

"This is my boyfriend, Charlie," I said, motioning with my shoulder toward Charlie, who was sizing up the surroundings.

"Lucky guy," Karen said, shaking his hand. "Hey, everyone," Karen said, turning to the gaggle of hipsters standing in small circles. "Say hi to Amanda and Charlie." The low din died down, and for a second I could swear I detected snickering.

"Make yourselves comfortable," she said. "Let me get you some wine." Karen took the bottle from the crook of my arm, walked us over to the makeshift bar on a table in her living room, grabbed a corkscrew, and opened it. "Help yourself to grub. I wouldn't call it haute cuisine but if you like vegan chili, you've come to the right place." She elbowed Charlie in jest.

I felt a tap on my shoulder. "So," the guy said. "Did I hear you work at FAIR News?"

"That's right," I nodded, though I didn't recall Karen announcing that.

"What the fuck are you doing here?" he asked. I couldn't tell if he was joking or drunk or neither.

"Don't worry," Karen said to him in a stage whisper. "She's one of us."

"I'll take that wine now," I said.

Karen splashed a hefty pour into a water glass and leaned in closer to me. "Listen, there are a couple of people here who would be very interested in talking to you."

"Oh?" I said. "Who?"

"There's a woman from the Daily Beast and a guy from TVNewser and I thought—"

"Oh, no," I said, feeling the little hairs on the back of my neck stand up. "I don't want to do that."

"Hey, no worries," she said throwing her hands up and taking three steps back. "You don't have to talk to them. I'm just sayin' if you *were* game, they'd love to have a conversation about FAIR."

"I don't want to," I said. "I'm not here to talk about work." I looked over at Charlie for backup but his eyes were open to the possibility.

"I get it," Karen said. "But just so you know, they're cool. They'd keep everything totally confidential. They're *very* interested in hearing how decisions are made over there, ya know? Why the network's decided to be all-in on Fluke. There's word that Benji Diggs and Fluke go way back. Maybe Fluke is financing FAIR—or the other way around . . ." She raised her eyebrows at me expectantly, like maybe I'd answer that question. When I didn't, she turned to Charlie and kicked her tone to upbeat. "So, Charlie, what do you do?"

"I teach at NYU, in the history department."

"Really? I went there. Political science. We must know lots of people in common."

"Let's see," Charlie said, thinking. "Professor Halloran?"

"Of course! He's a riot. There was one day when I was late to class . . ."

Charlie and Karen began trading school stories and I turned to look around the room. My eyes fell on a small cluster of guys in their twenties, clad in jeans and T-shirts. The short one seemed to be pointing in my direction, but retracted his hand when he saw me staring. I cocked my head and walked toward them.

"Can I help you guys with something?"

"You're Amanda, right?" one asked.

"Yes."

"Right, we recognize you."

"Oh, yeah? You guys watch FAIR News?" I asked.

"Oh, fuck, no," one said. The others cracked up.

"We saw you last night on Rachel Maddow's show," another explained.

"Oh." My stomach twisted.

"She did an entire segment on you," the first one added.

"What did she say?" I asked slowly.

"She said that you were a Fluke apologist and you're, like, very sympathetic to his followers. And I guess, you don't, like, do much fact-checking."

A bubble of bile burst in my gut. "Funny, she never called me to check her facts or get my side. I guess other news networks don't need both sides."

"I saw a clip of you on the *Daily Show*," the shorter one said. "Do you like being on there?"

"What do you think?" I snapped. "Would you like being mocked on national television?"

"Any publicity is good, right? Isn't that what you say in your biz?" the second one asked, shrugging. "Hey, did you really say that the protestors are more violent than the Fluke freaks?" At that, I noticed one of the silent guys reach into the pocket of his jacket. He didn't pull anything out but I thought I saw the outline of his knuckle press something. He looked up quickly and our eyes locked.

"Where do you guys work?" I asked him.

He glanced at the others.

"A think tank," one said.

"Really? Does it have a name?"

"You wouldn't know it. It's a nonprofit."

"Um-hum," I nodded.

"So can we ask you a question?" the first guy said.

"Depends."

"Why do you work at FAIR News? I mean, I'm sure you could get a job at a real network." He said it as compassionately as a college career counselor.

"And where would that be?" I pressed, though I had a hunch.

"Anywhere else. ABC, NBC. One guy I graduated with went to be a researcher for Gabe Wellborn. I mean, I know that's the pinnacle, but maybe someday you could work for him instead of someone like Benji Diggs."

I felt my jaw clenching. "You don't know what the fuck you're talking about," I said, lowering my voice so as not to yell. "You don't know the first thing about Benji Diggs or Gabe Wellborn. Benji Diggs is trying to get both sides to talk to each other. And by the way, Fluke's followers are real people. They have real feelings, too. They bleed when they're hit in the head, too."

The guys exchanged nervous glances, like, "Hey, get a load of the crazy lady," which only spurred me on. "You guys should get out more often and expand your minds. And I don't mean with edible marijuana. I mean by meeting people outside your little orbit. Try seeing the other side sometime." I turned around, my face hot, and felt their stares lingering on my back.

I scanned the room for Charlie, suddenly desperate to grab ahold of his hand. The party had gotten more crowded, and I found myself avoiding eye contact while searching for shelter, like a bathroom where I could hide. *Charlie's probably bored senseless by now. The faster I find him, the faster we can get the fuck out of here and go home to my couch and share a pint of chocolate ice cream. There he is, thank God.*

Over near the makeshift bar where I'd left him, Charlie stood next to Karen, in a circle of people holding beer bottles and laughing, riveted by some sort of gag Karen was reenacting.

"So Professor Halloran says, 'This isn't a bank, Burke. You can't just come here and make deposits when you feel like it,' and he tosses my paper back at me with the pages flying like confetti!" Karen's hands flew up and sent a handful of cocktail napkins fluttering up in the air. Everyone squealed in surprise.

I tapped Charlie on the shoulder. "You ready to go?"

Charlie turned and looked at me. "What? We just got here. It turns out Karen and I know lots of the same people. She was a TA for Halloran! How funny is that?"

"Hilarious," I said, stone-faced. "Can I talk to you for a second?" I grabbed Charlie's arm, tugging him away from the circle and into the kitchen. "Listen, something's up here," I whispered. "Everyone's staring at me. I feel like I'm wearing a scarlet letter. F for FAIR. We need to go home."

Charlie walked to the sink, where he put down his empty beer bottle then stuck his hand into a tub of ice and extracted a new one, grabbing an opener off the counter and popping off the top.

"What are you doing?" I asked. "You're taking one for the road?"

"Listen, Amanda, I don't want to rush out of here. When is the last time we went to a fun party? We used to do this a lot, remember? Maybe you should talk to some of these people. This is your opportunity to let everyone know about the stuff going on at FAIR. Don't you want to expose the crap they do with Fluke, the producers' pathetic research packets, the fact that Benji Diggs decides what you should report based on ratings?"

"Actually, no, Charlie," I said. "I don't want to be a mole. I like being a journalist, remember?"

"Good luck with that," Charlie snorted.

"What does that mean?"

"I mean good luck at FAIR News. You always wave the journalism flag, but they're silencing you. Benji won't even let you report the housekeeper story."

"I told you. He said we need to get the woman. He doesn't want to cover rumors. That should be a good thing!" I took a deep breath to calm myself down.

"Look, let's not talk about work. For once. Let's just have fun here tonight."

"But I don't feel comfortable here. I feel like I don't belong in this crowd anymore. They hate FAIR News. They don't get what I'm trying to do. They don't care about hearing the other side. They don't even think there is another side."

"Conservatives don't care about the other side either," Charlie pointed out.

"Right! The country has retreated to their corners! And I'm out here in the wilderness, trying to call everybody to the middle for a conversation. It's kind of a lonely place." I was hoping that was the point when Charlie would throw his arm around me and tell me I wasn't alone. We were in this together.

"That's a nice notion, Amanda," he said. "But it's naïve. You can't have it both ways. You've got to pick a side. These are our people. You've spent so much time at FAIR, it's like you've forgotten who your friends are."

"I do pick a side, Charlie," I said more emphatically. "In my personal life. And in the polling booth. But the rest of the time, if we all just stay in our comfy corners, then we're not going to find solutions or even hear each other. You're the one who talks about Tip O'Neill and Ronald Reagan fighting by day, then sharing drinks in the White House at night. I mean without that, we might as well divide into two separate countries right now. The Divided States of America."

"I'm okay with Texas and Alabama seceding, frankly," he said with a smile, and I felt like he hadn't heard a single other word I'd said.

"Guess what? It's not just those states," I said more loudly, trying to get his attention and using my thumb to point back at the partygoers. "Do you know there are more people who call themselves conservative in this country than liberal? What are you going to do? Ignore the whole heartland?"

"Amanda, take it down a notch. The people at this party are nice people. These are our friends. If you feel like they're singling you out, why don't you just tell them that you're working at FAIR for the paycheck. Everybody understands that."

"Because that's a total cop-out! Yes, I need the paycheck. But I'm also trying to accomplish something. Look," I said, smoothing out my tone and trying a new tack, a more practical one, to get Charlie to understand, "the producers at *Wake Up,* they're really just kids. And you're right, they have no clue what journalism is. But I think I might be getting through to them. They're doing some better research, they're checking their facts more. I've gotten some of Topher's stupid pitches killed. You know, baby steps."

A crooked smile pulled on Charlie's cheek. "You think you're changing FAIR News?"

"Yes, I think I might be," I said with conviction, hoping I was right. "Fatima is going along with my suggestions. She's pressing the producers to be more true and equal."

"True and equal? Listen to yourself, Amanda!" Charlie said. "It's like you have Stockholm syndrome. You're buying the bullshit that Benji is feeding you. You think that jackass Ro-ob"—Charlie stretched his name into two syllables—"is a journalist? He's an idiot!"

I retracted my head as though Charlie had thrown a jab, though I didn't know why that one stung. "Maybe you're the one with Stockholm syndrome," I said, my voice ticking up again. "Maybe you're not dealing with the fact that the country is bigger than Brooklyn."

"Yeah, I get it, Amanda. We're in a bubble. But that doesn't mean you need to pander to the redneck racist homophobes in the rest of the country."

My eyes grew wide. "Oh, that *is* what you think. You think that people in the Midwest and South are redneck homophobes. You think the Fluke followers are all racists." I shook my head. "I used to think that, too. But now I know them. I hear them." At that moment, I realized I was using my pointer finger to jab Charlie in the chest, so I stopped. "And here's the kicker. Those people like watching me on the news. So maybe if they *are* all as narrow-minded as you think, maybe I have a chance to expand some minds. Maybe I could make them open to compromise. Maybe I could help heal the division. I'm in a position to do that!"

"Wow," Charlie said slowly, staring at me and shaking his head. "That's quite a messiah complex. You really think you can bring the nation together by working at Benji Diggs's Fluke factory? I think, Amanda, that you are genuinely confused."

I stared at Charlie and felt sick that I'd ever considered sharing the silly idea that we would someday visit Tom and Joyce. God, maybe I *was* confused.

"You tell yourself you're in journalism to change the world, but you're the one who's changed," Charlie went on. "Your clothes. Your hair. Your politics. You care more about your viewers than what real people around you—" he gestured to the party. "Okay, I'll say it—educated people think about what you're doing."

"Yeah, Charlie," I said, my voice now sharp and sardonic, "I'd say what I'm doing on national TV is a tad more important than whatever these bloggers are writing."

"Ah, so you admit it," Charlie said, taking a step away from me. "You like the fame and power. This isn't about hearing both sides. It isn't about being *fair*. It's about you and your childhood dream."

I stared up at his face. "Why don't you want this for me?"

Charlie paused. "All yours, Amanda," he said, putting down his full beer on the counter and moving past me to walk away.

"Wait, are we leaving?" I asked.

"Yes," he said, "but not together."

Chapter 24

Right and Left

I'd never noticed how quiet my apartment could be on a Sunday morning without Charlie making coffee and giving a running commentary on the Week in Review section. I slumped onto the sofa and tried to think back to how we'd gotten to this point. We seemed a long way from our best times. And it was painful to remember. Our trip to Orcas Island last year. The two of us with his friends, grilling fresh salmon. One night after a couple of bottles of red wine, we'd taken turns reading aloud from a David Sedaris book. We'd laughed and laughed and it seemed to me that night that Charlie and I were meant for each other and we should get married and live off the land in farm-to-table harmony, or whatever that translated to in Midtown Manhattan.

God, was Charlie right? Had I put my career above my love life? Had our relationship always had issues? I couldn't remember now how I'd felt before.

I looked at the phone, wishing I could call Laurie, but 9:00 A.M. was way too early for her to be conscious. I dug in the sofa cushions for the remote and clicked on FAIR's weekend show, which was covering another Fluke SUCCESS! rally, this one in Wisconsin. I flicked it off and reached for the phone.

"Did you get the article I sent you on the health-care system?" Mom started after answering.

"Got it, thanks," I said. The fact that my mother considered herself my primary source for news usually amused me, but this morning it made me want to hang up.

"So did you watch Margot's special with Virginia Wynn Thursday night?" she asked.

"Uh, no. I was a little busy at the Fluke rally, remember? But I saw some clips online."

"Wasn't she so impressive? I don't mean Margot, I mean Virginia Wynn. She's so smart and all of her ideas on gun violence are smart and commonsensical. She's working with the Brady Campaign! That's why I can't understand why anyone would ever oppose them."

I sighed. "Because that's not who she should be working with, Mom."

"What do you mean? They're the foremost authority on gun control."

"Yeah, that's my point. That will never move the needle, because she's preaching to the choir. What Wynn should do is go to New Hampshire, or Texas, or Alabama, and go to a gun show. And sit down with all the people there and hear *them*. You know? All the people who think she's out to get them. Get *their* ideas on stopping gun violence. See what *they're* willing to compromise on."

Mom snorted. "That's never going to happen."

I sighed. "I know that."

"I have a funny story to tell you," she rolled on. "So, you know the neighbors Joe and Sally, who I told you are big FAIR News fans? Particularly Joe. He's probably seventy years old and he loooves you."

"Ah yes, my fan base . . . old men," I said, trying to sound upbeat, hoping not to have to tell Mom about my fight with Charlie.

"Yes, well, they were asking about you, as they always do, and how it is that I'm a liberal and you're a conservative Fluke fan! I laughed and assured them you're a good liberal, too. That covering Fluke is just your job."

I sat silent on the other end of the phone.

"Amanda? Are you there? Did I lose you?"

"I'm here."

"I'm right, aren't I?" Mom asked, her voice getting a note higher. "You're still a liberal, aren't you?"

I sighed.

"Amanda?"

"I'm not even sure what that means anymore, Mom."

"What do you mean you don't know what that means?"

"I mean, I guess I'm tired of having to fit into a liberal or conservative box. Why can't they both have good ideas? I've been struggling with this, Mom. Maybe you can help me. Can we play a little word game?"

"Okay," she said, her voice tilting upward with apprehension.

"Describe liberal in three adjectives."

"Well, let's see," she started. "I'd say generous."

"Yup, I'd say that, too," I replied. "But I learned something shocking last week. Conservatives actually give more money to charity than liberals. Can you believe that?"

"No," she replied, "I can't and I don't. I've read it's actually the lower class that gives a larger percentage of their income to charity than the upper class."

"Hold on," I said. "We did a talking point on this. It is true that the poor give a larger chunk of their money to charity than the rich, which is amazing, you're right. But it's conservatives who do most of the giving. I read an article on how conservative households give thirty percent more to charity each year than liberal households. Oh, and get this! They also volunteer more of their time. And give more blood!"

"I find that hard to believe," Mom said after a moment. "That must be from one of those right-wing outfits that does pseudo research."

"It was in the *New York Times*. Oh, and by the way, conservatives are also happier than liberals!" I said, almost slapping my own forehead.

"I don't remember seeing that," Mom said, terse. "Well, maybe Republicans give more money because they make more money than Democrats."

"Nope. The study adjusted for income. In fact, the liberal families on average made more money than conservatives. See, Mom, we have these notions about the other side, and I gotta tell you, it's been mind-blowing for me to find out where I'm wrong."

"What about Charlie's friend John you told me about? The one that started that arts program that brings theater and dance and poetry into impoverished schools," she countered. "*That's* what liberals stand for."

"You're right, Mom. And you know what John told me the last time we had dinner with him? That the teachers' unions are bleeding the system dry. So dyed-in-the-wool Democrat John, altruistic do-gooder, thinks tenured teachers and lavish pensions are the death of the arts. Does that make him a liberal or a conservative?" I asked.

Mom tsked. "I guess you'd have to ask him. But I would also say that a defining characteristic of being a liberal is tolerance. Conservatives are intolerant of anything that threatens their values."

"Again, I agree with you. But maybe liberals are only tolerant of their own causes, like climate change and gay marriage—not of conservative causes like gun rights and lower taxes."

"Well, you seem to have given this more thought than I have. I don't have other examples at the moment," she said. "This is just what I feel and have always felt about liberals. We're more kind."

"I've always thought that, too, Mom. And I'm giving it a lot of thought lately because I interview people on both sides every day, and it's weird, these Fluke supporters are also kind. They said the crew and I could stay at their house last week in New Hampshire."

"That's nice. You could have watched them write their vile signs."

"Liberals have vile signs, too, Mom. There were a lot of f-bombs on posters."

Mom sighed and I could tell our little game was wearing thin. "Look, honey, these are interesting issues and I'm glad you're thinking about them. I just don't want to see you lose yourself and what you stand for. What does Charlie think?"

I paused, last night coming back like a stab wound. "He thinks I'm losing myself."

Mom was quiet on the other end, then, "You know there's more to life than just your job."

She didn't have to say "like having a family," I heard it and at the moment it felt painfully out of reach.

"Listen, Mom, I'm trying to figure it all out. How to be fair to both sides and solve problems. And what being successful means to me."

"It's terrible that Victor Fluke has co-opted that word. I can't hear 'success' without feeling ill."

"Well, this might make you feel better. Laurie thinks she is on the verge of getting the housekeeper to speak. She's been working on it for months. And if that happens, Fluke's supporters will finally see the truth about him."

"Well, I know you're doing your best, too, sweetheart. And just remember, there's a lot in life we don't get to choose, but you do get to pick your own path. I can't remember who said that."

"I think it was Oprah."

"Probably," Mom said.

"Thank you, Mom. I'll try."

Chapter 25

Hard Out

3:20 A.M. The sky was pitch black, as usual, but somehow it felt darker when I left for work twenty minutes earlier than usual. I'd spent most of the night sad and anxious, tossing from side to side, thinking about Charlie. At 2:30, I gave up. It wouldn't hurt to get out of bed, get my mind off our fight, and get a jump on the research and articles I hadn't had the energy to read over the weekend.

When I keyed into my office, I saw a FedEx box sitting in the middle of my desk, that hadn't been there when I'd left on Thursday. The label was marked for Saturday delivery. It took me a couple of seconds of looking at the return address to connect who Joyce Keller was. Opening it, I found a note resting atop tissue paper.

> *Dear Amanda,*
>
>   *Thank you for coming to check on us. The nurses told us you stopped by. We're fine, just some cuts and bruises. I guess it comes with the territory. Hope you'll come back up sometime and see how real Granite Staters behave. Until then, we want you to have these for your outdoor assignments.*
>
>   *Sincerely,*
>   *Joyce and Tom*

I reached through the tissue paper and felt something fuzzy, then pulled out two mittens, clearly handmade, striped in garish yellow and brown yarn. Never in a million years would I wear them, but I found myself pressing them against my heart and holding them there.

I picked up my phone to call Charlie and tell him about the gift and how nice Joyce was to think of my cold hands instead of her bruised back. But then I remembered, I couldn't share the story because he wouldn't see it that way. So I stood still in the middle of the room, wondering what to do. I walked to my chair, dropped down into it, turned on my computer, and took out a notepad. *Dear Charlie*, I wrote, then stopped. *I'm sorry,* I wrote, then stopped and crossed it out. Sorry for what? I put down the pen and stared straight ahead for a couple of minutes, trying to figure out how I felt and how to write it. But nothing came. I pushed aside the notepad and clicked open my email, and at the sight of the first message my heart jumped. I smiled and exhaled. Oh, thank God, a message from Charlie.

TO: Amanda
FROM: Charlie
RE: Urgent
Look at this. A student sent it to me. It's anonymous. Scary. You've gotta get the hell out of there.
C

A link to a viral video was not what I was hoping for. Still, I clicked on it, then jerked back in my chair as discordant notes droned out from the speakers and cartoonish red blood dripped down the screen. A headless torso popped up, growing bigger as it moved closer. An ominous automated voice filled the speakers: "We are watching you, Amanda Gallo. Beware. Your support for gun lovers and antiabortion extremists will come back to haunt you. Stop worshipping at the altar of Victor Fluke. We will not sleep until you are silenced." The video stopped there and cut to black. A shiver ran across my shoulder blades, and I jumped up to look out the window into the dark night. Down on the street sixteen floors below, I could make out a lone shadowy figure standing in the middle of the block. What was he doing down there? Was he waiting for me? *My God, Amanda, get a grip. He's probably just trying to hail a taxi.* Plus, FAIR News has guards like Stanley . . . who was sleeping when I walked in. I turned back to the screen, afraid to touch one of the keys for fear of the ghoulish image popping back up and blaring back at me again. With shaky hands, I picked up the phone and dialed.

I could hear Charlie fumbling with the phone. "Hello?"

"Hey," I said.

"Who's this?"

"It's me! Who do you think it is?"

"Oh, sorry, you're coming up as 'Unknown.' What time is it? What's up?"

"I just saw that terrifying video you sent."

"Yeah, scary stuff."

"No kidding." I stood up and peered out the window into the dark again, but the guy was gone.

"If this doesn't give you a reason to run screaming out of that building, I don't know what will." Charlie's voice was losing its sleep layer and gathering steam.

"Who are these people that think I support Victor Fluke and that I love guns, or whatever the fuck they said?"

"Why wouldn't they?" Charlie said.

"Are you fucking kidding me?" I shouted. "He's a guest on the show! It doesn't mean I support him!"

"Here's the thing, Amanda," he said, "live by the sword, die by the sword. If you didn't work there, none of this would be happening. But this is the world you *choose* to work in."

"Charlie, this is scary. I was hoping you could lend some support right now."

There was only breathing on the other end, until he said, "Yeah, I've been trying, but I guess I don't know how to do that, Amanda. I can't tell you how to sort this out, and it seems like you don't really want me to. I've told you how I feel, but that's not what you want to hear." He paused, then said, "I need to focus on my work, too. Midterms are around the corner. I think we should take a break for a bit while we figure out our careers. Just get a little space."

His words hung in the receiver.

"But what about after things calm down?" I asked, because I had a horrible feeling he meant permanently.

"I don't know, Amanda. Let's cross that bridge when we get to it."

"Yeah, okay."

I didn't want to hang up, so I just listened until I heard the click on his end, then I put my head down on my desk and kept it there until my tears made a small puddle on the wood. I tried to banish the memory of our first date from my head. We'd gone hiking, and he'd put his arm around me for the first time, and from our 4,000-foot vantage point, it felt like together we could take on the world. Charlie and I had been together for two years, and now in the space of a few months our relationship had fallen apart. In fact, I couldn't call it a relationship anymore. My boyfriend and I were in a "spaceship."

A swoosh sound surprised me and for a second I thought it was an email from Charlie wanting a redo. But it wasn't. It was an intraoffice email. From RLahr.

RLahr: Checking on you. Saw the onslaught over the weekend.
   Think you can cross Rachel Maddow off the Xmas card list!
AGallo: Did you see that creepy headless video?
RLahr: What video?
AGallo: Some freaky video threatening me for my Fluke coverage.
RLahr: Send me the link. FWIW, I thought you crushed it out there.
   Did you see Fluke's tweet?
AGallo: No. What now?
RLahr: He loves you again.
AGallo: That's all I need.
RLahr: He said you're a "great journalist."
AGallo: Coming from Edward R. Murrow, that's a real compliment.
RLahr: Me or him?
AGallo: Him. You're Ron Burgundy.
RLahr: Hey! I resemble that remark. What's the plan for today?
   Need me to back you up on the rally stuff?
AGallo: I hope it's over. I don't have a plan beyond waiting for BNN
   to get the housekeeper to talk.
RLahr: Quick! Get those pajamas ready!

At that, I actually laughed out loud. After drowning in depth, Rob's shallowness felt like a salve. I grabbed a napkin from my drawer and blew my nose, then used my ring fingers to wipe my tears, delicately, like Jess had trained me to do when putting on concealer. *Conceal the tears. Slather on the news face. Man, maybe TV is soulless.* There was a sudden knock and I jumped. Rob pushed open the door.

"Oh, you scared me!" I said, putting my hand over my heart.

"You okay?" he asked, seeing my face. "What happened?"

"Oh, uh, nothing. Just that creepy video message scared me a little."

"I just watched it. That's scary shit. I bet we could get security to trace who posted it."

"Can they do that?"

"I'll find out. I'll email them the link. But hey, in the meantime, I figured you could use a bodyguard to take you downstairs," he said, holding out his arm, "cause is there anything more manly than a guy in a lilac shirt heading to the makeup chair?"

Chapter 26

Suzy Berenson

"Hello?" I answered my office phone tentatively, wondering why the PR department was calling. *God, I hope I didn't screw something up on the air.* It had been almost a week since my reporting at the Fluke rally was criticized and I'd tried to be as careful as possible about every word out of my mouth, so as not to inspire another Rachel Maddow segment or set off another social media tsunami. I became intensely neutral, avoiding declarative statements, thereby making *Wake Up, USA!* deadly dull. Rob tried to draw me out of my stiffness by cracking jokes and asking me direct questions, but I was afraid to cross the Fluke haters, who continued to send nasty tweets, or piss off the Fluke followers, who might stop watching. "A month away from Election Night and we're on a ratings roll. Keep it up!" Benji told us via Fatima. "Keep the Success train rolling!"

"Amanda, this is Susan in PR," the woman on the phone said. "Benji wanted me to check your availability to appear at his charity fund-raiser tomorrow night. As I'm sure you know, Benji gives a lot of money to cancer research, and this is his annual gala. Unfortunately, he's out of town this week and won't be able to make it, but he'd like you to attend."

"Oh, okay," I said.

"Also, Katie Couric was supposed to be the emcee for the night, but she just dropped out. Benji is asking if there is any way you would consider emceeing. He knows it's last minute, but he's in a bind. I've looked over the duties and they sound fairly straightforward, just prompter reading and schmoozing. You'd be giving Julie Andrews a Lifetime Achievement Award. Oh, and you'd be sitting with the prince and princess of San Marino. I've emailed you a link to last year's gala so you can check it out."

I clicked on the link and saw Katie Couric and Robin Roberts and Meredith Vieira, along with famous actors and musicians, all smiling in their black-tie finery. And look who the emcee was last year! Suzy Berenson! Oh, my God, I'd truly be following in her footsteps!

"Benji asked for you specifically . . . unless you're not available."

"I'm available! It looks wonderful."

"Very good. We'll arrange a car for you."

"But, um, it looks very fancy. I'm not sure I have anything to wear on short notice . . ."

"I suggest you call Meg. I'm sure she can find you something."

"Look at this one!" Meg's assistant gushed the next afternoon, as she petted a beautiful black frock with long fluffy feathers around its hem.

"That's my favorite," the other assistant swooned.

Surveying the rack of jeweled gowns, freshly delivered from the designers' showrooms, I lifted the feathered one and stared at it. "Wouldn't I look like a fancy ostrich in this? Maybe I should do a more basic ball gown."

"Hush," Meg silenced me with her hand. "Take off your clothes."

Meg's go-to command. I could only imagine how it worked on her husband.

Together, the three worked like fairies, fluttering around me, tugging, zipping, and cinching me into the feathered dress, and when they were done, Meg declared, "Voila."

I spun around to face the full-length mirror. I didn't look like Big Bird—I looked like a starlet about to accept an Oscar. I picked up the lint brush from Meg's desk and spoke into it. "I'd like to thank members of the Academy."

"It doesn't get more fabulous," Meg said, her reflection marveling at me in the mirror. She folded her arms in satisfaction. "That's the one."

"What about shoes?" I asked and awaited Meg's admonishment that I should have dealt with this before three P.M. on the day of the gala. Meg and the girls simultaneously looked down at my brown clogs and frowned.

"You'll need something strappy," Meg said, pointing to my feet, "and you get rid of those monstrosities."

"What about jewelry?" I asked. *Jesus,* I thought, hearing myself, *I am really ill prepared for these events.*

"I'm sure you have something glittery," Meg concluded.

"Not exactly," I said, taking a mental inventory of the hodgepodge of tangled costume jewelry in a box on my dresser.

"Now step out of this gown. We'll pack it up and have it delivered to your apartment. And remember, take pictures!" Meg pushed me toward the door and out of her office. I looked at my wrist to check the time and realized my watch had stopped. *Bad timing, literally.* I grabbed my coat and raced across Fifth Avenue, through traffic, and swung open the door to a Diamond District jewelry shop, breathless.

"Is the watch guy upstairs?" I asked of a bald man behind a glass case.

"Yeah, he's right up . . . hey, wait a minute!" the old jeweler said, standing up. "You're not that girl I see on the news, are you?" he asked, studying my face. "Amanda Gallo, right?"

I was about to blow past him when something sparkled inside his case, catching my eye, and I stopped to admire the rows of rings and bracelets shining through the glass. "Wow, you're good," I said, wagging my finger at him but not looking up, unable to take my eyes off the incandescent jewels beneath his face. "Very observant."

"I watch you all the time. You're my favorite. I don't watch anything but FAIR News!"

"Thank you. How nice to hear," I said distractedly, placing my hand on top of the glass case, which was warm and begging to be stroked.

"You need a watch battery?"

"Well, yes, I do," I said, snapping back to reality and my race against time. "I'm getting ready to host a very fancy gala. The prince and princess of San Marino will be there," I said, trying to sound matter-of-fact as I registered the man's age—in his seventies—and his apparent willingness to help. "I'll be presenting Julie Andrews with a Lifetime Achievement Award."

His eyes widened. "Dame Julie Andrews? She's my girl." He smiled and cupped his hands to his chin like a boy with a crush. "Hey, I have an idea!"

"Oh?" I said, raising my eyebrows.

"Let me show you some of my jewelry. Maybe you could wear some tonight! I design it all here myself. All made in the U.S.A.!"

"Go U.S.A.!" I said.

"Here, take a look at this." He reached into the case and pulled out a diamond necklace with carats to make Elizabeth Taylor blush. "This would be perfect on you." He let me run my finger along it as he bent down into the case again, this time to extract a huge diamond-encrusted flower ring with a glimmering yellow stone shining in the middle.

"My God, that's stunning," I whispered.

"It's a Canary," he said.

I turned the ring over, pretending to study its setting but scanning its price, handwritten in small black numbers: $38,000.

"Oh, I couldn't possibly afford—" I stopped to slip it on my finger.

"Don't be silly," he said. "Take it! I'll let you borrow anything you like here. I know you're good for it. I know where to find you!" He winked and gave me a warm smile. "How about these beauts?" He pulled out a pair of long, teardrop earrings, each dripping with a dozen little diamonds. I flipped to their price tag: $22,000.

"And of course, you'll need a new watch! How about this one?" he asked, holding up a platinum model with a gleaming diamond face. "I won't take no for an answer," he said. "Let me pack these up for you." He reached for a small silk purse and placed the watch in it, then laid the earrings gingerly on top. I curled my hand around the flower ring, hoping he wouldn't pry it away.

"Wear the ring home," he said. "All I ask is that you keep them safe and send me some pictures." He placed the stuffed purse in my left palm, then took my right hand in his, the ring shining upward. "It's like it was made for you."

"What's your name?" I asked him.

"It's Harold. They call me Heshie. Think of me tonight and tell Julie Andrews Heshie says hello."

. . . . .

I stepped out of the town car into a street lined with limos and an impossibly glamorous crowd milling on the sidewalk: women in mermaid-shaped sequined gowns, their shoulders draped in pashminas to guard against the brisk October night. A red carpet had been rolled down the stone steps and along the sidewalk. I stood behind a long-legged woman in sheer black hose and offered a silent note of gratitude to Meg and the feathered dress. Clutching the frayed silver satin purse I'd had since college graduation, I made my way into the throng, and for a moment I felt the pang of Charlie's absence, though I had a hard time picturing him in this crowd.

"Amanda! Over here!" A tall, pretty brunette in a little black dress called to me from the edge of the rope line, waving a walkie-talkie in her hand. "Yes, I've got Amanda Gallo here," she said, speaking into the device, then to me. "We need to take some pre-event photos with you and the prince and princess. I'm sure you know this, but you must refer to the prince as His Serene Highness . . ."

"Um, no," I said, "actually, I didn't know that."

"And you may call the princess 'Her Serene Highness,' or, if you'd prefer, 'princess,' which, of course, is pronounced 'prin-chi-PAY-sa' in Italian."

"I like that. Prin-chi-PAY-sa," I repeated.

"Okay, step this way. I'll bring you directly to the VIP section."

We scooted through the crowd, up the red-carpeted stairs, through the doors of a grand ballroom, and smack into the backs of two dozen photographers pressed up against a red velvet rope that cordoned off the VIP section from the rest of the gala. Four intimidatingly broad men in black suits and ties, speaking into their sleeves, flanked the area.

"Yes, right away," my handler chirped into her walkie-talkie. "I need to leave you here for your photos while I locate Julie Andrews."

"Oh, okay," I said, watching her flit away. I turned to move into the VIP section, but it was blocked by the red rope attached with a big metal clasp to a solid metal pole. I reached down to unlatch the hook.

"Hey! Whaddya doing?" barked a gravelly voice.

I looked up into the barrel chest of a man wearing a black suit jacket with a round pin on his lapel, and deduced he was one of the prince's security detail.

"Can't go in there," he said, looking over the top of my head.

"Oh, sorry, I was told I had to show up here for photos."

"Who you with?" he asked, not looking down.

"I'm with FAIR News. I'm the emcee tonight."

"What's your name?"

"Amanda Gallo."

The bodyguard looked at me for the first time. "Italian?" he asked.

"Yup." I nodded, and could tell from the faint crease in his cheek that he approved of the answer. "What's your name?" I asked, anticipating the connection. Italians loved to compare hometowns and family names.

"Sal Lamarughini," he said, lowering his lids toward me, with a nod, as if his melodic name were just for my enjoyment.

"Wow, that's beautiful," I said.

"So you work for FAIR News?" he asked, stepping back to size me up.

"Yup," I answered, knowing there was more.

"You've got some real Fluke lovers there, huh?"

"I guess," I said.

"You conservative?"

"Nope."

He moved his lips around as if gnawing on the info. "I'm forty years in law enforcement and we're a conservative bunch, generally speaking. But Fluke makes us look like pantywaists. He's hard core. Funny for a Hollywood actor, right?"

I let out a sniff. "You don't think he could be, oh I don't know . . . *acting,* do you?"

"Yeah, sometimes I do think that. So you like it there?" Sal jutted his jaw toward me. The Italian question mark.

"Yeah, I do."

"They good to you there?" he continued, his chin punctuating the question.

I paused before answering, wanting to linger here in this moment with my new friend Sal and his seeming understanding that I might work somewhere for reasons other than politics and that I could work someplace and not be defined by it. "Yes, they are."

He smiled. "That's all that matters, kid."

"Thanks, *paisan*."

"Ha!" He laughed, then jerked around, as though he'd seen something out of the back of his head and touched his earpiece. "Come on, let's go! Prince is ready for you."

Sal pulled back the velvet rope and I saw the prince and princess both lift elegant hands to summon me to the front. I squeezed past the scrum of paparazzi and scooted up next to the prince, unsure of where to stand or where to look. I had a terrible feeling there might be some international protocol that walkie-talkie girl had forgotten to tell me. "Right here! Over here!" the photographers yelled. The prince guided me to his right side and placed a calming hand around my shoulders. I reflexively reached my jittery arm around his waist and gripped his tux jacket, then froze. *Shit! I'm pretty sure I should not be touching the prince! Oh, God.*

Click, click, click. The cameras flashed white bursts. I forced my face from pained mask to awkward smile and tried peeling my hot hand from its death grip on the prince's jacket without him feeling it, one finger at a time. Just as I was about to attempt a subtle lift of my arm from around his back, the prince leaned down to my left ear and whispered, "Try to pretend you're enjoying this." He straightened back up, still smiling for the cameras.

"All right, everyone. All right. Thank you very much," he said, gently stirring the air in front of us with his hand, signaling that his patience with photos had expired. "We'll see you all inside the ballroom." I saw Sal make a sharp arm gesture, clearing the paparazzi and shepherding the Serene Highnesses through a velvet side curtain.

I stood alone, momentarily lost, scanning the ballroom for walkie-talkie girl to go over my script. *There sure are a lot of beautiful people here.* I caught the profile of one tall, wildly handsome guy, chatting with a beautiful young woman in a beaded gold gown. The guy's brown hair casually fell across his forehead, catching the light. He cast a winning smile at the girl, and she laughed coquettishly, so at ease in his tuxedoed life. *He must be a movie star,* I thought as he turned in my direction. Yes, he does look familiar.

"There you are," he called, lifting his hand to wave, then flashing that smile at me.

Holy shit. How could Rob look so different here? His cheeks were flushed, and his face more smooth than it looked under Jess's cakey makeup. Gone was any trace of the waxen facade he wore on the set.

"Wow, Amanda, you look smokin' hot," Rob said, walking right up and staring at me.

"Thanks, um, you, too. I didn't know you'd be here."

"Yeah, PR roped me into it. How about some champagne?"

"Oh, no, I can't," I said. "I have official emcee duties." I felt a quick but distinct vibration coming from my clutch and pulled out my phone to check it. "That's the rundown," I told him. "Oh, look, you'll never guess who we have on tomorrow."

"Wait, don't tell me!" Rob said, putting his hand up like this was a real game. "Virginia Wynn?"

"Close," I said. "Victor Fluke."

"No way!"

"Ugh," I said, reading the rundown. "He's coming on to talk about his plan to get rid of undocumented immigrants. Or, you know, Ameri-*can'ts.*"

"That's original," Rob said.

"Shit. I should go research some immigration stats," I said, putting the phone back in my clutch and hoping the next time I checked it, it would say something different.

"Don't worry," Rob said, stroking my bare arm. "Think of all we'll have to talk about in the morning. We can show photos from tonight. Viewers will eat it up."

"Well, then let's start snapping some selfies, cause I have to leave right after emceeing. I turn into a pumpkin at nine."

"You got it, Cinderella," Rob said, grabbing my hand and turning to lead me deeper into the ballroom. A waiter with a tray of champagne flutes came toward us and Rob used his free hand to slide two stems between his fingers, then glided his hand from the tray to me. "Just one," he said.

"Okay," I said to humor him, though I planned to put it down as soon as he wasn't looking.

Without warning, Arthur Dove appeared at my side.

"Well, hel-lo, you two," he said, sweet as shoofly pie. His evil Twitter twin nowhere in sight as he kissed me on the cheek and gave Rob a man hug.

"Mr. Lahr, you smell good!" Dove said.

Rob nodded, as if he were used to the men of the world complimenting his scent. "It's my pheromones," he explained. "I can't turn them off. Even middle-aged men from Texas can't resist them."

Dove laughed. "I bet that's a real problem, but I wouldn't know. I just rely on a shower and soap before these events. That's probably why I'm not in the company of a beautiful woman like Amanda."

I glared at him. "It'd take a lot more than a shower, Arthur."

"Ouch," he said. "What did I do wrong?"

"Gee, I don't know. Maybe the last ten nasty tweets about me that you've sent out."

"Oh, don't pay any attention to those," he said. "It's all in good fun."

"Not for me, it's not. When people tell you to kill yourself, it's not that much fun."

"Oh, don't be so susceptible to that stuff."

Rob put his arm on my shoulder to steer me away from Dove. "I hear we'll see you bright and early tomorrow, Arthur."

"Yup. I'm the first face you see in the morning and the last one you see at night."

"Nightmare," I said, under my breath, moving away.

"You're hurtin' my feelings, Amanda," Dove called.

"What's going on?" Rob asked when we were out of earshot.

"I've had it with him. He acts normal when we see him, then he goes into attack mode if I dare ask Fluke a question he doesn't like. I think he's a monster. And I pray after November 8 I never have to spend another morning with him."

"I don't know if Arthur Dove's going to go away that easily," Rob said.

We walked the rows of round tables with bodacious red rose centerpieces until I spotted our table, directly in front of the stage. I circled, reading the names on place cards just above the soup bowls: Ms. Amanda Gallo, Mr. Rob Lahr, His Serene Highness of San Marino, Her Serene Highness of San Marino, Dame Julie Andrews, Ms. Suzy Berenson . . . I stopped.

"Oh, my God! Rob, look who's at our table!" I pointed at the place card as though it might self-destruct before he could see it. "We're sitting with America's Sweetheart!"

"Yeah, and?" Rob looked like he was waiting for more.

"Suzy Berenson's my idol. My mom and I watched her every morning when I was growing up. She's the reason I got into TV news!"

Rob's dimples flared like he was trying to stifle a laugh. "Well, then, this must be your lucky night!" He clinked his champagne glass against mine, then made his eyes super wide and whispered, "Don't look now, but your girl crush is right behind you."

I swung around to see the one and only Suzy Berenson floating toward me, radiating sparkle. She smiled beneficently as admirers circled her, asking for pictures. The flashbulbs made it look like she'd been sprinkled in pixie dust and glittery goodness. I could hear her twinkly laugh as she approached.

"Suzy Berenson, hello!" I gushed, sticking out my hand. "I'm a huge fan, I've watched you every morning since I was a child!"

I saw a quick twitch of her left eye, as though a piece of lint had hit her.

"And you were practically a teenager then!" I added, fast. "I mean, you still look like a teenager."

"Why, thank you," she said, smiling her sagacious smile. "You're clearly a woman of discriminating taste . . . and diplomatic instincts."

"It's true," I went on, still holding her hand, refusing to let go. "You were an inspiration for me throughout college. I studied your delivery and tried to emulate you. Not terribly well, according to my journalism professors, but that's another story."

Suzy laughed. "Well, I'm happy to hear someone was doing something productive at college. I just did a story in Rhode Island, where college kids are engaged in activities that are, hmm, how should I phrase this, more *re*-productive in nature."

"I saw that one! Who knew that universities had such flourishing escort services?" I said.

"I know," Suzy agreed, then we nodded at each other. I couldn't stop staring at her.

"Well," she said, attempting to free her hand, "I was actually just looking for my table somewhere in this vicinity."

"Oh, it's right here," I said, excitedly pulling her to her seat. "We're sitting together!"

"Then this must be the cool table," she said, placing her shiny gold clutch down next to my sad silver one. "Oh, goodness, look who's with us!" Suzy said, pointing at the next name card. "Julie Andrews is at our table!" Suzy grabbed my arm to show me.

"You'll never wash that arm again," Rob whispered into my other ear. I tried elbowing him away but he wouldn't budge. "Julie Andrews is Suzy Berenson's Suzy Berenson!" Rob whispered, before straightening up and gallantly pulling out my chair, then Suzy's, on either side of his. "Ladies, shall we sit before the soup gets cold?"

The prince and princess approached the table, smiling regally. The prince nodded at me. "Ah, very good. I see I'm seated next to Amanda. I know how she enjoys photographs."

Rob took his seat between Suzy and me just as the official event photographer pressed the three of us closer together for a picture. *Snap!*

"Amanda, I'm sorry, I didn't catch your last name," Suzy said, leaning over Rob to face me. "And what's your connection to our esteemed hosts this evening?" I could swear a golden halo surrounded her.

"Oh, I'm Amanda Gallo, I'm emceeing the event tonight."

"Oh, that's wonderful. What a relief," Suzy said to the table as she smoothed her napkin on her lap. "I thought I had read that some anchor bimbo from FAIR News was emceeing."

My soupspoon dropped from my hand, clattering onto the saucer, and for a second I couldn't breathe. My eyes darted to Rob, who looked down into his bowl.

"I thought that was an odd fit," Suzy continued. "I mean, having a fake news anchor host this elegant affair."

"Well, that's funny," I began, trying to swallow the lump bloom-ing in my throat, "I *am* from FAIR News. But I assure you nothing about me this evening is fake."

The prince and princess offered courtesy laughs. "Those ear-rings are lovely," the princess said in a sweet Italian accent, attempt-ing, I knew, to change the subject.

"Just a second," Suzy said, grabbing the side of her chair and turning her body to stare across Rob at me. "You're from FAIR News? But you seem so smart and . . ." she paused, "sensible."

"Thank you, I think," I said.

"Seriously, how can you work there? Didn't you have to sign a manifesto vowing to prop up Fluke? I just read a Pew study on how much airtime you've given him. It's outrageous."

"We do have Fluke on a lot," I said, fighting against the constric-tion of my throat. "And those are always our highest-rated quarters. Clearly, the American people want to hear what he has to say."

"We had a Bengal tiger on my show last week. It rated well, too. But that doesn't mean we put the tiger on every week," Suzy said.

I turned my body toward Suzy and raised my voice. "Something's happening in this country. You can try to ignore it and distract your-self by playing with exotic animals but that's not the way to solve a problem."

The princess, who had been pretending to search for something im-portant in her purse, closed and rested the jeweled clutch on the table.

"Oh, really," Suzy said sarcastically. "I admit I don't watch FAIR News. But I've seen clips on the *Daily Show*. It sure looks like FAIR is giving Fluke a pass. That dreadful morning show, whatever it's called, that has him on constantly, with that insipid anchor. He's the worst. What's his name?"

"Rob Lahr," Rob said, turning to Suzy and offering his hand for a shake.

Suzy's body retracted until she bumped into the back of her chair.

"It's clear you've never seen our show," Rob noted cheerfully, "which is surprising. I'd think a journalist of your 'caliber,'" and here Rob used air quotes, "would want to watch her competition. You know, to see who's gaining on her."

"I don't consider FAIR News the competition," Suzy said, with an expression that could curdle the cream of artichoke soup.

"Well, that must make it easier to sleep at night. But if you check the ratings, and I bet you do," Rob sang flirtatiously, bringing his first finger close to Suzy's body like he might tickle her, "you know that your show is losing viewers every month and our show is adding them. And in case math isn't your strong suit, that's not a winning formula."

The princess sat stoically, hands folded in her lap, looking down. The prince rearranged his salad and dessert forks.

"Congratulations," Suzy said. "You've cornered the market on low-income, low-information, pickup-driving viewers. They aren't exactly advertiser friendly. I think we're doing just fine with our upper-income demographic, thank you very much."

"*That's* an interesting business model," Rob responded, "catering to advertisers over viewers. Let us know how that works out. But I bet you're feeling a little nervous. I bet you know that your network is a dinosaur. And it may not happen this year, but you're headed for extinction."

I suddenly tasted the sharp tang of blood in my mouth and realized I'd pulled a piece of skin from my lower lip with my teeth. "You are in the information business, correct?" Rob went on. "Or do you only do animal stunts and cooking segments? Amanda and I cover news and issues. Do you still call yours a news program?"

I looked at Rob and felt in that moment that he'd gone from being my cohost to becoming my friend.

"Hellooo everyone," Julie Andrews sang as she approached the table in a flowing peach gown. "Don't you all look lovely. Sorry I'm late. It looks like you're already having a grand time."

"Amanda, you're up." It was the walkie-talkie girl, tapping me on the shoulder. "Time for you to begin the program!"

Shit!! I'd never rehearsed the script. I stared at Rob and bit my lip again. He nodded assurance and nudged me up with his eyes. I stood, took a big swig of champagne, and headed for the podium. As my high heels teetered up three rickety wooden steps, Sal Lamarughini appeared from behind a black curtain and offered me his hand.

"Knock 'em dead, *paisan,*" he said. I nodded nervously and approached the podium.

"Good evening, everyone," I started, a little too loudly into the mic. "Allow me to welcome the prince and prin-chi-PAY-sa here tonight, along with Dame Julie Andrews," I read as the teleprompter scrolled. Then the prompter stopped and so did I. It said in parentheses, (AD-LIB INTRO HERE.) *Fuck! No one told me I'd have to ad-lib.* I shut my eyes, hoping if I couldn't see the audience, maybe they couldn't see me. A few long seconds ticked by, then I steadied myself against the podium and opened my eyes.

"Um . . . I'd like to extend a warm welcome to everyone here on this chilly October night. It's a pleasure to be with you all." I could see hundreds of blank faces staring up, waiting. "It's wonderful to be here. First, because I'm rarely up past eight P.M." A few people offered courtesy chuckles. "But mainly because you're such an impressive crowd. New York is a diverse place with lots of people holding lots of opinions. In my job as a newscaster during this election season, I interview many of the most opinionated people in the country. But tonight there can be no debate about our mission as we come together to fight cancer. And I can think of no one who better personifies goodwill than Dame Julie Andrews. In her illustrious career, she's demonstrated how to rise above the fray and face challenges with grace. So tonight, let's all make a commitment to emulate her sunniness, even if you happen to be confronting a storm cloud."

I looked down at the tables, a sea of darkness under the bright spotlight, until I could make out the outline of Rob's face and saw him offer a wink. "So without further ado, may I introduce . . . Dame Julie Andrews."

The crowd clapped as Julie Andrews walked onto the stage and I made my way back to the table. Suzy Berenson had vacated her seat and disappeared. I sat down, took another big swig of champagne, draining the glass, then collapsed against the chair. Rob reached under the table and squeezed my hand.

"Thank God that's over," I shouted to Rob as the band struck up loud swing music, signaling the dancing portion of the evening and my cue to head out to my waiting town car. I took one last gulp of Suzy Berenson's untouched champagne and stood up.

Rob leapt to pull my chair out, then brushed crumbs off his tux. "How 'bout we move to the bar for a nightcap?"

"I can't," I said, reaching for my purse. "I have to go."

Rob cocked his head to the right, causing his hair to fall onto his forehead in a boyish way. "Just one? Come on, prin-chi-PAY-sa," he smiled. "Don't we need a postgame wrap-up?"

I did want to wash down the bitter Suzy aftertaste. "Okay."

Rob grabbed my hand and led me across the crowded dance floor to the candlelit oak bar adjacent to the ballroom. He held up two fingers to the bartender.

"Two glasses of Veuve, please."

"What a night," I sighed, taking my seat on a barstool, then lifting my hand to press on my left temple.

"Dear Diary," Rob started, using his finger as a fake pen, pretending to write on his cocktail napkin. "It's me, Amanda. I met my idol, Suzy Berenson, America's Sweetheart . . . correction"—Rob stopped, pretending to erase the entry—"make that, America's Flaming Bee-atch." He crumpled the napkin and pitched it across the bar like a baseball. "Did you hear that load of horseshit coming out of her mouth? Our high-end demographic . . . Blah, blah, blah. Why doesn't she go get a half-caf venti cappuccino, no foam, extra hot, with a lid stopper so she doesn't spill it on the leather seats in her hybrid Lexus as she heads to the Hamptons?"

"Wow," I said, impressed by his on-the-fly characterization. "You seem to know her intimately."

"I know her type," Rob said. "Pretends to be 'of the people' on the air, then takes a private jet to P. Diddy's White Party to avoid the unwashed masses. I'm sure she thinks anyone west of the George Washington Bridge is a redneck."

Hearing that word made me think of Charlie, and it gave me a sad, unsettled feeling. Maybe Charlie should marry Suzy Berenson.

The bartender gently pushed two glasses of champagne across the shiny wood toward us. I put mine to my lips and let the bubbles burst into my mouth and tingle down my throat.

"And how about that part about me signing a manifesto?" I said to Rob, shaking my head, unable to shake the accusation.

"Don't listen to a word she said, okay Amanda? She can't hold a candle to you. On any level."

"Thank you, Rob," I said, reaching for his hand to pat. "I appreciate everything you said back there. I really do. The problem is I happen to agree with her." I took another gulp and looked off across the bar.

"What does that mean?" Rob asked, placing his first finger under my chin and drawing my gaze back to him.

"Face it, we don't challenge our guests enough, especially Fluke. And these poor kids on the staff *think* they're producing a newscast, but they have no earthly idea what journalism is." *God, now I sound like Charlie.*

"You think Suzy Berenson's morning show is journalism?" Rob asked. "I mean, if you want to learn about the best fall accessories for your pet, then yes."

"Look, *Wake Up, USA!* is not really 'True and Equal.'" I was starting to lean forward on my barstool, toward Rob, beseeching him. "I don't blame Suzy for thinking FAIR News may be responsible for the downfall of journalism. And without journalism, you know where that leaves us? We're supposed to be the watchdogs of government and politicians. Without us, well, that is the end of democracy. I mean, we might be ruining civilization." I took another gulp.

"Are you drunk?" he asked.

"Maybe."

"Is it possible you're using hyperbole for effect?" Rob asked, nodding at me, like one would a naughty five-year-old.

"I don't think so, Rob," I said, girding myself against the bar. "I do feel like boiling myself in hot water after some of those segments with Arthur Dove. The show crosses the line and you *know* it and you don't do anything about it! You're not even trying to solve problems!"

"That's not our job," Rob said.

"That's our mission statement!"

"Not *really*," Rob chided. "That's a Benji gimmick. Our job is to rush into the fire of breaking news—and when no news is happening, to have a fiery conversation in a well-lit studio. Our job is to make good TV."

"But don't you see, Rob? You're not putting out the fire. You're fanning the flames!"

"Way to run with a metaphor!"

"I'm serious, Rob. If you want to be a fireman, stop masquerading as a journalist! This is what is so frustrating about you! You actually know the facts. But you dance around them like they don't matter. It's like you only want the heat, not the light."

I braced for what I knew would happen next: Rob would stand up, probably toss a twenty onto the bar, flip me off, and walk out. And then he'd stop talking to me, like Charlie had done. I reached for my purse to avoid having to sit alone too long in the aftermath of Rob storming out.

"Okay," Rob said after a long exhale, then sat still and looked straight at me. "What should I do differently? I'm all ears."

"That's funny," I said, "I heard you were all hands." I had to beat Rob to whatever punch line he was planning.

"I'm being serious, Amanda," he said, leaning toward me. "I think we have something. It's working. The viewers love us together. If what I'm doing upsets you, let me hear your suggestions."

I put down my champagne and turned my barstool to face him. "For starters, we can't let everyone with an agenda or some crazy opinion say whatever shit they want to on national television. When they lie and make false claims, we shouldn't book those guests again. They have to be fact based, and when they're not, you should call them on it."

"Fair point," Rob said calmly.

"Plus, I know moderate voices don't make for good TV, but extremism is not good for the country. Our guests say some extreme things to get attention and it's toxic."

"I hear ya," Rob said, still looking at me intently. "Some of our guests go too far. I'll give you that. But that's the risk of live TV. We don't know what the guest is going to say before it comes out. It's unpredictable. And admit it, that's what makes our show interesting and more spontaneous. You're leaving out the fun parts."

"Some of it *is* fun," I agreed.

"Remember that piglet and puppy race?" Rob asked. "That was pretty funny."

"You mean when Larry announced we had 'a wiener'?" I said.

Rob shook his head with resignation. "Larry."

"*That's* the crazy part about *Wake Up*," I went on, picking up my champagne flute again and pointing it at him. "Sometimes it's really fun *and* sometimes it's really toxic. That's quite a hybrid, you know. It's almost like we should invent a new word for our brand of news that combines fun with toxic."

"Hmm . . ." Rob thought about it for a second. "How about foxic?"

"Yes!" I slapped the bar. "We're foxic!"

"I want to figure this out with you," Rob said, looking at me. "What else do you think I should work on?"

"Well, let's see. You have a bad habit of saying some words over and over again. It's maddening."

"Like what?"

"God, where do I start? You say 'from the get-go,' and 'let's unpack this.' Oh, you love to say 'touché.'"

Rob looked away, like maybe I was hurting his feelings, then nodded. "Roger that."

"Ah! That's another one!"

"Okay, okay. Too many touchés? So that's it?"

"You would never agree to do what I think we should do."

"Try me."

I took a deep inhale. "The election is one month away. What if we really hold Victor Fluke's feet to the fire? What if we really ask him the tough questions? How about we do a real interview with him, where we don't let him spin? How 'bout we bring up the housekeeper? Our own October surprise."

Rob looked up and to the left, like he was watching the movie of that future moment play out on the mahogany bar. "We do that, it's a one-shot deal," Rob said. "It would piss off Fluke. And chances are he would never come back."

"I disagree. He likes being on TV too much to boycott it."

"But he might go to the competition."

"Well, there you have it," I said, putting down my glass. "I knew you wouldn't want to do it. That's the problem. When push comes to shove, you don't have the balls to do it."

"Excuse me?" Rob said. "Don't make me drop my pants right here. I'll do it."

"Honestly, Rob, aren't you embarrassed that we sit there every morning like we've never heard of the housekeeper scandal?"

"Yeah, sometimes. But then I look at my paycheck and I feel a lot better."

"Rob, I'm telling you, this would put us on the map in a different way. Suzy Berenson could never question our journalistic credentials again. Plus if we confronted him, it would be a coup d'état. A ratings bonanza, in your language."

"Keep talking French," Rob said. "It's sexy."

"I'm serious!" I said, slapping his arm.

"And sexy," Rob said. "Okay."

"Okay, what?"

"Let's go for it. Let's nail him."

"Are you drunk?" I asked.

"Drunk with possibilities," he said.

"So are you in or out?"

"Oh, I'm in, darlin'."

"Okay, then." I steadied myself to glance down at Heshie's diamond watch. "Oh, my God, it's ten thirty! I have to go home. I haven't even studied the rundown yet. Tomorrow's going to be a disaster. I have to get up at three A.M.!"

"Really? That's weird," Rob said, "because SO DO I!"

I let out a whoop of a laugh, champagne almost coming out my nose. "Sorry! I forgot we're in the same boat."

"If there's one person on Earth, Amanda, who understands what your life is like, it's me," Rob said. "I get it. I get you."

"So then why don't you need to go to sleep?"

"Because I'm having a good time with you." Rob smiled that winning smile of his and I felt my chest flutter for a second, which I chalked up to the champagne. "Look," he said, "I understand how hard you prepare and how well you want to do. You and I are more similar than you like to admit."

"Oh, really?" I said, raising an eyebrow at him.

"Yes, really. I want us to do well, too. Only you and I understand how challenging our jobs are. And all the sick social media stuff. And Fatima, and Topher, and Larry." Rob stood up from his barstool and moved closer to my legs. "Only you and I know how 'foxic' it is."

"You make it seem like none of it matters to you," I said, and I could feel his pant leg brush against my bare leg.

"It matters a lot to me," he said. "I know what an incredible opportunity this is. That's why I'm grateful. I know what else is out there, and I know you don't find chemistry like ours." Rob put his hand lightly on my knee. "Trust me, tomorrow will be fine. You're so sharp, you can anchor the show with half your brain tied behind your back."

"I hate to phone it in, Rob," I said, sensing now would probably be a good time to get up and leave. "Plus I need more beauty sleep than you."

"No, you don't," he said, giving me a long look. "You're gorgeous. I haven't been able to stop staring at you all night."

Shit, there was that feeling again in my chest. Rob's body pressed into my legs.

"How about just one more glass?" Rob put his finger in the air for the bartender and slid his other hand around my waist. "We'll share it."

Chapter 27

Blow the Break

My God! What is that racket? Something was making a loud chirping noise, startling me out of a dream in which I was falling, falling . . . the sudden drop leaving me short of breath. My eyes tried to focus in the dark room. *Holy shit! My alarm!* How could it be 3:15 A.M. already? When I checked the clock mere seconds ago, it was 1:21.

I threw off the covers and caught sight of the crime scene. Lying on the floor, my feathered dress in a heap, shoes scattered, and, near the foot of the bed, an exhausted condom. And there, a foot away, another one. I tried to make out a strange object hanging from the lampshade. I squinted to discern its amorphous shape in the dark, until I realized it was my bra. *Good Lord.*

The night was a blur of Rob's skin and mouth against mine, with a few crystalline moments coming back: his strong arms wrapped around me, his warm mouth on my neck. My chest tingled remembering it. Jesus, this guy's a professional. His kisses were smooth and his mouth tasted sweet. *Don't fall for it, Amanda, whatever you do.* I bent down to gather the evidence and dash to the bathroom before Rob woke up.

"Hey," he reached for me. "Come back."

"It's three fifteen!" I said. "The car comes in half an hour. And I think you should take a taxi, so we're not showing up in the same car." Even in my champagne haze, I'd already thought that one out. "I've got to jump in the shower."

"You're right," Rob said, sitting up, suddenly alert. "We don't have a minute to spare. I'd better shower with you."

Against my will, I laughed. "Something tells me that wouldn't save any time." I grabbed a towel from the chair where I'd left it and started toward the bathroom.

"Hey, slow down," Rob said, his voice serious now. He reached for my arm and pulled me back down to the bed. He wrapped his arms around my waist, pressing his warm body against my back. "You're amazing," he whispered. I closed my eyes and could feel my heart pounding.

The town car pulled up to the studio door and I stepped out into the bracing night air, a baseball cap pulled over my wet head, my brain aching from champagne. A second later, Rob's taxi pulled up to the curb directly behind mine. He hopped out and waved.

"Hey, Amanda, fancy meeting you at this hour!" he called, his voice the only sound on the deserted block. "What are the chances?" he asked, striding toward me, looking more handsome than he should, in his black pants and rumpled white dress shirt, tuxedo jacket in his hand. "Wow, rough night?" he asked, his eyes twinkling. "Looks like you didn't get much sleep."

"I'm glad you're enjoying this," I said, hoisting my bag onto my shoulder and steading myself on the sidewalk.

"Oh, very much," he smiled.

We walked up to the side entrance. Through the glass doors we could see Stanley sleeping upright in a chair, arms folded across his chest, passkey in hand. Rob rapped on the glass doors and Stanley startled awake, then leapt to let us in.

"Good morning, sir," Rob said to Stanley, chipper as if it were nine A.M. "Look who I just happened to run into outside. My car coincidentally pulled up at the exact same time as Amanda's, so that's why we're arriving together, both with wet hair."

Stanley stared at us blankly.

I shot Rob a look, then turned and marched straight to the elevator, willing myself not to look back at him, though I could feel his eyes on me.

"Nice bumping into you, Amanda," he called.

I didn't turn around. I couldn't think about Rob . . . or his lips . . . *stay focused!* The elevator lifted, the loss of gravity adding to the light, fluttery sensation in my chest. Maybe I'm still drunk. I leaned against the metal wall, trying to block the images drifting in from last night:

Rob pulling off his tux, his body pressed against mine. *Dammit, stop thinking. How did my bra get on the lamp? And what the hell did I do with all that jewelry? Shit! Focus!* It was impossible to imagine getting through a three-hour show. Staggering into my office, I clicked on my computer and I stared at the rundown for a few seconds, but it looked like a scrambled word cloud. My head was aching in earnest now. It was 4:30. I threw on a bright red dress and ran to the elevator.

5:55 A.M. I raced into the studio, straining to appear calm. Using peripheral vision, I could see Rob going over his notes and whistling to the music. Bruce unzipped my dress halfway, wrestling with my bra strap and the mic pack. "Good tune," I said to distract myself. It took every ounce of discipline not to glance over at Rob on the sofa.

"It was Rob's choice," Bruce explained. "I didn't know he'd ever heard of Neon Trees. I think you're rubbing off on him."

I gulped a mouthful of air.

"Good morning, Amanda," Larry said. "You've got two minutes to air."

"Sorry, guys, I'm moving a little slowly," I said, sitting down two feet to Rob's left, careful not to look at him. "I had an event last night that ran late."

"What was it?" Larry asked.

"It was Benji's charity fund-raiser honoring Julie Andrews."

"Sounds fancy," Larry said, "like something they wouldn't let Rocco into."

"Or your mother," Rocco replied.

"How was it?" Larry asked.

Rob stopped typing and sat still, pretending to study his notes.

I paused, trying to decide how to characterize the night, then decided to just go with the truth. I said, "It was wonderful."

Rob exhaled and inched closer to me, making the skin on my arm prickle. *Focus!*

"Quiet down, everyone," Larry yelled to the crew. "Move over, Rob. Give Amanda some breathing room. You're on top of her. We're live in twenty seconds."

"Shit," I said, my hands shaking. "Can I read through the cold open?"

"You don't have time," Larry answered. "We're up in ten, nine, eight . . ."

I tugged on the hem of my dress, which was riding up, and stared at the teleprompter. *What are we talking about again?*

"Four, three, two . . ." Larry signaled for me to read into Camera 2 as the prompter rolled.

"Good morning, everyone," I began. "New investigations into whether Virginia Wynn's campaign violated any election laws by allegedly registering undocumented immigrants to vote. Victor Fluke will be calling in with his reaction."

I turned to Rob and saw his dimple made a dent in his cheek, as if just for my benefit. "And stick around till the end of the show, when we have a famous pickpocket here to see what he can steal from us! *Wake Up, USA!* starts right now!"

The music rolled.

"Hey, everyone, thanks for tuning in bright and early," Rob began, fresh as a daisy, as though he weren't up all night rolling around in my sheets. Of course, this was second nature to him. He's probably sat here a hundred mornings after various hookups. "Before we get started, let me thank Amanda for a great night."

My head whipped toward him.

"I had the pleasure of watching her emcee a terrific event last night. She helped raise a record amount of money for cancer research." Rob smiled at me. "And, man, you should have seen her," he said into Camera 2. "She was spectacular. Anyway, I got lucky, I mean, I was lucky to be a part of it. We'll show you some pictures later. Now, on to our top story . . ."

8:45 A.M. "You've got ninety seconds to get back to the sofa!" Larry yelled to me from the studio door as I raced toward him with the last remnants of the bagel I'd inhaled in the greenroom, trying to shake off my fluttery feeling. "The next guest is Fluke via phone," Larry read off his rundown as I squeezed past him. "Amanda, you lead."

Fuck! My throat tightened. Time to do what I'd promised myself I'd do. I'd prove to everyone, Charlie, Laurie, Suzy Berenson, Rachel Maddow, the *Daily Show,* Mom, that I was a journalist, not a Fluke stooge.

Rob started to say something to me, but Larry interrupted.

"Amanda, Rob, sit down, please!" Larry motioned for us to get back to the sofa. "In seven, six, five, four . . ." Larry pointed to Camera 3. I took a sharp breath.

"For many months, Victor Fluke has claimed Virginia Wynn violated election laws by registering undocumented immigrants to vote. This morning we have an update. Victor Fluke joins us now by phone."

"Good morning, Amanda."

This was the moment—to finally ignore the Fluke-friendly angle and go with the real story. "Mr. Fluke, you've said that illegal immigrants are sponges on society. But before we get to Virginia Wynn's alleged action, voters deserve to know your history—"

"Well, first of all," he said interrupting me, "nobody knows how many of these foreigners are feeding off the American people, flooding our country, and stealing our success. Then they have children here, but those children should not be U.S. citizens. They're Ameri-*can'ts.*"

"But our Constitution says if you're born here, you are a U.S. citizen."

"Well, I think that's wrong, and we should send those children back to their real homes. It's like Dr. Martin Luther King, Jr. said: 'An unjust law is no law at all.' People should follow their conscience rather than unjust laws."

I'd been listening for an opening and Fluke delivered one. "Mr. Fluke, is that what you do? Do you reject laws that you don't believe in? I'm sure you're aware of the allegations that you yourself hired an undocumented housekeeper. Did you ignore the very immigration and employment laws you now claim must be enforced?" By the time I got it out, my heart was beating so hard I was sure it was being picked up by the microphone resting on my breastbone.

"I'm sorry, I don't know what you're talking about."

"Amanda!" Fatima yelled in my ear. "Get back to his plan!"

"Mr. Fluke, as you know, there are witnesses who say you employed an undocumented worker from Haiti for three years as a housekeeper. They also say you bought her a home in Arizona so she could remain in the country. Is that true?"

"Rob!" Fatima yelled. "Get in there!"

"Amanda, I've got to tell you, I am very surprised to hear this coming from you. This is a smear campaign coming from Wynn's people, who, as we know, stole the nomination by registering illegals to vote. You realize no alleged maid has ever come forward. The thing that makes FAIR News so trusted is that you don't engage in rumor and innuendo, that is, until now."

"Mr. Fluke, do you know a woman named Martina Harrow?" I asked.

"Who?" he said. "I'm not . . . familiar . . . with that name." There was a long pause at that point, during which Fatima and Fluke were both silent.

"Mr. Fluke?"

Silence.

"Mr. Fluke, are you there?" I repeated.

"We lost him," Fatima said.

"Sounds like we've lost Victor Fluke," Rob said. "We'll fix our audio issues and reestablish contact as soon as possible. Let's take a quick break. More of *Wake Up* when we come right back."

"We're clear," Larry said.

I took a deep breath and braced myself for whatever was about to happen next.

"You fluked him!" Jeremy said, coming out from behind Camera 1 and applauding.

"Wow!" Casanova said, doubling over behind Camera 3 as if needing to catch his own breath.

"He hung up on you," Rocco said. "What a chicken."

"What a *phony*," Larry said. "He must have some real *hang-ups* about the housekeeper."

Rob reached over and touched the top of my hand. "You did it."

I gnawed on the inside of my cheek and nodded at him.

"Amanda, we'll talk at the pitch meeting," Fatima said in a serious voice that was impossible to read—until I realized she didn't know how she felt until she saw the fallout or pickup. "I'm waiting for a call from Benji," she said.

"Well, that's going to do it for us today," Rob said into Camera 2. "Tomorrow on *Wake Up, USA!*, a boy who Velcroed his whole house!"

The commercial rolled and Rob leaned close to me. "We're foxic," he whispered.

I moved away before the crew could see us sitting too close. I was so drained, it was all I could do to gather my papers and stand up.

"Amanda, can I see you for a second?" Larry asked from his side of the studio.

"Catch you at the meeting?" Rob said, our eyes meeting. I nodded and he flashed that movie star smile, then bounded out with what looked like an actual spring in his step. I limped over to Larry, who I thought might be about to tell me I'd been fired, but instead he glanced around to make sure no one could hear us, then put his head close to mine. "Something's going on with Rob."

"Oh?" I said, staring past Larry to the studio door Rob had just exited.

"I've worked with the guy for a year. He's acting funny. He's happier." Larry leaned closer to my face, "I think he likes you. And I mean, *likes* you."

I nodded, trying to match Larry's concerned expression. "Hmm, well, anything's possible, I guess."

"Yeah, so be on guard. I mean, he's a great guy, but bad news for women."

"Um, yeah," I said, suddenly sane again. *What was I doing? Of course Rob is bad news.* "Thanks for the heads-up."

Chapter 28

Bury the Lede

I shut my office door, then leaned against it, sliding down until I landed like a sack of bones on the floor. Resting my head against the door, I tried not to think about last night, because when I did, I got that tingly feeling in my chest. *Had he really said that? Had we really done that?* My skin shivered, remembering his.

I had a good twenty minutes until the pitch meeting so I kicked off my pumps then crawled on all fours to my comfy old brown sweats, lying in a pile in the corner. In the past few weeks, out of sheer postshow exhaustion, I'd given up all dress-for-success pretense and begun going to the pitch meeting in my equivalent of pajamas. Today would be no different. I kneeled, yanking my dress over my head, and before I could hang it up was hit with a wave of exhaustion, leaving barely enough energy to pull on the sweatpants. Never before had a scratchy beige carpet looked so inviting. I reached up to my shelf of sweaters, grabbed a beautiful, pink cashmere one, then balled it into a pillow and plopped it on the floor under my head.

My office phone rang loudly, hurting my ears. Once, twice, three times. I heaved my body back up from the floor and reached for the receiver.

"Hello?"

"Hey, got a minute?" It was Rob's deep voice. "I want to talk to you. Can I stop by?"

I felt my heart jump. "I'm actually heading out to grab a coffee before the meeting," I fibbed, hoping to avoid him seeing the clothing explosion on my floor.

"Can you swing by on your way out?" he asked. "I'll make it fast."

"Um, sure."

I slid my hideous clogs on. Catching my reflection in the full-length mirror: It was all bloodshot eyes and chapped lips. Cinderella really did vanish at midnight last night. I was back to my mere mortal self; from bejeweled in diamonds to downtrodden in brown sweats. Maybe last night's love potion will have evaporated, too. That would make life so much easier.

I knocked on Rob's office door.

"Hold on," he called from inside. A moment later, he swung open the door. He was out of his business suit and stood in old jeans and a T-shirt that showed the muscles in his arms. He didn't look tired, he looked good. It was almost too much for me. *So this is how he slays his victims.*

"Oh, look, it's Amanda Gallo," he announced to the pod of producers sitting outside his door, quietly working at their desks. "She's here to drop off some important paperwork!"

He grabbed my wrist and pulled me inside, shutting the door behind us. Then he put his arms on either side of my head, pinning me against the wall and leaning his body toward mine, stopping before we touched. My lips were near his warm neck.

"I can't stop thinking about you," he whispered. "I can't concentrate on anything else."

"Come on," I said, fake-trying to push him away. "You always keep your cool."

"Amanda, I need to see you again. Have dinner with me tonight."

I looked into his eyes, just six inches from mine. I wanted to kiss him right there but stopped myself. An office romance? With Rob Lahr? What the fuck was I thinking?

"I'm exhausted, Rob. I've got to go to sleep. This is all kind of complicated, you know?"

"No, I don't," he said.

"Come on, an office romance? Everyone butting into our business? Larry's probably already figured it out. Who's next? Angie?"

"How about this?" he offered. "I'll make dinner for you at my place. Very low profile." He stared into my eyes, waiting for a response, and in this light, his eyes looked turquoise. "Amanda, we can do this. We have something special here. You must feel it, too."

I did feel it, but I didn't say that. "The pitch meeting is in ten minutes. I'm still reeling from the Fluke stuff. Can we talk about this later?"

Rob straightened up and let his arms fall to his side. "Sure thing, Principessa. Let me know when. I'll be here." He squeezed my hand, then let go and opened the door. "And thank you very much, Amanda," he announced to the startled producers. "I'll be sure to look over those time-sensitive documents!"

I lumbered into the Think Tank and dropped into the seat next to Morgan, who overnight had turned his shaggy, dyed-black hair into a spiky Mohawk. I stared at the side of his head, marveling at how much mousse it must take to make hair stick straight up like that.

"Way to challenge Fluke," Tiffany said to me. "That was awesome."

"Thanks," I said, feeling a strange combo of tired, sick, and awesome.

"You should have seen the look on Rob's face when you went there," Tiffany said. "He was, like, floored. He was totally not expecting that."

Yeah, he was.

"Rob was speechless," Jada said. "We were watching his face in the control room. It was like he couldn't take his eyes off you."

Shit! There was that flutter again.

"I just saw Rob in the hall. He's in such a good mood today," Tiffany noted. "Weird."

I rubbed my temples.

"Hey, Amanda," Morgan said, casually turning toward me. "Are you and Rob fucking?"

I thought I might throw up on the table. "What are you talking about?" I said with more outrage than necessary, turning to glare at him, but careful not to catch Tiffany's eye.

"Nothing," he shrugged. "It just hit me when I was watching the show today. Neither of you are married. You know, he's a good-looking guy. You guys have great chemistry on the set. That's all."

The little hairs on my neck prickled like pins. "Spare me your perverted fantasies," I said too adamantly.

"Hey, my bad," Morgan said, shrugging at Tiffany then turning away like he thought I was overcaffeinated.

"Where is everyone?" Tiffany said. "It's freezing in here."

I was starting to sweat. I stared at the door, wondering if it was too late to get up and run out. I checked my watch and saw I was still wearing Heshie's diamond-encrusted one. Shit! Had I showered with it on? And what had I done with the rest of the jewelry? *God, I've got to get home.* Just then Rob breezed through the threshold.

"Hello, Team Fun!" he said to everyone. "How about a hand for Amanda, sticking it to Fluke in epic fashion? She took the bullshitter by the horns." He turned to me and ignited that sparkling smile.

I flattened my mouth, trying not to look flattered, or happy, or excited or nervous or guilty, so I was pretty much out of facial expressions by the time I pretended to scribble a brilliant pitch idea into my notebook.

"Jesus, it's cold in here," Fatima noted, coming in and taking her seat. "Let's move through this quickly so we can get out of here."

"Oh, look, Morgan saved a seat for me," Rob said, sauntering to my side of the table, then grabbing an empty chair from against the wall and forcibly moving Morgan's chair four feet to the right in order to wedge his own chair directly next to mine. "I think Amanda could use a little body heat."

I shot him an icy stare.

"Great, now it's cold *and* awkward," Morgan mumbled.

Fatima put down her iPhone and eyed Rob. "What's wrong with you? Why are you so . . . excited?"

"Just livin' the dream, Fati."

"Don't call me that."

Rob's knee moved toward mine, as if by accident, closing the tiny space between our legs until they touched. He left it there and I felt the electrical charge, so I crossed my leg in the other direction.

"Has anyone heard from Benji?" Tiffany asked.

"Not yet," Fatima said warily, then picked up her phone to check it again. "But I'm sure I will. In the meantime, let's hear some pitches."

"I was thinking we should do something on what's going on in the Sudan," Morgan started.

"What are we, CNN?" Fatima interrupted.

"I saw a special where Clooney went to this village and, I mean, the scale of the genocide is getting worse by the day."

"Next," Fatima said. "Tiffany, go."

"So, there's a new drug coming out to fight acne."

"Uh-huh," Fatima nodded.

"Basically, it's like a wonder drug. You wash your face with it and it makes the acne disappear."

"Ooh, I like it." Fatima said. "Book one of our medical contributors."

"I think I have our new slogan," Rob offered, raising his hand. "*Wake up, USA!* From ethnic cleansing to facial cleansing!" He kicked me playfully under the table.

I grabbed my pen, scribbled on my notebook, and slid it to Rob:

Knock it off

Rob read the message, nodding silently as though he were taking my suggestion under advisement, then lifted his pen thoughtfully and composed a response. He slid the notebook back:

Have dinner with me

"What do you think of that, Amanda?" Fatima asked.

"I'm too tired to think about food."

"What?" she said.

"Um . . ." I swallowed, straining to rehear the intern's pitch.

Rob piped up. "I think generally stories about the tax code are a little wonky, but if we make it about class warfare, that could work."

I stared at him, wondering how the hell he could be so cool and collected. *He really is a professional lady-killer,* I thought. *Remember that.*

Just then, Fatima's and Rob's phones buzzed simultaneously. They both glanced down.

"And here we go," Fatima said. "Google Alert for Amanda Gallo. A new Arthur Dove tweet. '@AmandaGallo falls for fake news.

@VictorFluke will no longer appear on @WakeUpUSA. #success fulman.'"

Morgan made a whistle like something falling out of the sky.

"Fuck! I have to go deal with this," Fatima said. "Meeting adjourned." She turned to me, dead serious. "Don't go home. Benji just emailed. He wants to see you."

Chapter 29

Feet to the Fire

"Oh. Em. Eff. Gee!" Melissa said as I entered Benji's outer office. "You were amaze-balls this morning."

Since I'd been here last, there'd been some redecorating. Gone were the treadmills and high keyboards; now Benji's gaggle of assistants were typing on normal keyboards atop their regular desks, while trying to maintain their balance sit-bouncing on oversized exercise balls that I suspected were ordered after Benji read somewhere of the ergonomic advantages of developing one's core strength and spine alignment.

"I can't believe Fluke hung up on you on live TV," Melissa said. "He's officially cray cray."

"Totes," I heard myself say, as though I were her college roommate.

"Benji's on a phone call," she whispered. "I'll tell him you're here."

"Hey, you," Benji called out his door, and he waved me in. His breezy casualness surprised me, and I felt better. Clearly, he wasn't angry with me.

I walked in to find Benji on his Bluetooth, talking and pacing the floor, tossing a stress ball back and forth in his hands. He motioned for me to sit on the sofa. His ankles were tanner than the last time I'd seen them.

"So you'll send me the quarter numbers and then we'll put something out in all the trades, plus the *Times* and *WaPo*. Cool? Good. You're the man," he said with a grin, and I knew instinctively that whomever he was talking to replied, "No, you're the man." And then on cue, Benji laughed.

"Oh-*kay*," he said, hanging up but still distracted, clipping a stack of papers on his desk, then nodding at it as if mentally check-ing a box. "So," he said, walking over to me and sitting down.

"Hi," I said.

"You've had quite a morning."

I made my eyes wide and nodded at him. "You could say that."

"'The Fluke Hang-up.' I'm already seeing that headline everywhere. Politico, The Hill, The Wrap, TVNewser. Getting a lot of pickup."

There was something about the straight way he said it, his just-the-facts-ma'am delivery, that made me feel uneasy.

"Yeah," I said, "I wasn't expecting him to hang up. I thought for sure he'd have some good answer. I mean, he had to know he'd be asked about it at some point."

"Yeah, yeah. No, I think he just wasn't expecting it from us, which is part of what made it so great. The unpredictability of live TV."

"Oh, good," I said, exhaling. "I'm glad you liked it, because I felt I had to ask him. The housekeeper story had become the elephant in the room, and he's never had to address it head-on."

"Yeah, yeah. No, I get it," Benji said. "I mean, you're a journalist. That's what you do. You ask the tough questions. You get the story."

"Exactly," I said.

"No, no, it was great. The only issue is that it really pissed off Fluke."

"You saw Dove's tweet?"

"No, he called."

"Really? Fluke himself?"

"Yeah, no, he says he won't come on again, unless you apologize on the air."

A pang of nausea hit me. "Seriously?"

"Yeah, I mean obviously you can't do that. Issuing an apology is the last thing we should ever do. FAIR News can't be issuing apolo-gies for asking tough questions."

I nodded with relief. "Of course not! That's my job. I didn't do anything wrong."

"Right, right. Of course not. No, I know that," he said. "Other than you did go way off message for the FAIR News brand. I know Fatima explained to you that we couldn't touch the other side until we *had* the other side."

"Well, we *do* have the other side. I mean we don't have the woman, but we have evidence that they had some sort of relationship. I've seen the real estate records that he bought her a house."

"Documents can be forged," Benji said. "And I think I've been pretty explicit about getting both sides. We needed the woman in order to do the story. We don't just repeat rumors. But look, what's done is done. There might even be a way to capitalize on your rift with Fluke. Your Twitter followers are going through the roof. I mean, a lot of them are your haters, of course."

I shrugged and looked out the window, trying to think of the right Fluke follow-up segment for tomorrow to advance the story. Maybe I could get Emilia the nanny on.

"So I'm going to have to pull you off the show," Benji said.

"What?!"

"Don't worry, it's not forever. Just till things settle down."

"What does that mean?"

"Look, we're very close to beating CNN and Fox for the entire quarter. We're like thirty thousand viewers shy of them in the demo. But I think in the next couple of weeks before the election we can close the gap. Do you know how huge this is for a start-up network? Our projections didn't have us coming close to them for five years! That's a big feather in our cap and you should feel very proud of that."

"So then don't pull me! The show is doing great! Maybe it will do better now that people know we'll hold Fluke's feet to the fire!"

"Well, we can't overlook the Fluke factor. I'd like to think the success is whatever you and Rob are doing, but let's face it, when Fluke's on, the numbers skyrocket, and when he's not, they dip. So look, let's just get through the election. Then if we win the quarter, we get huge bragging rights and I can roll out the publicity blitz I'm planning across all media platforms and FAIR News will officially be on the map in a major way."

"Benji, you can't do this. You cannot punish me for asking a question."

"Don't think of it like that. Think of it like you're getting a little break. Not having to wake up at three A.M. every day? Trust me, you'll be thanking me in a few days."

My heart was pounding. "What if I get the woman?"

"What do you mean?"

"I mean, what if I can get the housekeeper to talk?"

"Well, that would be the prime-time event of the year. The October surprise to beat all others. We'd win more than the quarter. Hell, I'd blow up your current contract and quadruple your salary for that. Can you get her?"

"I don't know. But if I can, will you put me back on the show?"

"Of course," Benji said. "In the meantime, Margot's in, starting Monday."

"What about Rob?"

"Rob stays on, of course. He didn't go rogue. He likes stardom too much to jeopardize it."

Chapter 30

Terminal Break

I staggered into my kitchen and dropped my bag, reaching out to brace myself against the counter. I narrowed my eyes and tried to focus on the silver sink faucet to see if there was one or two of them. Between Benji and Rob and Fluke, I was dizzy—so dizzy that on the subway home I'd developed a case of double vision. I was starting to see two of everything; even now the faucet was its shiny self with a fuzzy shadow faucet hovering just up and to the side. *What is happening to me?*

I thought of the story I'd done a few months ago about a transgender teenager who'd felt so trapped in her body that she became physically paralyzed and unable to walk. Only after she told her mother that she was a boy could she move again. *Am I experiencing some sort of bizarre psychosomatic manifestation of my effort to see two sides? Maybe I do need to pick a side. Fuck. Dr. Phil would have a field day with this one. Or maybe I'm dehydrated. I have GOT to get in bed and sleep this off. All of it.*

I reached for the faucet, happy to feel the metal in my hand, something solid to hold on to, then as I went for a glass, I saw a piece of scrap paper lying alone in the middle of the counter.

Amanda
    Saw the Fluke interview. I'm so proud of you. I'll stop by after class.
        Love,
        Charlie

I put my hand to my mouth. *Charlie. Oh, my God.* He hadn't been in the bedroom, had he? I couldn't remember what state I'd left it in. I looked at the note again, trying to read between the lines to tell if our spaceship had landed, then I rushed to the bedroom to check the scene of the crime. The sheets were knotted like ropes, as if I'd been tossing and turning all night. There on my nightstand was Heshie's necklace and watch and earring. *Oh, thank God.* But wait, my double vision must be playing tricks with me. I walked closer and put my hand on the pieces to separate them. Only one earring . . . where the hell was the other earring? *Tell me I didn't lose one of the fucking earrings!*

I dropped to my knees and ducked under the bed, fishing around wildly, but pulling out only a linty sock. I stood up, shut my eyes, and fell face first into bed.

When I opened my eyes some time later, the nightstand next to my bed had another nightstand next to it, like a hologram. *Had I missed my alarm for the show? Jesus, what day is it?* I reached for the diamond watch, and squinted at its face to try to turn the four fuzzy hands back into two. Three o'clock, it said, though I didn't know if that meant afternoon or the middle of the night. Sitting up, I could see it was light out, and then slowly, slowly the pieces came together, landing like a rotten egg in my stomach. *It's three P.M. I slept with Rob the womanizer last night. Fluke hung up on me. Benji pulled me off the show. And wait, wasn't there one more bad thing? Oh, yeah. I lost Heshie's earring. Hey, at least it's only one. That'll only cost $11,000 to replace.* I fell back down onto my pillow.

Rolling over, I saw the spot where Rob's head had been, and before I could stop myself, I drew the pillow to my face to see if it still smelled like him. Then it all came back, the sweet smell of his neck as he pulled me toward him. His deep kisses. My hands in his hair. How was he such a good kisser? *Dammit!* My cell phone rang on the nightstand behind me. Unknown number.

"Hello?" I murmured.

"Hi," Rob said, softer and more tentative than I'd ever heard him. "You asleep?"

"Ah, no, not really. I was just lying here . . . thinking about you, actually."

"Hold that thought!" he said. "I'll be right over."

"I don't think that's—" He'd hung up. I tried to force myself to be annoyed that he was coming over and then I tried to be angry that Benji had pulled me off the show and not Rob. But for some reason, I only felt excited.

I lay dozing in and out of a dreamy haze until my buzzer sounded and I got out of bed.

"Special delivery," Rob said into the intercom. I pressed the button to unlock the downstairs door and waited for him to climb the flights, my heart quickening.

"Hey," he called, taking the last two stairs in one stride and heading straight for me until our bodies almost touched. He reached into his pocket. "I have something I believe is yours."

"What is it?"

He pulled out the missing earring.

"Oh, my God! Where did you find that?"

"In my mouth," he said.

My jaw dropped.

"Kidding!" he said. "I felt something sharp in my tux collar and it was your earring poking me."

I grabbed it from his fingers. "I was going to have to liquidate everything I owned to pay for that."

"I got your back, baby," he said, wrapping his arm around me, then placing his hand on the small of my back and bringing my body to his.

"Come in, come in," I said, pulling away before the old lady in 4E could pop her nosy head out the door.

"How ya feeling?" he asked, following me in.

"Terrible," I said. "Benji pulled me off the air."

"What? No! Why?"

"Because Fluke's threatening not to come on if I'm there."

"Fuck," Rob said, setting his jaw and shaking his head. "Who's he putting in?"

"Margot," I said.

"Oh, no!" Rob said. "Listen," he said, taking my hand, "this won't last long. Margot sucks. Without you, *Wake Up* is a different show, a much worse show. Benji will see that. And Fluke will get over this. He's not going to go dark in these last weeks of the campaign. He needs us."

"I don't know," I said. "The whole thing is making me sick and dizzy. Do you know that I've developed double vision? I mean even now, you look blurry to me."

"Hmm. That's not good. Come, you'd better lie down." Rob put his arm around me and steered me to the bed. "Here, let me make you comfortable," he said, fluffing my pillow.

"Oh, you're so helpful."

"Yup. I'm a giver."

I didn't resist as Rob gently lay me down on the rumpled covers, then lay down next to me. He pulled my hips to his until we were an inch apart. "Let Dr. Lahr see what's wrong." He pressed his lips to my forehead. "Hmm . . . you feel hot. You better take off your clothes."

"I didn't know you were a doctor," I murmured.

"Yup, I studied medicine in college," Rob said, slowly pulling down the zipper of my sweatshirt, then tracing his finger from my lips down my neck. "Well, okay, female anatomy," he corrected.

"I should've known," I said.

He leaned in to kiss me. Goddammit, he was good at that. I was running my hand through his hair when he stopped and hoisted himself up on one elbow, looking down at me. "Amanda, I want you to know something. I don't ever feel this way about someone. This is different. I want you to know that. I know you must feel it, too."

I did feel it, in every part of my body . . . except my head, which told me it couldn't possibly work.

"Listen, Rob. It all feels a little complicated—"

"It doesn't have to be."

"I don't know," I said, starting to work his T-shirt up to his shoulders to take it off. I wanted to feel his warm skin against my chest again, while I told him why it would never work. "Maybe we should—"

The buzzer sounded and I froze. Rob continued to unzip me.

"Wait," I said.

"Ignore it," he said, kissing my neck.

"Wait, what time is it?"

"Who cares?"

"Oh, my God! I think that's Charlie! Get up!"

"What? Charlie?"

"Yes, Charlie said he was going to stop by later. Oh, my God!"

"What the fuck, Amanda?" Rob said, sitting up.

"Fuck!"

"Just ignore it."

"I can't! He has my keys. Shit. You gotta go!"

"What do you mean?"

I could hear footsteps padding up the stairs. There was no time for Rob to get out the door without running right into Charlie.

"I don't want him to see you. I need you to go into the bathroom. I'll get him to leave. Just give me a minute!"

Rob blew out an exasperated breath. "Whoa, Amanda. Why can't he see me? Wait, are you still with him?"

"Just one minute, Rob, please!" I pushed Rob into the bathroom and shut the door. I could hear the key turning in the lock. The door swung open.

"Hey, babe," Charlie said, offering me a puppy-dog smile.

"Hi," I said, breathless, straightening my sweatshirt and yanking up the zipper.

"Whatcha up to?" he said, coming in, taking off his jacket, and setting it on the chair like he always did.

"Um . . . not much. I was actually just napping."

"Napping? At this hour?"

"Yeah, I'm actually not feeling so well. I went to a gala last night, um, for Julie Andrews. I think I caught something," I said, praying that Rob couldn't hear that through the paper-thin walls.

"Well, I wanted to stop by and apologize. I saw what you did with Fluke this morning. And I'm so proud of you. I knew you would take a stand. You just had to find your footing. I'm sorry if I was too harsh about all of this." He came toward me, wrapping me in an embrace.

His arms felt so familiar that I lost myself for a moment, thinking how much easier it would be to stay right here forever. As long as neither of us ever needed to use the bathroom.

"Thanks, Charlie," I said into his shoulder before attempting to wriggle out of his arms. "I really appreciate you saying that. And I'd love to talk more about it but I'm not feeling well. I think I need to go back to bed. Can I call you later?"

"Sure, of course, babe. Can I get you anything?"

"Oh, no, thanks," I said, peering over his shoulder through my bedroom door and spotting last night's bra still dangling from the lampshade.

"And you know what else I was thinking?" he asked.

I shook my head.

"How about we make it a long weekend in DC when we go down to the White House Halloween Party? I know of a great little hotel on Capitol Hill and we can have a romantic weekend."

I'd forgotten that at one time we had planned to go to the White House together. "Yeah, sure, that sounds good," I said, handing Charlie his coat and swinging open the door for him to leave.

"All right, I'll let you get some more rest. You do look a little peaked."

"Yeah," I said.

"Mind if I just take a leak first? I raced right over from class," Charlie said, laying his coat back down and heading toward the shut bathroom door.

"Um . . . wait," I gasped. Charlie's hand was on the doorknob.

"What?" He turned around.

"I don't think it's working."

"Oh, really? I'll have a look," he said, pushing open the door.

My throat closed. I stood motionless waiting for what, I didn't know. A yell? A punch, maybe? Seconds later I heard only the sound of Charlie peeing. How was that possible? Had Rob snuck out when we weren't looking? Was there a window in the bathroom? I racked my brain. I heard a flush, then the sink running.

"All right, babe," Charlie said, coming out of the bathroom. "Seems to be working fine now." He came over and wrapped his arms around my back, stroking the back of my head. "I'll look forward to your call later. I love you."

"Okay," I nodded mechanically. Charlie grabbed his coat and offered a wave as he headed out the door. I watched the door shut, then darted back to the bathroom. I opened the door and stared mystified at the small, empty space. Suddenly, the shower curtain was ripped loudly to one side.

"Oh, my God!" I said covering my mouth. "Wow! Great disappearing act," I tried. "Sorry about that sitcom timing. I think I saw a scene like this on *Friends* once." I attempted a laugh.

"What the fuck was that, Amanda? I had to watch your fucking boyfriend take a piss. This is so fucking uncool." Rob was seething as he stepped out of the bathtub.

"I'm sorry, Rob."

"You didn't tell me you were still with your boyfriend."

"I'm not. I don't think. I mean, we were taking a break. At least I thought we were."

"So which one is it, Amanda? Are you broken up or not? You can't have it both ways." Rob stared right at me. Gone was any trace of the smooth operator from last night. His face was red. "Cause I don't want to be your rebound guy or your revenge guy or whatever this is. I don't know what game you're playing, Amanda. But it sure as shit doesn't sound like you're being honest."

I took a defensive step back. "Oh, really, Rob? Were you being honest when you said you had my back? How about that? We had a deal to confront Fluke and you fucking bailed on me. You hung me out to dry and now you're on the show and I'm off. What game are *you* playing?" I didn't know where my rage was coming from, but there was no turning it off. I felt it ramping up.

"That's bullshit, Amanda. I was going to confront him with you. I was ready. But he hung up!"

"How convenient!" I yelled. "You had ample opportunity to do it before then!"

"By the way," Rob shouted, "you didn't say we were doing it today. You decided to pull the trigger without even telling me. You know, we're supposed to be a team, but you don't get that."

"Come on, Rob. You were never going to do it. Even Benji said you didn't have the guts to do it!"

Rob flinched, then he shook his head and let out a snort of disgust. "Fuck this, Amanda. I don't like this. I never lose my cool like this. I'm outta here." Rob opened my door then slammed it behind him.

PART III

True and Equal

Chapter 31

P. O. V.

In the week since I'd been pulled off the show, I'd barely left my house. At first, I tried to keep working. I got dressed, put on some makeup, and went in—but I ended up sitting in my office, without any reporting assignment or anchor slot, simply watching waves of conflicting election polls scroll down my computer monitor, and Virginia Wynn's smile grow increasingly rigid. Things weren't going as planned—for either of us. So after a few days, I stopped going to work. I also stopped getting out of sweats. And showering. Mostly, I lay on my sofa.

I had seen Charlie once, the day after the blowup with Rob. I was still reeling—but my double vision had gone away, almost at the very moment I realized I'd been too focused on trying to see two sides: Wynn/Fluke, liberal/conservative, Charlie/Rob. Maybe my lens was wrong. Maybe there was more to full understanding than being able to simultaneously see black and white. Maybe life was a kaleidoscope, with lots of angles and colors all at once. That morning, in a search for wisdom, I'd looked up the Nietzsche quote that Laurie had mentioned months ago and realized she'd missed a vital piece.

It was true he'd said there are no facts, only interpretations, but he'd gone further. He said the only way to see the truth is to look at multiple perspectives. "The more eyes, different eyes, we can use to observe one thing, the more complete will our 'concept' of this thing, our 'objectivity,' be."

Charlie came through the door holding a bouquet of orange chrysanthemums. They were in season now and the corner deli had dozens of them in buckets by the street, but from Charlie, who rejected Hallmark moments, it was a truly tender gesture.

"Let me start," he'd said, kissing me, then sitting down. "I've thought a lot about this. I was unfair to you. Of course your career is important. I wasn't sensitive enough. I messed up. I want to make it clear that I get that. And I think you've turned a corner, too. It was great how you went after Fluke. I mean, if you can do more of that, I think you can take him down by Election Day and make a real mark in history."

I nodded, since it pained me too much to tell him Benji had pulled me off the air. I had a horrible feeling Charlie would say he told me so. "I don't think it's my job to take down Fluke. That's the job of the Wynn campaign—and the voters themselves. It's my job to shine a spotlight and highlight hypocrisy. On all sides."

"I know," Charlie said. "But Fluke doesn't have a side and people don't understand that. The World's Most Successful Man? It's all mythology. And you're on the front lines. You have a moral impera- tive to educate people, don't you?"

"No, that's you," I said. "I have a moral imperative to bear wit- ness to history, even the stuff I don't like, in as honest a way as I can," I said, then I sighed. "And maybe it's not the job of journalists to solve problems. Maybe that *was* always a gimmick. But somehow just reporting problems doesn't feel like enough anymore. I want to help both sides understand each other. You know? I think it's impor- tant to feel understood."

"Yeah, sure." He paused. "Understanding is good."

"So I don't think I can do this anymore," I told him.

"Yes, you can," he said. "Maybe FAIR News *is* the perfect place for you. You can speak directly to your lunatic viewers in these next couple of weeks and tell them how dangerous he is."

"No," I said flatly, "I mean this. Our relationship. I can't do this anymore."

"What does that mean?"

"It means I don't want a relationship based on liberal politics or anger at conservatives or hatred of Fluke. I know those things are really important to you and I hear you and I respect you for that. I just wish you heard me."

"I do hear you. You feel trapped. You signed a three-year contract and you have to make the best of it. I understand that. I do."

"I do feel trapped, Charlie. But not only at work. I don't want to be put in a box of Democrat or Republican or liberal or conservative. Maybe it's okay to be a little of everything. Maybe if that were an option, people wouldn't be so polarized. I want the freedom to feel however I feel. I want to ask whatever questions I want and be with whomever I choose, regardless of how they vote."

"What does that mean?" he asked.

I didn't tell him it meant that I was pining for Rob. Or that I felt like Rob had understood me in a way that no one else did.

"I know you think I have to pick a side," I went on to Charlie. "And of course I'm against Fluke. That's the easy part. The harder part is staying open to different sides."

"You know what they say," Charlie said, tilting his head at me. "Standing in the middle of the road will only get you run over."

"Maybe," I said. "But somewhere in the middle is also where problems get solved. And I don't think you'll ever be comfortable with me staying there."

Charlie looked like he didn't understand. I shut my eyes as he closed the door to my apartment, knowing it was possible that my best chance at the future life I wanted was walking out.

Hard to believe that was more than a week ago. It could have been six months ago or yesterday, for all I knew. Days had a funny way of bleeding together when not separated by work. I looked at the clock. 7:30 A.M. *Time for the breezy talking point to break up the hour.* I reflexively reached for the remote. The TV was set to FAIR, as it was every morning when I couldn't help myself and tuned in, hoping for a sign that Rob missed me, even though he hadn't returned my calls or email.

"And that's why I encourage women to *rebel* against the power structure, the men that keep us down," Margot was saying. "That's what the *R* stands for. Of course, it could also be for the silent *rage* we feel. I know it's not nice to feel angry. It can be scary, but I say, let it out!"

Oh, Jesus, not this again. Who signed off on this? Is Fatima on vacation or something?

Ever since the day Benji gave me the *Wake Up, USA!* slot months ago, Margot, it seemed, had channeled all her outrage into writing a soon-to-be-published self-help book titled *ROAR: The Four Female Empowerment Words to Find Your Inner Beast.* In anticipation of the book launch, she'd created a Women's Power Forum, as she called it, but which I suspected was really a local Junior League lunch that needed a last-minute pseudo celebrity. The book had allowed Margot to find her voice and she wasn't about to let viewers forget it.

"Now the *O* in R-O-A-R is for *outdo*," she went on. "That's what we as women need to do. Outdo, meaning outperform everyone else. That way the bosses can never take your job away from you. Outshine your competition! Run circles around them! And be *outspoken* about it. Toot your own horn!"

Overbearing, I thought.

"That's what's made Mr. Fluke so successful," she was saying. "He trumpets his own success. And you should, too! We'll get his take on all this when he's on the show just a few minutes from now."

Outrageous, I thought, saddling up on Fluke's "Success" slogan to sell books to his followers. How *obvious*. And *obsequious*!

"*Adamant*," she said. "Give yourself permission to be stubborn. Women are always the ones to cave in. But we don't have to anymore! We don't need to yield to others' *agendas*."

"Asinine!" I yelled at the TV. How could Rob sit there and suffer through this? He looked miserable. I was dying to text him. I could send something breezy and quippy—but I had tried that, with a "Make it stop!" text a few days ago when Margot was on a different *ROAR* rant. He hadn't responded and I worried that he didn't know what I was referring to. What I really needed to do was to see him and apologize and tell him that I had broken up with Charlie. And I needed to do it in person, not over email.

"*Relax, recharge,* and *regroup*," Margot continued. "The three *R*'s. We women take care of everyone else, but we need to *remember* ourselves."

"That's four *R*'s, you dummy!" I shouted. "*Redundant*!"

And with that, I let out a guttural howl at the TV, low and long, until I'd emptied my lungs. It wasn't a scream exactly, it was more like a growl, something painful and primal. A lot like a roar. "Dammit!" I yelled. *This ROAR shit is catchy!*

"Is that you making the noise?" Mom asked from behind me.

I turned to find her in a bathrobe. "Oh, God, sorry, Mom." I'd forgotten in my crazed state that Mom was in my bedroom sleeping, having arrived last night for a visit to try to cheer me up.

"What are you watching?" she asked. "It sounded like a wildlife program."

"It's *Wake Up, USA!*" I said, gesturing to the screen.

"Isn't it terrific that Margot's written a book for women? I wonder if that came out of her Wynn interview. Now, are women's issues something you might be able to focus on?"

"Oh, God, Mom. Margot's no champion of women's rights, believe me. She's more concerned with her gel manicures than equal pay."

"Sweetie, I hate to see you so upset. I know you miss being on the show. When does this quarter end anyway? That's what Benji's waiting for, yes? The quarter?"

"I don't know. I haven't heard from Benji. I left him a message Monday but he hasn't called me back."

"What about your agent?"

"Jake hasn't heard from Benji either. He told me to see this as a vacation." He'd actually said, *Do you know how many of my clients are trying to get paid for doing nothing? Congratulations!* "Jake says I should relax." I stopped myself before I added "recharge and regroup." *That ROAR stuff just makes sense!*

"Well, I do think it's nice that we get to spend some time together," Mom said. "You haven't had a moment to breathe since you started this job. Everyone is extremely stressed out by the election. It's nice you get a break."

Mom had moved to the kitchen, where I watched her putter around, opening cabinets, attempting, I knew, to fix herself a cup of tea, as soon as she figured out where to find the kettle, a tea bag, the mug, and some sugar.

"Let me make that for you," I said.

She waved me off. "You sit down and relax, I'm fine."

I looked at the TV and turned up the volume. "Let's unpack this," Rob was saying now, in my living room, but not, of course, to me.

Mom came and sat next to me. "Do you think it's time to ask

Benji to let you out of your contract? I mean, you've certainly given
FAIR News a good shot. Maybe it's not the right place for you."

I shut my eyes.

"Maybe you could go back and work with Laurie and Gabe
again?"

I let out an exhale.

"Maybe you should be a producer, like Laurie. Would that be
easier? Being on air just seems so much more competitive."

"Mom, this is it. *This* was my dream. And I'm not ready to give
up on it. Yes, it is competitive. Not everyone gets to work for Benji
Diggs. And I don't want to throw away that chance."

"I understand. I'm just concerned it's not panning out."

"Well, I had a plan. I figured Laurie would get the housekeeper to
talk and then she'd help *me* get the housekeeper. She talks to the
woman's lawyer all the time," I said, omitting the part about Laurie
sleeping with him. "And then if I got the housekeeper, Benji said I'd
be back on the show and he'd give me a prime-time special, and a
bigger contract."

"And you could win your Peabody," Mom smiled. How she re-
tained these tidbits from past conversations, I'd never know.

"Exactly. That's what I've been waiting for, but that plan's not
coming together. The housekeeper won't talk. Even Laurie's powers
of persuasion aren't working."

"I guess you have to decide how much time and energy you want
to put into waiting on that plan. Maybe there's another plan."

"Maybe."

"Well, I know you'll come up with it as you always do. And remember, ultimately you don't have to do what Benji or your agent or
Charlie or even I tell you to do. As Shakespeare said, 'To thine own
self be true.'"

"Okay, Mom, as soon as I figure out what that truth is, I'll do it."

And that's when it hit me. Maybe Laurie would never get the housekeeper. And maybe it was time for me to take matters into my own
hands. Watching the clock, I paced around until noon, an acceptable
hour in any time zone, and when Mom went on her stroll through

Central Park, I went to my desk and logged on to the Internet. For a second I allowed myself to be distracted by a tweet that had popped up from my old pal.

@WakeUpUSA not the same without @AmandaGallo.
#bringbackamanda

I gave a sad smile to the screen. At least good ole @FrankinFresno missed me. This one's for you, Frank, I thought as I zeroed in on what looked like it might be the right number and dialed.

It rang three times before a woman's voice picked up. "Hello?" She sounded distracted.

"Martina Harrow?" I asked.

There was a pause. "Who is this?"

"My name is Amanda Gallo. And I'd like to talk to you."

Chapter 32

White House

I was sure I had the right person the minute she said, "Yes, Amanda Gallo. I know you. You asked Victor about me."

"Yes, that was me!" I told her.

"And he hung up. That man made me furious." She spoke quickly, her Creole lilt smoothing the words together.

"Did you see that on TV?" I asked.

"Yes, I saw it. I wanted to kill him that day. He don't know who I am? He needs his head examined. Trust me, he knows very well who I am."

This was encouraging. Martina hadn't hung up on me as she had on Laurie. And she was already giving me great stuff. She was angry with Fluke, which boded well for me. But I had to play my hand right—tap into that anger, convince her I was her ally. "I *know* he knows you," I told her, like we were old friends. "I've seen the evidence. So why would he say that?"

"I'll tell you why he would say that. He's lying!"

That sounded like as good an opening as I'd ever get, so I went for it. "So what was your relationship with him like?"

She paused. "I'm sorry. I do not want to talk about this. I need to go now."

"Fuck!" I yelled after she hung up. And so it went for three days. Two steps forward, one step back. She'd give me a couple of juicy morsels, but when I pushed for an interview, she'd hang up.

By the fifth day, I'd almost convinced her that we'd spoken so much on the phone, I might as well fly out there to talk in person. No cameras. No commitment. Just a conversation.

"But one problem," she said. "My lawyer. He wants me to talk to BNN. He says there's a person there that I have to talk to. Just a minute, I wrote down the name—"

"Laurie Prodder!" I yelled before she could say it.

"Laurie Prod-der," she said.

"She's my best friend! Tell your lawyer you want Laurie and me to do it together. We'll come out there together. And you can talk to both of us at the same time. Kill two birds with one stone. I'm sure he'll agree. Let's plan on it," I said, getting ahead of myself, because it was time to seal this deal. "We can do it tomorrow."

"No, tomorrow's no good. Wednesday," she said.

"Okay! Wednesday it is! That's gr—" I stopped upon looking down at my wide-open calendar, every day white with space. The month had only one thing written on it, in big, bold, red ink on Wednesday, October 26. WHITE HOUSE HALLOWEEN PARTY. "Great," I said flatly.

"Is there a problem?"

"No, no, no. Not at all," I said quickly. "That just happens to be the day of this Halloween party . . . not a big deal . . . it's going to be at the White House . . . um . . . but not a big deal at all . . . so Wednesday it is," I said, trying to inject excitement back into my overly glum voice, which even I could hear.

"Oh, no, no, no. You don't miss that party. It's like Carnival back home. You go to that. We'll do it on Thursday."

I hung up and pressed my fingers to my mouth to contain the excitement. Getting Martina would be the granddaddy of October surprises. Everything—my career, my connection to Rob, the election, was about to turn around.

Sitting on the hotel bed, I ran my fingers again across the hand-engraved gold lettering on the heavy-stock, creamy, ecru stationery. "The President and First Lady request your presence at the White House Halloween Party." I'd been certain that since Benji had taken me off the show, I'd be crossed off the guest list. But then Susan in the PR department called to tell me that I was expected to go—to show what a united FAIR News family we are. I shut my eyes in silent prayer that Rob was going, too, and I would have the chance to see him face-to-face. FAIR had gotten a block of rooms at the Hay-Adams. Maybe he was here already. Maybe he was in the room next to mine. I felt that old fluttery feeling at what might happen next.

Of course, in case Rob wasn't inclined to talk to me, I had a plan. And I'd lugged the main component of that plan on the train down to DC, where it now sat on the other queen bed, staring at me: half of our old Rubik's Cube costume. I'd snuck into the *Wake Up* pod yesterday afternoon when I knew no one would be around and found it in a back corner, my heart skipping a beat when I saw that Rob's half was missing. Maybe Rob was too lazy to have gotten any other costume and, lo and behold, we would be stuck together for the night.

I pulled on nude tights and stepped into the cardboard box, tugging at the sides and securing the big black electrical tape straps over my shoulders. I had hoped that the tights, pumps, and box around my midsection would give me the vintage air of a sexy 1950s cigarette girl. But standing in front of the mirror, with my yellow squares facing forward, I saw Sponge Bob. "Oh, for fuck's sake," I said out loud. "Why didn't we do the Kardashians?"

I bumbled down the hallway to the elevator cursing, half hoping Rob might stick his head out of one of the rooms, see me, and start laughing. And then this silence would be over.

The White House was across the street from the hotel, thank God, because walking in a cardboard box that stretched from breastbone to mid-thighs was not easy—it required a waddle, back and forth, in tiny half steps that made crossing the street time consuming and hazardous. Taking my place at the back of the queue that stretched down Pennsylvania Avenue, I felt someone grab my arm.

"Amanda!" It was timid Emily Galen. "HI! Oh, I'm so glad to see you! What are you?" she asked.

"Half a Rubik's Cube," I said.

She looked down at my squares and knitted her brow.

"Rob is supposed to be the other half," I explained.

"Oh, that's cute!" she said. "I know he'd much rather share a costume with you than Margot."

"You do? Did he say that?" I asked too fast.

"No, I haven't seen him. But the show is terrible without you. What's going on?" she whispered.

"Fluke says he won't come on if I'm there."

"That's terrible," Emily whispered. "But it was so great when he hung up on you."

"Well, I think things are about to change. I have a plan," I told her, crossing my fingers and holding them up.

"I hope so," she said. "Want to see my costume?" she asked, looking abashed and adorably naughty as she opened her raincoat to reveal a French maid's outfit. "Get it?" she asked. "I'm Fluke's maid."

"You vixen," I said, thinking how different the steadfast real housekeeper I'd spent the past week talking to was from that caricature.

Wending our way forward in line, I looked around, hoping to spot Rob and growing more and more anxious that he wasn't there. It was hard to tell who was who, since everyone was in costume and a striking number of guests were wearing Fluke masks.

"Is that Matt Lauer?" I asked, pointing to the fourth Fluke I'd seen, this one taller than the others, standing next to a completely recognizable Al Roker dressed as Olaf the snowman from *Frozen*.

"No, that is," Emily said, pointing to Matt Lauer in a French maid's costume. "The one in the Fluke mask must be Savannah."

I turned and spotted Cleopatra, her hair in Roman plaits and a toga sticking out of the bottom of her fur coat. "Diane Sawyer," I whispered to nobody.

We stepped into a giant white tent, where security was checking IDs and sending people through the magnetometer. My cube, of course, didn't fit.

"I'm going to have to check the inside of this box," a security guard said.

"Of course you are," I said, looking behind me, half hoping to hear Rob chime in with "That sounds dirty!" The guard grabbed a metal detection wand and stuck it into each of my armholes, wiggling it back and forth.

"Is this a Rubik's Cube cavity check?" I asked, attempting to josh through the humiliation.

The security guard's lips stayed flat, then he nodded a go-ahead to one of his coworkers and I did my best to amble out of the tent and up the stone stairs in a crab walk. At the entrance, the big, wooden, white doors swept open.

"Welcome to the White House," one of the two Navy cadets holding the brass door handles said.

I was enveloped by golden light and music.

"I was working in the lab, late one night . . ."

A dozen schoolchildren dressed as little goblins stood at attention in the grand marble foyer singing an a cappella "Monster Mash" in front of a small crowd of costume-clad guests.

A familiar face came toward me. It was Margot in a navy blue uniform, cap, and empty hip holster. A politically correct police officer, I assumed. I scanned the wall, looking for a quick getaway, but realized there is no easy out for a woman in a cube.

"Amanda!" Margot said with a sticky smile. "You're the last person I expected to see here."

"Well, here I am," I said.

"*What* are you?"

"I'm a Rubik's Cube. Well, half of one. Production thought of it. This was their idea for Rob and me."

"Oh, dear," she said, shaking her head in pity. "Once again, you surrender to someone else's idea of who you should be. That's what women do. I don't know if you've bought a ticket yet to my Women's Power Forum next week, but I strongly suggest you go online and purchase one. I'll be leading workshops on how to stop being subjugated by men. You need to develop a stronger self-image."

"Sounds interesting," I muttered, thinking it took a particularly intact self-image to sport half a cube. "So is Rob here?"

"Oh, yes. He's dressed up as a fireman. We took a viewer poll and they voted for policewoman and fireman."

I almost winced from pain.

"Sorry," said someone who had knocked into me in a spot-on J. Lo get-up. I let the crowd's momentum push me past Margot and down a long corridor with big, framed photos of previous White House parties, including a 2 x 3-foot photo of President Clinton trimming a Christmas tree with a thirteen-year-old Chelsea.

I stopped in front of a doorway to a library, with an ornate cornice above its threshold. Staring in, I watched a gaggle of Dumbledores serving drinks. Moving on, I lumbered toward a grand staircase and made the awkward shuffle up it, clutching the bannister and being bumped by people passing on the left. At the top, the stairs emptied into a grand ballroom, in the middle of which sat a long table covered by a bright orange tablecloth and a lavish buffet: silver platters filled with giant slabs of roast beef next to little bowls of fresh horseradish; big china plates of roasted potatoes and bright green haricots vert; an overflowing silver terrine of giant shrimp, raw oysters, and stone crab claws. On the wall behind the smorgasbord hung an enormous portrait of George Washington in a heavy gold-leaf frame. I popped two oysters on my plate, then slid one into my mouth, wondering what Washington would make of this scene.

"Hey, you," said a deep voice behind me and I felt a tap on my shoulder. I turned to see Rob's face, his blue eyes beaming and his celebrity smile turned on. He was in yellow fireman pants with red suspenders dangling at the sides, a plastic fireman hat, and a tight red T-shirt, none of which, I noticed, incorporated any colored cubes.

"Oh, hi!" I said, quickly putting down my plate and giving an inadvertent flap of my arms against the side of my box. "I see you decided against the Rubik's Cube."

"Yeah," he said, "it just seemed silly. Though now that I see you in it—"

"Yes?"

"I think I made the right call."

"Gee, thanks," I said, forcing a laugh. "Just leave me hanging."

"Guess that makes us even," Rob said with a cock of his head, and I felt the jab right in my chest. "Quite a shindig, right?"

"Yeah, it's incredible," I said, staring up at Rob, wishing that he didn't look so damn good and that I'd worn anything but a multicolored cube.

Behind Rob I spotted Emily waving. "Let's get a picture of you two! Reunited and it feels so good," she sang. "Now Amanda, you stand right here, like so." She moved me into position. "And Rob, you get over here. And put your arm around Amanda . . . hmm, let's see, this box doesn't make it easy. Try putting your hand here, right on her shoulder. Now hold that position!"

Emily walked backward and played around with her iPhone while we stood frozen.

"Is your boyfriend here?" Rob asked, not looking at me.

"Get closer," Emily called, and we instinctively tilted our heads toward each other until the camera flashed.

"No," I said, freeing myself as quickly as possible so I could face Rob. "We broke up. For real and for good. You know, after you and I . . ." I trailed off, staring into his handsome face. "Listen, I've been trying to get ahold of you. I really wanted to apologize and explain myself . . . and tell you how much I regret—"

"There you are!" A tall brunette ambled up behind Rob. She wore a tight, low-cut black leotard that exposed her perfect cleavage, plus black tights and black thigh-high boots. Her only discernible nod to a costume was a thin black headband with cat ears.

"Hi," she said to me as she rested her chin on Rob's shoulder. "Wait, let me guess. You're a Lego?"

"I'm a Rubik's Cube," I said, flapping my arms against the outside of my box again. "Well, half of one."

"I don't get it," she said.

"Me, neither," I said.

"Oh, Amanda, this is Barbie," Rob said.

"Barbie?" I repeated. *Literally?*

"Hi," Barbie smiled, not taking her head from Rob's shoulder.

"And you're a . . .?" *Slutty cat*, I wanted to say.

"Oh, just a black cat. I know, not creative. But, you know," she turned her head to smile at Rob, "firemen rescue cats who get into trouble."

"Yeah," I said, feeling that oyster work its way back up.

"So, do you two work together?" she asked. "What do you do at FAIR?"

"Oh, um, you know, try to find truth and justice."

"Amanda's an anchor," Rob said.

"It must be great to be on TV," Barbie said.

"Um, yeah, sometimes."

"Let's go grab some champagne," Rob said to Barbie, starting to steer her away. "Nice to see you, Amanda. Show's not the same without you," he called over his shoulder as I watched them walk away.

I stood staring straight ahead, watching the crowd laugh and jostle around me, feeling as alone as I'd ever been. I wanted to go back to my hotel room, now, but as I turned to leave, I heard a minor commotion near the door and saw bodies circling around someone. When the cluster parted, they revealed Wonder Woman in a bright blue skirt with white stars, a gold headband, and a red cape. She wore a W across her chest.

"Over here, Senator Wynn," the White House photographer called, taking a knee in front of her and snapping a pic. I'd spent so much time over the past year focused on Victor Fluke, I realized now I hadn't studied Virginia Wynn closely enough. I didn't know her every facial expression and hand gesture the way I did Fluke's, and for that I felt failure. I elbowed my way to the front of the crowd to watch her, before realizing I'd become part of her photo op. I stayed. If nothing else, I'd have a memento of the historic, albeit shitty, night that I finally made it inside the White House. And God willing, someday I might look back on this photo and forget that Rob and Barbie were a two-headed fire-cat couple and only remember that I'd met the future president.

Watching the partygoers ahead of me taking pictures with her, I realized I might have about five seconds of an exchange with Wynn, shorter than an elevator pitch. *Hello, Senator. How 'bout a sit-down interview before the election?*

"Good evening," a young Hermione wearing a Wynn pin said. "Would you like your picture taken with Senator Wynn?"

"Yes, please."

"All right, hand me your phone. After these folks, you can step over, I'll snap it, then move off to the right as quickly as possible."

"Got it."

"Who's next?" the senator asked. I stepped forward. Upon seeing me, she cocked her head sideways. "A Rubik's Cube?"

"Congratulations, Senator," I said. "You're the first person to guess that correctly."

"I suppose it helps to be of a certain generation. Tell me your name and affiliation?" she asked as we both turned our bodies sideways for the photo, my cube almost sideswiping her.

"Amanda Gallo. FAIR News. *Wake Up, USA!*"

"I see," she said. The camera flashed and I knew that was my cue to move along.

"Nice meeting you," she said.

"Senator, I'd love to interview you."

Wynn looked directly at me, then smirked. "I don't think that would be the best use of our time."

"Why's that?"

"Hasn't your program focused solely on Fluke? Not sure what my campaign could get out of an appearance there."

"His supporters need to hear from you." I told her. "Maybe you could sway some of them. And if you win, you'll be their president, too."

"I've learned there are some minds you can't change," she said. "And some minds are not even worth trying."

"I don't believe that," I told her.

"Move along," her handler instructed, handing me my phone and shepherding me off to the right, leaving me spun around and needing air.

Was that true? Should I give up on trying to get viewers to hear different perspectives? Were people unswayable? It was a question I didn't feel prepared to answer dressed as a lonely cube. I needed to go. I clambered toward the exit, doing my crusty crab walk until I was down the stairs, out the door, and back in the stiff night air. It had started to rain, leaving a slick sheen on the marble stairs, which I had to navigate by alternately sliding and hopping, landing in puddles that soaked my pumps. "Dammit!" I cursed as the construction paper on my sides wilted and warped into a limp, wet mush.

If there's one thing sadder than half a Rubik's cube, I realized, it's half a soggy Rubik's Cube. "Get this thing off of me," I muttered to myself, before spotting a trash can on the corner. "Must . . . get this . . . off!" I furiously clawed and ripped at it until the box was in tatters and I'd stuffed it into the garbage can.

"There!" I shouted triumphantly. Then I looked down. I was in a nude leotard, nude tights, pumps, and no pants. "Oh, come on!"

"Amanda Gallo?" someone called.

I turned as a cell phone flash went off in my face. "Hey! Love watching you!" A middle-aged couple under an umbrella gave me a thumbs-up, then locked arms and hurried on.

I looked upward at the heavens. "Make this happen, Martina Harrow. I want to believe in what I'm doing again. Help me find my path."

Chapter 33

October Surprise

"Do you want a *People* or an *Us Weekly*?" Laurie asked, perusing the magazine rack at the gift shop.

"I want both, but I'm morally opposed to paying for either. I'll only devour celebrity gossip for free at the doctor's office. Now, of course I can't tell *you* whether *you* should buy it." I waved a big bag of candy at her. "Do you want M&M's? What's a girls' getaway without M&M's?"

"Yeah, that's good," she said. "And can you grab me a soda?"

"Where you ladies headed on your getaway?" the clerk at the cash register asked.

"Surprise!" I said to him, then elbowed Laurie.

He looked confused. "Is it a surprise for her?" he asked. "Or you want me to guess?"

"No. That's where we're going. Surprise, Arizona."

"For real?" the clerk said. "What's there?"

"Nothing," Laurie said quickly. "My parents live there, sooo, just getting away for the weekend."

"Sounds fun, ladies," he said, handing over the plastic bag with our snacks.

"Stop talking," Laurie said to me under her breath as we left the store. "Do *not* say anything more to anyone about where we're going. We've waited too long for this for you to blow it now."

"Shit. Sorry," I said, hit with panic that since I'd been off the air I'd gotten rusty and forgotten how to cover sensitive, top-secret things. Even the freelance Phoenix camera crew couldn't know what we were up to. I'd instructed them to be on location this afternoon, and wait for us outside, away from the house.

I slid down into the big leather business-class seat. Laurie dropped her heavy black bag with a thud, fished out a *Vanity Fair*, then collapsed into her seat, lowering big sunglasses from the top of her head down over her eyes.

I watched the slow line of passengers with expressionless faces sift by us and tried to think of a cover story if by chance someone we knew also happened to be bound for Phoenix. That's when a handsome older woman in a caramel-colored mohair coat, matching cashmere sweater, and expensive blond hair stopped at our row.

"Hey, I know you," she said.

I looked over at Laurie, slumped down in her seat, hiding behind her shades, and waited for her to acknowledge the connection, probably someone she had once interviewed.

"Amanda Gallo, right?"

"Oh," I said, surprised.

"I love watching you in the morning. Love your energy. But I haven't seen you. Have you been off?"

"Uh, yes," I said, startled that someone other than me and Frank in Fresno had noted my absence. "I've been on assignment. But I'll be back on very soon," I told her.

"I'll be watching," she said. "And I looove that very cute cohost of yours. Lucky girl." She gave a flirty smile as she and her bag rolled on.

"My God, these FAIR News watchers are everywhere," Laurie said, shaking her head. "How can she like that cohost, Ron, Rob, whatever his name is?"

"Cause he is cute," I said, though I felt a little queasy saying it out loud. "I mean, he looks like a movie star, for God's sake."

"I guess," Laurie muttered, turning the page of her magazine. "If you put a bag over his personality."

"Why, what's wrong with his personality?" I asked, kind of wanting to hear why Laurie thought he was so bad, to remind myself.

Laurie lowered her sunglasses and narrowed her eyes at me. "Oh, no," she said.

"What?"

"Are you having a thing with that guy?"

I froze, not wanting to say yes to Laurie or no to myself.

"For real?" Laurie said, leaning toward me. "Is that why you and Charlie broke up?"

"No," I said. "No, not really. I don't know. It's been a confusing time."

"Go on," Laurie said, training her unblinking laser eyes on my face. *So this is how she extracts scoops from unwilling subjects.*

"Don't Prodder me," I told her. "Your eyes are burning holes in my face."

"How was the sex?" she asked. "Cause that guy looks like he'd be good."

"Ladies, can I get you something once we've taken off?" The flight attendant smiled down on us.

"Two vodka and sodas please," Laurie answered. "Extra limes."

"Oh, no, I can't," I said. "I don't want to drink before our meeting."

"Those are for me," Laurie said. "Hair of the dog. I was up way too late last night at some sports bar with a college friend of Fluke's trying to find out whether Fluke did drugs in college."

I sighed. "And what would that prove? So did you."

"I'm not running for president," she said. "And I'm not a sanctimonious dick. So do you like that guy?"

I looked down and exhaled slowly. "Yeah, I do. Did. He's different than he seems on the air. But I don't know. Maybe I was wrong. Anyway, I realized I liked him a little too late."

"What happens when we get Martina? And you're back on the show with him?"

"I think he's moved on."

"Don't worry," Laurie said, putting her glasses back over her eyes. "I'm sure when you're back on the show, you'll rekindle your studioship. Or is it a sofaship?"

I turned away and forced open the window shade in time to see us racing down the runway. Then I felt the lift and watched the ground sink away, the nose tilting toward the sky.

"Can you shut that window?" Laurie groused. "It's too bright."

"Okay, let me get out my notebook," I said, turning to focus on the task at hand. "Let's strategize on how we're going to tackle the Martina interview." I clicked my pen into ready position as Laurie reclined her seat into the rest position. I could see her eyes close through her sunglasses. "So, Laur, what's our plan to get her to talk? I mean, when we first go in, do we just let her talk or right away press her to go on camera? Should we good cop, bad cop her? Or maybe we should both play the empathy card, cause when I talk to her, I think she really wants to be heard. Or what are you thinking?"

"You know," Laurie said, talking but not opening her eyes, "I don't really have a plan. I just go in knowing that I'm not leaving till I get her to talk."

"Well, that makes it simple," I said, wondering how in Laurie's world things always worked out. Maybe that was the secret to success: trust that it will happen and don't leave till it does. I put my notebook down and tugged on the window shade, leaving a small opening at the bottom so I could watch the clouds float by.

Chapter 34

The Scoop

It took two hours to drive from Phoenix to Surprise, Laurie behind the wheel, me navigating. When we got to Martina's street, Laurie crept the rental car up the block until I saw a mailbox with the number 27 in front of a neat Spanish bungalow. "That's it," I told her.

At the sight of the short brick path and small cactus garden, my pulse quickened. This was it. This was the moment, more than any other, that my entire future hung on—the exclusive that could change the course of history, and definitely get my job back. I thought of all the other times I'd imagined some story was make or break, and shook my head at my naïveté. All those other stories, in those other towns, at other stations, felt like a lifetime ago. This one mattered most.

I saw the unmarked van, a couple of doors away, and knew it was the freelance crew. The driver rolled down the window when he saw me walking up in his side mirror.

"Hey, guys," I said, not bothering with introductions, since if this didn't work out, I knew we'd never see one another again.

"So, whadda we got here?" the fotog asked. "We doin' this inside or out? Cause if it's in, you gotta give us time to set up some lights. These little houses can be dark. What about mics? We only brought two. Do both of you need to be mic'd? Cause it might be better to boom it."

"Not sure yet," I said, having learned my lesson from the store clerk not to say too much. "Give us a few minutes and hopefully we'll be right back and then you can bring all the equipment in."

"Okay. We'll stand by to stand by," the sound guy said, then reclined his seat back again.

I took a deep breath and started up the walkway to the front door. I looked at Laurie to make sure she was ready, then knocked. For a solid minute there was no response, and I chewed the inside of my cheek, shooting a worried glance at Laurie and listening for footsteps.

"I hope she hasn't changed—"

At that, the door opened, just wide enough for half a woman's face to show.

"Martina?" I said, and I could tell she was considering saying, "No. No Martina here," but instead, after a pause she said, "Yes?" like she didn't know what this was about.

"I'm Amanda," I said. "Thank you for letting us come."

"I thought you'd get here earlier," she said. "I forgot I have to be somewhere at four." She gestured to the watch on her wrist that read 3:30. "So maybe come back tomorrow?"

No! I wanted to cry, until I heard Laurie say, "No problem at all. This won't take long."

There was a momentary stillness. "May we?" Laurie asked and took a small step toward her. Martina reflexively stepped back, opening the door for us.

Martina was a petite woman with dark skin, round brown eyes, and wavy hair pulled back in a ponytail. She was not beautiful, nor was she unattractive. Her smooth skin made it hard to peg her age. Forty, maybe forty-five. She wore a solid blue tunic with pretty embroidering that looked hand sewn. A glossy image of Fluke's wife flashed in my head. A former Dallas Cowboy cheerleader who had worked her way up to becoming an NFL scout, known for her tough negotiating skills—and legs. Looking at Martina, I thought of Fluke and what this contradiction said about him.

"Thank you for letting us come," Laurie said, handing Martina the bouquet of flowers Laurie insisted we stop and buy. Part of the Prodder handbook.

The living room was spotless and generic, neatly furnished with a neutral sofa and an armchair. The only hint of Martina's island background was a hutch displaying some colorful pottery and masks. Martina accepted the flowers and disappeared for a second into the kitchen. She came back with a ceramic vase that she set in the middle of the coffee table.

"How about we put them right . . . here," Laurie said lightly, moving the vase to the side table and positioning the flowers petals forward. She might as well have plugged in a key light while she was at it, and I made serious eye contact with her to stop being so bald-faced about setting up a good shot for the fotog. Besides, she was distracting me from my effort to identify some good B-roll opportunities. I'd spotted a photo on the wall that looked like it could work. It showed a small house, painted canary yellow, with a roof of orange clay tiles, surrounded by lush green palm trees with what looked like a teenage girl standing in front of it, not smiling but giving off an air of comfort with her surroundings.

"Who's this?" I asked Martina, pointing to it.

"Me," she said.

"Oh, that's nice," I said. "Was that your house?"

"Yes," she nodded, "in Cap Haitien."

"It looks nice," I said, as if I were looking at a travel brochure. "Is that where your family lives?"

She shook her head no. "They were killed."

"Oh, gosh, I'm sorry." That wasn't the icebreaker I was hoping for. I was afraid to ask more, but she was looking at me, so I said, "What happened?"

"The hurricane."

"Hurricane Katrina?"

"No. Hurricane Georges. My parents died."

"Oh, that's terrible. I'm so sorry." This was not going well, but I couldn't help myself. "How old were you?"

"I was twenty-two. The house was washed away."

"And then where did you go?"

"It was very dangerous. There were armed robbers. So I took the boat to the U.S."

I could feel Laurie giving me the side-eye from the coffee table. She had one hand digging in her massive black bag, and gave me a circular wrap-up-this-convo gesture with the other.

"So, Martina, I hope you don't mind if we sit," Laurie said. "I know you want to do this quickly. Can you tell us how you met Victor Fluke?"

Martina's voice was so quiet, it was almost inaudible. "I was working at a restaurant in Miami and he came in."

"Right. And you got to know him there. And eventually, he asked you to move to Los Angeles to work as his housekeeper. So . . . what can you tell us about Victor Fluke and how he treated you?"

I thought Martina could probably use a little more warming up before we launched right into Fluke, but hey, Laurie was the expert in this department.

Martina cleared her throat. "He treated me well. He was very nice. Very good to me. Good to all of us who worked there. He paid very well."

"And he paid you off the books, yes?"

"Oh, yes, always off the books. He paid most of us in cash."

Laurie turned and nodded at me, like, strike one against Fluke.

"Right, because you did not have a work visa. And he was not paying taxes for you?" Laurie said.

"I cleaned the house," she went on, "took care of the laundry, watched the kids sometimes." Martina was fidgeting while talking and I noticed her hands trembling.

Laurie leaned in. "And what was your relationship exactly with Fluke?"

"It was fine," she answered quickly. "Mr. Fluke appreciated the work I did."

"Well, if it was all fine and normal, then why did you leave? And why did you move here? Did he buy you this house?"

I took a deep breath. Laurie was getting agitated and moving too quickly.

"It was fine. He was a good boss," Martina said, ignoring the question. "I don't like the things he says now. The 'sponges' and the 'illegal leeches' nonsense. This man is crazy now. It's not him."

"And that," I told her, "is what is so important for the country to hear and understand. That Fluke is being hypocritical and unnecessarily cruel. So if I can get our camera crew in here, they can set up very quickly—"

"Oh, no," Martina said. "I don't want any cameras. I don't want to talk to any cameras."

"But that's why we're here," Laurie said, looking over at me with disgust, like Martina's cold feet were my fault.

"No, no. I didn't know there'd be any cameras," she said, turning to me with an imploring stare.

"Well," I said as gently as possible, "when you and I talked on the phone, you said you wanted to tell your story."

"Yes, but just to you. Not to any camera."

Oh, for the love of God. Not another one of these. I couldn't count how many times I'd had to explain to a reluctant interview subject that if a tree falls in the forest, and there's no camera there, *NO ONE CAN HEAR THE STORY! It has to be ON CAMERA. That's what we do in TV news!*

"See, Martina," Laurie started, in her *TV News for Dummies* voice, "people won't trust us if we tell your story without you. They need to hear it from you." Laurie might as well have said, *Hey lady, I flew all the way out here with a hangover, now stop dicking around.*

"I'm sorry, I have to go now," Martina said. "I have a doctor's appointment."

"No problem," Laurie said. "We can shoot this outside your doctor's office. On a bench or something. It doesn't have to be in your house."

"One more minute, Martina," I said, leaning in and placing my elbows on my knees, which suddenly put me lower than Martina's eye level, and felt right. "When you and I spoke on the phone, you were mad at Victor. Can you tell us why?"

"Because he say he don't know me."

"But he does know you."

"Yes, yes. Very well. And I didn't like that."

"And can you tell us what your relationship was like with him back then?" I asked gently. "What was special about it?"

Martina shut her mouth and looked off to the left. I could see her biting her lip, like her mouth was fighting her brain over whether to talk. Then I saw her eyes start to water.

"We say, *espwa mal papay.* In my country, the pawpaw tree, it will flower, but it will never bear fruit. Do you understand? I loved him," she said. "I know it was wrong but I fell in love. I hoped . . ." She trailed off and looked someplace over my shoulder.

"And you had a romantic relationship?" I asked.

"I know it wasn't right. I know that," she said. "I'm not like that, but I fell in love with him. But not now. Now he says all this foolishness. That's not the person I knew."

"It's okay," I said, nodding at her, trying to ignore Laurie's restless foot, moving back and forth, back and forth, like it was itching to jump up and fetch the fotog.

"And then when I heard him say he don't know me . . ." Martina shook her head and looked off again as the tears spilled down her cheeks.

Laurie looked over at me, widened her eyes, and used them to point at the door and, I knew, the crew waiting outside in the van.

"Martina," I said, "I think the American public needs to hear your story. You know Victor better than most anyone."

"You mean on the camera?" she asked.

"Yes. On camera."

"Oh, no. I can't do that."

"Yes, you can," I told her. "I promise we can take it slow. I won't let you say anything you don't want to. If you say too much, we can edit that part out. We'll only use what you're comfortable with."

Martina sat still for several moments, looking down at her folded hands in her lap. "Excuse me," she finally said. She got up and disappeared through a door just off the kitchen into what I assumed was a bathroom. Laurie and I exchanged nervous glances.

"Let me see what time it is," Laurie said, getting up and going to her bag to retrieve her phone. "Okay, it's three fifty-five. I think she's gonna bail. Maybe we should get the crew in here right now."

"Oh, God, no," I said, springing out of my chair. "I think she's gonna do it. Give her a few minutes. This stuff is *so* good. We've got to get her to say it on camera."

That's when we heard Martina throwing up. At first I thought maybe she was just coughing, but after a few seconds, it was pretty clear she was having a violent reaction to something. I looked at Laurie and put my hand to my forehead, pressing my fingers to my scalp, trying to keep my brain from exploding.

"I say we get the crew in here before she can leave," Laurie said.

"I say we—" my thought was interrupted by the sound of the bathroom door opening.

"I'm sorry," Martina said, clearing her throat and coming back into the living room. "I think it would be better if you came back to-morrow, earlier in the day."

"Just one more minute, Martina," I said, gesturing for her to come sit back down next to me. "I know when we spoke on the phone it was important to you that we get this right. So let me make sure we have all the details. You were undocumented, yes? You worked for Fluke off the books, correct?"

"Yes," Martina said.

"And during that time, you fell in love with him?"

"Yes."

Before I could finish my thought, I heard a thud. I looked to my right and saw that Laurie had dropped her ginormous purse on the floor. I shot her a barbed look for breaking my flow.

"Oops, sorry," she said. "Just making sure my ringer was off. Please proceed."

"And you had a romantic relationship," I went on, "even though he was married at the time."

"Yes," Martina nodded. And Laurie nodded. Strike two. Fluke's bullshit marriage stance officially blown to bits.

"But I'm still unclear on why he bought you this house. Why did he buy you a house?" That's when I heard another slam. This one sounded like a screen door. *Damn fotog! I told him not to come in until I called him!*

"Mommy?" a girl's voice called from the back of the house. "They let me go early today because the kids had soccer practice—" A teen-ager burst into the living room and stopped when she saw us. "Oh! I didn't know there was company over."

Martina looked at the girl and cleared her throat. "I forgot to tell you, *ma doudou*. These are the ladies from that senior center. They came to interview me for the job."

I nodded at Laurie and tried to affect the look of a kindly volun-teer from a senior center as I stared at the girl, who looked eerily fa-miliar, like maybe she was a cousin of mine, or like I'd seen her on a TV show, though that seemed impossible. And then the hair on the back of my neck prickled. I knew where I'd seen her—in Victor

Fluke's face. She looked like a young, female Fluke. I tried to keep my eyes from popping out of my head and my mouth from saying, "Holy shit! Hand me that Peabody *now*!" I turned to Laurie, whose eyes had turned into exclamation points.

"This is my daughter, Chrissy. So now that she's home from her work, you should probably go."

"Oh, don't leave because of me," Chrissy said quickly. "Do you need me to be a reference for my mom? She's an excellent worker, I can tell you that." Chrissy pulled out a chair.

"We'd love to hear about that," Laurie said, turning her body immediately toward the daughter. "You must be very proud of her."

"Oh, my goodness, yes. It hasn't been easy for her, being a single mom. I'm sure she told you, my dad died when I was just a baby," Chrissy said, shaking her head with the old loss. "So it's just been me and her my whole life. And sometimes it's been a struggle, but mom has always worked hard to keep this home and to have food on the table."

"Oh, yes," Laurie said. "Yes, she was just telling us."

"Of course, I try to help. I work."

"How old are you?" I asked.

"I'm fifteen."

"Where do you work?"

"I babysit. I take care of two kids. It doesn't pay a lot, but it helps. And if Mom can work at the senior center, that will help a lot."

"Yes, of course," I said, and was tempted, right then and there, to offer Martina an imaginary job at the senior center. "You sound like a good team," I said instead.

"We are! It's like Mom always told me, 'You don't get to choose your parents but you can choose—'"

"—Your path," I said slowly, finishing her sentence and gripping the pillow on the sofa, because it was all getting overwhelming. "I know that expression."

"Right, and I lucked out with Mom." Chrissy got up and went over and gave her mother a hug around the shoulders. "I'm going to go change. Nice to meet you. My mom is the best. If you hire her, you'll never be sorry." Chrissy gave a wave, then went into a bedroom. Martina sat there, looking shell-shocked.

"Martina," I said softly, "I see why you're scared to talk to us. I understand now. But this isn't right. Does Fluke know he has a daughter?"

"Oh, yes," she whispered. "He took me to a doctor. He said it was to make sure the baby was healthy, but this doctor was trying to trick me."

"What do you mean?" I asked.

"He kept asking if I was sure I wanted to make a baby. He told me it would be very easy to stop the pregnancy."

I didn't have to look at Laurie for that one. I could read her mind. Strike three. Fluke wanted to ban abortion—for everyone except his pregnant girlfriend.

"Did he ever support you?" I asked. "Ever provide child support?"

She shook her head no. "He didn't want his wife to know."

"How have you supported your daughter?"

"I work. Different jobs all the time. And sometimes, if things are very bad, then Social Services helps."

Laurie jotted that in her notebook, then said in her all-business but quiet voice, "Martina, Victor Fluke has gone after people on government assistance, he's gone after immigrants. He calls children of immigrants 'anchor babies.' He calls them 'Ameri-*can'ts*.' He says he wants to outlaw abortion. But he operates with a different set of rules for himself. You can tell that story better than anyone."

Martina shut her eyes and tears poured out of the corners. "I can't," she whispered.

"Yes, you can," I told her. "We'll take it very slowly. You don't have to say anything you don't want to." I hoped if I said it again, it would reassure her and seal the deal.

"I can't let my daughter know I've been lying to her. She can't find out that Victor Fluke is her father. She hates that man. She yells at the TV when he comes on. She calls him Victor Fake. I can't do this to her. I'm all she has. She trusts me." She wiped her tears and shook her head. "I can't."

"Martina," I started, but she stood up and walked to the door and opened it.

"You have to go now," she said. "Right now."

I stood up from the sofa and reached for my bag, waiting for Laurie to work her special magic. Surely Laurie had something up her sleeve for this very occasion that could stop this derailment and get Martina to do the interview, expose Fluke, and get me back on the sofa with Rob. But instead, Laurie reached for her big black bag and walked to the door. "Thank you, Martina," was all she said, then nodded at me to follow as she walked out.

Once outside, I put my fingers to my eyebrows to try to keep myself from crying. I shut my eyes, took a couple of deep breaths, and when composed, I walked up to the crew van. "Sorry, guys. It's no-go. Sorry to keep you out here for nothing."

"Hey, no worries," the fotog said. "That was the easiest twelve hundred bucks we've made in a long time."

Laurie and I stood silent on the sidewalk watching the crew drive away. Then I turned to her and shook my head. "Fuck. I really thought we had her for a while there. This is horrible."

Laurie smiled at me. A cat-that-ate-the-canary smirk that gave me a hopeful lift. Maybe she had a plan after all.

"What?" I asked.

"I got it," she said. "I got the whole thing."

"What do you mean?"

"I mean, I recorded it on my cell phone. We got it."

"Laur, you can't do that."

"What do you mean? I did it."

"Yeah, but you can't use that."

"Oh, I'm using it. And you should, too."

"Laurie! We didn't get her permission. She didn't agree to that."

"Doesn't matter. Arizona is a one-party-permission state. We're golden."

"Laurie!" I grabbed her by the wrist. "You can't air this. I promised her we wouldn't use anything she didn't want us to."

"Yeah, you shouldn't have said that. But I didn't promise anything. And don't worry. I won't say I recorded it. I'll say BNN 'acquired' the cell phone video from a source."

"Laurie!" I involuntarily clutched my stomach because I thought now I might throw up. "You cannot air an off-the-record conversation! You know that."

"She didn't say it was off the record."

"She doesn't know to say that! She doesn't know those rules. Stop playing this game."

"Me? What game are you playing? We came out here to get the story. We got the story."

"No, we didn't! She doesn't want her story to be public. She would never have talked to us if she thought you were taping her. She would never have let us into her home!"

"Come on, Amanda." Laurie sighed. "You think the reporter who got the cell phone video of Mitt Romney saying that 'forty-seven percent' stuff asked Romney for permission to air it? How about Anthony Weiner? You think he gave the *New York Post* permission to show his dirty texts? Sometimes cell phones change the course of history—and this is one of those times."

"That's not fair, Laurie," I said, shaking my head. "Martina isn't a politician. She's a source. And you cannot burn a source! You protect your sources. That's the first rule they teach you in journalism school. She trusted us!"

Laurie cocked her head at me. "Don't worry. I don't think we're going to be needing this source again."

"I'm not worried about us. I'm worried about her! That's off-the-record information."

Laurie set her jaw. "Amanda, this isn't your Journalism 101 class. It's a different world than it was ten years ago. We'll be lucky if no one else breaks this story before tonight. Who knows what those crew guys heard. Maybe they planted a listening device on the window. Maybe Suzy Berenson has put two and two together by now. Maybe some blogger has figured out where to find Martina."

"Laurie, you can't do this! This is a real person. Martina and Chrissy are real people. They're not just 'good gets.' This is not 'fly in, get the gore, fly out!' This will ruin their lives. You heard what Martina said about her past in Haiti. If this comes out, she'll be deported. Have you thought about that? She is all her daughter has!"

"I don't get what you're doing right now," Laurie said, staring at me. "We came here for the story. We got the story. This is the biggest story of our careers. It's the story of a lifetime. You think Woodward and Bernstein shouldn't have run with the Watergate story because it was going to ruin someone's life? Not every story has a happy ending for all the players. Sorry. But we *got* the story we came for."

"But Laurie, it's not *our* story. It's *her* story. And she's not ready to tell it."

"I don't think that's right, Amanda. It's *all* of our story. Fluke paid her off the books—that's tax fraud. He didn't pay child support, and she's on welfare—that's every taxpayer's problem. If he wins, he's going after undocumented immigrants and their children. Maybe we'll be *saving* Martina and Chrissy by doing this." Laurie was staring straight at me, her arms out. "In one fell swoop, his followers see who he really is."

"I get that, Laurie!" I said, grabbing both her arms. "But slow down. I have an idea. I think we can get her to talk. She was close to doing it. I'll get us a hotel room and we'll come back here first thing in the morning and convince her to do it. We still have twelve days before the election. We have time."

"You can do that. But I'm not. I'm not sitting on this for another day."

Suddenly I had a new thought that could stop this runaway train. "Have you checked your phone to make sure it's there?" I asked. "I bet the audio is terrible. It's probably unusable."

She hit the play button and I heard Martina say, "I can't have my daughter know I've been lying to her. She can't find out that Victor Fluke is her father. She hates that man." Clear as a bell.

"God, this app is incredible," Laurie said, marveling at her own phone. "You can hear things like a mile away. I gotta call Gabe and figure out how to get this on tonight. Shit, it's already 7:30 in New York. I really hope the fucking lawyers can vet all this in the next three hours. I bet you can get FAIR News legal to approve it by the time *Wake Up* starts tomorrow. You want your old job back? This is the answer."

Yes, of course! That was the answer. I'd call the FAIR News legal team and toss this one in their laps. Surely the lawyers would find a way to justify using the clip. They'll argue its newsworthiness and national import, and then, hey, whatever the lawyers say goes. Yes! A higher authority would relieve me of this guilt and sickening feeling, and then I won't have a choice in the matter. I waited for the feeling of relief to wash over me. But instead, the nausea got worse, making me double over and take deep breaths.

"Shit," Laurie said, still looking at her phone, "I'm not getting service here and I gotta put this video into Dropbox. I say we go to the airport. I'll find a Starbucks and get this to New York. It's up to you what you want to do with it."

"Laurie, we won't be able to put this one back in the bottle once it explodes. You've got to think long and hard about the unintended consequences here."

"Let's go," Laurie said, opening the car door. "I'll think at the airport."

At 7:30 P.M., I looked up at the big TV monitor in the gate area of my red-eye flight and held my breath. I hadn't seen Laurie since she dropped me off at the curb and went to return the car and make her calls. And she hadn't responded to my texts pleading with her to give it one more day for the smoke to clear so we could make a rational decision. I put my hands together in prayer position and stared up at the open to Gabe's show, praying that Laurie, or at least the lawyers, had made the right decision.

"Good evening," Gabe said. "Tonight we begin with violence that's broken out at another Victor Fluke rally, this one outside of Pittsburgh. We go live now to our chopper reporter over the scene . . ."

I exhaled and hoped I was right—that the network lawyers had put the kibosh on it. Laurie and I could regroup and I could devote the next ten days or however long it took to convincing Martina to tell her story. I sat there in the hard plastic chair for the entire hour, to make sure there was no mention of Martina. And when Gabe's show was over, I reached for my phone and sent an email to Fatima.

TO: Fatima
FROM: Amanda
RE: Housekeeper
I tried. She won't do it. Sorry. Getting on a plane back.

She responded right away:

TO: Amanda
FROM: Fatima
Tell her we'll give her a ton of promotion and airtime. We can make it an hour special!

I snorted, then typed.

TO: Fatima
FROM: Amanda
She doesn't want to be on AT ALL, not for a second, much less an hour.

TO: Amanda
FROM: Fatima
Tell her we'll fly her out here. Maybe she wants a free trip to NYC! We'll put her up at a great hotel. We can get her B'way show tickets!

Good God.

TO: Fatima
FROM: Amanda
She won't do it.

Then I turned my phone off, grabbed my bag, and got on the plane, waiting for Laurie to take the seat next to me. But she never came.

Chapter 35

Hot Mic

The flight landed at JFK just before six in the morning. I was dehydrated, grungy, and achy, and couldn't wait to get home and take a hot shower. I fell back in the taxi and looked out the window at the cars filled with commuters already humming to work, realizing I didn't really have anywhere to go and maybe I wouldn't ever have a morning show to go to again. Then I sat up with a start, remembering that I hadn't turned my phone back on. When I did, it started pinging like a pinball machine.

> TO: Amanda
> FROM: Fatima
> RE: Housekeeper
> SO PSYCHED YOU GOT HER!!!! WHAT TIME CAN YOU BE HERE??

> TO: Amanda
> FROM: Fatima
> RE: Housekeeper
> We have you in at 8:45, unless you get here earlier. That way we tease your interview all show!

> TO: Amanda
> FROM: Fatima
> RE: Housekeeper
> HAVE YOU LANDED??? CALL ME IN THE CONTROL ROOM!!!!

I dropped the phone to my lap and put my hands to my face, my fingers over my eyes. *What the hell is happening?* My phone chimed a text, which I hoped was Laurie, but when I looked, it was Rob.

Hey! Great work in Arizona! Congrats. What time will you be here?

I felt the familiar sensation of my stomach dropping off the top of a roller coaster, and typed as fast as I could, my hands shaking.

What do you mean? I don't know what's happening.

F'ing Suzy Berenson trying to scoop you! he typed right back. **How fast can you get here with the video?**

What video? I typed back.

I sat in the taxi chewing the inside of my cheek waiting for Rob's response, watching the clock, wishing I could call him, but I knew *Wake Up, USA!* wouldn't hit a commercial until 6:18. I dialed Laurie's number and when it went straight to voice mail, I yelled into it, "What's happening? Call me!" Then I bit my nail, watching my phone until 6:18.

"Hey, what's up?" Rob answered, like we'd never stopped talking, like he was picking up a conversation that we'd had half an hour ago.

"What do you mean, 'the video'?" I asked. "What video are you talking about?"

"I mean the cell phone video of your sit-down with the maid. BNN is teasing the hell out of it. Suzy Berenson is about to run a clip of it."

"But how did you know I was there?"

"Because I can hear your voice. And I can see you. Or a part of you, at least. I'd know that dangle anywhere," Rob said, like it was our private joke and we were still in the habit of sharing private jokes.

"Fuck! I didn't get it. The maid didn't say yes. That conversation wasn't supposed to be recorded. I don't want that on the air!"

"Uh, welp, I didn't know that and I emailed Benji that it was you and I was super psyched for you. So . . . uh, Fatima has a slot for you at eight forty-five."

"Oh, no!" I said, hearing a beep. "Fuck! That's Benji on the other line."

"Congratulations!" Benji said. "You kicked *ASS* out there! This is the *get* of the century. Need you to do *Wake Up*, then I'm plugging you into the daytime lineup, and then we're putting together a prime-time special tonight like I promised. So how close are you? What time will you be here?"

"Benji," I said, "I didn't get it."

"What do you mean?"

"I mean, the housekeeper didn't say yes. That stuff is not supposed to be out there."

"Well, hey, it's out there. And you *own* this. This is your scoop. You're on the video. Or your foot is. It's already getting a ton of buzz. I'm not giving BNN your scoop."

"But it's not my scoop—"

"It *is* your scoop, Amanda. I had PR put out a press release five minutes ago that FAIR News's Amanda Gallo got the first interview with the maid and that it's a bombshell. This is huge for us—and it's huge for you! I'm having legal draw up that new contract I promised. Man, did you deliver! Now stop being modest and get in here, you superstar." He hung up.

My Twitter feed was on fire, lighting up with the news. Both sides already pissed at me.

WTF? @AmandaGallo going after @VictorFluke? #gotchajournalism

@FAIRNews is so far up Fluke's ass, @AmandaGallo will do a hit piece on the maid. #lightweight

Only @FrankinFresno was in my corner.

You're all haters. Let's not judge @AmandaGallo till we see the intv. I predict a total showstopper. #amandaluv #thedangle

I ran up to the side anchor-only door. Stanley swung open the door with his shoulder so he could give me a round of applause. "I hear you got a big exclusive! Good for you!"

I hauled ass down the hallway, past Angie and Jess's stalls, and past even the studio, until I got to the control room door and burst through. I could see Rob and Margot on six monitors, sitting on the sofa, looking anxious. From the row behind the director, Fatima was giving instructions through her headset. Next to her in the second row were three other producers and writers on headsets. And behind all of them, Benji was pacing.

"Here she is! Come here, Superstar," he exclaimed upon seeing me, and extended his arms for a hug, then stopped. "You look like something the cat dragged in. We gotta get you into hair and makeup. This thing is blowing up. Wellborn is about to go on Berenson's show to break this story. Those fuckers are calling it their exclusive. We need you on set pronto. Where's your video?"

"There is no video," I told him. "It was recorded on a cell phone. I don't have it," I said, without mentioning that I had Laurie's text with a Dropbox code for where to find it.

"Whoa! What do you mean?"

"I mean the housekeeper doesn't want to tell her story. She's not ready," I said. "She has her reasons and they're good ones. She doesn't want it out there."

"Well, it's out there, all right. BNN is teasing that there may be some love child! Does Fluke have a love child? Tell me you got B-roll of you playing patty-cake with a baby! Come on! This is too good. Now saddle up and get out there."

"I don't have anything!" I said, desperate for someone in there to hear me. "I didn't get the story."

Benji sighed. "All right, so, Fatima, pull whatever you can off BNN's air. Maybe they already put some of the video on their website. If not, use their tease—but blow it up so we don't see the BNN bug. Look," he said, turning to me, "it's not ideal, you should have gotten it on your phone, but get out there on the sofa and start talking about it."

"I'm not going on!" I said, and that's when everyone turned around. "I don't want to air off-the-record information."

"Oh, boy," Benji said. "How about we table this conversation until after you break the story? Let's do it now and ask for forgiveness later."

"It'll be too late then," I told him.

"It's already too late," he said. "People know you were there. Now if we *don't* run it, they'll say FAIR News is in the tank for Fluke, that you're burying the story to protect Fluke, the very fucking thing they accuse us of! This is bigger than you, Amanda. The election is eleven days away. Now is the time for FAIR News to make its mark. And I'm ordering you to get out there."

"She doesn't want to do it," Rob said. I turned to see that Rob had entered the control room, leaving Margot on set by herself.

"Yeah, I'm picking that up, Einstein," Benji said to Rob. "But you're both missing something. I'm not *asking* you to report this. I'm *telling* you to report it. This is not a democracy. This is a business. I have shareholders to think of. Now, get out there and report it!"

Something in his argument clicked with me—not the shareholders part, the "report it" part.

"Okay," I said.

"Good, good," Benji said, before making a circular motion around my head with his finger. "Can somebody get Angie and Jess in here for some triage?"

"No," I said, looking at the monitors and the commercial for life insurance that seemed to be screaming at me. "There's no time. I'm going on now."

Rob swung open the door and we ran down the corridor to the studio, where Bruce was waiting to attach my microphone and earpiece.

"Thirty seconds back," Larry said. "And welcome back, Amanda. We've missed you."

I darted to the sofa and took a seat on the opposite end from Rob, with Margot between us, making a vain attempt to smooth my wrinkled jeans.

"Guys, listen very closely," Fatima said. "Here's the plan. We bong in with a FAIR News Break, you get right to Amanda. She breaks the housekeeper news before BNN can. Amanda tells the story for a minute, then we'll pull the housekeeper video from BNN as soon as they air it. Got it?"

"Can you repeat all that?" Margot asked. "I'm unclear on what's happening."

But it was too late. I heard the familiar, ominous breaking news bong, then watched the monitors wipe to the big red BREAKING NEWS graphic, and then to the three of us on the sofa.

"We have some major breaking news at this hour regarding presidential candidate Victor Fluke," Rob said into Camera 2. "Our own Amanda Gallo is here in studio with more. Amanda?"

"Um, yeah. I do have a bombshell of a story," I said, then stopped to take a sharp inhale, unsure of what on earth was about to come out of my mouth. "It's a story I've been working on and wanting to tell for a very long time. So let me give you a bit of the backstory. I've learned a lot this past year at FAIR News, covering this crazy election with its flood of information and misinformation. And I've spent a lot of time trying to see both sides and to bring you the news in as, well, *fair* a way as I can.

"So, how do I decide what stories to report?" I went on. "Well, one pretty good test is that when the thought of reporting something makes me feel sick, I probably shouldn't do it. Of course, that wasn't the litmus test we used here at *Wake Up*. No, we went for ratings over real reporting. Titillation over information. And we justified it because you kept coming back for more. But some stories that get great ratings don't deserve to be broadcast."

"What are you doing?" Fatima yelled into my earpiece. "Get to the maid story!"

"For instance," I continued, "I don't think we should show videos made by terrorists. Those videos draw a lot of eyeballs to the screen and they get big ratings. In fact, they're so popular, in pitch meetings we call them 'terror porn'—just a little news humor for ya," I snorted. "But no amount of ratings are worth showing that hatred. Just like I don't think we should say the names of gunmen in mass shootings. We know they crave notoriety and I don't want us to fulfill their wish. See, I've also realized that's my job as a journalist—to use good judgment, even if it doesn't mean good ratings."

"Get to the housekeeper, now!" Fatima said, and I could hear Benji yelling behind her.

"And that brings me to the story of the housekeeper," I said. "Yes, I did sit down with her and I tried to get her to share her story. But she was crystal clear that she was not ready to do that. She has her reasons, and I respect them. And it's not because I'm a stooge for Victor Fluke or in the tank for him or any of the other things you'll accuse me of. It's because I think I should highlight hypocrisy without destroying someone who happens to be caught in the crossfire. More important, I promised her I would not reveal her story, and I'm going to keep that promise today. Because really, as journalists, that's all we have: our credibility. I know people don't trust the media. And I want to win back your trust by keeping my promises—to our sources and to you."

"That's enough, Amanda!" Fatima said.

"And I want to say something about journalism," I went on. "We always joke in newsrooms, 'Hey, it's not brain surgery.' And we forget that it *is* about life and death for journalists all over the world who are killed by powerful people who don't want the truth known. Journalism, at its best, does shine a light—on corruption and abuse and injustice. I know it seems harder and harder to know what the truth is, but real journalists are still trying to find it and bring it to you.

"And for those of you who say you hate the news media and that we're the lowest life form, let me say, you have no idea how much you'd miss us. Just ask the people in North Korea or Russia what they'd do for a free press. So, yeah, do we get it right every day? No. These judgment calls are not easy. But we wrestle with them and fight about it and hope to feel proud instead of sick at the end of each show."

"Rob, get in there," Fatima yelled. "If she won't tell the maid story, you do it!"

Rob nodded seriously into Camera 2, like he always did to let Fatima know he heard her, then said, "Go on, Amanda."

I took another gulp of air. God, it was hot in here. "As for our motto of True and Equal, we claimed balance by having Fluke *and* his critics on. But personal attacks are not news, and letting two sides hurl insults at each other does not create balance, it creates bitterness. Plus it's just plain toxic." At that I reflexively looked over at Rob to see if he remembered that private joke. Rob looked at me with soft eyes, like maybe he remembered or maybe he just felt sorry for me.

"I've also come to believe that being 'objective' should not be our goal." *Sorry, Professor Jordan!* "Reporters are not robots, devoid of feelings. Yes, we have preconceived notions about stories. Of course we have opinions and biases, even when we do our best to fight them. We're human. So instead of being objective, I've tried to be open—to ideas and people and concepts that I'd never before considered."

"Larry, wrap her!" Fatima yelled. Larry took a step closer to the sofa so I could see him. But his hands, normally so active with swirling time signals, were folded neatly across his chest.

"And I speak for everyone here," I said, looking over at Casanova, then Rocco, "when I say we want to be proud of what we do. Our studio crew shows up in the middle of the night every night to bring you this show. And when we get something wrong, it makes us all look bad. It turns out some stories do have a right side. Some people do lie and cheat and steal—and it's our job to call them out, which we did not always do. And for that, I'm sorry."

"Margot, say something! Stop her," Fatima yelled.

"Women don't need to always apologize," Margot announced to Camera 2. "Empowered women *empower* women. As I write in my new book *ROAR*, available now for preorder at Amazon—"

"Bruce," Fatima yelled, "cut Amanda's mic."

Bruce scrambled over to his audio board and fiddled with some dials and all of a sudden I could no longer hear Margot plugging her book. Bruce smiled at me.

"Rob, get in there," Fatima yelled. "We hit a terminal break in ninety seconds!"

Rob nodded his head and looked straight at me. "You're right, Amanda. We blew it. There were a lot of things we should have done differently." He turned then to address the viewers. "We've made some good TV here at FAIR News, but we've also made the country more angry and divided."

"Yes, Rob!" I said. "We focused on the fighting rather than the solution."

"I know," Rob said, leaning past Margot to look at me. "Yelling at each other was not helpful. It drove us apart—I mean, the country apart. I believe in keeping my word, too," he said, turning to Camera 2. "And I'm going to prove you can trust me." I looked at the side of Rob's face and wished he was talking to me rather than the audience.

"Is this a talking point?" Margot asked.

I knew this was probably my last shot, so I turned to Rob to speak directly. "I let you down, too," I said. "I didn't believe that it could work and I didn't admit how I really felt and I ended up complicating things."

Rob turned to face me. "It was more complicated than I was making it. You know, when I want something, I want it. But you were trying to slow down and make sure it was right. I shouldn't have rushed it. I'm sorry, too."

"Good!" Margot said. "More men should apologize more! I'm *A for adamant* about that."

"It wasn't your fault," I said to Rob, trying to read those deep blue eyes to see if he still felt anything other than sorry. "I should have given you a chance, you know, *from the get-go*. I mean, if you really want to *unpack this*."

Larry hoisted his paper coffee cup at me and took two swigs.

"Roger that," Rob said, then gave me a wink.

"*Oh, touché,*" I responded.

"Wait, what are we talking about?" Margot asked.

Rob smiled that winning smile at me. "But here's some good news. It's not too late."

"It's not?" I asked, looking straight at him.

"I sure hope not."

Margot looked around. "Are we still on the air?"

"I want to make this work," Rob said. "And I'll show you how easy it can be."

I wanted to believe him. "But what about Barbie?" I asked.

"Who's Barbie?" Margot asked. "Does anyone know what's happening?"

"Yeah, that didn't work out so well," Rob said. "It turns out, no one can replace you. No offense, Margot."

"Actually *O* is for *outdo*," Margot said.

"We're hitting the terminal in five seconds!" Fatima yelled. "Wrap!"

"That's gonna do it for *Wake Up, USA!*" Rob said to Camera 2. "Who knows if we'll see you tomorrow."

"And we're clear," Larry yelled as we cut to commercial. Then one by one the crew guys started clapping.

Rob stood up, stepped past Margot, and sat down next to me, then took my head in his hands and kissed me.

"What's happening?" Margot asked. "Is it sweeps?"

"Looks like Rob's sweeping Amanda off her feet," Larry said.

Rob looked at me. "You're a total showstopper," he said.

"I have a feeling that was my last show," I told him.

"Well, if Benji fires you, someone bigger and better will hire you." Rob pressed his palm into mine and interlaced our fingers and I squeezed back. "This is just the beginning," he said.

I stared at Rob and felt a strange déjà vu. "Showstopper," I repeated. I'd heard that word somewhere recently. . . . "That's so funny," I said. "That's the express—" I stopped as a jolt of electricity shot up my spine into my brain. "Wait a second . . . that's the same expression Frank in Fresno tweeted earlier." I narrowed my eyes at Rob and started to feel a weird sensation in my stomach. "Are you in cahoots with Frank in Fresno? Are you two friends or something?"

Rob kept his eyes trained on mine, but tilted his head in a beguiling way. "I'd say it's the 'or something.'"

I tilted my head back at him, trying to read his face, then my mouth fell open. "Wait, you're Frank in Fresno?!"

"Guilty?" Rob shrugged and made a pained face like he expected me to slap him.

"What the hell, Rob?"

"Hold on!" he said, lifting his hand in the stop sign. "I can explain! When the show started, I didn't think you wanted any support from me. You didn't seem to be, umm, how should I put this, a Rob Lahr *fan*. But I wanted to work with you. I knew we'd be the best team. I always wanted it to be you."

"So you turned yourself into a foot fetishist?"

"You make it sound like a bad thing," Rob said. "And about that dangle, may I say: You. Are. Welcome."

"Has Rob been a real heel?" Larry asked.

"Sorry to break up this freaky love fest, or whatever weirdness we're all hearing in the control room. You know your mics are still hot, right?" Fatima said into our earpieces. "Benji wants to see you *BOTH* in his office. Now."

Chapter 36

The Kicker

Rob and I marched down the hall and I felt like I might explode from the boomeranging sensations of being with Rob and being about to lose my job.

"What if we're *both* fired?" I asked when the elevator doors shut.

"Then it's 'Good morning, Cincinnati!'" Rob said in his best Ron Burgundy voice. "'Bob, is that a Bengals tie you're wearing? What a spanking they took last night, huh? Now give us the seven-day forecast, you animal!'" Rob stopped and blew out a stream of air from his mouth that told me he was more nervous than he was pretending.

"Hey, Rob," I said, drawing his attention away from the third floor button that he pressed again though it was already lit up. "Thank you. I know you didn't have to say any of that on the show."

He nodded, seriously this time. "I'd run into a burning building for you, Amanda."

We marched single file, me in front of Rob, into Benji's waiting room.

"Awesome sauce!" Melissa exclaimed upon seeing us, then bounced over on a pogo stick. "Do you know you guys are trending on Facebook right now? You're right behind the maid story. There's even a hashtag for you two called #Romanda. How adorbs is that?!"

"Come in here, my dynamic duo," Benji called from the threshold of his office. Rob and I exchanged looks then walked toward him. "Come, come, sit down," Benji said, gesturing not to the cowhide sofa this time, but to two chairs parked in front of his desk with two matching stacks of white paper in front of them. "So. That was interesting," he said. "Amanda, you made your lofty points about journalism, which are getting good buzz on social. I mean, it's not as good as the fucking maid story would have been. BNN is going to crush us in the numbers today."

I braced myself. Here it comes. The end of the show and our jobs.

"So I'm rethinking everything. I want to go in a different direction," Benji said. "The election is almost over, thank God, and it's time to think about what's next. I've got an idea and, frankly, the timing could not be better. I've been watching the trend lines for the past month, ever since the research department gave me the latest focus group findings. Turns out, the audience says they're sick of politics, sick of conflict. The minute the election is over, they want us to move on. And you know what they all say they want?"

"Free pizza," I blurted, because that's what I heard they got at those focus groups, and also because I was delirious.

"Ha! Good one," Benji said. "Close! They all want *good news*. They're tired of terror and violence and politics and anger. They want more pet stories and hero profiles and babies doing silly things. We can be ahead of the curve on this. Hell, I don't even have to change the name of the network. Think of FAIR News as in *My Fair Lady*. It just works!"

Rob and I turned to each other and nodded along, like, yeah, that makes total sense.

"And that's where you two come in. You're like the perfect good news team. You know, your speech about *journalism* and *trust*, and keeping promises, blah, blah, blah. You two will be my good news couple. And you are a couple now, yes? Look, it's none of my business. But even if you're not, I think we should plant the seed that you *are*. Cause how great a marketing tool is that? Unity. Love. Forgiveness. You guys are a slogan machine!" Benji's face lit up. "Good News Times Two! True Blue News! The Better Together Team. I'm spitballing here. We could stage an elaborate proposal on the air. And Rob, you could pop the question out on the plaza! Think of the ratings you'd generate with the months of wedding prep. Jesus," he said, slapping his hands together. "I gotta pinch myself."

"Yeah, that's good stuff, Benji," Rob said. "And believe me, the idea of marrying Amanda is very tempting. I mean, if you could get her to go along with a stunt like that, which won't be cheap."

I raised my brows and looked over at Rob, cause I had no idea where he was going with this. But Benji did.

"Oh, yeah, yeah, of course. No, no. Don't worry, I've thought of that," Benji said. "That's why I've had these two contracts drawn up. Feel free to glance through them quickly. I think you'll be very pleased with the terms," he said, pointing to the papers in front of us, which had lots of small print. "I've added first-class travel and accommodations when you're on the road, higher clothing and car allowances, some prime-time specials for you to front. And, as you'll see on page five, I've bumped up your salaries considerably."

I flipped to page five and thought it must a typo. I'd never seen that many zeros before. "Oh, my God, yes, hand me a pen!" I almost yelled—until I remembered that sometimes Benji's dreams were not in my best interests, and, oh yeah, he didn't have a fucking clue about journalism.

"Hmm," Rob said, tapping a pen on the desk "This looks a little thin, Benji. I mean, for all the marketing and sales promotion you're asking us to do."

"Yeah, no," Benji said quickly, "we can work that out. I mean, obviously this is just a starting point."

"I don't know, Benji," Rob said, like he was really disappointed. "I see it's for four years with no outs—and I just don't think Amanda and I are ready for that kind of commitment. I mean to you."

"Those terms are negotiable," Benji said.

Rob scratched his head. "I'm not seeing more vacation time in here. Amanda and I are going to need a lot of vacation. In fact, Benji, can you add a rider in which those first-class accommodations extend to personal travel as well?"

Benji said, "Sure, sure. I don't think that will be a problem."

"Good," Rob said. "And we'd like that provision to begin today. There's a flight to St. Bart's at two P.M. that we'd like to be on. We could use a long weekend getaway before Election Day. This campaign has been exhausting for all of us. So if travel could arrange that, we'd appreciate it."

Benji looked at us. "All right, so if I meet those conditions, we've got a deal?" He extended his hand for a shake and for a second I almost took it. Benji's idea sounded soft and delicious to me—like a bowl of whipped cream or a fluffy pillow. Then something shifted and I got that stomachache again.

"I don't think so," I said, surprising myself. "I understand that people want good news. And doing that would make our jobs a hell of a lot easier. But I don't think the answer is more water-skiing squirrels. Regardless of who wins the election, our jobs should get harder, not easier. We have to get back to being watchdogs of government, not junkies for conflict. We're going to have to be more open-minded and fact based, in case our president is not. We're already being accused of bias by both sides, so we're going to have to convince viewers that we hear them and they can trust us. So, yeah, dancing baby videos do sound like a fun distraction, but there's too much at stake for a funfest. Sorry, guys, I'm out."

Benji picked up his stress ball from the desk and squeezed like he was giving it chest compressions. "I like where you're going with this, Amanda," he said. "You're right. We shouldn't make the show more fun. Every other morning show already does that. Let's counterprogram! Let's make ours deadly serious! We can call it *What's at Stake* or *Democracy in Danger*. Or *DefCon1*. Nobody else is doing this!"

"Or *Into the Fire*," Rob said, smiling at me.

"Or *Cooler Heads Prevail*," I said back.

"Look, we can massage all that later," Benji said. "Right after you guys sign the contracts."

"I have an idea," Rob said, standing up. "How about we take these with us? Because Amanda has a lot of thoughts I want to hear about how to make the show better. She and I will brainstorm on the beach. Cool?"

"Uhh . . ." Benji said.

Rob grabbed his contract off the desk, then I did the same, trying to affect his same swagger, but accidentally sweeping the pen off the desk in the process.

Rob held out his hand to me. "Ready?"

I took his hand and prayed he knew what the hell he was doing.

"Hold on," Benji said, following us out the door and past Melissa, who was peeking out from behind her monitor. "This offer doesn't last forever! I need to hear from you in the next forty-eight hours."

"Not a problem," I told him. "As long as we have cell service on the island."

"Guys, this is bullshit!" Benji said, positioning himself in front of us now and blocking the way out. "You're not going to hold me hostage to your pseudo honeymoon."

"Don't worry, time flies when we're having fun." At that, Rob thrust his hand out, I think to high-five Benji, but his palm connected with Benji's right shoulder, causing Benji to lose his footing and topple backward into the ball pit.

"Oh!" I gasped, watching Benji's body slip down into bright blue, yellow, and red quicksand.

"Rob!" Benji yelled. "This is *not funny.*"

"Have a ball while we're gone!" Rob said, then grabbed my hand and we ran out.

"Oh, my God!" I said once we were out in the hall. "Did you mean to do that?"

"Not really," Rob said, making his eyes wide at me, then biting his lower lip. "But I think it worked."

"I would have gone with a handshake."

"Yeah, point taken," Rob nodded. "Do you need to swing by your office to grab anything before our tropical brainstorming session?"

"I need to swing by my house to grab some clothes and a bathing suit."

"You know, it's really clothing optional there. I find clothes cramp the creative process."

"Oh, don't worry. I rarely travel with enough."

Rob and I got off the elevator and headed for the front door. Just then, my phone rang.

"Don't answer," Rob said. "I don't want anything to stop this."

I looked at the caller ID. "I have to," I said. "It's Laurie."

"Hey! Did you see the news?" she asked.

"You mean the part where you violated every tenet of journalistic credibility? Yeah, I saw that."

"No, that there's a book deal in the works. Publishers are throwing offers at Martina and Chrissy. A mother-daughter memoir."

"Oh, my God!"

"Oh, and the president saw Martina's story. As his last act in office, he's issuing an executive order to keep her in the country for a new public service campaign. She'll be the face of undocumented workers."

"Peabody Award, here you come!" I told her.

"Shit, I gotta go. There's a mob chasing Fluke down the street. I need to get video! Call me later."

"What'd she say?" Rob asked.

"The usual," I said.

Rob held the door as we left the building and headed to the black car at the curb. A sign in the window read GALLO AND LAHR.

"Oh, look," Rob said, pointing. "The name of our new show." He stopped me right there and pulled me in for a kiss.

"I like the sound of that," I said, looking into his eyes. Then I turned to look back at FAIR News, my attention drawn to the red neon ticker gliding around the middle of the building, usually blaring the latest headlines, but I saw that Benji had already made an adjustment. He'd turned the ticker into a tease: "Keep it tuned to FAIR: Real News Starts Now."

Author's Note

Covering presidential elections is a strange business, and I've done my share of it. Starting in 2000, riding on John McCain's Straight Talk Express through New Hampshire, I learned that political campaigns are lively, interesting places where facts can fall victim to the blood sport of winning at any cost. Just ask John McCain's illegitimate daughter—who never existed, other than as the brainchild of an underhanded opponent.

In 2004 and 2008, I returned to New Hampshire, chasing candidates along the trail. Before John Edwards's campaign was scuttled by scandal, I went to so many of his whistle-stops that I could recite his stump speech word for word as he delivered it, which always cracked up my cameraman.

By 2012, I was the anchor of a national cable morning show, trying to navigate my way through another tumultuous primary season filled with colorful characters and outlandish claims. I regularly interviewed the candidates, from Herman Cain to Michele Bachmann, trying to get them to answer questions and stick to the facts. It took a lot of mental energy to process the ethical issues that came up when deciding which stories to cover—or not cover. What do you do when you know someone isn't being honest? How do you check your own bias at the door? What happens when your boss tells you not to touch a story? What's wrong with wearing pants? I didn't have the answers back then, but handing these challenges to a fictional character somehow helped me figure it out.

Publishing a book, I discovered, takes a long time (this was a news flash to a deadline-driven broadcast journalist), and I learned that by the time this book would hit the shelves another presidential race would probably have come and gone. But I'd already seen enough campaigns to make some safe bets: the next presidential race would likely include a female candidate making a historic run, and a male candidate, who by dint of a larger-than-life persona and TV exposure would be able to break through a pack of prospective opponents. In addition, I thought there was a good chance that certain perennial issues would make a comeback: immigration, voter fraud, gay marriage, funding for Planned Parenthood, gun control, et cetera. I also had a hunch a personal peccadillo or two might crop up. They always do.

If as you read this novel you start to wonder whether I'm psychic, the answer is: I knew you were going to ask that. I can't count how many times my editors, agent, and I would gasp in amazement at how something I'd already written came true in the 2016 election. (Senator Wynn dressed up as Wonder Woman long before Kellyanne Conway ever had the idea.) The parallels between my fictional world and the real one became so striking that at one point my editor begged me to share future lottery numbers with her.

But, it turns out, truth is stranger than fiction. As prescient as some of these pages were, I could not have predicted where we'd find ourselves after the election of 2016. And I didn't try. This book was not designed to be an answer to a world in flux or a treatise on geopolitics in a precarious, anxiety-filled time. Let me be clear: this book is not an autobiography. While it's informed and colored by my almost three decades in TV news and the crazy cast of characters I've met along the way, it is not a tell-all. It's a composite of the interviews, dilemmas, questions, and laughs I've experienced over the course of my career.

Being a journalist isn't easy, but it's the best job in the world, and for the most part, I've loved every minute.

Now if you'll excuse me, I have some breaking news to cover.

Acknowledgments

A lot of people told me I should write a book. But it was my friend J. R. Moehringer who insisted I do it and helped put the wheels in motion. He said it would be easy. I don't know whether to thank him or sue him.

To figure out how, I consulted a host of talented writers, literary minds, and general geniuses who took time from their own important projects to read my manuscript or offer guidance. Peter Goldberg, Jay Sures, Lauren Wachtler, Paul Montclare, James Carville, Aline Mc-Kenna, Eric Zohn, Susan Mercandetti, and Gary Ginsburg. I owe a particular debt of gratitude (and sincere apology) to those who suffered through early drafts and had to indulge my painfully rudimentary questions: Adrienne Brodeur, Matt Danilowicz, Phil Lerman, Caroline Sherman, Harrison Hobart, Svea Vocke, Patrick McCord, Tish Fried, Jaimee Rose, Leslie Kaufman, Elizabeth Sheinkman, Jay Weiss, and Alexander Wright.

As always, my friends' enthusiasm and feedback were invaluable. Their smart words and funny expressions color every page: Maria Villalobos, Gillian Kahn, Lori Burns, Susan Flannery, Rosalyn Porter, Amy Fanning, Lu Hanessian, Daniella Landau, Jennifer Snell, Jennifer Donaldson, Beth Halloran, Brian Kilmeade, James Rosen, Mary Ann Zoellner, Megan Meany, Deirdre Lord, Charlie and Blyth Lord, Tim and Allison Lord, Lisa Lori, Nyssa Kourakos, Duncan Hughes, Cameron Stowe, Ben Tudhope, Stephanie Szostak, Stefanie Lemcke, Annika Pergament, Jane Green, Emily Liebert, Lauren Cohen, Allison Winn-Scotch, Karen Vigurs-Stack, Coco Grace, Sally Kohn, and Jennifer Rivera.

To my CNN colleagues, Chris Cuomo, Rick Davis, Amy Entelis, Allison Gollust, Ken Jautz, Neel Khairzada, Javi Morgado, Jim Murphy,

Izzy Povich, and David Vigilante, your support and friendship mean the world to me during these tumultuous times. It's an honor to work with such stellar journalists. And Jeff Zucker, who renewed my faith in the power of TV news. You truly changed my life.

To the remarkable Carole DeSanti at Viking, who got Amanda immediately, I can't imagine being in more thoughtful, experienced hands. You kept me focused on what mattered, even during some dark days. Your keen vision made the book and me better. Someday we'll laugh about all of it. Very soon. Over wine. I promise. Thanks to Brian Tart, Andrea Schulz, Lindsay Prevette, Carolyn Coleburn, Rebecca Marsh, Kate Stark, Lydia Hirt, and Mary Stone for all of the energy and enthusiasm. Christopher Russell at Viking and Svetlana Katz at WME were soothing presences through it all.

If writing a book is like birthing a baby, this was one hell of a gestation period. It's a long story but this novel was more like producing quadruplets—and Hilary Liftin was the perfect midwife (and editor) through the long labor. Wise, compassionate, and indefatigable, this woman gets it done. I hope to never write another word without her. She is a godsend.

In literary circles, there's a game of high-level chicken to see who can heap the highest praise on Tina Bennett. So, let me say, she is the sharpest, most insightful collaborator a writer could ever have. She willed Amanda into existence out of a brown paper bag passed on a street corner (literally). She knew how to prod and press and when to prop me up. One of the best parts of writing this book was getting to hang with her. (Your move, Malcolm Gladwell!)

I cannot imagine a more supportive family than the one I'm blessed with. During this arduous process, my husband Tim Lewis buoyed my spirits, offered keen advice, kept the kids' schedules, and only occasionally asked why I hadn't had time to organize a playdate. I love you for that and so much more. My children, Alessandra, Francesca, and Nathaniel, cheered me on and gave me excellent suggestions for the story line and cover art. And a huge thank you to Savi Sinanan, without whom none of this could have happened. My brother Andrew is always a steady sounding board. I'm also blessed with very cool in-laws: Catherine and Alex, Suzanne and John—as well as the awesome

Sherman clan. My parents-in-law, Karen and Stan Lewis, act as my own personal fan club. Thank you for all of your love—the feeling is mutual. And to my biggest champion, now and always, my mother Elaine Camerota (who wants you to know she's nothing like Amanda's mom—and she'll send you an article to prove it). Mom, your wealth of wisdom has guided me my entire life. You are a wonderful editor and mother. I wish my stepfather Mike were here to enjoy this. I hear him, along with Gram, Poppy, Eileen, and Dad, cheering from beyond.